British
Bachelors
Fabulous & Famous

British *Bachelors* COLLECTION

January 2017

February 2017

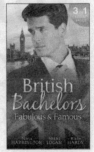

March 2017

April 2017

May 2017

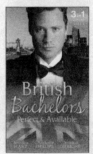

June 2017

British
Bachelors
Fabulous & Famous

Nina
HARRINGTON

Nikki
LOGAN

Kate
HARDY

Published in Great Britain 2017
By Mills & Boon, an imprint of HarperCollins*Publishers*
1 London Bridge Street, London, SE1 9GF

BRITISH BACHERLORS: FABULOUS & FAMOUS © 2017
Harlequin Books S.A.

The Secret Ingredient © 2014 Nina Harrington
How to Get Over Your Ex © 2013 Nikki Logan
Behind the Film Star's Smile © 2014 Pamela Brooks

ISBN: 978-0-263-92793-1

09-0317

Our policy is to use papers that are natural, renewable and recyclable products and made from wood grown in sustainable forests.
The logging and manufacturing processes conform to the legal environmental regulations of the country of origin.

Printed and bound in Spain
by CPI, Barcelona

THE SECRET INGREDIENT

NINA HARRINGTON

Nina Harrington grew up in rural Northumberland, England, and decided at the age of eleven that she was going to be a librarian—because then she could read all of the books in the public library whenever she wanted! Since then she has been a shop assistant, community pharmacist, technical writer, university lecturer, volcano walker and industrial scientist, before taking a career break to realise her dream of being a fiction writer. When she is not creating stories which make her readers smile, her hobbies are cooking, eating, enjoying good wine—and talking, for which she has had specialist training.

CHAPTER ONE

ROB BERESFORD STEPPED OUT of the black stretch limo onto the red carpet outside London's newest and most prestigious art gallery, slowly rolled back his shoulders, and stretched out to his full height.

Rob ran the fingers of his right hand through his mane of collar-length dark wavy hair in a move he had perfected to draw attention to what, according to the Beresford hotel group marketing department, was his best feature.

'Make sure that your fans see that fantastic head and shoulders shot,' his agent, Sally, kept telling him. 'That's what your millions of lady followers will be looking for. Make the most of it while you can!'

Ah. The joys of self-promotion.

After twenty years in the hotel business Rob knew the drill inside out.

He gave the press what they wanted and they loved him for it. They had seen him on good and bad nights and both sides played the game when it suited them.

It was a pity that the paparazzi made more money when he was playing the bad-boy celebrity chef than on all of the other countless occasions when he was working in the kitchens creating the award-winning recipes for the Beresford hotel restaurants.

They wanted him to misbehave and throw a tantrum and

grab a camera. Punch someone out because of a careless remark or lose his temper over an insult to his family or food.

The Rob Beresford they wanted to see was the young chef who had become notorious after he physically lifted the most famous restaurant critic in Chicago out of his chair and threw him out of the Beresford hotel restaurant when he dared to criticise the way his steak had been cooked.

And sometimes he was tired enough or bored enough to let them goad him and provoke him into a stupid response, which he instantly regretted.

Press the red button and watch the fireworks. Oh, yes! *But not tonight.*

For once he was not here to celebrate the Beresford name or promote his TV show or best-selling cookery books. Tonight was all about someone else's success. Not his. And if that meant that he had to act out his part in public yet again, then so be it.

He was wearing the costume; he had rehearsed his script. Now it was time to act out his part until the star of the show arrived.

Tonight he needed the crowd to love him and play up the success of the art gallery. And the artist whose work had been chosen to be exhibited for their prestigious grand opening event. Adele Forrester. Fine Art Painter. And his mother.

But inside his designer clothing? *Inside, he was a wreck.*

Even the photographers in the front row only a few feet away could not see the prickle of sweat on his brow on this cool June evening and he quickly covered up the tenseness in his mouth with a broad smile so that no one would ever know that, for once, Rob Beresford was more than just nervous.

He was dreading every second of the next few hours and would only be able to relax when he was safe back in the hotel room with his mother, congratulating her on a stunning exhibition that was bound to sell out fast.

The plan had been simple. They would arrive together, his mother would smile and wave a couple of times and Rob would escort her sedately into the exhibition to the sound of applause from her faithful fans and art lovers. Proud son. Star mother. Winner all the way.

So much for that plan.

The past week had been a blur of rushed last-minute arrangements and then a twenty-four-hour cold virus, which had been going the rounds in California, had knocked her out for most of the day. Followed by a serious attack of first-night nerves.

Until an hour ago he'd thought that he had succeeded and his mother was dressed, made up and ready to go, smiling and happy that after eight years of preparation her work was going to be shown in public.

But then she had made the mistake of peeking out of the hotel front entrance, seen the press pack and scurried back into the room, white-faced and breathing hard. Trying to control her panic while pretending that it was about time that she walked down the red carpet on her own. After all, this was her special night. No need to wait. She would make her own grand entrance. Why did she need her handsome son stealing her spotlight?

Right. She was forgetting that he knew her. Only too well.

So the limo had driven around the corner with him inside alone. While she cowered inside her hotel room, going through the relaxation exercises one more time. Afraid to come out and walk a few steps down a carpet and have her photo taken.

And just the thought that his beautiful mother did not

think she was ready or good enough for this crowd was enough to make his blood boil.

They had no idea how far she had come over the past few years to get to the point where she could even think about turning up in person to an exhibition of her paintings.

And they never would.

Fifteen years ago he had made his mother a promise.

He had given her his word that he would protect her and take care of her, and keep her secret, no matter what. And he had kept that promise and would go on keeping that promise, no matter how much it had impacted his life and the decisions that he had been forced to take to keep her safe.

He had stayed in Beresford hotels in cities close to the major psychiatric specialist units and turned down gigs in restaurants other chefs would kill to have worked in, just to make sure that his mother had a stable environment when she needed one.

Not that she liked cities. Far from it. He had lost count of the times he had made mad dashes to airports wearing his chef's clothes so that he could keep her company on a long flight to the latest new creative retreat that she had heard about, that afternoon. And suddenly it was the only thing she needed to complete her work and *she had to go that day or the rest of her life would be in ruins*.

No time to pack or organise anything. Then she was on her way, usually without the things she needed, but it had to be done now.

So he had to drop everything and go with her to keep her safe. Because when she was manic she was amazing, but there was one universal truth: whatever soared high had to come back down to earth. Fast. And hard. Sometimes very hard.

Walking down a red carpet and smiling was a small

price to pay for being able to support his mother financially and emotionally.

Rob scanned the rows of photographers lined up behind the mesh barriers on either side of the narrow entrance and acknowledged some of the familiar paparazzi that followed him from event to event whenever he was in London with a quick nod and a wave.

The rest of the pack jostled for position at the barricade, calling out his name, demanding pose after pose.

Fans held up signs with his name on them. Cameras flashed wildly. All desperate to capture a rare evening appearance from the chef who had just been shortlisted for Chef of the Year. Again.

Spotlights hit him from every angle.

He turned slowly from side to side in front of the floor-to-ceiling poster for the gala exhibition of new work from Adele Forrester, making sure that her official photograph and the poster would always be the background to any of his photos.

One hand plunged into his left trouser pocket. One hand raised towards the crowd. Wearing his trademark pristine white shirt and dark designer suit. No tie. That would be too conventional. A call to look this way then that was answered with a swagger. He rolled back his shoulders, lifted his chin and went to work the crowd.

It had taken him every day of the past ten years to create an image and a brand that served him and the Beresford family well and now was his chance to use it to help his mum.

A pretty brunette in her twenties held out one of his recipe books, stretching towards him, her stomach pressed against the metal barrier and shoulders so low that he had a perfect view down her deep V-necked top into a very generous cleavage.

Rob quickly stepped forwards, grin locked in place, his pen already in his hand, and signed a flourish of his name on the cover page while the crowd went mad behind her, screaming and calling out his name at ear-damaging volume.

He walked slowly down the line, signing yet another recipe book—one of his early ones—then a poster from his restaurant-makeover show.

And then the questions started. One male voice and then another.

'Is Adele turning up in person tonight for the show or has she done a runner like last time?'

'Where have you hidden your mum, Rob?'

'Have you left her behind in that treatment centre? Is that the only kind of artist retreat she knows these days?'

'Are the rumours true about her retiring after this show?'

Louder and louder, closer and closer, the questions came from every direction, more pointed and all demanding to know where his mother was.

They were goading him. Pushing him harder and harder, desperate for a reaction.

They wanted him to explode. To push the camera down someone's throat or, even better, give one of them a black eye.

A few years ago? He would have done it and taken the consequences. But tonight was not about him and he refused to let the press win, so he pretended to have developed sudden hearing loss and politely ignored them. This of course made them goad him even more.

Nine minutes later he had walked the whole of the line, smiling and laughing towards the waiting crowd, leaning in for the compulsory mobile phone shots.

Then just like that the press turned away as the next limo pulled up and, without waiting for permission or a good-behaviour pass, Rob turned his back on the crowd and photographers and strode purposefully down the last few feet of red carpet, through the open door of the art gallery and into the relative calm of the marble atrium where the other specially invited guests were already assembled.

This preview show was the one exclusive opportunity for the art critics to admire and study his mother's work without having to share the gallery with the general public. That was the good news. The less-good news was that it had been the art critics who had descended on his mother like a pack of rabid wolves when she had imploded at her last exhibition in Toronto.

Having a screaming and crying nervous breakdown in public was bad enough, but for her tormented and terrified face to be captured for ever by the press had made it worse.

Instead of defending her for her fragile creativity, they had condemned her for being a bad example to young artists for her excessive lifestyle.

But that was eight years ago.

Different world. Different faces. Different approach to mental illness. Surely?

Rob paused long enough to take a flute of chilled champagne from a passing waiter and was just about to launch into the media crew clustered around the gallery owner when he caught sight of his reflection in the installation light feature.

A sombre dark male face glared back at him, his heavy eyebrows low above narrowed eyes and a jaw that would be a better fit on a prizefighter rather than a patron of the arts.

Yikes! Maybe not.

He didn't want to terrify the critics before they had even had a chance to see the artwork. And most of them seemed to be enjoying the refreshments.

A quick scan of the room confirmed that unless there

was a back door through the kitchen, he was trapped. Unless… Yes! There was one person who was taking time to actually see the paintings instead of networking over the catalogues and free booze before the food was served.

A pretty blonde woman. Correction. Make that a very pretty blonde. She was sitting completely alone at the far end of the gallery, away from the hustle and noise from the street. Her gaze appeared to be completely engrossed in the artwork in front of her.

Rob turned away from the other guests, nodding to people as he passed, and started strolling down the gallery space, taking the time to scan some of the twenty-two paintings that he knew inside out.

He could give the critics a full history of each and every brush stroke. Where and when and what mood his mother had been in when she painted them. The hours spent debating locations and the quality of the light. Desperate for each work to be perfect. Flawless. Ideal.

The despair that came when they did not match up to her exacting standards.

The joy and delight and laughter of walking along beaches day after day, which only seemed to make the darker ones blacker. Like the time he was called out of a business meeting when she set six of his favourite canvases on fire on the hotel patio in a barbecue pit. That depression had lasted weeks.

These paintings truly were the survivors.

Especially the canvas that the blonde was looking at that very minute.

Rob exhaled long and slow. He should have known that a critic would be drawn to such a totally over-the-top sentimental and emotional piece.

It was good—no doubt about that.

But it was so obvious that his mother might as well be

standing there waving a banner telling the world that she had painted it in a dark time when the depression had almost become too much and she'd had to go back on the much-hated medication again.

It was probably the only piece that he had suggested to his mother to leave behind in her villa in Carmel, California. It was just too personal and way too deep to show to the world.

Too late. Because there it was. Not the biggest painting but the most intimate and revealing in the whole collection.

But just who was this woman who had obviously spotted the best picture in the room?

Rob stood to one side, sipping his champagne, and watched her for a few minutes in silence, his gaze scanning her pose, her body, her clothing, taking it all in and trying to make sense of what he was seeing.

She certainly didn't look like one of his mother's art critic pals or the hyenas back in Toronto. Failed artists every one of them. Far from it.

Straight blonde hair falling to her shoulders, she was wearing a sleeveless aqua dress and he could just make out a line of collarbone above a long, slender, elegant neck, surprisingly overlaid with muscle as opposed to starved thin like most fine artists he had met.

And she really was stunningly pretty. A break in the clouds outside the window shone a beam of sunlight onto the cream-coloured gallery wall, which reflected back from her skin. It became luminescent and pale. No artificial tan for this girl. She truly was all white peaches and cream.

But what were her hands like? At the moment they were pushed flat against the bench on either side of her body, palm down, but as he watched she lifted her shoulders and her hands clasped around her arms as though she was cold.

The air conditioning was certainly chilly but it was more than that. She was holding on to herself.

Totally wrapped up in her thoughts. Contained. Calm. Her gaze locked on to the painting as though it was the most important thing in the world. She was transfixed. Oblivious to the world. Totally caught up in the painting.

Because she got it. It was so obvious.

And for the first time that day—no, make that the first time this month—he felt that little bubble of a real smile pop in his chest.

Perhaps there was at least one art critic in the room tonight that was going to make him change his mind about their species?

Now all he had to do was find out her name and…

'Rob. So pleased that you could make it.' Rob blinked away his anxiety as the gallery owner came forward to shake his hand and, with one pat on his shoulder, guide him back towards the entrance to introduce him to several of the press who were clustered around the media table.

He glanced quickly over one shoulder back to the blonde, but she had turned slightly away from him to take a call on her mobile.

Later. He would find out a lot more about this woman… later.

Lottie Rosemount chuckled into the mouthpiece of her mobile phone. 'You really are shameless, Dee Flynn! But are you quite sure that Sean does not mind me using his hotel for the fundraiser? He is doing me a seriously big favour here.'

'No need to panic, oh, great organiser lady.' Dee's familiar laughing voice crackled down the phone. 'Let's call it one of the many perks to having a boyfriend who just happens to run his own hotel chain. Sean expects you to invite the great and good of London town and fill his hotel to bursting. And once they see how fabulous his new hotel is? Job done.'

'Oh, is that what it is. A perk? Nothing to do with the fact that the lovely Sean would jog to the moon and back if you asked him. Oh, no. But I am grateful. You are a total star! Thanks, Dee. And have a great time in the tea gardens.'

'I will, but only if you stop worrying, missy. Yes, I can hear it in your voice. Just because a few hundred people will be turning up on Saturday night doesn't mean that you have to be nervous. They will hardly notice that Valencia has not turned up. You wait and see.' Then Dee's voice changed to a breathless gasp. 'Sorry, Lottie. They're calling my flight. Miss you, too. But we need the tea! Bye, Lottie. Bye.'

Lottie held the phone in her hand for a few seconds before clicking it closed and exhaling. Very slowly.

Worried? Of course she was worried. Or should that be terrified?

She would be a fool if she wasn't.

What if the fundraiser was a flop? There were so many creative people bursting with talent who needed a helping hand to get started living their dream. Scholarships to help gifted chefs find training was only the start. But a big start in more ways than one.

Pity that Dee had to be in China this week. She could have used some moral support.

Especially when the celebrity chef she had booked as the main attraction for the fundraiser had just cancelled that morning. It had taken months of pleading and cajoling before multi-award-winning chef Valencia Cagoni had finally agreed to turn up for the night.

Yes, of course Lottie understood that Valencia was still with her family in Turin because both of the four-year-old twins had chickenpox and were grounded as infectious ty-

rants. And no, Valencia was way too busy with the cala-
mine lotion to think of another chef who could step in at
such short notice and take her place.

Thank you, Valencia, my old boss and mentor. *Thanks
a lot.*

Panic gripped her for a few seconds but Lottie willed it
back down to a place where she kept all of the suppressed
fear and suffocating anxiety that came with taking on such
a huge responsibility.

This fundraiser had been her idea from the start, but
if there was one good thing that her father had taught her
it was that she always had options. All she had to do was
think of one. Fast.

Lottie shuffled from side to side on the hard seat and
tried to get a comfier position. She was going to have to
give the gallery owner some feedback before his paying
customers started complaining about having frozen bottoms.

On the other hand, this was not a museum and she had
been sitting in one place a lot longer than she had planned.
Wealthy clients looking for artwork to adorn their walls
would not be perched on the end of a leather bench for more
than a few minutes while she had been sitting there for—
Lottie checked her watch and snorted deep in the back of
her throat in disbelief—twenty minutes.

Amazing.

This was the first time in weeks that she had been able
to steal a few minutes to enjoy herself in between running
her bakery and organising the fundraiser and she was quite
determined to enjoy every second of it. Because she probably would not find another slot before the event.

But she had always been the same. Every time her
mother bought a new piece of art for one of her interior
design clients, it was Lottie who had the first look before

the piece was shipped off to some luxury second or third or, in one case, eighth home around the world. That was all part of her mum's high-end design business.

If Lottie saw something she liked she took the opportunity to appreciate it while she could. It was as simple as that.

Having the time to enjoy works of art was probably the only thing she really missed in her new life.

Of course she had known that running a cake shop and tea rooms would not be a nine-to-five job, but, *sheesh*, the hours she was working now were even longer than when she worked in banking.

She loved most of it. The bakery was her dream come true. But when her photographer friend Ian had casually mentioned that he was looking for a caterer to serve canapés and mini desserts for the opening of a new gallery specialising in contemporary art she had jumped at the chance.

Lottie's Cake Shop and Tea Rooms needed a photographer to take images for the bakery website and Ian needed food for the gallery tonight. Now that was the kind of trade she liked and it had nothing to do with her old job working the stock market.

Lottie glanced back at the main reception area.

She could hear the visitors start to arrive and gather in the bar area that had been opened up onto the stunning patio overlooking the south bank of the Thames on this cloudy June evening. The weather was warm with only a slight breeze. Perfect. Just the way she liked it.

Her skin did not do well in hot sunshine. Too fair. Too freckly.

Much better to stay here for a few minutes and enjoy this painting all to herself while she had the chance before the evening really got started.

The food was all ready to be served in the small kitchen behind the bar, the waiting staff would not be here for another ten minutes, and even the artist had not made an appearance yet.

So she could steal another few minutes of glorious self-indulgence before she had to go back to work.

This was her special time. To be alone with the art.

Lottie waggled some of the tension out of her shoulders and rolled her neck from side to side before lifting her chin and sighing in pleasure.

Most of the exhibition was high-art portraits and landscapes in oils and multimedia in a startling bright and vibrant colour palette, but for some reason she had been drawn to this far corner of the room. It was away from the entrance and the drinks table but was bright with natural light flooding in from the floor-to-ceiling windows.

And the one picture in the whole collection that was muted and subtle.

It was a small canvas in a wide red glass frame just like all of the others.

But this one was special. Different. She had seen it in the catalogue for the exhibition that her friend Ian had created and had been immediately drawn to it.

It was hard to explain but there was just something about the image that had taken hold of her and refused to let her go.

Lottie's gaze scanned the picture.

A middle-aged woman in a knee-length sleeveless red dress was standing on a sandy shore edged with pine trees and luxuriant Mediterranean plants. She was slender and holding out her arms towards the sea.

Lottie could almost feel the breeze in the chiffon layers that made up the skirt as they lifted out behind her.

The woman's head was held high and tall and there was a faint smile on her lips as she stared out to sea, reaching for it with both hands while her pale feet seemed totally encased in the sand.

It was dusk and on the horizon there were the characteristic red and gold and apricot streaks in the misty shadows that stretched out to the horizon. Soon darkness would fall but Lottie knew that this woman would stay there, entranced, until the last possible moment, yearning for the sea, until the very last of the day was gone.

While she still had a chance for happiness.

A single tear ran down Lottie's cheek and she sniffed several times before diving into her bag for a tissue, but then remembered that she had left them back at the cake shop, so made do with a spare paper napkin she had popped into her bag for spillages.

Last chances. Oh, yes. She knew all about those.

Until three years ago she had been a business clone in a suit, trapped in cubicle nation in the investment bank where her father had worked for thirty-five years. All she'd had to do was keep her head down, say the right things and do what she was told and she'd had a clear career path that would take her to the top. She'd even had the ideal boyfriend with the right credentials on paper just one step higher than her on the ladder.

How could her life have been more perfect?

The fact that she hated her job so much that she threw up most mornings was one of the reasons she was earning the big bucks. Wasn't it?

Until that one fateful day when all of the pretence and lies had been whipped away, leaving her bereft and alone. Standing on a beach like the one in the painting. Holding out her arms towards the sea, looking for a new direction and a new identity.

She wasn't balls-of-steel Charlie any longer, the girl who had walked away from her six-figure salary and the career track to the top of her father's investment bank to train as a pastry chef. Oh, no.

That girl was gone.

The girl sitting with tears in her eyes was Lottie the baker. The real girl with the real pain that she had thought she had worked through over these past three years but was still there. Catching her unawares at moments like this when the overwhelming emotion swallowed her down and drowned her.

For the first time in a long time she had allowed her public face to slip and reveal that she was hurting.

Foolish woman! Exhaustion and unspoken loneliness made her vulnerable. That was all.

The paper napkin was starting to disintegrate so she stuffed it back into her bag.

Maybe at the end of the night when everyone was heading home she could steal a few minutes with the artist and ask her about 'Last Chances'.

Who knew? Maybe Adele Forrester might be able to answer a few of her questions about how making the most of last chances could change your life so very much. And what to do when all of the people and friends that you thought would stick by you decided that you had nothing in common with them once you jumped ship and stopped answering your calls.

Starting with that, oh-so-perfect-on-paper boyfriend.

Yes, maybe Adele had a few answers of her own.

With one final sniff, Lottie blinked and wiped her cheek with the back of her finger. Time to repair the damage to this make-up and get ready to rock and roll. She had two hundred portions of canapés to plate out.

Busy, busy.

Yes, she should really make a move now. Oops. Too late. Lottie sensed rather than heard someone stroll closer and stand next to her, so that they were both looking at the canvas in silence for what felt like minutes but was probably only seconds.

'It's perfect, isn't it?' Lottie sniffed as yet another tear ran down her cheek, preventing her from turning around and embarrassing herself in front of a complete stranger.

'Absolutely perfect. How does she do it?' Lottie asked. 'How does Adele capture so much feeling in a flat image? It's incredible.'

'Talent. And a deep feeling for the place. Adele knows that beach at all times of day and season. Look at the way she blends the ocean and the sky. That can only come from seeing it happen over and over again.'

Lottie blinked again, but this time in surprise.

He understood. This man, because it was a man's voice and definitely a manly pair of designer trousers, was echoing the exact same thoughts that were going through her head.

How did he do that? The tremor in his voice was instantly calming and restorative. Someone else saw the same things in this work that she had. How was that possible?

It was unnerving that he knew what this painting was all about and could talk about it with such passion.

And then the harsh reality of where she was struck home and she felt like a fool. Ian had told her that this was a preview show for art critics and media people. This man was probably a friend of Adele Forrester who knew perfectly well the history behind the picture.

Maybe he could answer her question?

Lottie lifted her chin and shuffled sideways on the bench so that she could look up into the face of the man standing by her side.

The room froze.

It was as though everything around her slowed down

to treacle speed like a DVD or video being played in slow motion.

The laughter and gossip from the clusters of elegantly dressed people gathered around the gallery owner became a blur of distant sounds. Even the air between them felt colder and thicker as Lottie sucked in a low, calming breath.

Was this really happening?

'Rob Beresford,' she said out loud, and instantly clenched her teeth tight shut.

Thinking out loud had always been her worst habit and she'd thought she had it beaten. Apparently not. Her mouth gaped open in confusion.

And why not?

Rob Beresford. Her least-favourite chef in the world. And the man who had single-handedly tried to destroy her career.

CHAPTER TWO

'IN THE FLESH.' Rob shrugged. And without asking permission or forgiveness he sat down next to her on the flat leather-covered bench and stretched his long legs out towards the exhibition wall. 'I hope that you are enjoying the exhibition. This piece is really quite remarkable.'

Lottie tried to make her senses take it in. And failed.

Rob Beresford.

Of all the people in the entire world, he was the last person she expected to meet at a gallery preview show.

He looked like a picture postcard of the ideal celebrity chef. Stylish suit. Hair. Designer stubble. Damn the stylist who had his clothes pitched perfectly.

But underneath the slick exterior the old Rob was all still there.

She could see it in the way he walked. The swagger. The attitude and that arrogant lift of his head that made him look like a captain of some sailing ship, looking out over the ocean for pirate ships loaded with treasure.

He had not changed that much since their last meeting almost three years earlier.

When he had fired her from her very first catering job.

Just thinking about that day was enough for an ice cube large enough to sink the *Titanic* to form in the pit of her stomach.

She had only been working as an apprentice in the Beresford hotel kitchen for three months when the mighty Rob Beresford had burst into the kitchen and demanded that the idiot who had made the chocolate dessert go out into the dining room and apologise in person to the diner on his table who had almost broken his teeth on the rock-hard pastry he had just been served.

Apparently Rob had been totally humiliated and embarrassed. So he'd needed a scapegoat to blame for the screw-up.

In one glance the head pastry chef had nodded in her direction and the next thing she'd known Rob had grabbed the front of her chef's coat and used it to haul her up to his face so close that she could feel his hot, angry, brutal breath on her cheek. His anger and recrimination had been spat out in the words that would be burnt into her heart and her mind for the rest of her career.

'Get out of my kitchen and back to your finishing school, you pathetic excuse for a chef. You don't have what it takes to be in this business so leave now and save us all a lot of wasted time. Nobody humiliates me and gets away with it.'

Then he'd flung his hands back from her jacket so quickly that she had almost fallen and had had to grab hold of the steel workbench as Rob had stabbed the air. 'I don't want to see you here tomorrow. Got it?'

Oh, she'd got it, all right. She'd understood perfectly how unfair and how prejudiced these chefs were. She had waited until the sous chefs had stopped fawning at him and plated up new desserts before slipping out to grab her coat and escape from the back door before the pastry chef, skanky Debra, who had been so drunk that she could barely stand never mind make decent *pâté sucrée* that evening, could say another word.

From that moment she had vowed to be her own boss. No matter what.

Which begged the question…what was he doing here tonight? In an art gallery of all places? Buying art for the restaurants? That was possible, but not fine art. No, it was much more likely that there was someone in the room who could advance his career in some way.

See and be seen was Rob Beresford's motto. It always had been, and from what she had seen of him in the press and TV, nothing had changed. And if he had to pretend to have some knowledge of the pieces, well, that was a small price for his personal advancement.

The humiliating thing was he did not seem to have recognised her. She had been consigned to the box where all of the other sacked apprentices went to be forgotten. And she had absolutely no intention of reminding him.

Lottie ran one hand over the back of her neck to lift her hair away from her suddenly burning skin as a flash of anger shot through her.

Rob's powerful, low voice seemed to resonate inside her head and a whole flutter of butterflies came to life in her stomach.

His presence filled the space between them and she felt crowded out, squeezed between the ivory-painted wall and the bench. Last time he had towered over her, his eyes like burning lasers, and she refused to let that happen again.

Not going to happen. This time she was the one who glared at him face-to-face.

Hard angles defined his jawline and cheekbones but they only made the lushness of his full mouth even more pronounced.

At some point his nose had been broken, creating a definite twist just below the bridge. Thank heaven for that. Otherwise this Rob Beresford had all the credentials for being even more gorgeous than the last time that they had met.

As Rob reached for a champagne flute the fine fabric of his shirt stretched over the valleys and mounds of his chest muscles, which came from a lifetime of hard work rather than lifting weights in a city gym. There really was no justice—that a man who could create dishes as he could was good-looking, too.

Shame that he knew it.

In one smooth movement he pushed the sleeve of his designer dinner jacket farther up his left arm, revealing a curving, dark tattoo that ran up from his wrist. It seemed to match the design that peeked out in the deep V of the crisp white dinner shirt he was wearing unbuttoned. No tie.

For a tiny fraction of a second Lottie wondered what the rest of the design looked like on that powerful chest. Then she pushed the thought away. Body art on a chef? Oh, that made perfect sense...not.

Typical exhibitionist. Just one more way to draw attention to himself.

In the small world of high-level cooking it would be impossible not to run into Rob Beresford at the many chef award ceremonies where she was with the lesser mortals sitting in the back row.

And of course there was his TV show. It took guts to walk into a strange kitchen and tell the chef that the way they had been running their restaurant needed to be turned around and he had all the answers.

The TV audience could not get enough of the fireworks and tears and family trauma that came with having a complete stranger telling you how to run your life after years and years of working day and night. It had to be the third or fourth season. Why did these places apply? Madness. She certainly would never do it.

He was precisely the kind of man she had come to despise for the games that he liked to play with other people's lives. Pushing them around. Uncaring and selfish.

Harsh? Maybe. But true all the same.

What had she promised herself the day she walked out of the bank? No more lies. No more kidding yourself. No more second best. And no more putting up with other people's games.

Rob Beresford was a player.

And she had no intention of being part of his little game.

Then he lifted his head and looked at her. No. More than that. He seemed to be studying her. She had been expecting those famous piercing cobalt-blue eyes to give her the beauty-parade head-to-toe assessment.

He didn't. His gaze was locked on to her face as though he was searching for something, and finding it. Because one corner of his mouth turned up into just the hint of a smile, which only drew her attention to that kissable mouth.

'I think we have met before somewhere, but I am embarrassed to say that I have forgotten your name. Can you help?'

His voice was hot chocolate sauce on top of the best butterscotch ice cream and had all the potential to make her silly girl heart spin just fast enough to make breathing a challenge. More American than it used to be but that was hardly surprising. In fact, if anything, that trace of an accent only added to the allure.

Could she what? Oh, was that the best he could do? Try and make her feel guilty for causing him embarrassment?

She was almost insulted.

Surely the famous Rob Beresford had better pickup lines that that? Or perhaps he was not on top form. There was certainly something different about Rob. A little less arrogant, perhaps? Not surprising. He certainly got around, if you could believe the hotel and catering trade press.

'Oh, please. Does that line still work?'

Rob's eyebrow arched and a sexy smile designed to defrost frozen food at twenty paces switched on like a light bulb.

'Occasionally. But now I am even more intrigued. Put me out of my misery. Have we met before?'

'We might have.' She blinked and then casually turned back to face the canvases on the wall in front of her. 'But then again I didn't expect to find you in an art gallery. Have you changed direction? Or perhaps you want to meet a different type of girl? They do say that museums and galleries are very popular with single people these days. So tell me—how do you come to know Adele Forrester's work? You seem to be something of a fan. Am I right?'

She heard Rob take a short breath. 'I might be. But here is an idea. You seem to be very curious about me and I am curious about you. What if I answer one question then you have to answer mine? Simple trade. Question for question. What do you say? Do we have a deal?'

Lottie raised her eyebrows, then squinted at him. 'Can I trust you to keep your word?'

'Now I am offended,' he tutted. 'Absolutely. Just this once. And I promise not to ask any personal questions. Scout's honour.'

'You were never in the Boy Scouts!'

'Two weeks on the Isle of Wight getting sunburnt and learning to light fires. I remember it well. And you haven't answered my first question.'

Lottie could almost feel the prickle of interest build under her skin as his gaze stayed locked tight on her face.

Maybe she could take a few minutes to chat with him? Equal to equal? Pretend that they had never met? It would make a change from talking to Ian about the fundraiser and the photography shoot he was planning. It might even be amusing to see him struggle to recall where and when they last met.

'Okay,' she casually replied as though she didn't care either way.

'Okay? Is that it?'

'That is all you are going to get from me, so take it or leave it,' Lottie replied with a small shoulder shrug. 'And I get to go first. My question. Remember?'

'Right. Yes, I know Adele Forrester and, yes, I am a huge fan of her work. Love everything that she has ever exhibited and a lot more besides. Happy now? Good. Because now it is my turn to ask for the name of my inquisitor. Because whatever paper you are working for has certainly chosen the perfect character for their entertainment section. So. What name shall I look out for in the Forrester review?'

Lottie nibbled on the inside of her lip to stop herself from smiling. Ah. So he thought she was one of the art critics. *Perfect. She was officially incognito. This was going to be fun.*

'Charlotte. But you can call me Charlie. I answer to both.'

'Charlie,' he repeated in a low voice, then blinked twice before shaking his head from side to side. 'An art critic called Charlie. I should have known it would be something like that.'

His trademark collar-length hair swung loosely in front of his face as he moved, then he flicked his head back out of habit rather than design and a low rough chuckle rumbled deep in his throat before he laughed it away.

'Thank you. I needed that. And does Charlie come with a surname?'

Patience. There was no way that she was going to allow

this arrogant man to win his little game. Her surname would instantly give the game away.

'You are so impatient. That is a completely new question. It's my turn now.'

Lottie tilted her head towards the canvas and pushed her lips together. She had met enough art critics through her mum to give a decent enough performance for a few minutes.

'This is such an interesting piece. But it seems so different from the other paintings in the exhibition. Most of the landscapes are luxuriant, and the portraits jump off the page—they are terrific. But this one is more…'

Lottie waved her hand in the air as she tried to come up with the perfect description and failed.

'Introspective?' Rob whispered. 'Was that the word you were looking for? The colours capture Adele's mood. Every artist has shades to their work and their character. The dark makes the light seem brighter. Don't you find?' And with that he turned and gave her a smile that had nothing to do with teeth and everything to do with the warmth of genuine feeling that illuminated his face, from the gentle turn of those full lips to the slight crease in the corner of each eye.

After years working in the hard world of banking where a wrong call could cost millions, Lottie prided herself on being a good judge of character.

And this version of Rob Beresford threw her.

He meant it. He was so…calm and centred…and normal. At that moment he was simply a man in an art gallery having a conversation about an artist that he sincerely admired.

Where had that come from?

Was it possible that he had changed so much in the past few years?

'Would you call yourself an artist, Rob? The media certainly seem to think so.'

His eyes widened and just like that the tiny thread of connection that had been linking them together on this slim bench snapped with a loud twang and went spinning off into the room.

'Charlie! Every chef would like to think that they create art on a plate. Colours, tastes and textures. But an artist? No.'

With a quick toss of his head he raised his eyebrows. 'You surprise me, Charlie. Surely you don't believe everything you read in the press? I would hate to be a disappointment.'

'Ah. I knew there was a reason why I never wanted to go down the celebrity route. The price of fame. It must be so exhausting. Having to act out the part every time you show yourself in public when all you want to do is stay home and watch reality TV shows in your pyjamas with a cup of hot chocolate.'

'Drat. You have found one of my private fantasies.'

And then Rob paused and leant a little closer. *Too close.* Blocking her view of the rest of the room but forcing her to focus on just how full his lips were and how the dark hair on his throat curled into the open neck of his crisp white shirt.

He lifted his right hand and stroked the line of her jaw from ear to throat with the pad of a soft forefinger, his touch so light that Lottie might almost have imagined it.

But that would have been a lie because the second his skin met her face Lottie sucked in a sharp quick breath and her lips parted, revealing in the most humiliating way possible that she was not immune to his touch.

Just the opposite. She knew that her neck was already flaming red in a blush that engrossed her.

Which was more than humiliating; it was a bad joke. Rob Beresford's reputation with women was common knowledge in the catering world and the Beresford hotel kitchens had been alive with gossip about who he had seduced and then dumped in quick succession. She had seen it herself.

One single quiver of sexual attraction was not going to change her mind about him. It was biology and a much underused libido playing tricks on her.

Her gaze scanned his face.

At this distance she could see that his eyes were not just blue, but a blend of different shades of blue from steel-grey to the bright evening sky. Mesmerising. Totally, totally mesmerising. And quite shameless.

Because before she had time to protest, Rob cupped the nape of her neck with one hand and bent his head lower so that his nose was pressed against her forehead, his breath hot and slow and heavy on her face.

Without asking for permission she felt his other hand fan out on her lower back, taking her weight, arching her body down. Into his control.

His lips trembled and parted. *He was going to kiss her.*

Instinctively she slid her tongue across her parched lips but instantly saw his smile switch back on.

Damn. She had fallen straight into his little trap.

'What are you doing?' she breathed and raised both hands to push his away. 'You are being outrageous. Don't you ever go off duty? Please don't try and flirt with me, Mr Beresford.'

'There we go. Another one of those damn fantasies of mine.'

Rob pushed both hands down hard, slid off the bench and stretched to his full height so that when he spoke he had to look down at her with a huge grin on his face. 'After all, I would hate for you to think that I was acting out of character for some reason. That might be too much for your readers to understand. Because otherwise, who knows? It might actually cross your mind that I am simply here to enjoy the art on my night off.'

His gaze locked on to her eyes and held them tight in its grasp. Only now those blue eyes were more gunmetal than warm sea. Laser cold. Sharp. A cold shiver that had nothing to do with the icy air conditioning raised goosebumps along Lottie's arms and neck.

So this was what it was like to be at the receiving end of one of Rob Beresford's bad moods.

Not good. *So* not good.

The cold shiver turned to fiery indignation and Lottie pressed her lips together. What gave him the right to talk to a guest at an art gallery like this?

One more minute and she was going to jump up and give him just as much right back, starting with the last time they met. Maybe he could dish it out but could he take it when the tables were turned and he was on the receiving end? She doubted it.

Lottie curled her fingers into a tight fist and mentally came up with a couple of suitable put-downs from her banking days, but she never got the chance to use them. Because just like that he broke eye contact and rolled back his shoulders for a second before looking back over one shoulder at her.

'I've just had an outrageous idea. Plus it's my turn for a question. Care to join me on a tour of the exhibition? It's about time you gave me your expert opinion on the other paintings.'

Rob ran one hand back through his hair and tore his gaze away from the blonde and looked around the room. A trickle of guests was starting to wander into the exhibition space now and he inwardly cursed himself for being stupid enough to lose his temper and act out his frustration with this girl he had just met.

He was so tired of playing the fool for the cameras. Tired of allowing his emotions and excitement to get the better of him.

Just once it would be nice to be taken seriously.

He was Adele Forrester's only child. Did the press, like this cute blonde, really think that he had no appreciation of the art world after spending most of his precious free time in the company of a woman who was even more obsessed and passionate than he was?

'You want to hear my opinion of the other paintings, Mr Beresford? Is that right?'

He flicked his head towards the reception area. 'Absolutely. I think I just saw some waiting staff coming in. Why don't we find out what culinary delights the gallery have lined up for us this evening before the rest of your colleagues arrive? You never know. Some of them might even be edible! Oh—and, Charlie, tonight you can forget the Beresford. Right here, at this moment, I'm just Rob. Think you can handle that? Or are you scared of living dangerously?'

He offered her his hand and she lowered her head and stared at it, flicked her gaze onto his face, then back.

'Danger is my middle name. I think I can just about manage that. Rob.'

But just as she stood up her head bobbed to one side and she saw someone behind his back. 'Oops. Duty calls. I would love to stand around and feed your ego a little longer but I have to get back to work. Another time, perhaps. Have a lovely evening. Ciao.'

And with a tiny finger wave of her right hand she strolled—no, she sashayed across the room on four-inch heels as though she were made to wear them, giving him the most excellent view of the sweetest clinging dress above spectacular legs.

She had a waist he could wrap his hands around and meet in the middle, and the way she lifted her chin as she strode away?

Dynamite.

This girl moved as if she were gliding. Head held high and still, focused on the path ahead, determined. She was like a swan on the water, a perfect example of restrained elegance, both understated and explosively seductive.

Even the way she walked screamed out that she came from a background of old money plus an expensive education and all that came with it.

Either that or she was the best actor that he had ever met, and he had met plenty of actresses in the hotel and restaurant trade. Hollywood and Broadway. A class and C class. They were all the same under the slick exterior. Girls ready and waiting to say the words someone else had written for them.

But Charlie the art critic? Charlie was in a class of her own.

And in his crazy world, that was pretty unique.

Who was this woman and what had he done to upset her? He had met her before, that was certain. And from that frosty glare she had given him when he'd sat down next to her, chances were that it had not been one of his finer moments.

Now all he had to do was work out what terrible crime he had committed. Rob could never resist a challenge.

He was going to chase this woman down to her lair and find out her name before the night was out.

Maybe he could salvage something out of his nightmare of an exhibition after all?

'Charlie. Just a moment,' he said to her back, and strode after her across the exhibition space, back towards the reception area where waiting staff were stacking side plates and cutlery onto white tablecloths over polymer tables.

It had been a long day and his body clock was starting to kick in. Perhaps it was time to show his appreciation for the lady who had finally given him something to smile about?

With his long athletic legs and her shorter high-heeled ones, it only took Rob a few steps to catch up with Charlie, who surprised him by stepping behind the desk.

'Hold up. You never did give me your name. A business card. Email address. Phone number, if you are old school. Come on. You know you want to keep in touch. For…follow-up questions.'

Rob's voice faded away as he stepped closer.

'You're wearing an apron. Are you waiting tables?'

'You're right, the rumours about you could not possibly be true. You *are* more intelligent than you look,' Charlie said, and flashed him a glance in between giving directions to the very young-looking art-student waiters. 'But I can only hope that you have a sense of humour, as well. Because it's even worse than that. You see, I am not an art critic. Never have been. Probably never will be. I'm the chef who is taking care of the canapés this evening.'

And before Rob had a chance to take it all in, Lottie picked up a tray of steaming-hot savouries and thrust it out towards him like a weapon.

'Could I interest you in one of my humble pies? I think they are just what you need.'

CHAPTER THREE

'NOT AT THE MOMENT, THANK YOU. No. I think I'll pass.'

Rob picked up one of the business cards that Lottie had fanned out next to the condiments and the deep frown creased his forehead as he read the address out loud.

'Lottie Rosemount's Cake Shop and Tea Rooms? That's where Dee Flynn works.'

Lottie could practically see the cogs of Rob's mind work as his gaze ratcheted up one notch at a time from the business card past the platter of savoury canapés and finally to her face. Where it settled for one millisecond as the inevitable hit home.

'Please tell me that you're not Lottie Rosemount.' He finally groaned.

Her breath caught in the back of her throat for a second before she smiled it away with a quick flick of the head.

Busted! Playtime had officially just ended and it was back to work.

'Sorry. Can't do that. Life is so unfair sometimes. Don't you think? Welcome to my world, Mr Beresford.'

Shame. She had enjoyed being taken seriously as an art expert for a few minutes. Now it was back to being plain old Lottie the cake maker. It was always curious to see how people's expectations changed when she announced that she baked for a living, but she had not expected to see that stunned look on Rob's face. He was in the same business, after all.

Her body still tingled at the touch of his hand at the small of her back. One thin layer of silk was all that had separated his clever long fingers from her naked skin.

Time to jump in and take control while he was still at the glaring-in-disbelief stage. 'I did tell you that my name was Charlotte and people call me so many nicknames that it's fun to have a change now and then. Just for the variety.'

'Lottie Rosemount.' Rob nodded slowly up and down, then gave a low whistle. 'I don't believe it. So you like playing games with people? Lottie. Or do you have another nickname you prefer to use on social occasions?'

Games. *Hell, no.* He was not accusing her of playing tricks on him.

'Oh, no. Lottie works fine. As for playing games? On the contrary. It goes against my principles.'

His reply was a choked cough and he gestured towards the bench, which was already occupied by other patrons.

'But it was okay to string me along just now and pretend that you were an art critic. Did you even like that painting you were staring at or just doing it to impress me?'

She heard the annoyance in his voice and was shamefully delighted.

'I don't recall saying that I was a critic. And as for trying to impress you? Well, someone has a very high opinion of themselves. For the record I have always adored contemporary art and I love these pieces. Especially that painting. If that is okay with you? Or are you one of those people who think that the catering staff should stay in their place? Out of sight. So that they are not able to embarrass the management.'

His back stiffened and instantly Rob seemed to grow about five inches taller.

'No. I am not one of those people, Lottie. Far from it, actually.'

The words whirled around inside her head at the confused signals. He was acting as if she had insulted him. Well, that was rich.

'Good. Because I do love that painting and was pleased to have the chance to see it. So, seeing as we share a common interest, I think it only fair that I share my other passion with you before the masses of starving media arrive.'

'You have more than one passion? Please, carry on. I would hate for you to feel that you cannot act on your principles. *Heaven forfend.*'

Ignoring the sarcasm was not something Lottie found easy, but she got through it by focusing on opening up a new batch of bakery boxes.

The next thing Rob knew he was holding a dessert plate with a piece of cake on it. He lifted it to his nose and sniffed.

'Lemon sponge?'

'I do hope that you enjoy it. The gallery gave me strict instructions that Adele Forrester had specifically requested two desserts. Individual dark chocolate tarts and lemon drizzle cakes. A special order from a fine artist. Now that, Mr Beresford, I could not fake. Dig in.'

His lips closed around the forkful of cake and her gaze locked on to those lips.

She had never seen such sensual lips on any man before and, oh, boy, they looked good enough to eat. The tip of his tongue flicked out tantalisingly and wiped away a smear of lemon sauce.

A flash of raw and unadulterated attraction hit her hard. Unexpected and entirely inappropriate. Strange how it felt seriously good.

Do that again. Please.

Lottie didn't realise that she had stopped breathing until

a very loud ringtone smashed through her foodie trance and she instantly whipped the other cakes onto the platters and arranged them artistically on the buffet table so that the guests could help themselves.

Saved by the bell.

Rob put down his plate and casually fished the mobile phone out of his pocket, checked the caller identity. And flicked the phone closed with a crisp clip.

'Interesting cake. But I have to go and meet another lovely lady. I'll be seeing you around.' He smiled at Lottie, then gave her an outrageously over-the-top wink. 'You can bet on it.'

See you around?

Of course Rob was going to see her around.

His half-brother, Sean Beresford, was totally in love with her best friend and business partner, Dee, and unless she had totally misread the signs, there would be engagement parties and wedding planning before the end of the year. And right there next to Sean would be his best pal, Rob.

She was going to have to put up with Rob for Dee's sake. But really? Trying to flirt with her in an art gallery? Sheesh. And why did he have to be so…so…him?

So who was this lovely lady anyway? Some A-list celebrity? Or that supermodel Dee had told her he was seeing?

Lottie casually turned her head so that she could see Rob's back.

He was making a beeline for the tall, elegant, very slender older woman who was walking on air through the doors leading into the gallery. One hand was high in the air, the other waving from side to side from the wrist in flamboyant over-the-top gestures.

The moment she saw Rob she gave a quick squeal, flung her arms forward and gave him such a warm and sweet hug that Lottie knew that they cared about one another. He seemed perfectly happy to hook her arm over his and escort her into the room, lighting their way with the kind of beaming smile that should be licensed to power companies.

But it was only when she stepped closer under the exhibition spotlights that Lottie realised she was looking at Adele Forrester. She recognised the characteristic high cheekbones and profile from the posters and exhibition catalogues that her friend Ian had created.

And it totally floored her.

Adele was lovely, happy, laughing and enjoying herself.

Well, that was one more illusion shattered! So much for the tortured artist who had painted that wonderful landscape of the woman on the shore looking for a last chance. She had clearly found her mojo because right at that moment Adele Forrester was the star of the show, Rob Beresford was her escort and they were both having a great time.

Rob Beresford and Adele Forrester.

This evening was certainly turning out to be full of surprises. Little wonder that he was a walking expert on the artist's work when they were clearly such great pals. Not lovers. She could see that. No. There was none of that awkward first touch. They seemed closer. Almost like best friends or family.

Curious. She had not expected that. Perhaps she should call Dee and find out if Sean had mentioned anything about how Rob knew an artist like Adele Forrester.

Instantly the gallery owner and several of the guests surged forwards to shake Adele's hand, smiling and laughing and crowding in to get attention from the star of the show.

Lottie tried to peer over their heads but it was no good. Adele was swamped.

And right on time the first batch of art-student waiting

staff emerged from the kitchen carrying platters of hot canapés straight from the oven.

It was show time!

He had known that this was going to happen.

Worse. It was entirely his own fault.

He should never have left his mum alone at the hotel with the champagne that the gallery had sent around and several packs of cold medicine.

He had taken his eyes off the ball and indulged in a little free time with a lovely blonde who had turned out to be the opposite of what he'd expected.

And now his lovely mother was as high as a kite.

Flying over everyone's heads but coming down to earth just long enough to make polite and quite sensible conversation with the very people who had the power to make her life miserable if she imploded.

He had let her down.

There was no other way of describing it. The most important exhibition of her career and Adele Forrester had just described her signature style to the art critic of the largest broadsheet newspaper in London as Californian rain.

The real problem was that she adored chatting about her art so much. This was her world and she was amazing. Truly. Grabbing her arm and dragging her away would not only be creepy, but annoying.

That wouldn't work. So he had switched to plan B. The oldest technique in the world. Distraction and diversion.

Now. How many lovely lady art critics could he charm just long enough for them not to notice that the artist they had come to chat to was totally sozzled? *Time to find out.*

'Lemon drizzle cake! Oh, how did you know that was my absolute favourite? You are a complete genius and I don't even know your name. How embarrassing. My son never makes me lemon drizzle, no matter how often I plead with him.'

Lottie grinned and loaded a plate with three squares of moist cake. 'Lottie Rosemount. And I am told that your agent made a special request, Miss Forrester.'

'Oh, one more reason why I love Sally so much. And please call me Adele.'

Lottie watched Adele dive into her bag and sneeze onto a lovely hand-embroidered hankie, which was now sodden. She squeezed her eyes together, then blinked a couple of times.

'Can you believe it? I wait eight years for an exhibition and I have to come down with a horrible head cold. Almost through it, but my head! It feels as though it is totally full of cotton wool. Excuse me, darling. Time for another of these cold tablets I bought this morning. They really are the perfect pick-me-up.'

Adele popped one into her mouth and washed it down with a huge slug of pink champagne before smacking her lips. 'Quite delicious.'

Lottie took a quick glance at the medicine box Adele had left on the table.

'Er. Adele, those are one-a-day tablets. Are you sure it's okay to take so many with alcohol?'

'One a day? Really? Oh. Well, that must mean that they work faster. Excellent.'

Adele rested a beautifully manicured hand on Lottie's arm and swayed slightly. 'As long as they get me through the night, sweetie, I am prepared to take the risk. I have waited a long time for tonight. There is no way that I am going to miss a single moment.'

Then her eyebrows lifted and a huge sweet grin illuminated the room. 'Ah. There's my son. Better load my plate up with those delicious-looking bites before he catches up with me and reminds me that it is way past my bedtime.'

Then Adele flashed a completely over-the-top dramatic wink before blinking in rapid succession.

'A girl can always use more pizza squares. Don't you think? Ah. Rob. Perfect timing as always. Give your old mum a hand and hold my glass while I sample these pastries, will you, kiddo? They all look *so* good.'

Lottie inhaled a long slow breath, redolent with the aroma of the last of the mushroom-and-anchovy croustade slices Adele was tucking into with great relish, before slowly sliding her gaze up Adele's arm into the face of Rob Beresford.

The man who had sat down on that bench and let her prattle on about the paintings without even giving one tiny hint about why he knew so much about Adele Forrester.

Because apparently this lovely woman with the amazing artistic talent…

Was his mother.

There were bad words to describe men like Rob. And *kiddo* was not one of them.

And he had been accusing her of playing games!

Oh, Adele. Where had it all gone wrong?

The snake waited until Adele was chatting to Ian before sliding closer to the serving area. 'Charlie… No. I mean, Lottie. Good. You are still here.'

Rob glanced from side to side before asking in a low whisper, 'I need a back way out of the gallery and I need it fast. Start talking.'

His fingers started tapping out a beat on the table and his whole body language screamed out impatience and frustration.

Lottie glanced over his shoulder at the cluster of giggling press ladies in regulation black who had their heads pressed together comparing their mobile-phone photos and shooting very unsubtle smoochy glances in his direction. Hair flicking and quick-fire reapplication of lip gloss seemed to be the order of the day.

'So I see,' Lottie replied with the same fixed, professional smile that she had used all evening, the one that made her jaw ache. 'The owner has a very useful gallery plan. You will find it just over there. Behind the barman's head.'

Lottie pointed to the large display on the wall next to the drinks table, which was slowly emptying as the remaining guests wandered out onto the terrace to enjoy the cool late-evening air before heading home.

'What's the matter, Rob? Need to make your escape before the girls pounce on you?'

The smile dropped from the handsome man's face and he half turned and flashed her the withering, contemptuous look that had made him notorious in the hard-nosed cookery shows, but had no place at all in a fine-art exhibition.

It was nothing like as angry as the look he had given her when he had fired her but Lottie reared back and pretended to dodge to one side. 'Oh, my. Are those daggers aimed at me? I do hope that the wind won't change because you would not want your face to stick like that.'

Then she leant forwards a little and winked. 'I worked in banking for many years. So the hard approach is wasted on me. Same goes for sighing loudly and frowning. Been there, done that. Not putting up with it a moment longer.'

Rob's eyebrows shot up and he stared at her in what looked like real astonishment.

To her delight the hard line of his mouth lifted up into the tiniest of smiles. 'Okay. Let's try it your way,' he replied in a low, hoarse voice that almost trembled with suppressed energy. 'Excuse me, Miss Rosemount, but could you please direct me to the back way out of the gallery through the kitchens?'

Her hands got busy stacking her bakery platters into a wide plastic crate. 'Of course, Mr Beresford. If you go through those two swing doors and walk about ten metres past the dishwasher there is a fire door to the main staircase to the building. It comes out at the loading bay at the back of the gallery.'

His reply was a quick 'thanks' as he strolled past her at jogging speed, one hand in his pocket as though he were boarding a yacht.

'You're welcome,' she murmured to his back.

What was that all about?

Or rather *who* was that all about?

Lottie swung the final platter and table cover into the carry crate and looked up to scan the room.

He certainly did not want to see someone here this evening. But who? Most of the critics had left when the food ran out and Adele had been around the gallery at least ten times over the last two hours, explaining each and every piece to them before returning to the bar for a refill.

Perhaps he had seen a former girlfriend he did not want to be photographed with? Or maybe one of the rival chefs on the bake-off contest had turned up and was itching for extra publicity.

There must be someone. Then a flash of blue sparkle just in front of one of the largest paintings caught her attention, followed by a peal of very loud and very over-the-top female laughter.

And Lottie's heart sank.

Because suddenly the reason for Rob Beresford's desire to explore other exits from the gallery became startling clear.

It was Adele Forrester.

And she had just staggered into one of the major installations from a very famous artist. It was by pure chance that the gallery owner had caught it in time to prevent a major disaster. On their opening night.

Ouch.

The problem was that Adele was treating it as a huge joke. Her hands were waving in the air but as she stepped forwards it was only too obvious that she was way too unsteady on her feet to be standing up.

Oh, Adele! Cold tablets plus champagne were a bad combination.

Any minute now she was going to fall over and embarrass and humiliate herself, which was the very last thing she needed!

Yep. *Back door.*

In a second she whipped off her apron and dropped it into the crate.

'Adele.' Lottie smiled as she strolled as casually as she could manage up to the stunningly dressed woman who was clinging on to the slightly intoxicated and more-than-slightly terrified gallery owner.

Adele turned towards her a little too quickly and her legs gave a definite wobble but Lottie stepped forwards, hooked her arm around Adele's, and took her weight before anyone had a chance to notice. 'I feel so guilty. I promised to save you some of that lemon drizzle cake you loved so much and now there are only three pieces left.' Then she grinned and snuggled closer as though they were the best of pals and intent on a girl huddle. 'I have kept them hidden in the kitchen for you. If you are ready?'

With one final laugh in the direction of the very relieved gallery owner, Adele clung on to Lottie and chatted merrily about how much she loved London. And cake. And champagne. But somehow Lottie held Adele mostly upright as they very slowly and sedately crossed the gallery and with one push they were through the doors and into the kitchen.

One bar stool and a plastic cake box later, Lottie could finally catch her breath and rub some life back into her arm. Give it five minutes and they would be on their way.

The sound of heavy male footsteps taking the stairs two at a time echoed up and Lottie closed her eyes.

Rob burst into the kitchen, his gaze taking in the scene, eyes flashing, dark and powerful. Accusing and angry. Full of that same fire and mistrust as the last time that they had met.

'What's going on?' he asked, and he jerked his chin higher with every word.

'Adele needs some air and lemon drizzle cake. I was helping her to get both. Okay?'

The Rob she had met three years ago had been obscenely confident of who he was. Master of the universe. Demanding and expecting everyone to worship his talent and magnificence. And that man was right here in the room all over again.

'I can take it from here. She's fine. Just fine.'

But as she nodded Lottie was incapable of dragging her gaze from those stunning eyes.

And the longer she looked, the more she recognised something so startling and surprising that it unnerved her.

Rob might appear to be the most confident and put-together and in-control man that she had ever met, but in those eyes she recognised anxiety and concern.

Something was worrying him. Something she did not know about.

'Have you organised some transport?' Lottie whispered, trying to sound casual so that Adele would not be scared.

'Don't worry about that,' Rob snapped. 'The most important thing is to get her out of here before she makes a fool of herself.'

Lottie smiled down at the lovely woman who was half leaning against the dishwasher and nibbling delicately at the cake, apparently oblivious to their conversation.

'Why? This is her party. Her work. Surely she is allowed to have fun at the opening night?'

'Not in front of these people. They are looking for any excuse to pull us down and sell the photographs to the highest bidder. They know me. And they know where to find me. The last thing I need is a scene. Not good at all.'

'*You.* They know *you.*'

Lottie stared at him open-mouthed and then shook her head in disbelief. 'Oh, I have been so stupid. I actually thought that you were concerned that your mum might embarrass herself on her big night. When all of the time you were more concerned about how this might look to the press pack waiting outside the front entrance. You and your precious image are the only things that matters.'

'You don't know what you are talking about,' he whispered, and she saw something hard and painful in those dark and flashing eyes.

'Oh, don't I? You would be surprised. I know a lot more about men who put their so-called appearance above everything else than you think.'

She could feel her neck flushing red but there was nothing she could do to stop it.

How many times had her father used the same expression? The last thing he wanted was a scene. How often had she stood next to him at company functions afraid to speak or even move, because he had given her strict instructions to stay silent and keep in the background? Don't make a fuss. You are an embarrassment. No one likes a show-off.

And never, ever, do anything that would put him in a bad light.

The one time she got drunk after a multimillion-dollar client signed with her and she arrived home in the middle of her parents' bridge party, happy and loud and laughing, her mother was so disgusted that she asked her to go to her room and stay out of sight in case her guests saw her.

No mention about her happiness. It had all revolved about her father's carefully stage-managed and totally fake image. Everything her family did was to make sure that the rest of the world never saw a crack in the carefully constructed outside persona.

He had been a tyrant, a bully and a liar. And a con man.

And now Rob was acting in exactly the same way.

She felt so angry with him she could hit him. The egotistical creep. Her fingernails pressed into her palms as she fought the urge to throw open the kitchen door and leave Rob to sort this mess out on his own.

'This is really good cake. Is there any more?'

Adele!

Guilt and shame shot through Lottie so fast that it blasted away her contempt for Rob and left her with a lovely lady who needed help.

In a click the fog that was clouding Lottie's brain cleared. It was Adele that mattered here, not Rob.

'Absolutely,' Lottie replied. 'In fact I am on the way to the bakery right now. Would you like a lift? I can drop you off at the hotel later if you like? When you're feeling a little steadier.'

'Great idea,' Adele replied and tried to pick up one of the wine glasses draining in the dishwasher tray. 'Oh. My glass is empty.'

'No problem. I have lots of lovely coffee and tea back at the bakery. And then when you get back to the hotel, your son here—' and at this point she flashed him a narrow-eyed squint '—can make you some lovely hot chocolate. How about that?'

Adele staggered to her feet and held out her arm. 'Lead the way. Cake ahoy.'

'I'm coming with you.'

'No can do. This is a two-woman delivery van. And Adele is quite happy in the passenger seat.'

Rob grunted and waved back to his mother, who was sitting quite sedately in the van with her seat belt already fastened, looking vacantly and very glassy-eyed down the lane behind the gallery.

In the end Lottie had given way and skipped ahead with her bakery crate while Rob had helped his mum negotiate the quite steep staircase to the delivery bay.

'Then drive to the hotel and I'll follow in a black cab.'

Lottie took a calming breath and then lifted her chin and leant closer to Rob so that she could talk to him through clenched teeth. 'And watch Adele fall out of the van onto her face in front of the cameras? Oh, that would be a good idea. Not a chance. Your mother needs somewhere to go for a couple of hours to rest and recover before she heads back to the hotel.'

Her hand flipped up. 'Dee is away in China and I have a spare room your mum can use if she likes. Next question.'

He stepped up so that their chests were almost touching.

'My mother is my responsibility. Not yours.'

Lottie narrowed her eyes and stared up at Rob. His face was in shadow from the street lights and security lamps, making the hard planes of his cheekbones appear even more pronounced.

'Let me make something very clear. I am not doing this for you. I am doing it for Adele. Bully.'

'Let me make something clear. I am not letting her out of my sight. Kidnapper.'

They stood there, locked in a silent stand-off as the air between them positively crackled with the electricity that sparked in the narrow gap.

And into that gap drifted a completely obvious but daring idea.

She needed a replacement chef for Valencia Cagoni at the charity fundraiser and Rob needed transport in her van. Maybe there was a way they could both get what they wanted?

Lottie inhaled a long slow breath through her nose as the plan took shape.

'There might be one way you could persuade me to let you travel in the back with my bakery trays. If you can lower your pride, of course. I realise that would mean coming down in the world from the kind of transport that you are accustomed to.'

A thunderous look and a lightning-sharp glare were joined by a hand-on-hip move that would no doubt terrorise any lesser female. But Lottie held her ground as he slowly walked around to the back of her white delivery van and peered inside.

'The back of the van?'

She nodded slowly up and down. Just once. 'There is a charity fundraiser on Saturday evening at the catering college we both went to. You were notorious. I was a star. The big-name chef who was lined up to attend can't make it. So I have to find a second-best alternative. I suppose you would do as a last-minute stand-in. Or do you want to go home in a taxi?'

His nose twitched. Ah. Perhaps there was still a faint sense of humour lurking there behind the scowl.

'One evening. Charity fundraiser. That's it.'

'Absolutely.' She grinned. 'Leap in.'

CHAPTER FOUR

'WELL, THE WAY SEAN TELLS IT, Rob was squeezed into the back of your delivery van all the way back to the bakery and you took every corner at speed just to make sure that he would be tossed around in the back as much as possible.' Dee giggled down the phone. 'Shame on you, Lottie Rosemount. Although…I would have liked to have been there to see it.'

'I don't know what you mean,' Lottie replied, with the phone jammed tight between her shoulder and her ear. 'A good dry-cleaner should be able to get the stains out of his trousers. Although chocolate and double cream sticky smears can be tricky, especially on cashmere.'

'You should try getting soy sauce out of a silk top!' Dee laughed and Lottie could visualise her friend wiping her eyes before sniffing. 'Now here is the thing, sweetie. I haven't told Sean that Rob was the head chef who fired you from your job when you were an apprentice. Secret squirrel, just like you asked. So the boy wonder is still in the dark at why his devilish charm is being wasted on you. At the moment. But you know how much chefs love to gossip and the fundraiser is at a Beresford hotel. Rob is bound to find out one way or another. So-o-o…it might be time to fess up and call it equals before the big night.'

'Equals? Oh, no. Rob Beresford doesn't get away that

easily. A twenty-minute van ride through central London does not match up to being fired from your dream job for something you did not do. I think I can stretch the retribution out for a little bit longer.' Then Lottie put down her mixing spoon and took the phone in one hand before asking in a low voice, 'Does that make me a bad person? Because I don't want him to turn me into an evil witch.'

'True. That coven look is so last year. But don't worry. You just want to make the boy suffer as payment for the horrible mistake he made when he let you go. His loss. I understand that perfectly. You have to get it out of your system and this is your chance to do it. And maybe have a little fun in the process. Am I right? And now I am going to be late. Email. Later. Bye.'

Lottie put down the telephone and thought back to that moment when she had turned around to find Rob Beresford sitting within striking distance of her and fun was not the first thing that came into her mind.

The sound of laughter rang out from inside the tea rooms and Lottie looked up as one of their regular gentlemen customers held open the door for two elderly ladies whose hands were full of shopping bags and the three cake boxes containing all they needed for a spectacular sixth birthday party for a very special grandson.

Her regular crowd of early shoppers were still enjoying the special-offer breakfast special. Cheese and ham panini followed by a freshly baked and still-warm blueberry and cinnamon muffin washed down with as much tea as they could drink. Good tea, of course. Dee Flynn might not be spending much time in the tea rooms these days but she made sure that the tea was as good as ever.

Sunlight flooded into the cake shop from the London street and bounced back from the cream-and-pastel-coloured walls.

This was how she had imagined it. Years ago when she was working the corporate life and popping into coffee shops for a triple espresso and a paper sack full of carbohydrates, fats and sugar just to get through the morning.

Her bakery. Her cake shop and tea rooms.

It was all real. She had done it. No, correction. She had not done this all on her own.

Lottie smiled and reached out for a spatula but then let her hand drop onto the worktop.

She missed Dee more than she would ever admit. Dee had been the one and only person she had asked to join her and it had been such fun planning the cake shop and tea rooms together. A girl who had a passion for baking and an Irish girl whose idea of heaven was the contents of the wonderful mystery packages that used to arrive from tea gardens all over the world.

But then Dee had fallen for Sean Beresford and now her life was one huge adventure. Exciting and thrilling. Her tea import company would go live by the end of the year and she was loved by a man who was almost good enough for her.

One day soon Dee would be off for good, leaving her alone. Again.

A woman's voice lifted up from the chatter and Lottie looked up in time to see a handsome couple in business suits laughing together as they strolled hand in hand down the pavement, a cake box swinging from the man's arm like an expensive briefcase.

From the side view the blonde in the designer suit and high heels looked so much like the old version of herself that Lottie clasped hold of the workbench for support.

Not so many years ago she had been that girl. Hard-working and driven, but happy to eat out in fine restaurants several times a week with the man her father thought was suitable boyfriend material.

Strange. She had taken it for granted at the time that one day she would move to the next step and marry the young executive, take the standard maternity leave and create a pristine and perfectly run home of her own with her two perfectly mannered children around her. One boy. One girl. All part of the grand master plan her parents had slotted her into.

The problem was she had bought into the whole family thing from the start and she still wanted it. Only this time the family she wanted was going to be very different from the one she had grown up in. That was not negotiable.

Cold, icy silences at torturous formal mealtimes would be replaced by warm, real interest in what the people around the unpolished practical pine kitchen table were thinking and doing. Helpful and supportive. Wanting the best for her children and being there for them no matter what happened and what choices they made. Working with a man who she could love as a real partner for the long haul.

A man who did not insist that every surface in the house was sanitised and polished daily in silent obedience by the slaves of women who were his token wife and daughter.

So, overall the precise opposite of what she had grown up in and survived.

Yeah. Well, that was the dream.

And her life at that moment was the reality.

No boyfriend. No family. No children of her own. And no prospects for creating that family unless something changed in her life or she made it happen.

When was the last time she had shared a meal cooked by someone else with a man who she could call her boyfriend—or even a lover?

When was the last time she had even gone on a date?

Lottie stood on tiptoe to watch the young executive couple press their heads together, happy and oblivious to how blessed they were, before they turned the corner and moved out of sight.

Drat Dee for showing her just what she was missing in her life.

One day she would find someone who she could trust enough to share her life and dreams with. One day.

When the phone began to ring again, Lottie had to take a moment to blink away stupid tears before picking it up.

'Lottie's Cake Shop and Tea Rooms.'

'Good morning, Miss Rosemount. I trust that you slept well.'

It was Rob!

Her foolish girly heart skipped a beat and her stomach flipped so hard that she had to grab the mixing bowl of icing before it slithered off the worktop.

Sleep? How did he expect her to sleep? It had taken hours to settle a very bouncy and over-stimulated Adele into Dee's room and persuade her not to munch the entire contents of the biscuit displays. Followed by several hours of tossing and turning as she replayed the scenes with Rob on repeat inside her head.

Breathe. All she had to do was breathe normally. Keep it casual. That was the key. Lottie's mouth curved up into a smile. He was totally in her control, and that felt disgracefully good.

'Splendidly, thank you,' she lied. 'Good morning to you, too. I hope that the bruises have faded?'

'Not yet,' a low rough voice replied. 'Those packing crates were lethal.' Then he gave a low cough. 'I was wondering if my mother was awake yet. We had agreed to catch up about her plans for the day.'

Ah. So that was why he had phoned. He was worried about how his mother was.

Okay. She got that. As long as Rob remembered that *she* was the person who had invited his mother to stay in Dee's room overnight, for the simple reason that she liked Adele Forrester and the poor woman was in no fit state to face the press.

And definitely *not* because her son Rob had looked desperate.

'As of ten minutes ago your mum was snuggled under Dee's duvet and snoring lightly. That cold medicine and champagne combination make a very effective knock-out potion. It may be a while before she surfaces.'

'Fine. See you in an hour. Try and get her up in time. *Ciao.*'

And then he put the phone down on her. *Unbelievable!*

Lottie glared at the handset in disbelief for a few seconds before shaking her head and returning it to the wall bracket.

That man had no manners whatsoever.

Lottie sniffed and picked up her spatula and got back to work filling an icing bag with the luscious soft-cheese-and-orange-zest icing for the mini carrot cakes that were already lined up in their cases and waiting for a soft swirl of Lottie's special recipe topping.

The cheek of the man. Just because he was a celebrity chef with his own TV show and food awards up to his armpits did not mean that he could simply order her about and expect her to say, 'Yes, chef,' like one of his kitchen brigade!

Lottie tossed the spatula back into the bowl and squeezed the piping bag down until she had formed a perfect swirl in the bowl.

But at least one good thing had come out of it all. Robert Beresford, international chef and gossip-columnist golden boy, had promised to turn up for the fundraiser at the hotel. And she was going to hold him to that, no matter what happened.

'Oh, can I lick the bowl out? Please? You know I cannot resist your icing! Mmm, delish.'

Lottie chuckled as her friend and part-time waitress wiped her fingertip around the scrapes of icing left in the glass mixing bowl and popped it into the mouth. 'Oh, that is *so* good,' Gloria moaned. 'When are you going to give me the recipe, woman? My girls would love me for ever.'

Lottie threw her head back and laughed out loud. 'What are you talking about, Gloria? Your three girls already think you're a goddess because you work here and go home loaded with edible swag every afternoon. And what about that handsome husband of yours? How did the chocolate melting-middle brownies go down last night?'

'Go down? Oh, yes. I am going to need a regular supply, if that boy has the stamina to keep up with me,' Gloria replied with a waggle of her eyebrows.

Lottie glanced quickly at the tables, then leant across and wiped the icing from Gloria's cheek. 'You are terrible! And setting a bad example for the customers.'

Then she flicked her head towards the counter. 'How are we doing out there? Ready for the carrot cakes?'

'Girl, we are always ready for that carrot cake. Pass them over and turn the oven on to make the next batch. They'll be gone in an hour. And before I forget, the gals have been asking me about the Bake and Bitch club meeting next week. What special treat do you have lined up?'

Lottie winked and started washing up. 'Wait and see, Gloria. You are just going to have to wait and see.'

Rob stared out of the floor-to-ceiling office window at the overcast sunless skies of central London in June. It was hard to believe that only thirty-six hours earlier he had been eating barbecue in the glorious Californian sunshine with his restaurant brigade.

His eyes felt heavy, gritty, and ready to close, but just as Rob rolled back his shoulders his talent agent, Sally Richards, finished the call on her mobile phone.

'Good news. The first reviews and photos of the exhibition are all looking brilliant. The only photographs I have seen are when she left the hotel for the event last evening. Adele smiled sweetly on the way out and gave them a lovely wave before jumping into the limo. Not a word about her staggering home early the worse for wear. So relax, Rob. You got away with it.'

'By the skin of my teeth and through the back door. What a nightmare,' he replied and then covered a yawn with one hand.

'So are you ready to rock and roll? Because I have to tell you, I have a tube of under-eye concealer in my bag and you need it more than I do. Did you get any sleep at all on the flight? Eight hours, wasn't it? Nine?'

Rob snorted a reply to the one talent manager he had used since he first stepped out from his dad's Beresford hotel chain and started making a name for himself.

'That was the New York leg of the journey. I had to stop en route from California to check up on a few things at the Beresford New York office. Then the traffic was horrendous. So I missed my flight to London and had to battle with the usual airport media scrum. So all in all just about a typical day's travel in the crazy world I live in.'

'Hey. That's why you love it so much!'

Rob looked around and blinked at Sally a few times before collapsing down on the leather sofa with a grin. 'If you say so, but these past few months have been a nightmare, Sally. My mum...well, you know my mum. Hates medics.

Always has done. She promised me that she would start taking the medication as soon as she finished the final piece for this exhibition, but I don't know. I called her from the airport yesterday and she sounded high as a kite. But last night she was so doped up with cold medicine it was hard to know what was going on inside her head.'

Rob ran his hand back and forth over his mouth and chin. 'It's been eight years since her meltdown at the last exhibition. Eight years, Sally! And the press are still baying for something juicy to say. I thought that if I came here I could provide some sort of diversion. You know what they're like. Why bother with a clever artist with a fading reputation when she has a TV celebrity as a son? Who knows? If we goad him enough we might be able to set off some of those fireworks and get some photographs to sell to the highest bidder. And they have the perfect ammunition to do it with.'

Sally walked around and perched on the edge of the desk.

'Did you manage to keep it together?'

There was something in Sally's tone that made Rob sit back on the sofa and look up. 'Barely. I would not give them the satisfaction. So don't give me that look. I played nice and did not punch anyone, no matter how much I wanted to. Happy? Because I know that voice. There's something else going on here. Fire away. Let's get it over with.'

'Observant as ever.' She smiled and paused long enough to reach across the desk and pass a bundle of printed sheets across to Rob, who glanced at them once before tossing them onto the sofa cushion.

'You cannot be serious. I've just finished filming the final TV series and it practically killed me fitting everything in. I've done the interviews and press calls and earned that money. And now they want me to do another series? What is that all about? We've been down this road before,

Sally. Mum needs me to be close at hand. Travelling across the States then flying back to get her through this exhibition has been tough on both of us. She needs me to be in California. And I really need to get back to work in the Beresford kitchens. Sean has hardly seen me this year and I have been relying way too much on the chefs I trained. Time to get back to doing what I do best. Working with food and creating amazing dishes for the Beresford hotel chain.'

Sally raised both hands in the air. 'I did what you asked me to. I made it clear to the production company a year ago that you have had enough of the restaurant makeover show for TV. One more series and that's it. But the audience figures are soaring higher month on month, Rob. Viewers cannot get enough of you. Look at the numbers, Rob. This is crazy money. Sign the new contract and you don't need to work again unless you want to. Ever. This could be just the opportunity you need to build up that emergency fund.'

Rob paused, then glanced up at the woman who had looked after his interests since he was seventeen. 'Come on, Sally. You know this was never about the money. Every penny I have earned on the TV shows and personal appearances has gone into my mum's account.'

'And last time I checked, the investment plan we worked on was doing very nicely and bringing in a respectable income to cover her not-so-little spending sprees. But how long is that going to last? You are top news at the moment. But once you move back into your kitchen the focus will shift onto the next hot new chef and Rob Beresford will not be the man of the moment any longer. And you can stop glaring at me. Because I'm not the only person who has got their head about that fact. So far I have had three enquiries from documentary film companies. Every one of them wants the exclusive rights to a behind-the-scenes exposé of the real Rob Beresford. And if you don't take part they will make them anyway. That's the way it goes.'

There were a few seconds of silence before Rob responded in a low voice. 'Are you telling me that someone else is planning to write my life story without even asking me?'

'Absolutely. That's why you should think about it. Because you know what would happen if they did. They are bound to focus on the one thing we've worked hard to keep in the background.'

Rob pushed himself shakily to his feet and walked stiffly over to the window, his shoulders rigid with stress. 'My mother would not survive. It took her months to pull back from the last bout of depression and I can't force her to take the medication while she is painting. It has to be her choice. That was what we agreed.'

'Then tell the story the way you want to before somebody else does.'

'Tell my story? You think the readers would want to know about all of the gruelling years I spent in hotel kitchens? There is nothing exciting and glamorous about that way of life.'

Rob rolled back his shoulders and winced. 'Speaking of which, I have an appointment with a baker and something tells me that I had better not be late.'

Sally coughed low in her throat and looked at him over the top of her spectacles. 'A baker? Today? I thought you would be spending time at the gallery with Adele.'

'I'll explain later, Sally…if I survive.'

It was mid-morning before Rob pushed open the door to Lottie's Cake Shop and Tea Rooms and stepped inside.

And almost whirled around on one heel and went straight back out again.

Because he had just walked into what looked like a children's tea party, complete with ear-damaging levels of laughing, calling out and crying, some sort of jangling music, and a group of toddlers swaying their bodies from side to side and waving their hands in the air just in front of the serving counter while the girl he now knew to be Lottie Rosemount was conducting the dancing with a large wooden spoon.

She was wearing wide-leg navy trousers and a floral T-shirt covered with a large navy apron with a picture of a cupcake on it. Her blonde hair was tied back in a high ponytail and a pretty navy-and-white headband drew attention to an oval face that even without a trace of make-up still managed to be stunningly pretty.

This was the place that Sean's girlfriend, Dee, loved so much?

He had survived restaurant opening nights that were quieter and more in control than this!

After a ninety-hour week and several international flights the last thing he wanted to do was join in a school party. His job was to earn the money so that his mother never had to worry about having nothing in the bank ever again.

But when could he ever refuse her anything?

She was the one and only woman on the planet who he had promised to take care of for as long as she needed him.

And he kept his promises. Even if that meant turning up to a small high-street bakery on a weekday morning.

'Thank you, ladies and gentlemen,' Lottie called out. 'That was simply amazing. Disco dancing and sporting stars of the future. No doubt about it. And don't forget, the Yummy Mummy club meets at the same time next week. So if you are ready to say the word about the one thing we all love best in the whole world...wait for it, Helena, and please stop doing that, Adam…three…two…one. Let's have a great big…*cake*!'

Rob winced and half closed one eye as the wannabe dance troupe screamed out the word and then they all burst into a barrage of yelling and screaming and calling and jumping up and down.

All he could do was stand to one side as the actually very yummy mummies wrestled their little darlings into submission and baby buggies and in some cases reins and shuffled past him towards the entrance and the busy London street outside on the pavement.

Holding the door open for them seemed like a good idea. The first time.

Except that the second each lovely mummy spotted him smiling politely at them the forward movement onto the pavement slowed down to the point where a very rowdy and disorderly queue had formed in the cake shop.

'Hello, handsome. Has anyone ever told you that you look a bit like that horrible rude chef that shouts a lot on the telly?' The second girl shrugged. 'Only not as good-looking. Sort off.' Then she covered her hand with her mouth and laughed before shuffling off.

'I get that a lot. No problem,' Rob called after her with a quick wave before helping a very attractive brunette with her buggy. His reward was a beaming smile and a small business card popped into his shirt pocket with a cheeky wink while the little girl in the buggy amused herself by painting the jam from her donut onto the leg of his trousers.

Charming.

Five minutes later he had to physically unwrap the fingers of one charming cherub from his jacket and slide backwards into the cake shop. In an instant he closed the door tight behind him, his back flat against the glass, and exhaled slowly.

'It must be nice to be so popular.' A familiar female voice chuckled and Rob opened his eyes to see Lottie staring at him from behind the counter. 'Are you available next Thursday morning? I'm thinking of doing Zumba for the under-fives. You would be a great hit for the lovely mums.'

'Sorry. Previous booking. And please tell me that it's not always like that.'

'Oh, no,' Lottie tutted. 'Sometimes it can be quite rowdy.' Then she smiled. 'But brilliant fun for the kids. They have the best time and the mums have a chance to meet their pals. I love it.' Then she pressed her lips together. 'Do you drink tea?'

'Don't tell Dee but I would love a coffee,' Rob replied and stepped forwards to the counter.

Lottie pushed her lips out. 'Let me guess. Double-shot Americano. The breakfast of champions.'

Just for one split second Rob thought about calling her bluff but just the thought of that coffee was making his mouth water.

'Damn. I hate to be predictable. Hit me.'

'With pleasure,' she whispered and then shook her head, rolled her eyes skywards and turned back to face him with a small shoulder shrug. 'House rule. If you are a guest you have to eat something baked on the premises with your beverage. The donuts lasted thirty seconds but I have grown-up cakes galore.'

Then she turned away and continued talking but he couldn't hear a word above the hiss and explosive steam from the coffee machine.

'Sorry, I didn't catch that,' Rob said and strolled casually around the counter and stepped up to Lottie as she tapped out the coffee grounds.

In front of him was a kitchen about the same size as the one in his London penthouse apartment, except this kitchen was jam-packed with stainless-steel appliances and what looked like two commercial-size ovens. The air was filled with the most delicious aroma of baked goods. Spices and vanilla combined with the unique tang of caramel and buttery pastry and fresh-baked bread. Rob took a moment to appreciate the aroma.

'What do you think you are doing?' she muttered between clenched teeth and whirled around and pressed both hands flat against his chest and pushed hard.

'Nobody—and I mean nobody—comes into my kitchen without asking me first. Do you let strangers just walk into your kitchen? No. I didn't think so. Step back. All the way. And stay there. Thank you, that's better. Take a seat and I'll be right with you.'

Then she exhaled slowly and stepped back to the coffee machine, mumbling under her breath as she went.

'Apologies,' Rob said and raised both hands in the air. 'My fault entirely. I am so used to walking into other people's kitchens I forgot my manners.'

'Um, well, I hope that you remember at the fundraiser,' Lottie replied and stabbed the coffee spoon in his direction. 'The whole idea is to raise funds for scholarships to the catering college. Not scare the VIPs away.'

'Hey. I can play nice when the occasion demands,' Rob replied and hit her with his sweetest smile.

'That's good to know.' Lottie sighed as she strolled towards his table carrying a tray with two steaming cups of coffee that smelt so good his mouth was practically watering before he sat down.

She took a breath, put the tray onto the table, and then shuffled onto the chair facing him.

Watching him take that long, deep sip of piping-hot black coffee. Just the way he liked it. Perfect.

'Great coffee. And thank you again for helping my

mother out last night. It was very generous of you,' Rob added with a slight bow of the head. 'I appreciate it.'

'No problem. Adele has been no trouble at all.'

Ah. Adele had been no trouble? So why did she think he would be?

With a low growl Rob put down the coffee and folded his arms and sat back in his chair so that he could face Lottie. 'You don't have a very high opinion of me, do you? Help me to understand.'

She blinked a couple of times and swallowed a long sip of coffee before her gaze flicked up into Rob's face and their eyes met. 'You were right, last night in the gallery. We have met before. About three years ago I was one of the catering students who had won a place in the Beresford hotel kitchens right here in London. You were entertaining guests one night and came in to see us after the meal and…you fired me. Gave me the sack. Threw me to the wolves. Let me go.'

Lottie clasped her hands so tightly around the coffee cup that Rob could see the whites of her knuckles and there was just enough of a tremble in her voice to make the hairs on the back of his neck prickle to attention. 'Remember the pastry chef? Debra? The one who could barely stand up that night, never mind create something amazing? Debra was the one who had made the desserts. But I was the one who got the blame and the sack instead of her.'

Lottie paused and then lifted her chin, defiance blasting out from those green eyes with all of the heat of a fiery dragon. 'It was no secret that you were sleeping with Debra at the time so you were not going to fire the person responsible for that particular disaster, were you? So I went. And she stayed. Does that help to make things a little clearer, Rob?'

CHAPTER FIVE

EVERY SOUND IN THE CAKE SHOP seemed to fade into the background as Rob focused on the bitter words that had exploded from the lips of the pretty girl sitting so still across the small table from him.

Of course he remembered Debra.

A shiver of cold regret and bitter disappointment bubbled up.

His rules were simple and easy to remember.

They could have fun. They could have a fling and a great time together and while it lasted he would be the most attentive and faithful boyfriend that a girl could want. Then they would walk away and get on with their lives.

That was how it worked and he made damn sure that any girl he dated was very clear that he was not in the business of negotiating. They were either in or out. Black or white. Their choice.

Debra had lasted longer than most and they had enjoyed a pretty good relationship for a few months. Until the inevitable had happened. She had started pushing for a long-term commitment that he hadn't been prepared to give. She had kept telling him how much she loved him and how different she was from all of the other girls, so his rules did not apply to her. She was too special and different to be treated like one of the others.

She had not felt so special when he'd packed his bags and had been out of her door an hour later. In fact he recalled crying, screaming, and a humiliating display of begging.

It was weeks later that he'd found out through the gossip channels that Debra had been getting over his breaking up with her with the help of vodka and free hotel wine.

Lottie was the apprentice pastry chef who he fired that night to teach Debra a lesson and try and shock her into taking her life back.

Well, that explained a lot.

'I remember it well. I ended up taking Debra home to her parents a few days later and finding her the professional help that she needed. It was a great relationship while it lasted and Debra is a remarkable girl. I met up with her and her husband when they were in Los Angeles for a professional chef conference last autumn. They seem like a great couple who have a stunning restaurant together. I am happy for her.'

Rob slowly unfolded his arms and stretched them out across the table.

'That was a long time ago, Lottie. I made a choice. It was the right decision at the time and I have to stand by that. End of story.'

There was a gasp from across the table and Lottie stared at him, wide-eyed.

'The right decision at the time? For who? Your squeeze?'

She sat back heavily in the chair and blinked. 'Is that it? Is that the only apology you have for me? Because I have to tell you that, as excuses go, that is pathetic.'

'No excuses. It was my job to recruit top talent for the restaurant and Debra is a great pastry chef. I didn't know about her drinking problems until they impacted her work.'

Rob leant forwards from the waist and pressed the flat of his hand down on the pale wood tabletop.

'My only regret is that I allowed personal feelings to block my judgement. I should have spotted that Debra was in trouble weeks earlier and done something about it before things got out of hand. Instead I stayed away to give her some distance. The last thing she needed was me standing looking over her shoulder and shouting orders at her. That was my mistake.'

'What about firing me as some sort of scapegoat? I was incredibly lucky to find another placement the next day after some serious pleading.'

A smile crept over his lips and he tilted his head towards Lottie. 'Sometimes I'm just too sensitive and caring for my own good.'

'Really? I had no idea.' Lottie nodded but every word was dripping with venom. 'You hide it so very well.'

'On the contrary.' Rob shrugged. 'Take this charity fundraiser you conned me into.' His hand flipped up into a question before he reached for his coffee. 'I cannot wait to hear all about it. For a start, I would like to know who's running the show. Whose idea was it to create scholarship funds for trainee chefs? Because I hope that they know what they're getting themselves into. That is one hell of a lot of hard work.'

The blonde sitting opposite leant forwards, her forearms on the table until her face was only a few inches away from Rob's nose, and smiled sweetly. 'That's an easy question to answer. It was my idea. I know precisely what I have got myself into and, yes, it is a lot of hard work. And I wouldn't have it any other way.'

Then she slid back, lifted her chin and smiled before replying. 'This time I am the one who gets to set the rules and call the shots. And I can't tell you how liberating that is.'

Then she nodded towards the plate she had slid towards

him. 'Take now, for example. No coffee without something to eat. This time it happens to be my speciality pear-and-almond tart. Enjoy.'

Rob stared at the food, and then looked up into a pair of sparkling green eyes.

Only Lottie's eyes were not simply green. They were forest green. Spring-bud green. The kind of captivating green that knocked the breath out of his lungs.

It was hot outside, but it had suddenly become a lot hotter in this cake shop.

It must be the heat from the ovens.

Her attention was totally focused on him, and her head tilted slightly to one side as she waited patiently for his reply for a few moments.

Just for a second, her gaze faltered and a chink appeared in the façade through which he got a faint glimmer of something unexpected. Suspicion, maybe, but a fierce intelligence and power. It lasted only an instant. But it sent him reeling, before the closed-mouth smile switched back on.

Lottie polished a pristine fork on a clean corner of her apron before placing it next to the pastry on Rob's plate. 'You know how hard it is to make a name for yourself in the catering world. I was lucky and so were you. We had money and backup. A full scholarship is the only way most of these young people can afford to go to college and get the training they need to show what they can do. I happen to think that's worth spending time on. Just because I chose to become a baker does not mean that I tossed my business management degree into the nearest bin on the way into the catering college.'

She gave a small shoulder-shrug. 'Relax, Rob. The charity has a full-time administrator and a professional team running it. Any questions, talk to Sean. He has been through the details and offered the use of the Beresford for the event.'

Ah. So that was it. This girl thought that he was going to turn a charity auction into a Rob Beresford promotional event.

Was that really how she saw him? As a self-serving egomaniac? Well, this day was just getting better and better.

And with that she extended her free hand towards him, her eyes locked on his. Her gaze was intense. Focused. 'We made a trade last evening. One personal appearance in exchange for bed and breakfast. I need to know that we still have a deal this morning and you are not going to walk out on us.'

Rob stared at the food, then looked up into those sparkling green eyes, and took her hand.

It was warm, small, and sticky and calloused, with long, strong fingers that clamped around his. This was no limp, girly handshake. This was the hand of a woman who cooked her own food, kneaded her own bread, and washed her own dishes. The sinews and muscles in her wrists and forearms were strong and toned.

He was accustomed to shaking hands with men and women from all sides of the building trade every day of the week in his job, but this was different. A frisson of energy, a connection, sparked through that simple contact of skin on skin.

'I gave you my word. I'll be there.'

Her fingers gripped his for a second longer than necessary before releasing him, her eyes darting to his. The crease in her forehead told him that he was not the only one to have felt it. But to her credit Lottie nodded towards his plate. 'Good. Now that's cleared up, why don't you enjoy your tart? You still look as though you need it. Tough morning?'

He paused before replying. 'Yes, actually, it has been a tiring morning, and I'm sure it's delicious but I don't eat cake.'

Lottie sniffed and tilted her head. 'Well, that's a shame. Luckily I am confident that with your extensive culinary expertise you will have observed that this is not cake. This is a tart, which I made today, in this kitchen. At some silly time of the morning.'

Lottie gave her ovens a finger wave, and then moved to sit down on the corner of the table, her arms folded. 'Speciality of the house. And nobody leaves this kitchen without trying my baking. Including you, Rob Beresford.'

Her eyes ratcheted down to the pastry, then slowly, slowly, came back up to his face. 'I have heard the words and shaken on it, but now I want to see the proof that you want to cooperate with me. The success of the evening all depends on what you do in the next five minutes. So, what's it going to be, Rob?'

What Lottie had not expected was for Rob to reach out towards her. She forced herself not to back away as Rob picked up her left hand and kissed the backs of her knuckles before releasing it with a grin.

'We came to an arrangement. And a Beresford man always keeps his promises.'

Lottie uncrossed her arms and wrapped her fingers around the coffee cup as Rob glared at her for a second before picking up his fork and breaking off a piece of warm, fragrant tart.

Lottie Rosemount had no intention of letting the scholarship students down when it came to the simple matter of organising a fundraising event.

The last thing she needed was a celebrity chef turning up and questioning her abilities.

Even if that chef smelt of warm spice and looked as if he had stepped down from a photo shoot for a fashion magazine. She had never met anyone who could totally rock designer denim jeans and a white shirt.

Her eyes could not move from his wide, full lips wrapping around the cake fork.

She had to see his reaction when he tasted the combination of sweet almonds and warm spice with the aromatic juicy fruit of the ripe pear, which she had poached gently in spiced pear juice syrup until it was almost falling apart.

It had taken six trial batches before she was happy with the variety of pear and the cooking time.

Ah. There it was.

Rob's eyes fluttered closed for just a fraction of a second and then he chewed a little faster so that he could break off a huge piece of tart with his fork and pick it up with his fingers.

Oh, yes. He had got it. He liked it!

He was staring into her eyes now, the corners of his mouth turned up with a flicker of something that could have been amusement, interest, or more likely frustration that she had forced him into agreeing to come to the fundraiser.

A slight twinge of guilt flickered through her mind. She had been quite shameless. One overnight stay for a distressed artist in exchange for an hour shaking hands and supporting the charity. That was not too terrible. Was it?

'Mmm,' he murmured and drained the last of his coffee. 'Not bad. In fact, seriously good. Where did you say you trained?'

'Here and there. I finished my apprenticeship with Valencia Cagoni when you fired me. You can check the rest on my website later.'

The creases in the corners of his eyes deepened as Lottie inhaled a powerful aroma of spicy masculine sweat, which was sweet even against the perfume of the fruit and nuts in her food.

His gaze hovered over her ring finger, then flicked back to her face, eyebrows high.

'Not married? Or are you too rebellious to wear a ring?'

Lottie almost choked on a piece of pastry from her tart and quickly swallowed down a slurp of coffee before wheezing out a reply.

'Not married, engaged, dating, or anything else. Where would I find the time for that?'

'If you wanted it enough you would find the time.' His eyes flashed a challenge that was definitely hot enough to warm the coolest of breezes.

Wanted it? Oh, she wanted it. But it had to be the right man who wanted the same things. And so far they were thin on the ground.

'Not very high on my priority list at the moment,' she lied, but not very convincingly because that smile on Rob's face lifted into a knowing smirk of deep self-satisfaction.

Damn. She had fallen straight into his trap.

'So it's all work and no play for the lovely Miss Rosemount. That doesn't sound like much fun.'

'And your life is one great circus of constant amusement because your business runs itself. Is that right?'

Damn him for making her snappy.

'I never said that,' he replied with a twist of his head towards the door where a young couple was staggering in with a baby buggy and shopping bags.

She couldn't move. There was something electric in the few inches of air between them, as though powerful magnets were pulling them together.

At this distance, she could feel that frisson of energy and strength of the man whose whole professional life had been spent under the glare of public scrutiny—by choice.

This was the kind of bloke who was accustomed to walking into a cocktail bar or restaurant and having head waiters fawn over themselves to find him the best table.

Well, not this time, handsome!

She could stick this out longer than he could.

It was Gloria who saved him. Her friend came galloping down the stairs from the bedroom and third-floor studio and instantly twisted her mouth into a smile.

'Well, hello! You have to be Rob. You mum has been telling me *all* about you, scamp. I'm Gloria.'

With a laugh she turned to Lottie. 'Adele decided to take her breakfast to the studio with Ian. They're having a great time up there so I thought I would leave them to it.'

There was a sharp intake of breath from across the table. 'Ian?'

'My friend Ian Walker,' Lottie said. 'You must have met him last night. He was the photographer who worked with your mum on the exhibition catalogue for the gallery. Tall, thin, about forty. And a great fan of your mum's work.'

Suddenly Rob was standing ramrod-straight next to her, his back braced, and looking horribly tall, as though he feared the worst.

'Then I think it's time I caught up with them, don't you?' he said. 'So you have a studio?' he went on. 'That is different. I have been to plenty of artists' studios in my time but above a bakery? My mum and her pals would spend more time scoffing the goods than working.'

Her mouth opened and then closed before she answered him with a smirk. 'Ah. So this is going to be a first. And who said anything about artists? Prepare to be disappointed. Follow me.' Then she caught his smile and her eyes narrowed. 'On second thoughts, you can go first. Straight through that door. Then at the top of the stairs take a sharp left and carry on up to the third floor. You can't miss it.'

Rob took the stairs two at a time then slowed down to take the narrow second steps, conscious that Lottie was by his side the whole time.

His mother was alone with a man who he had never met; he certainly did not recognise the name. In his book, that meant trouble. *Lots of trouble.*

Especially when they stopped outside what looked like a bedroom door.

Lottie stepped forwards and gently turned the brass handle, casually swung open the wooden door and stepped through.

The walls and ceiling were painted in brilliant white.

Light flooded in from the plain glass windows, illuminating one single picture hanging over what must have been the original chimney breast.

Staring back at him was a life-size formal portrait of Lottie Rosemount—the impact of seeing her captured knocked Rob physically backwards.

He was so stunned that it took a few seconds for him to notice that Lottie had moved forwards and was chatting to a tall, thin, older man, who he vaguely recognised, standing next to a long table covered with a pristine white cloth.

His quick brain struggled to take in what he was looking at.

It was the complete opposite of what he had been expecting.

Instead of the chaotic blend of noise and bakery odours and general chaos he had walked into in the cake shop, the third-floor space was a haven of quiet sunlight and calm.

It was a separate world. *An oasis.* And totally stunning.

The studio had clearly been a loft and the ceiling was angled away into one corner, but half of the roof was made from glass panels, which created a flood of light into the centre of the room. The outside wall had two wide panels of floor-to-ceiling double patio doors. And sitting outside on a tiny patio chair, cradling a large white cup, was his mother.

She was wearing a silk kimono, her hair was already styled, and there was a china plate stacked high with *pain au chocolat* and Danish pastries, which he knew that she adored. Next to an open box of tissues.

'Darling. There you are! What a lovely morning. Do come and look at this wonderful view. Isn't it divine?'

Rob rolled back his shoulders and, with a nod to Lottie and Ian, who were totally engrossed in looking at some images on a laptop computer, walked out onto the narrow roof terrace.

He pressed his lips to his mother's hair and wrapped his arm loosely across the back of the chair as she blew her nose.

'How are you this morning, Mum? Cold any better?'

'Much. I have it down to sniffles. And I slept for hours! Hopefully I shall stay awake at the gallery today when the great British public arrive. It was such a shame that I did not last much of the evening.'

He rested his chin on her shoulder so that they were both looking out at the same panoramic view across the London skyline towards the river Thames.

'Now, tell me what you have been up to this morning.'

Perhaps it would be better not to mention last night after all.

His breath caught in his throat.

All of the Beresford hotels in the city had views over London, but this? Somehow being on this tiny terrace reminded him so much of the house where he had grown up with his dad. The window box full of red geraniums. The wrought iron railings. The tiled clay roofs that spread out with the old chimney pots. Church spires. And the faint sound of the busy London street just below where they were standing. Red buses, black cabs. The whole package.

He had missed this. He missed the real London.

'Couldn't have put it better myself,' he whispered. 'This is special.'

'It's wonderful. How clever of you to persuade your friend to allow me to stay here. Because I have to tell you, darling, your hotel is charming and so efficient but this place is divine and Gloria and Lottie have been perfect hosts. And the studio…'

Adele pressed one hand gently to the front of the kimono and Rob was shocked to see the faint glimmer of tears in her eyes.

'When I first came to London your father tried so hard to find me somewhere to work and the closest I came was somewhere just like this. A third floor of an old stone house that had belonged to one of the Impressionists. I loved it, for a while.'

Then she waved one hand. 'It was not to be, but that is past history and there is no point living with regret. Strange, I had almost forgotten how special this city is.'

'London? I thought that you hated it here.'

'Hated it?' his mother replied and turned around to face him. 'Oh, no, darling. I could never do that. I was so young and I simply couldn't find my balance.'

Then she looked out across the rooftops. 'We've both come a long way since then, kiddo. A hell of a long way.'

A killer grin lightened her face. 'This is wonderful and I intend to enjoy every minute of it before heading back to the gallery. So scoot. Go and talk to Ian. That man worked miracles with my catalogue and Lottie needs your help. Call me before you go. But in the meantime, I am simply splendid.'

And with that she snuggled back in the chair and picked up a flaky pastry and bit into it with moans of delight.

It was the happiest that he had seen her for weeks.

Well. So much for all of his concerns about finding his mother a wreck!

Perhaps he had to thank Lottie Rosemount for a lot more than he'd first thought.

He loved his mother very much.

Lottie exhaled slowly as the thought crept into her mind that she had made a horrible mistake.

She darted a quick glance towards the terrace where Adele was quite happily enjoying the June sunshine with Rob chatting so sweetly by her side, his arm draped so protectively close, and swallowed down a moment of deep humiliation.

She had been wrong.

Last night had not been about Rob trying to save his credibility and reputation at all.

It had all been about protecting his mother. Not himself.

That was why he had been so concerned about going to the hotel.

He had been terrified that his mother would embarrass herself and the press would be full of photographs of Adele staggering about looking half drunk and falling out of a limo onto the street in front of the cameras.

How could she have been so stupid?

When Rob Beresford had walked into that art gallery all she had been able to see was the man who had treated her so unfairly.

But what about the rest? It was gossip. Tittle-tattle scandal about Rob's many conquests and how he had ditched Debra without a moment's notice.

A low icy shudder ran across her shoulders.

She was a fool. No, worse than that. She had allowed her memory of what had happened when they had last met to cloud her judgement.

This was not just unfair, it was wrong.

Stupid, stupid, stupid.

She had made a total fool of herself by doing the very thing she'd promised she would not do again: judge people based on what they had done in the past.

And if she was guilty of that she was woman enough to put it right.

Right now.

'Rob.' Lottie smiled and strolled over to the terrace. 'Can I drag you away from Adele for a moment? You're an expert on recipe books and this is my first. Do you remember Ian? This lovely man has bravely taken on a very different kind of challenge: making my novelty birthday cakes look good enough to eat. Welcome to my budget photo shoot!'

On a white cake stand on a pedestal in the middle of a long table covered in a white cloth was a cake.

It had been shaped into a racing car Rob vaguely recalled seeing on movie posters for a children's cartoon film some months ago.

The long low body was covered with bright red fondant icing with a white stripe running down both sides. The wheels were white discs and the whole design looked so realistic it might have been mistaken for a toy. Except that Lottie had just finished icing liquorice round sweets in place of the headlights and steering wheel.

All in all a perfect cake for a car-mad little boy.

It was brilliant.

Rob stepped closer and nodded to Ian, who stopped work

adjusting a light stand and an elaborate studio camera system on a tripod to come forward and shake his hand. 'Good to meet you, Rob. Adele has told me a lot about you.'

'Really?' Rob answered and glanced towards his mother, who was now chatting happily to Lottie and eating croissants. *Because she has not said a word about you.* 'Congratulations on the exhibition catalogue. Everyone I spoke to last evening loved the layout.'

'It was my pleasure.' Ian shook his head. 'Although I confess that I didn't expect to meet Adele here this morning when I turned up to work on the charity cookbook Lottie is pulling together. Do you have an interest in food photography, Rob?'

'Me? Not at all. I leave that to the experts. I simply prepare the food and the stylists and photographers get to work on the recipe books.'

He quickly scanned the room, taking in the high ceilings and natural light from the skylight and tall windows. 'Has this always been a photographer's studio?'

'Not as far as I know. Lottie refurbished the loft as soon as she bought the place. It is quite something. And I need to get back to it or the cake will dry out. Later.'

A quick tour of the loft revealed that Lottie's taste in books ranged from classic French cuisine to high finance and shared the space with a fine collection of spiders' webs and dust.

At the far end, away from the windows, was a screened-off area, and Rob could not resist peeking behind the découpage screen.

A double bed with a Victorian carved wooden headboard was flat against the wall. Dressed with white bedcovers trimmed in lilac satin and a soft-looking duvet.

Feather. He could tell from the way it was made.

Hmm, interesting. He wouldn't be trying that bed out. Way too girly.

But who slept in a bed that size?

He was just about to investigate when there was a sharp cough from behind his back. 'Found anything interesting back there,' Lottie asked and he knew without bothering to look that she had her hands on her hips, 'Mr Nosy Parker?'

'My natural, insatiable curiosity cannot be contained, Goldilocks.'

'Goldilocks? What do you mean?'

Rob peeked at her over one shoulder and smiled. 'Thought so. I have discovered your secret hideaway. Not a bad spot. Not bad at all.'

'Actually, it's lovely. I don't mind sleeping in the studio for six months during the summer. It's not such a bad place to wake up in the morning.'

'And the rest of the time?'

Lottie strolled over to the screen and gestured to the terrace where Adele was just finishing off her breakfast.

'When I was in business my first Christmas bonus paid for an apartment in the city with a view over the Thames. At the moment I am renting it out to one of my former colleagues while she is working on a project in central London and wanted a home rather than a serviced apartment.'

Lottie dropped her hand. 'You know the statistics about how many restaurants and cafés never make it to their first birthday? Well, I am just coming up to eight months and—' she tapped on the wooden frame on the screen '—so far, so good. But who knows? Things change. People change.'

Then she paused. 'What gave me away?'

Then he gestured with his head towards the garment bags and clothing hanging on two garment rails behind the decorated screen. 'Designer clothing is not really Dee's style.'

'I could have put my clothes in storage but I prefer to have them handy. A girl has to be ready for all eventualities.'

'Is this what you are wearing on Saturday evening?' Rob picked up the skirt of a stunning slinky mocha-coloured satin slip with a lace trim and lifted his eyebrows before releasing it. 'Because I am not sure the Beresford Richmond is ready for this kind of allure. Va va boom.'

'Please don't touch the frillies. And my gown is going to be a surprise, so do stop looking.'

'Fair enough. What time shall I pick you up?'

'That's okay. I'm meeting you there.'

'Why, Miss Rosemount, surely you are not frightened of tongues wagging if we walk in together, are you?'

'Not at all. But I am going to get there early to help set things up. That's all.'

'Is that it? Or do you have a rule about not dating chefs?'

'Dating? Of course not. I don't have any problem with chefs. Far from it. I have spent three years working my backside off becoming one.' Her gaze locked on to his chest but slowly, slowly, lifted to his face. 'Just arrogant chefs with egos to match the size of their name on the menu.'

Lottie gave a small shoulder-shrug. 'Any girl who dates a chef who likes to have his name in the gossip columns knows what she is taking on and I am not just talking about the long hours and bad tempers.'

'Harsh. You could say that about any type of successful person, the kind that has earned that reputation through sweat and puts the work in for that success. Publicity is not a bad thing. Not when restaurants are closing every week. The press love me just as long as I give them something to write about. It's part of the job.'

'Ah. Well, there you have it. You can glory in the glare of publicity for the charity and we lesser mortals shall scurry around in the background making sure that everything is working. Win-win. I can hardly wait. It promises to be a very interesting evening.'

CHAPTER SIX

IT WAS LIKE going back in time.

Rob Beresford stood at the entrance to the park across the street from the West London Catering College where he had spent two of the most gruelling years of his life learning how to cook at a professional level.

The building might look a little cleaner and they had added more glass and pale colours to the entrance to make it look less like a prison, but otherwise it was just the same.

Somewhere in a storage unit in London there was a box stuffed with his diplomas and degree certificates for what the college liked to call the culinary arts and professional cooking.

From what he remembered it was mostly culinary sweat and manic activity fuelled by industrial quantities of cheap coffee and cheaper carbohydrates.

He had grown up in London and spent the first nineteen years of his life here. It would always feel like home.

And now he was going to a Beresford hotel to raise funds so that some other youngster with nothing but a fire in his belly could have a chance to show what they could do.

How ironic was that?

With a low chuckle he shook his head and strode out along the sunlit pavements and turned the corner, away from the college and into the world he lived in now. Sean had done a great job refurbishing the Beresford Richmond and Rob waved to the reception staff as he jogged up the staircase to the main conference room and flung open the doors to the cocktail bar.

He scanned the room looking for Sean or Lottie and walked slowly between the drinks tables, waving and saying a brief hello to familiar faces from the hotel and food world, flashguns lighting up his back as he tugged at the cuffs of his evening shirt.

He was a Beresford working the crowd in a Beresford hotel.

This was the one time he was willing to put his handmade tux on show for the press and wear his heart on his sleeve.

His father, Tom Beresford, had founded the Beresford hotel chain from nothing and worked hard to create a line of luxury hotels in cities around the world. But Rob admired him for a lot more than that. No matter where his mum had gone to find artistic inspiration, his dad had made sure that Rob had his own room and a stable home and school life. It had been a shock when his dad had announced that he was going to marry again. Until then it had only been the two of them. But she was so lovely. And as a bonus—he got a new brother.

And there he was. Sean Beresford. Hotel troubleshooter and the current manager of the hotel he was standing in, greeting the sixty or so especially invited guests in person, same as always. Charming but professional.

Rob took the initiative by thumping Sean on the back in a half hug. 'Heard that there was a charity auction tonight and thought I might pick up a few bargains. How about you?'

He was rewarded by a short snort. 'Dee is in China. Again. But somehow Dee and Lottie persuaded me to host their fundraiser here. I even agreed to be the master of ceremonies. So behave.'

'I am behaving! And well done on the refurbishment. This is a fabulous venue.'

'Thanks. Hard work but worth it. VIP events like this are a perfect way to get word-of-mouth publicity. Gold dust. I had no idea that Lottie knew so many people in high places.'

His brows came together. 'Lottie Rosemount?'

'Absolutely. That girl has a contact list to die for. If anyone deserves praise for making this benefit a sell-out it's Lottie. Oh, have to go. Enjoy the party! And I hope you like the food. We're trying that new event menu from the Beresford Paris which has been so popular.'

'Wait up. What are you serving? Surprise me.'

'Canapés followed by plated cold starters, three choices of hot buffet, salad and cheese. And I know you are going to sample some of everything because you always do before the desserts arrive.'

Sean gestured with his head towards the swing doors that led to the kitchen. Waiters were clearing away what little was left of the patisserie.

'I have a head chef in there who has been screaming at her brigade all night that Rob Beresford is in the room and they had better cook as though their jobs depended on it. Forget the other city chefs. You are the one my team want to impress. They are nervous wrecks in there! So don't worry about the food. Your job is to do the celeb thing. And good luck with that. See you later.' And with that Sean strode over to greet the cluster of new arrivals who had packed the reception area behind him.

Rob stepped to one side, and tried to bring his breathing back down to a level where he could control it.

What the hell was the new event menu from Paris?

He was supposed to be responsible for the entire food-and-drinks range across all of the Beresford hotel chain.

His mother's exhibition and the filming of the TV show had sucked every second of his life for the past few months but surely he would have heard about a new menu?

Why had no one told him about it? Or worse. They had told him but the message had got lost in the hundreds of emails he received every day.

Of course he had to trust the hotel chefs. He had personally picked them, got drunk with them and slayed them with cooking better than them. But as for trusting other people to create an entirely new menu? Forget it.

He needed to get to the hotel kitchens and find out exactly what they intended to serve at this function.

He glanced around the gilt high-ceiling dining room. Top hoteliers, company directors in designer suits, food journalists and, if he was not mistaken, several of the college lecturers who were responsible for what skills he had. So overall pretty much everyone in London with an interest in developing amazing new chef talent.

Brilliant for the charity. And a nightmare waiting to happen if this new menu was not totally spectacular.

And walking towards him around the edge of the room, one very, very pretty girl.

Lottie Rosemount. Only not the hard-working baker version of Lottie he had spent most of the day with.

This Lottie was dressed in a pale lilac cocktail dress that fitted her perfectly, the fabric draped close to her waist then flaring out over the slim hips to just above the knees. Then long, slim but muscular legs and high heels.

Tonight Lottie Rosemount was every bit the young female corporate mover and shaker he had seen at parties all over the world. Efficient. Brilliant. Organised.

Only he knew the real Lottie. The woman who had

taken a high-street bakery and transformed it into something spectacular. Doing what she loved to do, her passion. On her own terms.

When had he last met a woman like that? Not often. Oh, he had met plenty of glossy-haired girls with high IQs who had claimed they were doing what they truly loved, and plenty of lady bakers had studied business, but so few people were able to combine the two skills to create a successful bakery.

Lottie had.

Maybe that was why he connected with the elegant, stunning woman he was looking at now, though he had only met her a few days earlier.

They were different from other people.

Her life forces, her energy, sparkled like the jewels in the bracelet on her wrist. She was effervescent, hot, and so attractive he had to fight down that fizz of testosterone that clenched the muscles under his dress shirt and set his heart racing.

Just at the sight of her.

Rob watched Lottie chatting away to the other guests. He heard her speaking and replying to questions in French and what sounded like Russian. Of course. She must have studied modern languages for business.

He headed for the bar, anxious not to make a fool of himself, ogling the woman in the lilac dress, but she strolled across through to the other room, totally confident and completely at ease in this group of top decision makers in the catering world. It was the kind of ease that came from an expensive education. Hadn't she mentioned something about a management degree?

It was an education designed to open doors. And it had.

His education had been at the school of hard graft and a local college that would take in a boy with a police record and next to no academic qualifications past the age of seventeen.

He picked up a glass of sparkling water and turned back to the cluster of other guests at the same moment as Lottie started introducing some tough-looking lads to one of the college lecturers he vaguely recalled from his student days, going out of her way to make them feel relaxed and included.

He had got it wrong.

She was not one of the hobby bakers who opened a cupcake shop for a joke. A whim to keep her and her friends amused and give them somewhere to meet up to laugh at the poor schmucks who had to slave for a living.

Just the opposite

She had trained. Worked. Slaved. Knew what she was talking about.

People did not often surprise him, not after years in the hotel trade.

Lottie Rosemount was one of a kind.

Perhaps that was why his gaze stayed locked solid on that lovely face until she turned and strolled away towards the stage on Sean's arm to begin the charity auction, leaving Rob to stare after her. And the low back of her dress.

Whoa. Mind-blowing. Brain-blasting whoa.

What had he intended to do? Oh, yes. Find out what the hell was going on with this new menu he knew nothing about.

He caught sight of a waiter emerging from the kitchen with a platter of canapés. Then another, and another. His heart instantly sank. It was too late.

The food service had started. There was no way he was going to barge into that kitchen and start asking questions when the food was already on plates.

Plan B. He was going to have to find out the hard way.

By tasting every single dish presented to the guests at this event. And they had better be spectacular. Or he would want to know why.

'Well. What did you think?'

'I think he did a fine job.' Lottie smiled, her gaze focused on the stage. 'Consider me impressed. But don't you dare tell him that I said that. The students are thinking of joining his online fan club and they must have taken at least a hundred photos on their mobile phones.'

Lottie stood shoulder to shoulder next to Sean and they watched in contented silence as Rob chatted and laughed with the newest group of catering students. He had spent most of the last hour following the charity auction happily introducing the wide-eyed students to chefs who Lottie had held in awe for most of her life. Chefs who she had somehow managed to get to donate seven-course dinners as auction prizes were like putty in Rob's hands.

'There is one tiny little thing which I should mention. Did Rob come up with tonight's menu?'

Sean shook his head. 'Rob is responsible for the hotel standards but the executive chef at the Paris hotel sent over the recipes.'

Lottie slowly produced a printed copy of the menu that she had stolen from the table and passed it to Sean who groaned out loud.

'Oh, great, what's this? Marks out of ten? And what are these scribbles down the side and over the page?'

'Suggestions. Ideas. Proposals. And when it comes to that mess of a salad, a shut-down notice. Pomegranate seeds on the same plate as chopped walnuts, anchovies and smoked ham? It was a mess. But the rest?'

Lottie flipped the flat of her right hand from side to side

and sucked in air between her teeth. 'It was edible. But that is all I could say about it.'

Sean coughed. 'Don't hit me, but it sounds like you might enjoy working with that brother of mine and coming up with your own recipes.'

'Work with the mighty Rob Beresford? The very idea. I'm far too good. His ego would never recover.' Then she laughed and nudged Sean in the arm. 'Let's go talk to your chef and hear what she has to say about tonight's meal. I'd like to hear what she thinks.'

Then Lottie paused and shot a quick glance back towards the stage and her voice faded away. 'But after that I need to catch up with Rob about a very interesting phone call that I have just had with Valencia Cagoni. Your brother has some explaining to do.'

Sean snorted out a reply. 'Too late. He's seen you and is coming this way. Best of luck!'

Lottie lifted her chin as Rob sauntered over with a couple of students and waved towards the buffet table where a few remaining desserts were being demolished by the students before they were cleared away.

A wave of conflicting emotions coursed through her at the sight of his handsome face smiling at her. Confusion, disbelief, annoyance, and something alarmingly like respect were in the mix.

'Hi,' she said in a very hoarse voice, then covered it up with a quick cough. 'Fed up with signing autographs yet?'

'They're a great bunch.' Rob nodded and half turned to face the buffet. 'You were right about the scholarships. Half of those young men wouldn't be here if their fees were not paid. Good idea. I like it.'

He rolled his shoulders back and shoved both hands into his trouser pockets. 'I like it so much I am going to do something about it. Leave it with me. I'll come up with something to give that fund a boost.'

'Really?' Lottie squeaked. 'That's fantastic. Splendid. Great.'

There must have been something in her voice that made Rob turn and look at her.

'Are you feeling okay?'

'Never better. In fact I have just had the most fascinating chat with my old boss, Valencia Cagoni. Her twins are recovering from the chickenpox and she was delighted that I had found such an inspiring replacement chef for the fundraiser. But, of course, you know Valencia very well, don't you, Rob?'

Lottie whirled around and stepped closer to Rob so that the few remaining guests would not be able to hear their conversation.

'In fact, you know her so well that you sometimes pass on your personal recommendations for new apprentices in her restaurant.'

She took a breath and took one more step so that she could almost reach out and touch him if she wanted to. 'Apprentices like me.'

Her eyes narrowed. 'You were the one who persuaded Valencia to give me that training place. You made the call, you told her that I would be coming to see her and that she should give me a chance.'

'She told you.' Rob winced. 'Damn.'

Lottie stabbed Rob in the chest with her forefinger. 'You are responsible for my entire career. You!' Then she stepped back and looked around the ballroom. 'I still cannot believe it.'

His eyebrows lifted. 'Valencia Cagoni is an old friend from college. You needed a job in a hurry. I made the call. Happy now?'

'No, I'm confused.' Lottie blinked. 'Why didn't you just tell me that earlier and save yourself some grief? And Valencia never said a word. Not once in three years. She made me slave for that training post.'

'I asked her not to tell you that I had called,' Rob replied, and then dropped his shoulders back. 'You know how chefs talk. It makes it feel a lot sweeter if you had to fight for what you want and get it on your own merit, instead of who you know in the business. You had to work, and work hard. What you achieved was down to you, not me.'

Then he flicked one hand in the air. 'You know Valencia would never have taken you on unless she was convinced that you had talent. She is way tougher with her training than I am.'

'You fired me, and then set up my replacement training position. Why? Why did you do that?' Lottie asked, her voice trembling with emotion. 'I would really like to know because right now my head is spinning.'

'Because I knew Debra was never going to be a mentor to anyone with talent. You deserved a chance to show what you could do and Debra was not going to let another chef steal her star. Valencia needed someone who could step up. Okay?'

Lottie stared at Rob in stunned silence, her hands planted one on each hip, her gaze locked on to his eyes.

'Has anyone ever told you,' she breathed in a low voice 'that you are the most infuriating man alive?'

'Frequently.' He grinned. 'Has anyone ever told you that you are the prettiest and most persistent woman alive? Perhaps that is why I find you so intriguing.'

He glanced from side to side and then pushed out his elbow. 'We're done here. Might as well hit the road in style! How about it?'

Lottie glared at Rob's elbow, then at his face and then

back to his elbow, before sighing out loud and hooking her arm through his.

'This has already been one crazy evening. Why not go the whole way? Because I really don't know what to think about you any longer. First I think you are a complete… and then the whole image gets flipped over. It is so beyond annoying it's not funny and it's giving me a headache just thinking about it. I really don't have a single clue who you are, Rob Beresford.'

'Want to find out?'

CHAPTER SEVEN

'Is THIS LEGAL?'

'Behave. I need to clear my head and the main entrance is too far away. Fancy a walk?'

Lottie stared at the wooden sign that read in large letters: 'Keep Off the Grass', inhaled sharply, pulled her arm tight towards Rob and stepped over the low wooden white fence that separated the London pavement from the grass in the public park.

It only took a minute to skip across the grass and onto the path but her heart was beating a little harder when they were back on tarmac.

'You don't like breaking the rules. Do you?' Rob smirked.

He was observant, too. 'Not something I do very often. But I suppose it is a lovely evening and my headache needs an airing. Why don't we take a tour of the park? I haven't been in there for years.'

And it *was* a lovely evening, and Rob Beresford looked hotter than fresh bread just out of the oven. He smelt just as good, too.

Her treacherous heart had not completely got used to the fact that she was strolling along the pavement arm in arm with this dazzling man as he casually chatted to her as though they were old friends out for the evening.

Occasionally Lottie had to fire a hot glance in Rob's

direction to make sure that she was not in fact hallucinating and this was the same man who breathed dragon fire at trainees and made grown men cry on TV.

The arrogance and attitude were gone and in their place was this astonishing man who she now knew was responsible for kicking off her career with the finest award-winning patisserie chef in London.

And the transformation knocked the feet out from under her.

'Ian was telling me about your idea for a birthday cake book. I like it. Could be fun.'

'I think so. My cake shop is right in the middle of the high street and these days a lot of mums and dads simply don't have the time or, to be honest, the skill, to come up with that perfect birthday cake. So I get a lot of orders. And you would be surprised at how many are for old-style family cakes for grandparents and even great-grandparents.'

'Are you kidding me?' Rob asked with a lilt in his voice.

'Nope. That's one of the reasons why I started the Bake and Banter club. To teach adults how to bake a cake they can make at home which the family will love.'

She shifted closer to Rob to avoid a group of tourists who had their heads down, totally engrossed in their tablet computers and oblivious to other people on the walkway.

'You really get a buzz out of the baking, don't you?'

'More than I ever expected,' Lottie replied with a smile. 'So far I have made eight versions of that cartoon–racing car cake you saw this morning for little boys aged four to eighty-four and they all love it. Everyone is so different. Take next week, for example. The baking club want me to demonstrate how to make a chocolate birthday cake for one of our regular customers. Ninety years young. She wants loads of soft gooey chocolate icing. And three layers of chocolate sponge in the middle. Eat with a spoon. Whipped cream on the side. Delish.'

'Oh, yes, I remember what it was like to have my hands in sticky icing sugar and chocolate all day. Don't miss it a bit. But let me tell you—' he tilted his head closer to hers and half whispered '—for a working baker, you look fabulous.'

'Thank you, kind sir. My pleasure. You clean up nicely yourself.'

Rob exaggeratedly tugged with one hand at the lapel of the same dinner jacket he had worn for the gallery opening, while dodging the other pedestrians on the busy west London pavements. 'Oh, this old suit? Thought I had better make an effort as the star pupil.'

Lottie gave his arm an extra squeeze before snorting out loud. 'Shameless! Make that one of the many star pupils! How is your mum's cold?'

'She's feeling a lot better today and went to the gallery this afternoon before heading off to tea with her pals,' Rob replied as he negotiated around some dog walkers. 'So I am officially off duty for a couple of hours and, unless you are desperate to get home, I think this calls for a small delay! Look across the street. What do you see?'

He slipped his dinner jacket around her shoulders and held her within it for a few seconds, bringing up the collar so that he could flip the ultra-soft fabric around her smooth neck.

She pretended not to notice as his fingertips gently moved against her skin to flick the ends of her hair back over the collar.

'Thank you.' She smiled back in reply, conscious that the hard cheekbones of Rob's face were highlighted too sharply by the streetlight outside the swish, glossy shopfronts. He was too lean, but she knew that he had eaten something from every tray of the buffet at the hotel.

Maybe she could do something about that, if he stayed around long enough.

He smiled and surprised her by sliding around behind her, so that his arms were wrapped around her waist, holding her tight against him. She felt the pressure of his head against the side of her face as he dropped his chin onto her shoulder, lifted his left arm, and pointed.

Lottie tore her eyes away from Rob, and stared across to a very familiar sunlit stone building. Then laughed out loud.

'It's the old grand entrance to the catering college. We've come around in a circle.'

Rob nodded and looked up into the high carved stone entrance to what had been a 1930s art deco school of architecture before it was taken over by the catering school.

'The first time I walked through those doors I was seventeen, angry, bitter, and furious with the world and myself. I was a mess, Lottie. And maybe not someone you wanted to be around.'

There was something is his voice that compelled Lottie to look over her shoulder into his face. This was the young man, so full of hope and dreams.

'Why do you think that you were such a disaster?' Lottie replied with a smile, looking into his face. 'From my experience, most seventeen-year-olds feel that way.'

'Oh, girl, if you only knew the truth of it.'

Then something shifted in his eyes as though a darker memory had floated up to the surface.

And in that moment the mood changed. His brow was furrowed with anxiety, his mouth moved back to a straight line, and his body almost bristled with tension.

'Then tell me. Tell me the truth about why you were such a mess, because I really want to know.'

'That's one hell of a long story.'

'Then let's sit down and look at the college and reminisce together.' She looked around and spotted an old and not very clean wooden bench, which she covered with Rob's expensive jacket, liner side up.

'Ah. This is perfect.' Lottie shuffled back on the hard seat and folded her hands neatly on her lap.

'It is June. It's a relatively warm evening and I am sitting on your jacket, so there is no possible escape. I suggest that you start at the beginning and go from there. That usually works.'

'Are you sure that you're not an art critic? Because you are being damn nosy.'

'One of my terrible character flaws; nothing I can do about it. Once I take an interest in something I have to find out everything there is to know. So fire away. Because I am not going anywhere until I find out why you were so very angry with the world the first day you walked through those doors.'

'A-ha. So you are interested in me. At last she admits it.'

'I want to know what kind of family my best friend is getting herself into. So far Sean has been great, but are there skeletons in the Beresford family cupboard which will burst Dee's bubble? Not going to happen.'

'Skeletons? Lottie, there is a whole pirate ship of skeletons moored offshore all armed to the teeth and ready and able to cause mayhem at any minute they are released. The problem is most of them are about my side of the family. Not Sean's.'

'I don't understand. Sean told me that your mum and dad get on just fine even though they're divorced.'

'They do. I am lucky. Tom Beresford met my mother when he opened up the first Beresford hotel in New York City. She was living a bohemian life in an artists' colony in

the Hamptons most of the year, and holding exhibitions of
her work in the city when she needed funds. Well…' Rob
smiled. 'You've seen my mother. Gorgeous, fun, and so talented it's criminal. I don't blame my dad for falling for her
one little bit. She was even more stunning back then and
she must have really adored him to settle in the city. In the
end they had six great years in New York before we had to
move back to London to open the flagship hotel here. That
was when things started to change. It was my mum who
decided that she could not tolerate living here.'

'Did she hate London that much?'

'Not particularly. It was the sudden change in her routine that she hated. Mum likes her day and her life all laid
out, nice and simple and familiar. London was too much,
too fast, and she couldn't get used to it. In the end the only
way she could work was to go back to the Hamptons for a
couple of months at a time with frequent trips back to London to see me. I was only a toddler so I stayed here with
my dad and got used to airports.'

'That must have been tough. But there are people who
lead their whole lives like that. My dad used to boast that
one year he spent a grand total of fifteen days sleeping in
his own bed. The price of modern life.'

'It might have worked for your family but it didn't work
for mine. My dad made plans to move back to New York
but then my grandparents in Suffolk needed him and Mum
was staying away for longer and longer periods…and they
simply drifted apart. I was way too young to understand
what divorce was and nothing really changed in my life.
Until my dad met Sean's mum. Maria. And for the next ten
years I found out what it was like to have a mother who
was there every minute of the day when I needed her and
who even gave me a brother.'

'Sean. Of course. You loved Maria. Didn't you?'

'Adored her. Oh, I knew that I had a real mother. At birthdays and Christmas the house used to be full of Adele Forrester and her friends and extended family who used to descend like a whirlwind then disappear again for another six months leaving chaos behind them. But that was the way Maria and my dad liked it. Open house. Maria was a very special person and Sean was great. I had a family who were willing to put up with a very confused teenager and help him make some sense of his life and what he wanted to do with it. It was all good. It was too good.'

Rob flicked his arm out in a wide arc towards the trees.

'And then it was all taken away from me. And I went off the rails. Big time.'

'Maria. Of course. I am so sorry. Sean told Dee that she had died when he was young.'

'Unfair. So very, very unfair. One day when Sean is a lot older you might want to ask him about his mother's life as a refugee fleeing war and destruction. Only to die of cancer in a country where she thought she was safe with a family she loved and loved her right back in return. Because I can't talk about it without wanting to hit something very hard.'

Rob reached out and nipped off a large leaf from the bush growing behind their heads and slowly tore it into segments with his long, clever fingers as he spoke.

'You want to know about my skeletons? I was seventeen years old, I had plenty of money and a driving licence, and enough fury and anger in my belly to burn down most of London. And that is precisely what I tried to do. I had grown up in this city and knew precisely where to find trouble and distraction in any shape or form. Drink, girls, gambling, and the kind of people my dad would throw out of his hotel. The whole package. Sometimes I got away with it by being smarter and faster than the other guy. Sometimes I didn't and I have a police record to prove it. And a few broken bones along the way. My nose was a different shape then.'

'What did your dad do? He must have been frantic and scared for you.'

'The best he could. He was grieving and lost. Sean was desolate. And I was out of control and heading downhill faster than he could apply the brakes.'

'How did you pull back from that life to find your way to catering college?'

'The hard way. I woke up one morning in the bed of a girl whose name I couldn't even recall and I must have had twenty messages on my mobile phone. All asking me to get back to the house. My mum had got herself into a mess in Thailand. And I mean a mess. Three hours later I was on a plane to Bangkok.'

Rob exhaled long and slow. 'I had heard the words *nervous breakdown* but nothing could have prepared me for the emotional wreck I found in a Bangkok psychiatric unit. Her latest lover had stolen everything she had and left her broke and alone in the middle of nowhere. It wasn't the first time that had happened but this was the worst. But she was lucky. One of the other artists on the retreat was worried about her and sent out a search party. They found her on the beach the next day. Crying. Distraught. Irrational and terrified of anyone touching her or coming near her. It was one of the worst twenty-four hours of my life.'

'Oh, Rob. That's horrific. For both of you.'

'I made her a deal. It was very simple. I promised that if she came back to London with me and got some medical help for her problems, then I would take care of her. I would go to college and get the qualifications I needed to run the hotel kitchens. Sober and clean, a hardworking little drone. And that is what I did. I poured all of that bitter anger and fury at Maria's death into my work.'

The shredded pieces of leaf fluttered through the air.

'That's why I am not surprised people found me scary. I was so desperate to prove that I could achieve something that I refused to allow anything or anyone get in my way. *Relentless* is actually not a bad description.'

'Did she agree? I mean, did she come back from Thailand with you?'

'My mum went into the best rehab unit money could buy and I already knew that she was going to be there a long time. My dad was going to see her when he could get away from the hotel business and Sean went along when the unit said that she was stable enough to cope. But apart from that it was just the two of us against the world. I thought that was going to be enough to get her through this dark time in her life and magically turn her back to the lovely mum I used to know and everything would be back to normal again.'

Rob shrugged. 'I was so naïve about mental illness. So wrong. Badly wrong. Things have never been the same. Oh, she can go for a year or eighteen months without a major episode, and then she will fall for some hotshot man and life will be wonderful—until it isn't. And I have to pick up the pieces and start all over again.'

Lottie hesitated before replying. 'The other night at the gallery. Was that what you were worried about? That it was all too much for her and she would have a relapse?'

'No. I was far more worried about what the killer combo of cold remedies and champagne would look like to the real critics who were standing outside with their cameras. A good news story about an artist who has come back after eight years with a wonderful inspirational show does not sell. But give them Rob Beresford's rehab-refugee mother? Oh, yes. Let's just say that I was tired of giving them what they want.'

Her fingers slid across the bench and found his. 'Then Adele is very lucky to have a son like you to protect her.'

'Is she? I haven't always been there for her, Lottie. Not by a long way. I had replaced her in my life with Sean's mother at the very time she needed me as a son. And that sort of guilt does not go away easily.'

'But you kept that promise. That means a lot in my book.'

Her own eyes pricked with tears, and she laced her fingers between his, forcing apart his fingers, which had tightened into a ball.

Her touch acted like a catalyst, and he ripped his eyes away from the park and focused on her face as his fingers relaxed and squeezed hers back, leaving it to Lottie to break the silence.

Lottie stopped and turned so that she was facing Rob. 'I have an idea. And you can tell me to mind my own business, but here goes.'

She took a breath. 'I can see that you want to help your mum become the best she can be. I want to help. She is a remarkable artist and I adore her work. If you like, she can use my studio any time she wants when you are in London together. Room service, accommodation and as much lemon drizzle cake as she can eat, courtesy of the management.'

She clenched her teeth and pretended to duck. 'What do you think?'

Rob looked into her face for a few seconds, before replying in a low intense voice.

'You would do that? For us?'

'In a heartbeat, yes.'

His reply was to take a firmer grip of her hand as he rose slowly to his feet.

'Thank you, Lottie. Yes. I think that she would like that very much. Although I should warn you, for a skinny artist that woman can eat a hell of a lot of cake.'

Lottie looked up into Rob's face and what she saw there was like a light in the darkness. He was not used to being shown kindness and was trying to bluff away the depth of his feeling.

Hell, she knew what that was like. She simply had not expected it in him.

And just like that the resentment she had held for the past three years and all of the imagined angst popped like a balloon. Gone. Finished. Over.

Time to start all over again with the Rob she was with right here and now.

Hesitantly at first, then more firmly, she grasped hold of both of Rob's hands and slowly let him help her up from the bench and back on her feet.

And with that they walked casually, hand in hand, in silence, along the wide path as though it were something they did all of the time.

Rob could never know that her palms weren't sweating due to the warm breeze, but the gentle way in which his fingertips stroked the tender skin. Her gaze moved over the happy groups of smiling, chatty couples who strolled across the park. Anywhere except Rob. She wanted to look at him so badly it was almost a physical pain.

Except that would mean giving in to the sigh of absolute pleasure that was bursting to escape.

This was what it would be like if she were Rob's girl-friend. On a regular date.

Except, of course, this wasn't a date, was it?

This was a kind gesture to his brother's friend, who had been in the right place at the right time to help him out with somewhere for his mother to stay. That was all it could be. All it was ever going to be.

So, why not enjoy these precious moments and make the best of them while she could? These were the happy memories *she* would hold precious over the coming months when Rob and Adele had gone back to their exciting, busy lives, and she was merely a person they might see at social events with Dee and Sean.

In a few days she would be back in her normal, safe life. Which was just how she wanted it, wasn't it?

Her brain was so distracted by the unfamiliar thoughts and feelings whirling around inside her head that she didn't see the sudden break in the paving slab until the toe of her thin-soled evening sandal caught in the stone and she found herself falling forwards, hands outstretched. Into a pair of strong arms.

It was seconds before her brain connected with the fact that she was standing chest to chest with Rob with both of his arms wrapped around her body, her hands flat against his shirt front.

Just for a moment, Lottie closed her eyes and revelled in the warmth and the strength of his embrace. The exquisite aroma of aftershave, antiperspirant and clean pressed linen. Lemon, blended with the musky spice of light perspiration of the warm summer evening, and something else, something unique. Rob. His scent, his heat. And the strange magnetic pull that made her want to edge closer and closer to him every time they met. The pull that was going to make parting from him so very painful.

The overall effect was so totally intoxicating, that suddenly she felt light-headed and bent forward to rest her brow on his chest.

This was her dream, her fantasy. For a few precious seconds she could pretend that she was just like any other girl out for a stroll with her boyfriend. Pretend that this man cared about her, had chosen her, wanted to be with her.

A strong bicep flexed next to the thin fabric of her dress,

and her eyes closed in pleasure. It had been so long since she had been held like this!

Drat Rob. Drat. She couldn't do this. Why had she agreed to walk with him? He would be flying back to his real world, and she would be back to square one. On her own, holding it together.

'Are you okay?' Rob asked, with enough concern in his voice to bring a lump to her throat again.

His hands slid down as she pulled back and smiled up into his face, but instead of stepping away he simply linked his hands behind her back, holding her in place as she recovered.

'Yes. I think so.' She glanced down at her shoe. 'How clumsy of me. Thanks for stopping me from falling flat on my face.'

Lottie leant back so that she could focus only to find him smiling down at her, his eyes scanning her face from side to side, as though looking for something before speaking.

His lips curved back into a wide, open-mouthed smile, so warm, so caring that she was blinded by it. The warm fingers of one hand slid up her back as he dropped his head forward and nuzzled his chin against her hair. 'I'm pleased that I was here at the right time.'

Some part of her brain registered that she should make a response, and she forced herself to lift her chin.

Bad mistake.

Because at that precise moment Rob shifted his position and as she whispered, 'Thank you,' she felt the heat of his breath on her cheek. Lottie dared to slowly slide the palms of her hands up onto his chest. She could feel the hard planes and ridges of his body beneath her fingers. Emanating enough heat to warm deep inside her, melting away the last remnants of icy resistance that might have lingered there.

A young couple walked by, then a cyclist, but Lottie could hear nothing except the sound of Rob's breathing as his lips pressed against her temple, and the stubble on his chin rasping against her cheek for a second before he released his grip on her waist and slowly, slowly, slid his hand up inside his jacket, and onto the bare skin of her back above her dress

The sensation was so unexpected, so delicious that she inhaled sharply, gasping in air.

It was as though she had given him a signal of approval.

As his fingertips stroked her skin his soft, sensuous mouth slid slowly and tenderly against her upper lip in the sweetest, most gentle of kisses. It was so brief that Lottie had only seconds to close her eyes and enjoy it before he pulled away from her, his fingers sliding down from the small of her back.

Leaving her feeling bereft.

'Would you like some coffee? I know the perfect place.'

CHAPTER EIGHT

'I COULD NEVER get tired of this view,' Lottie murmured as she looked out from the patio outside the luxurious apartment over the rooftops of London in the fading dusk.

'Remarkable.'

Lottie looked over her shoulder at Rob, who was leaning on the kitchen-area worktop. Staring at her as though she were the most fascinating thing in the room instead of the view from the patio. Taunting her with one glance. How did he do that? She had met international bankers who could take lessons on how to make people squirm from Rob Beresford.

She felt like rolling back her shoulders and squaring up to him but somehow she suspected he would enjoy seeing how uncomfortable his ogling was making her feel.

The look he was giving her at that second could be classified as a fire risk.

For the first time since she walked out of the hotel elevator a quiver of alarm crossed Lottie's mind, making her breath catch in her throat.

What was she doing here?

She had worked with predatory sharks in banking and through her family most of her life and was well used to their tactics of luring the little fish into a shallow pool where they could not possibly escape.

This time she was the one who had voluntarily decided to enter the shark's territory with nothing more than her brain and her wit as protection. To do…what, exactly? Had she completely lost her mind?

Blinking away the butterflies of doubt and something close to alarm, Lottie watched as Rob broke his stare and strode over to the open-plan living space and shrugged off his dinner jacket, casually draping it on the back of a sofa.

The muscles underneath the fine fabric of his dinner shirt strained taut against the tug and flexed enough to make the hairs on her arms perk up.

And just like that the attraction she had felt towards him in the park sizzled and caught flame, making her inhale sharply and turn back to the patio.

By turning into the gentle breeze Lottie could feel the cool air calming the heat of her skin, and, reaching back, she lifted her long hair from her neck and let it fall onto her shoulders.

'Have you always lived in London?' Rob asked as he joined her at the metal railing, so close that their elbows touched for a second before he braced himself.

The heady muskiness of his aftershave blended with the coffee aromas and something on his skin that was so uniquely Rob to create a fragrance that was so addictive it should be banned. Lottie's chest lifted and fell as she indulged in the pleasure before she managed to pull together a reply.

'I spent some time in management school in America but apart from that, yes, I suppose I have.' Her gaze scanned the lights laid out before her. 'I love this city. I always have.'

'Then that is something else we have in common.'

Lottie let go of the railing and half turned to face him.

The light from the living room created a mosaic of shadows on his face, which added to the hard planes she knew were there.

London?

'I thought that you couldn't wait to get out of this city and your business was based in California? Your mother was telling me all about her wonderful studio home on the beach and…'

Understanding flooded in to replace disbelief and Lottie turned back to face the panorama in silence.

Now she was getting a clearer picture of this man. Remarkable award-winning chef moves to California to be close to his mother when she needs him. And in the process starts a new career in TV. Still a player. Still someone interested in what was in it for him…but…

'She seems very happy there.'

'She is. The exhibition is a hit and my mum is heading back to California as soon as it closes and the next lucky artist takes over. Which means that it is back to work for both of us. I probably won't be back in London for a good few months.'

'Wow. Do you have a home of your own to go back to?'

'If you mean bricks and mortar and a welcome mat? Not exactly. I've claimed the penthouse in the Beresford Plaza and my mum has a loft packed with boxes of my old stuff. Is decaf okay for you?'

'Perfect. Thank you.'

Rob strolled back into the kitchen, topped up his elaborate coffee maker with water, and added two large scoops of ground coffee from a canister, before pressing several buttons.

'Well, I can see your barista skills are just fine, but do you still find time to cook, Rob? You must miss running your own kitchen.'

His hands stilled on the worktop. 'Cooking as in chopping veg and making stock? Not for years.' Then he grinned. 'I have the fun of bringing new chefs into the hotels and seeing them learn and grow and do amazing things. Every one of them is so desperate to impress me they give us their all. Now that *is* magical.'

Lottie strolled back into the apartment as he spoke and every word seemed to penetrate her heart and touch something very deep inside her. This was the closest she had come to the real Rob Beresford. No pretence. Just Rob standing in a kitchen waiting for coffee to brew after a night at a function where he played a clever version of the persona he had created for the outside world to see.

And yet here she was. Alone with him. And suddenly that very idea became so heady with the rush that she deliberately stepped back one step so that she could look at him from the side.

Desperate to keep just out of the effective range of his devastating power of attraction that was sucking her closer and closer by the minute.

'So you understood what I was trying to do tonight? Raise funds to make that dream possible?'

Rob swirled one hand into the air around his head. 'Of course I understood. Lottie, the fairy godmother, wants to make sure that she has the support in place before she makes commitments that could change someone's life. No false promises. That makes sense to me.'

'Fairy godmother? I bet you say that to all the girls.'

Lottie gave a mini curtsey. This was a mistake.

Because at that precise moment Rob raised his arms to lift a tray from the shelf, and in the process his shirt rose high enough above the waistband of his low-rise smart trousers to reveal a couple of inches of toned, flat stomach.

Why was it that she had always been attracted to the athletic type?

Just when she thought that he could not be more gorgeous, he had to hit her with this. The irony of it all made her sigh out loud.

Bad head.

Bad heart.

Bad need for contact with his man.

Bad, full stop.

'What? Was it something I said? Or have you found a new hobby down there?'

Lottie hesitated before replying, desperate to avoid the harsh truth, so she started gabbling instead of ogling.

'I love my bakery so much it's hard to imagine living in hotel rooms full time, no matter how splendid the view.'

Rob chuckled. 'Don't worry about it. I'm used to living out of a suitcase.'

For a moment she wanted to run into Rob's arms, feel the strength of his body against hers, and tell him how attracted she was to him.

But she wouldn't. Because he was leaving and she was staying, and that was a recipe for disaster in anyone's cookbook.

No. She had to control herself, and fight this powerful attraction. She just had to. His life was in the fast lane of the cities she had left behind her.

Time to put the mask back on, drink her coffee, and swallow down her feelings. And get the hell out of there before she did something stupid. Like pounce on him.

Lottie watched in silence as Rob poured the coffee.

'That smells divine.'

'Special import from one of the hotel's best coffee roasters. Oh, if you're hungry for dessert you'll find some soft amaretto biscuits in that tin. My Italian pastry chef claimed he made them himself, but I know your standards are pretty high so I await the expert opinion.'

Rob watched as Lottie flicked open the clasp on the steel canister and brought it up to her face, inhaling deeply.

'Oh, this is heaven. Did Dee tell you that I adore Italian food? Or did you have a premonition?'

'Serendipity. It seems that we share at least some of the same passions, Miss Rosemount,' Rob whispered as Lottie slowly closed her lips around a piece of the soft round almond-and-apricot biscuit and groaned in pleasure, her eyelids flickering as her face twisted in delight.

It was the sexiest thing Rob had ever seen in his life.

His chef was going to have to hire extra staff to cope with all of the takeaway orders coming to this apartment, because there was no way he was going to sit opposite this woman in a restaurant if she was going to act out a movie scene with her food.

He froze, stunned, as he tried in vain to control his breathing…and various other parts of his anatomy that seemed to have woken up to the fact that he was within arm's reach of an amazing woman, and they were alone in this apartment.

Once they recognised him as the chef who they had seen on the TV, women tended to either get stuck into the whole celebrity lifestyle and the second-hand fame that came with being photographed hanging on to his arm, or hit on him straight away for the extra points on the famous name scoresheet.

He gave them what they wanted and they gave him what he wanted. Simple, straightforward. No grey areas; always black and white.

Lottie was as multicoloured as a rainbow. She was totally unfazed by his star ratings and had challenged him from the first moment they met in the gallery.

He admired her for making him change his routine and cut out his usual public performance.

In fact, he liked that more than was good for him.

Maybe it was going back to the Beresford hotel and then the catering college, but the fact that she had crept under his guard tonight to the point where he had blurted out his life story rankled him deeply.

He never told his story. Not to the press and certainly not to strangers. It was way too risky and likely to end up in a tell-all story in some sleazy newspaper, which Sally would have to pay to suppress.

So what did that say about Lottie?

Could he trust her? Dee was a special girl and his brother adored her, but Lottie was very different. Clever, witty, and on the surface an excellent businesswoman.

After a lifetime in the hotel business he prided himself on being able to judge people and every instinct in his body was screaming at that moment that she was someone who had no guile or hidden agendas. And yet there was something sad lingering under that very lovely surface.

Hell. He knew all about that. But it was strange to see the sadness and regret so openly on Lottie's face when she thought he wasn't looking.

Even stranger, it made him all the more attracted to her.

His heart was racing, hard and fast, as he stepped across to the refrigerator to bring out the milk, and took a breath of cool air, fighting to regain his composure. This was getting out of hand, and all he was doing was looking at Lottie!

It had been a very long time since he had wanted to be with a woman as much as he did at that moment.

Lottie chewed and hummed gently to herself as he pretended to move the meagre contents of his huge refrigerator around.

Was this what it would be like to have someone who loved you, and wanted to be with you, not just for an afternoon between international flights, but seven days a week? He had only met this woman a few days ago, and the connection was... What was it? A crush? Because it was a lot more than physical attraction, that was for sure.

In a few days he would go back to his normal life across the Atlantic. This apartment would be rented out, and his time here would be a memory. Left to his imagination.

If this was what Lottie did with biscuits, what would she be like in his bed? Naked, with his hands running over the soft skin of her stunning body, giving her pleasure.

Suddenly Rob found an excellent reason to plunge his head inside the chiller.

'I have white wine if you would like some,' he asked, casually waving the sealed bottle the sommelier had sent up. 'Or perhaps a twenty-year-old tawny port?'

'Thank you, but I have to be up early tomorrow morning and I am already starting with a headache. This has been a long day.'

He closed the door and looked at her, slack jawed. 'You're serious. You are actually going back to work on a Sunday?'

'Of course. One of my very special customers at the bakery is celebrating her fiftieth wedding anniversary tomorrow and I promised that I would bake a very special decorated cake and deliver it in time for their tea party.' And without asking or waiting for a reply she dunked an amaretto biscuit in the hot coffee, slid off the stool, and held a piece of it in front of his mouth so quickly that without thinking he leant forward and closed his lips around her fingertips.

Sweet, warm, intensely flavoured almond exploded onto his taste buds. It was superb.

It was one of those special moments when the food and the company and the location came together and he knew that the next time he tasted that biscuit anywhere in the world he would remember how Lottie looked at that moment. Her face was flushed with excitement and sparkling energy, her lips warm and plump and soft, and those stunning eyes were focused completely on his face.

The silence between them opened up.

Then the coffee machine pinged to tell him the milk was hot and he swallowed, suddenly desperate to keep Lottie close to him as long as he could stretch out the precious time they had left together. 'I am going to have to give that man a raise. But tell me more about this cake of yours. Why is it so important to you?'

'Why? Oh, that's easy. Lily used to be our housekeeper and the woman who taught me how to bake. I owe my entire career to the one person who made my childhood bearable. I think that's worth a cake. Don't you? And these biscuits really are so good.'

She turned her back on him, scrabbling to open the spring lid on the canister, only her trembling fingers let her down and the biscuit fell to the floor.

Before Lottie could reach down to scoop it up, Rob stepped forwards and slid his fingers onto each side of her waist, holding her firm. Secure.

He breathed in an intoxicating combination of luxurious fragrance, body lotion, shampoo, and Lottie.

She smelt fabulous. Felt. Fabulous.

He dared to inch closer behind her, until he could feel the length of her body from shoulder to groin pressed against him.

His arms wrapped tighter around her waist, the fingers

pressing, oh, so gently into her ribcage, and he was rewarded by a gentle but tantalising low sigh.

Rob smoothed her hair away from her face so that he could press his lips against the back of her neck.

'Dee told me that you gave up your job in banking to spend your life doing something you loved instead,' he said, and his low soft voice seemed to resonate against the side of her head. 'That takes guts. And passion. If Lily gave you even a hint of that, then, yes, the lady does deserve the best cake you can make. Even on a Sunday. But why do I feel that you are only telling me part of the story?' He paused and slid just far enough way so that he could run his fingers back through her hair.

'Why did you really leave your old life behind, Lottie? What made you give up a well-paying job and take a risk on a bakery? You must have had choices.'

He sensed her shoulders lift with tension but waited patiently until she was ready to fill the silence. 'I did. If I'm honest, I had too many choices. My parents couldn't help. My dad wanted me to move to France and a ready-made slot in an IT company he had started as a retirement project. But not one person thought that I had it in me to retrain for a completely new career and start my own company. And that...hurt for a while.'

He swallowed down hard, stunned by the calmness of her voice, and pressed his chin against the top of her head. 'Then they didn't know you. Their loss.'

A deep chuckle bubbled up from inside Lottie's chest and he could feel it through his fingers. 'You're right. They didn't know the real me at all. My boss, my friends—even my boyfriend at the time—thought I would be back to work and my old life within six months. They were wrong. I love it. I sold enough shares to make it happen, but with Dee's help I think we created something very special. I *am* Lottie's cake shop now, and I wouldn't want it any other way.'

'So you gave it all up? Career, lifestyle, everything you had?'

'I traded up. Some of the happiest times of my teenage life were spent helping Lily in the kitchen, experimenting with pastry and flavours and textures.'

'Any regrets?'

'Some. I thought the friends I had made at school and university would stay my friends. But that didn't happen. Suddenly we didn't have anything to talk about any longer. Packing it all in and starting a bakery was what you did for a hobby when you retired, not your life's work. So I've had to make new friends instead.'

'Wait a minute. Your boyfriend didn't support you when you were going through so much upheaval?'

Rob slowly but firmly turned her around at the waist until his gaze was locked on that stunning face, his hands resting lightly on her hips.

'You are a beautiful woman, Lottie. He was a fool to let you go.'

Lottie smiled and pressed the flat of her hands on his chest before replying in a low, hoarse voice.

'He didn't let me go. We both knew that our relationship had come to an end. He wanted to climb the corporate ladder and achieve his dreams in banking. I didn't want that life any longer and he didn't understand how I could leave it all behind and start again on a shoestring. So don't judge him—that wouldn't be fair.'

'Then he was an even bigger idiot. Although it does make me wonder.'

'Wonder what?'

Lottie leant back within the circle of his arms so that she could gaze up into his face, and the compassion and need that Rob saw in those wide green eyes fractured the frosting of ice around his heart like an ice pick and kept on picking away until the warm and vulnerable core was exposed to the world.

It destroyed him. Broke him. Blasted away the shell that he had built up.

So that when he did reply, every word came from the heart instead of the head before he had a chance to change his mind.

'I was simply wondering whether you'd be willing to give another bloke a chance to show you how stunning you are. Is that so outrageous?'

Lottie inhaled a sharp breath and her gaze scanned his face as though she was looking for something. And found it.

'No. Not so outrageous at all.' She smiled.

'Excellent. Then why not start right now? Today. With me.'

Lottie's brain froze.

Him? Rob wanted her to start dating him?

He was holding out the most delicious temptation and all she had to do was say yes and find out if his touch was as exciting as she thought it would be.

For a night or even a weekend, if she was lucky, she would find out what it was like to be the object of a man's desire again.

Until he left. And she would be right back where she started. Alone.

Her gaze scanned his face. He was serious.

As serious as the most forbidden fruit could be.

'You don't know how to give up, do you?' Lottie said with a shaky smile.

'Not good enough for you?' Rob grinned back.

And then he nodded his head up and down, just once.

'Ah. I see your problem. You're too afraid you might get used to the idea of having a fling? Maybe even like it. Yup, could be trouble.'

'Come on, Rob. Your life and work is in California and you've already told me that you don't plan to come back to London any time soon. I have my bakery and right now there are no plans to open a cake shop and tea rooms in Carmel. So thank you for the compliment, but you know it would never work out. I'm not interested in long-term relationships.'

'Good. Because that's not what I am suggesting. In fact, just the opposite. My rules are pretty simple: a short-term relationship between two consenting adults, no strings and no expectation of anything more than what we have for as long as we have it.'

She looked into those eyes. Fatal mistake. It meant she was powerless to resist when he moved forward and pressed his long, slim fingers either side of her head and tilted his head to lean in.

His full mouth was moist and warm on her upper lip, and she could not help but close her eyes and luxuriate in the delicious sensation of his long, slow kiss.

Her arms moved around his neck, he moved closer, and she kissed him back, pressing hotter, deeper, the pace of her breathing matching his.

Somewhere at the back of her brain a sensible voice was shouting out that this was not a clever thing to do.

Bad Lottie. Very bad.

His lips slid away down her jaw to kiss her throat so she could gasp a breath.

'Take a chance on me, Lottie,' he whispered as his cheek worked his way down the side of her neck to her collarbone. 'I want to be with you, get to know you. Will you give me a chance to do that? Can you learn to trust me that much?'

She forced her eyes open wide enough to see that his own eyes were closed, his face...oh, his face. She was so going to regret this. One of her arms moved around so that she could run her fingers through his hair. 'I don't know. It would mean that you have to be around long enough to find out. Can you do that?'

He looked at her, his fingers pressing on her back.

'I will be around long enough. Will you give me a chance?'

She looked at him so long her stomach knotted up, his eyes scanning her face as though they were begging her to accept him. There was something in those eyes that went through her skin and penetrated her heart, blowing away any chance of resistance.

There was a lot to be said for giving in to impulses.

Lottie found herself grinning back at him, suddenly drunk with the smell, the feeling of his touch on her skin, the power of his physical presence.

Her fingertip traced the curved fullness of this man's lower lip, and his mouth opened a little wider at her touch.

Lottie stared up at Rob, into his sea-blue eyes, and knew that he wanted to kiss her again. She focused on his mouth as his long fingers stroked the sides of her face.

It terrified her. And thrilled her.

She wanted him to kiss her. To make the connection she longed for. There was no way that she could freeze this man from her life—it had gone too far now for that to happen. Her lips parted and she felt his mouth against hers as her eyes closed and she let herself be carried away in a breathless dream of a deep, deep kiss.

Tears welled up in Lottie's eyes and she tried to turn away as a single bead escaped but it was too late. Rob wiped it away with his thumb, the gentle pressure stroking her cheek with such tenderness it took her breath away.

How could she have doubted that this man was capable of being gentle and loving?

Yes, loving.

Her gaze scanned the cheekbones of his face, the bumpy nose, coming to rest on the bow of his upper lip above the full mouth. She felt as though she had known him all of her life.

Her fingertip moved over the crease lines in the corners of his mouth and eyes, which she knew now were down to more than just laughter.

Life had not been easy for this man. His love for his mother had driven him to take risks. If he had become ambitious it was not for his own ego. He had made sacrifices for the people he loved and would do so again.

His hand slid from her cheek into her hair. Smoothing it back from her face as his lips pressed against her brow, closer, and closer.

Her heart was racing, blood surging in her ears and she forgot how crazy this was as she closed her eyes and sensed the raw moistness of his lips on one eyelid, then the other. One of his hands moved around the curve of her waist, drawing her body closer to his.

The delicious sensation of being wanted as a woman dulled any sense of control she might have had left.

There was only this moment in time. There was only Rob.

She needed him as much as he needed her. How had that happened? And why did it feel so absolutely right to be in his arms, feeling his fingers stroke her back and hair, his lips on the crook of her neck, his chin pressed against her jaw? She knew she would be powerless to resist if the heat of that mouth moved closer.

She wanted him to kiss her again, and again, and her

head shifted so that she could caress his chin and cheek. Her lips parted and she felt the touch of his tongue on her neck.

Heaven was about to happen.

The pressure of his lips increased as he moved slowly under her chin and nuzzled her lower lip, back and forth, and she was lost in the heat of his embrace.

His hand slid down her arm and up to the hollow of her back, moving in slow circles on her skin at her waist, sending delicious waves of heat and desire surging through her body.

Her eyes closed with pleasure. He was so good.

There was a movement at her waist. He had started to work on the buttons at the back of her dress.

She wanted him to. She needed him to. She wanted… him to stop!

Something inside her screamed and she jerked her face away from his, her eyes catching a flash of his passion, his desire for her in that split fraction of a second before he re-alised that she was leaning back.

'I thought I was ready for this. Truly, I did.' She forced in a noisy breath. 'And I'm not. I am so sorry.'

His brows came together until understanding crept back into the rational part of Rob's brain and he exhaled, very slowly. A couple of times. Before refastening her buttons, single-handed.

His arm was still around her waist and he used his free hand to stroke her cheek as he drew her closer.

She cuddled into his chest, listening to the beat of his heart, knowing that she was the cause of the palpitations and smiling at the need. The smell of his sweat combined with his aftershave filled the air she was breathing.

Lottie pressed her lips together then closed her eyes and blurted out the truth before she lost her nerve.

'I'm so tired of being average, and, most of all, I'm really tired of being so scared.'

'Scared?' There was concern in his voice. 'What are you frightened of? Me?'

'This. Intimacy. Letting go of my inhibitions and simply enjoying myself with another human being.'

She squeezed her eyes tight shut.

'I'm not a prude or frigid. That's not the problem. I just cannot let myself relax. It's totally ridiculous. I am an adult, I'm single, and I've had more chocolate profiteroles in my life than I have had orgasms. Which for a woman of twenty-seven is a disgrace.'

Instantly she covered her mouth with her hand. 'And I have no idea why I just said that.'

'A total disgrace. You're a beautiful woman, Lottie. You deserve to be adored. Fed chocolate ice cream in bed every night. Whatever you want.'

'Thank you. But adoration is not on my list of priorities right now.'

Her hand pressed against Rob's chest. 'I am vanilla ice cream. Nice, dependable. Can be excellent. But on the whole pretty unadventurous and average.'

The rumble of a deep-seated chuckle started low in his body but when he spoke the words were murmured through the lips pressed against her forehead as he hugged her closer.

'I happen to like good vanilla dairy ice cream. There is nothing wrong with that.'

'Now you're trying to be nice to make me feel better. Please stop. It's a lot easier if you slip back into the scamp role.'

'Then let me ask you a question. How many times have

you practised a recipe in that bakery kitchen of yours before you're happy to serve it to your customers?'

Lottie laughed out loud. 'Way too many. It always takes me six or seven test batches before I have something I love.'

'Right. Same here. The only way to get past average is to test yourself in a safe environment where you are in control and no one has to see the results but you.'

'Yes, I suppose so…but where are you going with this?'

'Just this. It seems to me that the lovely Miss Rosemount needs to connect with her sensuality in a safe place where she feels comfortable and secure. With a lover who she can trust.'

'Ah, that's where you're going. And I suppose you are the perfect candidate for the position? I mean job. Role. Oh, stop laughing.'

'I can produce references and commendations should they be required.'

'Your technical prowess is not in doubt. It's the trust bit that's the killer.'

'You don't trust me?'

'I don't know you! I've met Rob Beresford the chef and I've seen Rob Beresford the TV celebrity in action everywhere I look. And this evening I got to know Rob the teenage carer. But who is Rob when the only thing that separates us is a sheet and a whiff of bakery sugar?'

'You're looking at him right now.'

Rob held his arms out wide.

'How can you not know me? You've seen me with my mother and with Sean. My family are the people that matter in my life. All of the celebrity stuff is promotion, fluff, marketing so that I can earn a living. Look at me. Really look at me.'

'What you said earlier,' Lottie asked, her voice trembling

and hesitant, 'about only being interested in the short term. Did you mean it?'

The pad of his fingertip scorched a path down from her temple to the hollow just under her ear.

'Every word. That's the way I live. No long-term relationships. No heartbreak. Just two adults who know precisely what they are getting into from the start.'

'Is that what you told Debra? Because she was heartbroken.'

Rob exhaled slowly. 'Debra thought that she could make me change my mind, that she was different and special and that my rules didn't apply to her. They did, and she didn't like it. I'm not heartless, Lottie. I was sorry that she took it badly but it worked out okay for her in the end.' His fingertips started running up and down her forearm, and every hair on her body stood to attention in response. 'And it can work out okay for you, too.'

Lottie blew out sharply and stepped back, both hands in the air, palms forwards.

'Sorry, but this is a little too much.'

His response was a knowing chuckle that rattled around inside her skull, intent on causing disruption.

'You do realise that what you are suggesting is the nearest thing to training lessons! I mean, I've read women's magazines and mix with girls who have paid professionals to help them in that area in the past. And don't scowl like that—male escorts are not unheard of. You could probably do quite well in that line of work.'

'Thanks for the compliment. I will keep that career choice in mind if I should ever fancy a change in direction.'

He shook his head slowly from side to side. 'You don't get it, gorgeous. This is a one-time offer. You're tired of being ordinary. I see the extraordinary. We're both single, consenting adults and I would seriously love to get you naked and see what happens next. There. Is that honest enough for you?'

His head tilted to one side and he turned on the killer smile that could melt ice at fifty paces. 'So come on, Lottie, take a chance on a fling. You know you want to.'

'Wait a minute. It's one thing to brainstorm an idea, but making it happen and seeing it through are a whole different matter.'

'Then I'll make it easy for you. This is Saturday night and I am going to be in town for the next three days. Three days. Three interactive lessons. I could make a start tomorrow morning if you like.'

'Tomorrow! That's fast work, cheeky. Will there be an exam at the end?'

'Oh, darling Lottie, you've already passed the exam. This is the higher education course where anything at all can happen. And I cannot wait to get started. But if you're nervous—let's say that we have an introductory taster session. On the house. Now how can you deny yourself that little treat? Tomorrow morning at the bakery. How does that sound?'

Lottie flung her hands in the air. 'Crazy! That's how it sounds. In fact—'

She never got to finish her sentence because Rob stepped in the moment she began speaking, pulled her towards him with both hands spread flat against her back, and pressed his mouth against hers. Not forcibly. She would have hit him hard if he had tried that. No, his lips and mouth moved against her lips with such exquisite gentleness that Lottie opened her mouth wider and moved into the hot moistness of that irresistible kiss.

Helpless to do anything else.

A bristly chin moved across her cheek and down into her neck.

'I can't guarantee I'll be able to keep my hands off you. You are quite irresistible, Miss Rosemount. You know that, don't you?'

She grinned, unsure of her own ability to keep her hands off *him* at that moment, but that was not good enough, and Rob lifted her chin so that he could look into her smiling eyes.

'Seriously? This is the craziest proposal that I have ever heard in my life and, believe me, after my career in banking that's saying something. So on second thoughts, I appreciate your kind offer, but…'

Before she could blink his arm wrapped around her waist, turned her towards him and Rob silenced her by pressing his mouth against hers in a kiss that was so all-encompassing, so demanding, and so very, very delicious that breathing suddenly became unimportant.

The tip of his tongue touched her tongue, sending a shock of visceral desire to parts of her body that had been very short on action for a very long time. Desire: hot, real, undeniable.

Rob pulled her even closer, deepening his intense kisses until she was light-headed enough to want him never to stop. 'All you have to do,' he whispered, his mouth closed around her upper lip, teasing and playing with it to open as he came up for air, 'is nod once for yes.'

She managed to make a gentle nod, before his head lowered and he gave her the sweetest, most loving, lingering, whispering kiss she had ever had in her life.

'Quite irresistible. But it's getting late for a couple of early birds like us.'

His hands dropped to her waist and he stepped back, giving her the time to get her breath back.

'The gallery is closed on Sundays and my mother is spending time with friends tomorrow, so how about I pop over to your place in the morning? It's going to be fun.'

He leant forward as she nodded her reply, and kissed her on the nose before grinning.

'Try not to kiss anyone else in the meantime.'

CHAPTER NINE

WHERE HAD ALL of these people come from at 11:00 a.m. on a Sunday?

Rob squeezed his way past clusters of ladies with baby buggies chatting on the pavement tables outside a branch of a well-known coffee-shop chain, but kept his head down in case they recognised him.

He had to lift his arms up high as a couple of rampaging teens hunkered low on skateboards sped down the pavement, causing chaos. Couples arm in arm, men in running gear, cyclists in bright Lycra, older men carrying newspapers, all were mingling in a typical London street with the thundering traffic only feet away.

A low chuckle bubbled up from inside Rob's chest and he smiled at an elderly lady who was looking at a bookshop window—then caught sight of him. She was clearly making the connection between the poster advertising his latest cookbook and the man strolling down the pavement next to her. Then she shook her head and shrugged. No, how ridiculous, it couldn't be.

He didn't blame her for thinking that there was no reason why Rob Beresford should be walking down a London street on a Sunday morning.

Sunday mornings were Rob's one indulgence. Downtime from the mayhem of either a Saturday night restaurant service or a night spent at some hotel or business function.

There had been a time when he would stagger home in the early hours with some gorgeous girl whose name he had written on the back of his hand using her lipstick and the light from whatever bar they had met in, but by the time he sobered up she would be gone and so would her name.

The gossip press would be surprised to know that for the past few years he had been too exhausted to do anything on a Sunday but read the trade press from the balcony of his ocean-view penthouse apartment and fuel up with coffee and bad news about the economy. Business paperwork and phone calls and emails to Beresford hotels around the world took up most of the rest of the morning before he headed out to the beach to enjoy a long late lunch with his mum.

It was a routine that worked for him. A few hours' respite before the chaos of a new week and a diary that was booked months in advance. A week in one place? Unheard of. The last time was when the Beresford Chicago was hit with a norovirus outbreak, which had closed the entire hotel right in the middle of the conference season and he'd had to drop everything to fix the problem. Not good.

So taking a full week in London in June was a very special treat. Business—of course. He had meetings in the diary with both his dad and Sean to talk about the expansion plans. But that was not the real reason. The second his mother had been invited to be the opening artist for the new gallery, he had tagged three days' holiday onto the end of his work week. Recovery time. This might be the most important exhibition of his mother's career and was certainly going to be crucial in helping her get well.

And so far it seemed to be working. It had been a long time since he had seen her so happy and content and balanced. A very long time.

This Sunday was going to be his first real day off in eighteen months.

Strange, he had never even thought about it like that until the previous evening when Sean had sent him on his way and told him to take the rest of the weekend off for a change. Give his mother a break.

A weekend off. Now that really was a strange concept.

Was that why he had looked out over the London skyline from the penthouse apartment in the Beresford Richmond that morning and had only been able to think of one person that he wanted to spend it with?

Last night he had opened up to Lottie in a way that had startled him as much as it had surprised her.

He rarely talked about his past to people he had just met. Why bother? The media had done all of that for him.

But somehow Lottie had got under his skin and it mattered very badly that this girl understood the young man who had fought his way through catering college as a way to burn off his bitter anger and resentment so he could make good his promise to his mum.

Lottie's good opinion mattered. She was Dee's best friend, after all, and Sean was bound to let slip a lot about their life as teenagers. Yeah, that was a good plan. He could keep on telling himself that was the only reason he had blurted out his life story like a fool. Shame that was only part of the reason.

But in the middle of the night as he'd tossed and turned under his high-thread-count sheets, his mind had refused to let her go.

The image of Lottie's face as he'd kissed her whirled around into a hot dream where his fingertips explored every inch of her body from that stunning hair to the tips of those rose-painted toenails that had peeped out from her designer sandals.

So what if her vulnerability and beauty and inner strength had reached out and grabbed him and refused to let him escape?

There was a fairy story book his mother had used to read occasionally when he was small that told tales of beautiful half-bird-like women called sirens whose music and singing was so irresistible and alluring that sailors jumped overboard or crashed their ships on the rocks just to get closer to them.

Lottie the siren, that had to be it. The girl had magical powers. It was the only logical explanation. Otherwise things would get into seriously dodgy territory involving a pair of green eyes that made him want to move back to England so he could feel spring again, hair that he ached to run his fingers through and skin so unctuously peaches and cream he could eat it with a spoon. Or find out what it tasted like on his tongue, more likely.

Nope. He would stick to the siren idea. That was safer.

And since resistance was futile—best go with the flow!

Rob looked up at the front of Lottie's Cake Shop and Tea Rooms and ran a hand back through his hair.

He had not noticed that the sign was hand painted before and that the colours matched the interior decor. Stylish. Nice. Very nice.

Or the large sign that hung on a string in the half-glass door that read: 'CLOSED'.

Lottie closed the bakery on Sundays?

Damn. He had not expected that. Not when the pavements were full of potential customers all desperate for tea and cake. And she had mentioned baking some special novelty cake or something today?

By cupping his hand and peering in through the glass Rob could see that the lights were on in the kitchen, so someone was home. He rang the doorbell and kept looking. No movement. No reply.

He had not called in advance or made a specific arrangement. What if she had company? An out-of-town relative? A hunky rugby player of a first cousin whom she had called in as security because she had changed her mind about their little arrangement?

That had not been the impression he had got last night. Far from it.

His fingers closed around his mobile phone. Sean would know. And laugh his head off at the very thought of Rob checking up on Lottie's family and never let him forget it.

Scratch that idea.

Glancing quickly from side to side, Rob scrolled down his huge list of phone numbers until he found Lottie's and pressed the button hard enough for his finger to hurt.

Phone to his ear, he rolled back his shoulders as the call rang and rang and after a few long seconds a very croaky and sleepy voice answered, 'Hello.'

'Good morning, Lottie. Hope I haven't woken you. *I am here for my appointment.* Any chance you could let me in?'

There was just enough of a pause for Rob to ask, 'Lottie? Are you still there?'

He wanted to see her and tell her all the news about the exhibition, which was already almost a sell-out, and come up with some great ideas for a celebration party. Not have half a conversation through a glass door and down a phone.

'Rob? Oh. Yes. Sure.' And then there was a sharp intake of breath. 'Oh, no. I don't believe it. How stupid!' And then the unmistakeable clatter of a phone being dropped onto something solid.

Stupid? Who was she calling stupid? What was that all about? He had given up his free morning to spend time with her and she was calling him stupid? Or was there someone else in the room with her?

Rob flipped his phone closed and pushed it deep down inside his trouser pocket.

Either way this was a bad idea. Time to get back to civilisation.

Brow tense with frustration Rob was just turning away when he heard the sound of a key turning in a lock and whipped around to see Lottie peering out through a gap in the front door.

At least he thought it was Lottie. Those startling pale green eyes were almost grey behind the narrow slits of eyelids that seemed to be wincing at the bright sunlight bouncing back from the pavement. Her lovely blonde hair was tied back behind a stretch headband highlighting a very pale face with a bright red circle in the centre of each cheek. A perfect match for what looked like a pair of pink spotty pyjamas that she was wearing under her apron.

'Rob?'

'Still here. Although I don't know why after you just called me stupid.'

She blinked, then squeezed her eyes closed, then opened them a little wider but winced and closed them again. 'That wasn't you. It was me. I was the stupid one. I set the oven timer for my cake but fell asleep.'

A quiver around her upper lip was followed by a short gasp as she slowly turned and flung one hand in the direction of the kitchen. 'I burnt the sponges. They're completely dried out. I never burn my cakes. And it's their golden wedding today and it's meant to be really special and I feel… terrible. My head feels terrible.'

Then she half slumped and half collapsed onto the nearest chair. In a second her eyes fluttered closed and her head fell forwards onto her arm, which was stretched out on the table, so that Rob had to step inside the shop, close the door behind him and lean in closer to hear what she said next.

'I've caught your mother's rotten head cold. Everything feels fuzzy. And I think I need to have a little sleep now.'

'Oh, no, you don't,' he replied and quickly put one hand under each of her armpits and lifted her back to a seated position. 'Wake up, Lottie. Come on. You need to go and lie down for a while. Take a nap.'

She tried to shake her head but winced. 'Cake. Gloria. I need to call Gloria. Gloria can make the cake.' Then she blinked. 'Wait. That girl is hopeless at piping. I need piping.'

'Don't worry about the cake. I'll sort something out while you get your head down for half an hour.'

Lottie smiled at him. 'That sounds so good.' Then she blinked and stared at the Beresford hotel bag that he had dumped onto the table so he could pick her up.

'What's in the bag?'

'Amaretto biscuits.' He sighed and rolled his eyes. 'I thought you might like your own stash.'

'For me? That's nice. You're a nice man.'

'You wouldn't be saying that if you knew what I was thinking right now,' Rob replied through gritted teeth as he hooked one of Lottie's arms around his neck. 'Nice is not how I would describe it.'

Bright sunlight was streaming in around the side of the long roman blinds that covered the studio windows when Lottie turned over and dared open her eyes just a crack. Then a little wider.

Her head still felt as though it were stuffed with cotton and her throat was beyond scratchy but she could turn over without feeling dizzy, which was a major improvement on how she had felt earlier.

The pyjama top she was wearing had twisted into a knot under her shoulder and she wriggled into a more comfortable position in her bed and tugged the satin quilt up to her chin.

Wait a minute. She couldn't remember climbing the stairs to the loft and she certainly couldn't recall pulling the quilt from the shelf.

And just like that, fractured memories of opening the door to one of the best-known chefs on the planet came flooding back.

Groaning out loud, Lottie pushed up against the headboard and closed her eyes.

Oh, no! The one person on the planet who she did not want to see her looking like an extra from a really cheap horror movie had walked in at exactly the wrong time. He had probably run away screaming in shock.

Pressing the fingers of one hand to her forehead, she closed her eyes and tried not to picture what she must have looked like that morning after her silly attempt to make Lily's cake.

The cake!

She had to make a cake!

Blinking awake, Lottie rolled her legs over the edge of the bed and stared at her watch. Then looked again in horror. She had been asleep for hours! There was no way she had time to bake and decorate a cake before the tea party.

What was she going to do?

Run out to the supermarket and buy whatever they had left at this time on a Sunday afternoon? Or plan B, the freezer. She had cakes in the freezer. If she worked fast there might be enough time to quickly defrost a couple of sponge cakes, whip up some emergency icing and decorate with whatever she had handy. Forget the fine sugar work.

It would be tight but she might be able to manage it—if she got to work now.

Pushing her hair back from her face, Lottie stood upright, checked that she was steady. A quick splash of water on her face. A wince at the state of her hair. And she was ready for action. Sort of.

First step—find out what she could salvage in a hurry. Hopefully Rob had tossed the burnt cakes in the bin. So that left the icing.

Rob.

Had Rob really been here or had she imagined the whole thing? He had certainly played a starring role in her fevered dreams as she'd tossed and turned all night.

Yawning widely, Lottie slipped down the stairs to her kitchen, then her feet slowed.

She must have been even sicker than she had imagined because that wasn't her usual CD. Modern jazz didn't quite fit as background music for her cake shop.

She slid quietly in through the door. And froze in her stocking feet.

Rob was standing in front of the worktop.

His hands were rock steady but she could see that his gaze was totally focused and narrowed with concentration.

On the marble pastry board to one side was a panel of pale gold-coloured fondant icing that had been transformed with intricate precision into the most stunning crown of elegant and perfect edible lace that she had ever seen.

Her breath caught in her throat as he slowly and carefully lifted the fondant lace onto a sheet of baking parchment and then painstakingly placed the complete panel onto the sides of a round cake.

She dared not make a sound in case it disturbed him as he lifted away the paper. It was like watching a great artist at work.

'Behold one super-light sandwich cake. Four layers. Fresh lemon curd and pastry cream filling for the vanilla sponges at the top. My own special recipe Black Forest chocolate ganache for the two chocolate sponges on the bottom. Gold icing to cover. As ordered,' he said and stood back to check that the fondant was not moving.

'Lily prefers plain cake but Harry is a chocolate man,' she whispered through a throat that was tingling with emotion. 'It's wonderful, Rob. I love what you've done with the gold fondant. That lace design is gorgeous.'

Rob smiled back at her. 'No problem. All I did was follow the order you had pinned to the clip rail and checked the burnt cakes to make sure that you were going for two flavours. Gold lace seemed about right for a golden wedding cake. How are you feeling?'

Lottie took a few steps into the kitchen and sat down on the bar stool with her elbow on the bench.

'You mean apart from inadequate? Much better. I cannot believe that I slept for four hours. That's a first for me. But at least my headache has gone.'

'If it is my mum's cold you will be back to normal tomorrow. But in the meantime, take it easy. I've got this for you.'

'Now you're making me feel really guilty.' Lottie groaned. 'I have to do something to help.'

He walked up and down a few steps, then nodded. 'How about some gold ribbon around the pedestal? Think you can manage that? I want to finish the centrepiece before the fondant hardens up too much.'

'Got it.' She grinned and was about to slide off the stool when she blinked up at Rob, who was wiping away cornflour and icing sugar from what looked like an immaculate kitchen surface. 'What centrepiece?'

'Every wedding cake needs a centrepiece, doesn't it?

And I needed something to do while the cakes were cooling besides checking up on you.'

'You checked up on me?' Lottie blushed and self-consciously pulled the front edges of her pyjama top a little closer together.

The reply was a completely over-the-top wink. 'You snore beautifully. Has anyone ever told you that?'

'Must be my cold,' she replied and narrowed her eyes at him. 'Unfair. I'm not exactly dressed for visitors.'

'Oh, I don't know about that. You look okay to me.'

His voice was molten chocolate, which, combined with the heat going on behind those eyes, made Lottie squirm on her chair. It was the same look he had given her last night at the apartment.

How did he do it? It was as if he had an internal dial behind his eyes that went from calm, cold appraisal to steaming-hot mentally undressing in two seconds flat. And, boy, was it effective.

She was surprised that steam was not billowing out from the front of her jacket.

'Um. Cake. Let's focus on the cake. What are you doing for the…centrepiece? Oh, those are perfect.'

Lottie slid her bottom off the stool and stepped up to Rob so that she could look at the contents of the platter he had taken out of the refrigerator. She inhaled a long, slow breath and her right arm draped around the top of his jeans so that she could lean in closer.

Rob the master chef had shaped creamy gold-coloured fondant into three perfect calla lilies. The central stamen and stem were made from green crystallised angelica.

'Lilies for Lily. Why didn't I think of that?' she breathed, then held still as he laid them in a spiral pattern on the top of the icing-sugar dusting that covered the top sponge.

'One final touch. Crystallised violets. Just makes the gold pop.'

The two of them stood in silence for a second just staring at the cake with its golden crown before Lottie sniffed.

'I knew that you were good, but I had no idea how good.'

His reply was a low chuckle followed by a cheeky grin. 'Don't sound so surprised.'

But what mattered more than the words was the way his arm wrapped around her shoulder, drawing her to him, and then slid down the sleeve of her jacket, sending delicious shivers of pleasure up her arm.

He was overpowering. Too intense, too tempting.

Stupid cold. It was making her all weepy and sentimental.

He had made a cake that was far more nicely decorated than the one she had been planning. She had not asked him to do it. He simply had. Because he'd wanted to. Because he was caring and compassionate and right at that moment it was all a bit too much.

She was going to have to work extra hard to keep focused on why a fling with Rob would be a terrible idea.

The barriers between them had not gone away. Far from it. They were staring her in the face every time she looked at him.

She could do this. She could freeze him out to protect herself. She just had to.

Lottie made a dramatic gesture of checking her watch, and then slowly stepped out of the arc of his arms. 'Help! We're going to miss the tea party unless I get dressed in the next five minutes. And after all that work, you're definitely coming with me.'

Then, without thinking or hesitating, she stood on tiptoe and pressed her lips for a fraction of a second against the side of his cheek.

'Thank you for making such a beautiful cake. Lily is going to love it.'

Rob watched her shuffle back to the stairs in stunned silence, amazed by what she had just done. 'You're welcome. Any time at all.'

CHAPTER TEN

'LAUREL COURT RESIDENTIAL HOME. Second turning on the left. You can't miss it. Big stone house with a gorgeous conservatory dining room. The teas will be set up inside and then served on the lawn if the weather is warm.'

Rob flashed Lottie a quick glance from the driver's seat. 'Do you go and visit your friend very often?'

'First Sunday of the month when I can. I missed last week. Too much on with Dee being away. But Lily knows that I'll be there today.' Lottie looked at her watch and sucked in a sharp hiss. 'If we get there in time. Rotten cold. I hate being late.'

'With you on that. What? Don't give me that look. My life might be tabloid fodder but I keep my promises to people that matter. I do feel semi responsible for foisting my mother onto you in the first place, so if you want someone to blame for that cold, I am right here.'

'I can see that. Why else would I allow you to drive my precious delivery van? This is definitely a one-off in more ways than one. I'm not used to having a guest baker around the place. But it was good of you to offer to deliver the cake for me.'

Rob shuffled his bottom in the low seat and tried to get more comfortable but his gaze focused on the busy London street. He had already pushed the seat as far back as it would go but his knees almost touched the steering wheel. 'How do you drive this thing?'

Lottie laughed out loud and immediately started a coughing fit, which had her reaching for her water bottle. 'Oh, please don't make me laugh,' she replied with her hand on her throat. 'If you must know the van came from one of Dee's pals and was such a good price it was hard to turn down. It does the job. Oh. Here we are. Laurel Court. Just turn into the drive. The car park is on the left.'

Rob gritted his teeth in exasperation as he crunched the gears and slowed down to park in a narrow bay at the very end of the drive close to the house.

He sat drumming his fingers on the steering wheel for a few seconds and pushed out his lips before speaking. 'And you are sure that they know that I am just delivering the cake, right? Nothing else.'

'Absolutely.' Lottie nodded. 'I am a walking biohazard. The last thing I want is for Lily and her young-at-heart pals to go down with a twenty-four-hour head cold. Not at their age. Bad idea. It would slow them down, which is totally unacceptable. They are having far too much fun.'

Then she looked out through the windscreen and pressed her lips together. 'Too late to run away now. They've spotted the van. We would never get out of here alive if we tried to escape without delivering that cake.'

Then before Rob could protest, she rolled down the window and started waving like mad. 'Lily! We're over here. Come and meet Rob. He's my…sous-chef for the day. And he cannot wait to show you the fantastic cake he made, especially for you. Can you, Rob?'

Two hours later Lottie was driving down the side streets of London, her fingers wrapped around the steering wheel, grateful that it was late on a Sunday afternoon and the traffic was remarkably light.

Her headache was gone, her sore throat was already feeling a lot better, and the cotton wool that had clogged her brain was slowly easing away.

Which was just as well seeing as Rob was in no fit state to drive the van back to the bakery.

She slowed the van at the next set of traffic lights and grinned across at Rob, who was lying in the passenger seat with his head back and eyes closed.

'How are your toes doing? Any sign of movement yet? Or do I need to drive to the accident department?'

One eye creaked open and he slowly raised his head and glared at her. 'Did you know that they had hired a dance band? And every single lady in the place expected a samba and a foxtrot before we got to the waltzes. Even the gals with the walking frames. And forget my toes. They are so numb I wouldn't be a bit surprised if they were all broken. Oh, no, it's my rear end that got the most damage. Those gals need more medication!'

'Ah. Perhaps I should have warned you about the bottom pinchers. Don't worry. The bruising will fade away in a few days. But you have to understand, that was the best entertainment those girls have seen for a long time. Lily and her husband had the best time. You were a *total* superstar!'

'So you were watching me through the conservatory windows. I suspected as much. I hope you enjoyed the show.'

Enjoyed? Lottie had simply brought her knees up to her chest and watched in awe as this amazing man who she had only just met charmed and laughed and danced and at one point even sang along with the residents of the home as if they were old friends having a great party.

He had been remarkable. He *was* remarkable.

But it would only make his ego swell larger if she shared just how much she had enjoyed watching him having fun and being himself.

There was no bravado or false arrogance about this version of Rob Beresford. Just the opposite.

She had been granted a glimpse of the man behind the celebrity mask and she liked what she had seen. She liked it more than was good for her.

'I did enjoy it.' She grinned. 'But to be fair I think the wine served at the special lunch may have contributed to the merriment. That stuff is pretty lethal combined with the artificial colours in the jelly and ice cream they usually have for dessert.'

'Jelly and ice cream?' Rob repeated in disbelief. 'That explains why they liked the cake so much. In fact, they demolished the cake and asked me to pass on the message that it was so nice that could you please bring more next time you visit? And more chocolate. The chocolate sponge was a hit.'

'There you go. Praise indeed. Lily knows her cakes. And there are some advantages to being so tall. At least the cake made it to the buffet table in one piece before the girls saw it. They've been making cakes all of their lives. Any supermarket factory-made baking would go straight in the bin.'

His reply was a slow shake of the head. 'Last time I faced a crowd like that was at the international bake-off challenge in Paris. It was a battle but I survived.' Then he paused and tapped one finger against his lower lip. 'Actually, that's not such a bad idea.'

'What is?' Lottie asked as she set off again.

'Beresford hotels probably have six trainee pastry chefs at any one time. Boys and girls. It would be interesting to set up a contest and ask those ladies and gentlemen to pick the winner.'

'Interesting? It would be brutal.' Then she added with a grin, 'And Lily would love it. Great idea—go for it. Although I think an idea like that is worth a small favour.'

Rob groaned out loud. 'Go on. Am I going to like this?'

'The recipe for your chocolate cake, of course—and the icing. I think that would be a fair trade. And I would hate to let the residents down after they made a special request.'

'Mmm. Not sure. That's one of my specials. I think you would have to throw in an extra incentive to make me divulge something like that,' Rob replied with a low husky tone in his voice that set the hairs on the back of Lottie's neck standing up straight.

She dared to glance quickly at his face and immediately had to calm her racing heart and focus on turning into the lane behind her bakery.

The adrenaline-pumping heat of instant attraction coursed through her veins.

This was it. If she wanted to show Rob how attracted she was to him it was now or never.

Could she do it? Could she open up her heart, let him into her life, and not regret it?

Rob made the decision for her by calmly walking around the front of the van the moment she turned off the ignition, opening the driver's door, and taking both of her hands to help her to her feet, taking her whole weight and pressing her body against his.

'How are you feeling?' he asked as his gaze drilled holes into her forehead and messed around with her brain.

'Better. Would you like to come inside for some coffee?' she managed to reply in a throat that suddenly seemed full of sand. 'Cakes on the house.'

Her reward was a smile that would defrost large ice sculptures at thirty paces. 'I've been waiting all day to hear you say those words. Lead the way.'

At catering college there had been plenty of late-night drunken clinches in dark corners of bars and sofa cuddling, but whenever it had started to get more serious she had ducked out at the last minute. Sexual stage fright. She wasn't a prude, just cautious.

To the world she was Lottie the brave, Lottie the entrepreneur, Lottie the baker. But never Lottie the woman who was afraid to show how scared and vulnerable she was.

Always putting her own sexual needs and desires into second place. Waiting until she found someone who would not trample her into the ground. Waiting for the right man to share her bed with.

Well, tonight she was determined to throw all of her common-sense caution to the wind. She turned to Rob.

She wanted this gorgeous man with his wavy dark brown hair, blue eyes, and a body that was a work of art. She wanted to feel that sexy stubble on her skin and know what it was like to be the subject of his adoration. Then seduce him right back.

Okay, so he had seen her without make-up with the head cold from Hades, but her body was not too bad and she still shaved her legs. Now and then. He wouldn't be totally repelled.

So what if he was Sean's brother and she was bound to see him again?

She liked him. More than liked him. They were adults. They could handle it, couldn't they?

A shiver ran down her back. This was going to happen; she had to make it happen. No second best. This was her selfish-indulgence and for once in her life she was going to put herself first and enjoy life to the full.

Jogging into the kitchen, Lottie flicked on the CD player and turned up the volume as the lively saxophone music filled the air.

'So you do like jazz?'

She turned to find Rob leaning on the doorjamb. Watching her swing her hips from side to side in time with the music.

'Care to dance?' he asked, and held out his hand. 'I have been in training recently.'

She glided into his arms, his hands sliding along her slender waist until they rested lightly on her hips. Instinct rather than technique or practice made her lift her arms high and cup the sides of his neck.

The music and the sensation of his hot breath on her forehead acted like a hypnotic dream where their bodies automatically knew how to move in perfect harmony.

Her heart rate and breathing moved up another notch the second her forehead dropped forward onto his chest and again he matched her, heartbeat for heartbeat, his hands tightening on her waist and holding her closer and closer by the second.

A faint smile quivered across her lips as his hands slowly slid lower until they were smoothing down the fabric of the silk shirt dress that had been in the first garment bag she had come to in the loft. Just the pressure of the slippery fabric and the heat of his fingers cupping her bottom were enough to make her catch her breath in her throat and for a second his hands stilled.

Then she broke the moment by giving a very girly giggle and pulling her head back just far enough to look at him. It meant unlocking her hands from behind his neck but it was worth it to feel the hard planes of his chest beneath her fingers.

His smiling eyes were half open and focused totally on her face, hazy with promise and desire. Any doubt she might have had that he wanted her just as much as she wanted him were instantly swept away in that one look.

Heartbeat for heartbeat. Strong and fierce and hot and sweet.

'Rob. Do you have any of that chocolate icing left? Because I have a very ticklish spot just here—' and she pointed to the corner of her mouth next to her upper lip '—which needs a large dose of licking. Think you can help with that?'

He pulled her so quickly towards him that she almost toppled over as they took one step backwards until her back pressed against the wall of her kitchen. Out of sight of the street, she did not feel exposed when one of his hands shot up to cradle the back of her head.

Trapped between the hard wall and the harder length of his body, Lottie only had time for one sharp breath before his warm, full lips crushed down onto hers in a kiss so fast and intense that breathing took second place to keeping up.

His teeth nibbled her upper lip, sending shock waves of desire and wet heat surging through her body, making her beg for more and more. It was almost unbearable when that stubble grazed her throat and started making its way down to her collarbone.

'I have wanted to do that since I first saw you in the gallery.'

In a minute that mouth would be on her breast and it would be game over for any kind of sensible thought.

The silk dress was already a crumpled wreck with the writhing, but her brain caught up with the rest of her body just long enough to realise that ripping it off here might not be such a good idea.

'I'm probably still infectious, you know,' Lottie whispered, her eyes fluttering half closed in the heady, sensuous movement of his mouth on her throat.

'How are you feeling now? There is some colour back in your cheeks.'

'A lot better. But what about you? I could be contagious. I would hate to be the reason why the mighty Rob goes down with a shocking head cold.'

'I'll take the risk. My mum gave it to me first. Generous as always.' It was more of a mumbled murmur.

Lottie's mouth went dry. She should be embarrassed. This was what she wanted, wasn't it?

'Oh, right, I see.'

'Hey. Don't look so worried. This is meant to be fun.'

'I know. It's just that I had this vision of meeting you at one of Sean and Dee's parties and having to go through the embarrassed silence and awkward first kissy thing which always make me cringe.'

'Ah. The social etiquette of the former lovers who may or may not have parted as friends. That's the advanced course, but somehow I don't think that's going to be a problem for us.'

He tapped his middle fingers several times against his forehead. 'Smart. And we get on. Right?' His grin had the power to illuminate the kitchen. *Oh, yeah, we get on.*

A shiver quivered across her back that had nothing to do with the cool evening air.

Scary thoughts flittered through her mind and she tossed her head from side to side to shake them out, blowing out in short sharp breaths.

'I don't know if I can do this. Give in to my wild side. Because, actually, I don't even know if I have a wild side.'

'Are you kidding me? You are an angel dressed to tempt any man. Smoking.'

Lottie looked down at her crumpled dress.

'It will take me five minutes to change into a mini dress. Heels. Decent underwear. You can stay there and...'

'That would make it way too obvious.' He grinned and his hands got busy on the small of her back.

'Then I have one more question. Do you have a condom in your wallet?'

That made him stop what he was doing and look at her with a wide-eyed stunned expression before his mouth relaxed into the cheekiest, sexiest grin that she had ever seen.

'I told you that I was a Boy Scout. Prepared for anything.'

'Not for this,' she replied and nipped his throat with her teeth.

And she started to unbutton his shirt. Slowly and languorously, taking her time. Prolonging the pleasure.

A summer dawn was streaming through the patio doors when Lottie turned over in the bed and reached out for Rob's warm chest, but there was nothing there.

Propping herself up on one elbow, she blinked in the early morning sunlight and scanned the room.

Rob was standing at the wide-open window, his hands loosely touching the window frame. His long, muscular legs were languid and soft compared to the tension that was only too apparent in the wide shoulder blades that were almost touching in the middle of his back. He had tugged on his boxers, which lay low on his hips, but there was no mistaking the tightness of that magnificent backside.

Lottie inhaled slowly, locking the image into her memory. No matter what happened going forwards, she was never going to forget last night and what Rob looked like at that moment.

He was so gorgeous she could have looked at him all night and it would not have been enough.

The tattoo on his arm twisted into dark eastern symbols all the way up his biceps and across his shoulder, marking him as a warrior, a man of action.

Rob Beresford had just ruined her for any other man.

Fact. And the sudden realisation made her whimper slightly at the back of her throat.

He heard her, turned his head, and smiled.

'Hey, you.'

'Hey, you back,' she whispered when her throat finally recovered.

'Sorry. I didn't mean to wake you.' His smile made the very core of her body flutter with desire and affection. 'Go back to sleep.'

'Not without you.' She grinned and waggled her eyebrows up and down a few times and then gave him a very saucy and over-the-top wink.

Rob threw back his head and laughed out loud but as her reward he padded across the wooden floorboards.

But instead of throwing himself onto her and making her morning complete, he picked up her wooden chair and dragged it closer towards the bed.

Lottie shuffled up against her wooden bedhead and brought the duvet up to cover her bare chest, which was suddenly quivering with goosebumps in the cool breeze from the wide-open window.

'Are you okay?' She yawned. 'Did something wake you up?'

'No.' He shook his head and reached out for her hand, lifting it to his lips so that he could kiss the backs of the knuckles. 'I'm fine.'

It was one of the sweetest kisses of her life and Lottie's already tender heart just popped the last little restraining band and threatened to burst out of her chest with love for this man.

'Then what is it? What do you want, Rob? What do you ache for in the middle of the night?'

He chuckled and shook his head and tried to shuffle

off the chair but Lottie tightened her grip on his hand and held fast.

'Please, talk to me. Tell me. I really do want to know.'

He hesitated and his gaze hit the floorboards for a few seconds longer than she expected, which acted like a dagger to her heart. Just when she believed that she had made a connection, the real Rob was pulling away from her and going back into that shell he had made.

'Forget it. I'm sorry. It really is none of my business,' she whispered.

'No, don't do that. Don't knock yourself down. The only reason I am reluctant to talk about it is that it had been so long since...' he exhaled slowly '...since anyone got close enough to see that there was another side to me than just the flash exterior with the drama and the shouting. It's taking a bit of getting used to.'

'I know, same here. It works both ways, remember?'

'Yeah. I remember.' He smiled and his reply came out in a hoarse whisper that she had never heard him use before.

But for once, Lottie did not say anything, just held on to his hand and smiled.

Waiting.

And he was smart enough to know precisely what she was doing and still gave her an answer.

'What do you crave, Lottie? What would give you pleasure?'

'Right now?' She wriggled down onto the soft feather duvet. 'Right now I would like to be reminded what your body feels like on my naked skin.'

His reply was a low, rough growl. 'Hold that thought, gorgeous girl.' But then his voice changed. It was serious, low, and intense. 'But I'm curious. Who do you want in your life going forwards?'

Lottie blinked, a little more awake, and shuffled higher

onto the bedhead. 'Seriously, you want to talk about this now? Oh, okay.' She covered her mouth as a huge yawn swept over her, then swallowed before trying to clear her head. 'Well, I could lie to you and tell you that after last night's crash course I want more flings. More weekends of pure selfish pleasure to make up for what I've been missing. But that would be fluff and you would see through it in a moment.'

Rob nodded, then tipped his head in a salute. 'Then tell me the truth. I can take it. What do you crave in your life? What have you always longed to have and not yet found?'

Lottie looked at his handsome face for a moment. 'What I want in my life is an ordinary man who can love me and be the last face I see every night and the first face I see every morning when I wake up. A man who will give me children and love being a father, and is prepared to woo me with such delights as a courting cake if that is what it takes. Sorry if it sounds suburban and boring and a little bit average, but there it is. That's what I truly want.'

Rob nodded twice, then exhaled slowly. 'Thank you for that. I don't often get to hear the truth. And for the record, you could never be average, no matter how much you tried. He would be a lucky man. And what the hell is a courting cake?'

'A northern tradition.' Lottie laughed. 'It used to be that the girl had to prove her skills in baking by making the man she wanted a special show-stopper of a cake, but it seems only fair to let the boys have a chance, as well.'

Lottie propped herself up on an elbow and pushed Rob's hair back over one ear with her fingertip, delighting in the pleasure it gave her that she had the right to do that.

'But what about you, Rob? What are you doing next week, next month or next year? What do you long to do with your life? You have already achieved so much.'

He inhaled through his nose and raised both arms to cup his hands beneath his head, totally relaxed, but Lottie could see that telltale crease of anxiety in his brow.

'I need to get back to my real work in the kitchens. These past few years have been a crazy roller-coaster ride, what with the TV work and helping my mum get over her issues. Spending time in London with Sean has brought it home to me just how much I miss cooking.'

Then he chuckled and gave her a wink and a grin. 'And baking. How could I forget the baking? That cake I made for Lily was fun and I meant what I said about the pastry students. Yeah, back to the kitchens I go. Grease and fish guts will be flying in all directions.'

'Ah, charming! I'll stick to my bakery, thank you.'

Then she tilted her head and smiled at him. 'You haven't answered my question, have you?'

His reply was a deep, warm laugh that reached inside her heart and found a home.

'Touché. It's actually quite simple. I want to stop feeling so guilty. I want my mother to be happy and safe and well. And most of all? Most of all I want my life back so that I can take a risk on love. And that makes me the worst and most ungrateful son in the world. But that's probably hard for you to understand—you never had to face those sorts of problems with your parents.'

CHAPTER ELEVEN

LOTTIE BLINKED AT HIM in complete disbelief and then tugged his hand until he was sitting on the bed next to her.

'Oh, Rob. I had no clue how unhappy my parents were until I started going to visit friends and their parents smiled and laughed and touched one another. Apparently that was what real families did. They hug and cuddle and talk to their children. My parents never did any of those things. Oh, Rob, they were so cold.'

She exhaled slowly.

'So I set out to make my parents happy the only way I could: By being the perfect daughter, the girl who was always top of the class, captain of the netball team, and destined for a stellar career. I killed myself working so hard night after night to get a first-class degree then the scholarship to the top management school. All so that I could take my place at my dad's investment bank and make them proud of me.

'So that was what I did, Rob. I looked the part. The right clothes and hours spent on personal grooming. All geared up to make me fit into the well-oiled machine as the newest cog in the family investment company. I felt that if I stopped being perfect, stopped working day and night for my father's approval, even for a second, then he would reject me and stop caring for me and my life would collapse in on itself.'

'What was your life like?'

'It wasn't a life. Every morning I would travel in with my dad with a smile on my face while he ignored me and read the paper, and then literally throw up in the ladies' because I hated the work so much. But ten minutes later there I would be, sitting around the boardroom table with my father watching in stony silence while I gave a faultless presentation to the bored, listless people who were earning huge sums of money to make more money. I was dying inside every second and none of them knew.'

'What happened? Why aren't you there now?'

'Two things happened in the space of twenty-four hours that changed my life. One day I was an investment banker on a clear path to being the first female CEO of the company, and the next morning—I was unemployed and alone.

'Because, you see, it turned out that I was not so perfect after all. I wasn't even who I thought I was. There was a very good reason why my dad was never satisfied with my results. Most of my life had been one long lie.'

Rob took a sharp intake of breath but stayed silent, waiting for her to finish.

'My dad had his first mini-stroke at the age of fifty-eight. He went to the company doctor that morning, complaining of really bad headaches and leg pain. He had always insisted that we ate breakfast together in deadly silence before we left the house, so he was always wolfing it down. His normal meals were stress and caffeine and the occasional cigar. He had a flight booked for a big new client in Rome a few hours later and there was always a mountain of work to do. The doctor took one look at him and wanted to call an ambulance but he said no, he was fine. Just a headache. Stubborn, you see.'

Lottie smiled and released one hand to stroke Rob's face.

'I remember begging him to go and have a check-up and he just looked at me and said, "No. This is who I am. This is what we do. Hospitals are for wimps."'

Then she shrugged.

'Two hours later he collapsed at the airport waiting for his flight. I remember rushing to the hospital, terrified. But when I got there the first thing I saw was a lovely-looking woman who I had never seen before sobbing and distraught with her arms around him. And he was grinning and kissing and hugging her and trying to reassure her. Kissing and hugging this woman. When the last time he had touched me was to shake my hand at graduation. I didn't even know that he could smile.'

There was just enough shock in Rob's eyes for her to nod in reply.

'Oh, yes. My mother arrived a few minutes later and all became clear. This woman was his mistress. And had been for the past thirty years. She was his real love, the woman who had been there all the time when he met my mother, who had the money and family connections to get him to the top. Two hours later my world was turned upside down.'

Lottie dropped her gaze onto the tattoo on Rob's arm and her fingers traced the curving blade design up and down his skin.

'My dad and his mistress were in the hospital. And my mum and I were in a taxi. We must have sat in the back of that black cab in silence for ten minutes, totally shell-shocked and frozen, trying to deal with what had just happened, I suppose. And then she started talking, really talking. And that was when she told me—for the first time—that Charles Rosemount is not my birth father.'

'What? You mean that you had no idea?'

She shook her head. 'Not a clue. Apparently my mother

had spent six months studying in Paris a couple of years after she married and fell totally in love with another student who was already married. Love at first sight, the full thing. As far as she was concerned he was the love of her life and they had a passionate affair, which lasted three months.'

'What happened? I mean, they were both married.'

'They talked about divorcing on both sides but they cared about the people who loved them and the pain the divorce would cause was just too enormous and shocking. They couldn't do it so they parted.'

'But he was the love of her life. How does that work?'

'I don't know. She only found out that she was pregnant with me a few months later and my dad was delighted. Thrilled. I was going to be the glue that held their rocky marriage together. It didn't. He hated the disruption of having a new baby in the house and his glamorous, pretty wife suddenly could not fly out to entertain business guests at a moment's notice like she had before.'

'So they stayed married, knowing that they weren't in love.'

'They stayed together because my father absolutely refused to give my mother a divorce and made it quite clear that if she even tried to leave he would be awarded custody of me and she would never see me again.'

A hard expletive exploded from Rob's mouth. 'Why? Was he so power crazed that he would use a child like that? As a pawn in some game?'

'Totally. But it was more than that. He needed the perfect family for the perfect corporate image. It looked so good on his résumé. The immaculate house, the pretty, obedient wife and clever daughter. I was always just a piece in the fake home that he built around his ego.'

'What about your real father? What do you know about him?'

'I don't know anything. She was forbidden to speak to him again so he never knew that he had a daughter. And believe me that was a long night, talking and talking. I think I did a lot of shouting, too. I don't think either of us slept much.'

Lottie's face faded. 'But the next morning, my alarm clock went off at five a.m. and I leapt out of bed the same as always so I could be ready for a six a.m. breakfast meeting. Then suddenly I sat back down again on the bed because I was dizzy and light-headed. And as I sat there with my dizzy head this wonderful feeling came over me. Because I had the craziest idea.'

She looked up into Rob's face and took his hands in hers. 'It was over. I was not going back to work in the job I hated. My dad was going to take early retirement and move to France with his lover to the house they had lived in for years. And I didn't have to impress him in exchange for a token kind word any longer. For the first time in my life, ever, I felt free. And it was as though this huge weight had been lifted away from my shoulders and I could float up in the air like a miraculous dream.'

Lottie dropped her head and when she lifted it, she could feel the tears running down her cheeks. 'I was so happy I was laughing so loudly that my mother came in to check on me. She was worried that I had totally lost it in the shock of everything that had happened. But I hadn't. It had been years since either of us had laughed and felt happy and free and joyous. I felt as though the whole world had been opened up for me. I was finally free to do what I wanted.'

'And the first person you thought of was Lily, wasn't it?' Rob replied as he wiped the tear from her cheek with his finger.

Lottie nodded. 'Yes, yes, it was. The only time that I had been truly happy was when I spent time learning to bake. That was my joy; that was my delight. Not banking.'

She knelt on the bed and squeezed his hands. 'You know the rest. I reclaimed my life and I have never been happier. Never. But here is the totally odd thing. My mother is happy, too. Happy that I have finally found something I love.'

'It isn't the same. My mother has a lot of health problems.'

'I know. But things are different now.'

Rob raised his head and those amazing blue eyes focused on her with such intensity, and burnt with an unspoken question.

'You have me. From now on we are going to look after her together. If she wants us to. But in the meantime I think it's important that I should try to catch up with my sleep before I have to start baking. If only there was some way of getting warm fast. Can you think of any ideas? Oh, yes, that will definitely do the trick. Rob!'

Rob Beresford strolled down the high street with a spring in his step. He had walked back to the Beresford Richmond for a long hot shower, shave, and a change of clothes.

But for the first time in years, the driving urge to get back to work bright and early on a Monday morning was simply not there. When he popped into Sean's office and told his PA that he was taking the day off as vacation he didn't know which of them was more shocked.

The PA or himself.

And he knew exactly who to blame for this remarkable change of heart.

The girl he had kissed goodbye that morning as she lay

half asleep and as desirable as ever in a loft studio above a bakery.

The girl he had every intention of spending the day with. If he had the stamina.

What a woman!

She had matched him in every way possible and the sex was amazing.

He might just have found his match in Lottie Rosemount. But there was one area where he knew that he had the edge: in the kitchen. Back in the hotel his chefs knew his secrets only too well. It was time to put the *B* back in the Beresford pastry chefs and he knew the perfect place to practise some cunning recipes that would put them right back at the top.

Lottie's cake shop might not be an award-winning kitchen, but it had everything he needed to have some serious fun. Starting with the girl he was going to wow with his five-star baking. She deserved the best and that was precisely what he intended to give her. Followed by a very nice dinner at a wonderful restaurant and coffee in the penthouse. And this time she would definitely be staying the night.

Rob was still chuckling along when his mobile phone rang and he absent-mindedly broke the habit of a lifetime and flicked it open without checking the caller identity.

'Rob Beresford.'

'Oh, good morning, Mr Beresford. I do hope that I have not disturbed you. This is Rupert from the Hardcastle gallery. I believe we met the other evening when Adele introduced us at the opening event for her exhibition.'

'Of course. What can I do for you?'

'Actually I was hoping to speak to Adele. She's not answering her phone and we've had a very interesting offer from a buyer for several of her pieces. Perhaps you could ask her to get in touch.'

Rob's steps slowed. 'What do you mean, get in touch?

It's almost noon. I thought that she would be there with you by now.'

'Oh, no, Mr Beresford. That's just the problem. No one has seen Adele all morning and we cannot find anyone who knows where she is. Mr Beresford?'

Too late. Rob had already cut him off and was ringing his mother's number. Which rang and rang. Same with the number for her hotel room.

Cursing, he cancelled the call and rang the numbers she had given him for her friends, who answered on the second ring.

Adele? They had not seen Adele since dinner the previous evening when they had dropped her at the hotel. They had no idea where she might be.

He stopped in the middle of the pavement, not caring that the other pedestrians had to squeeze past him.

Dread slithered through his veins.

No messages on his phone. No message for him at the hotel.

He had taken his eye off the ball and his mother had gone missing.

He had been too busy falling for Lottie that he had broken his promise to his mother to take care of her.

The worst kind of scenarios cursed through his mind and he ran one hand over his face.

Think positive. She was always forgetting to charge her phone. He knew that. But she would never just take off and not let him know.

Something was wrong. Badly wrong. And he knew just who to blame.

And he was looking at that person in his own reflection in the shop window.

Lottie Rosemount giggled for the tenth time that morning at the tin of amaretto biscuits that had been waiting for her when she eventually made it down to the kitchen almost an hour later than normal.

Rob must have sneaked them in on his way out to get changed.

What a night!

Fast, slow, then faster. Wow. That man had ruined her for any other lover, that was for sure.

Focusing on making cupcakes and a slicing cake that were even vaguely what they should be was quite a challenge, but Gloria had been a star and taken care of the breakfast customers and baked some of her emergency stock of frozen croissants, French bread and Danish pastries to keep the shelves filled.

All she had to do was make icing worth eating, decorate the cakes and then get started on the quiche and filled baguettes, and the lunch menus would be ready.

And hopefully, if she was a very good girl, Rob would come back and see her.

Now that was something to look forward to.

Grabbing a tray of cooled double-chocolate pecan-and-hazelnut brownies, Lottie strolled into the cake shop and started loading the cake stand.

And almost dropped them all.

It was Rob, but not her Rob. This was the old Rob. His face was dark and hooded with a twisted expression of anxious disappointment and anger.

What had happened? He had only been gone a couple of hours.

There was something seriously wrong.

She put down her tray and slipped off her apron to go and meet him but before she could say anything he marched past her in stony silence and headed straight for the stairs.

Running after him, with a quick shrug to Gloria, Lottie was out of breath by the time she reached the studio.

He was pacing back and forth like a caged animal, his phone pressed to one ear. Then he flung it down on the bed and tore open the patio doors, practically jumping onto the terrace.

Lottie pressed one hand to her chest and willed her heart to slow down to the point where she could speak.

'Rob, you're frightening me. What's happened? Is something wrong?'

His shoulders rolled back as though he was bracing himself to tell her some terrible news and when his voice did break the horrible silence, it was as cold and terrible as ice.

'Mum's gone missing. Not answering her phone. Nobody knows where she is. I don't even know where to start.'

Lottie coughed and took gentle hold of his arm.

'But that's not true. Adele is with Ian. He phoned less than five minutes ago to let me know that Adele is in a department-store changing room buying a new dress for a cocktail party she's been invited to. She forgot to charge her phone so he thought he had better let me know where she was. In case we were worried. Oh, Rob.'

His face twisted into relief then fury and then relief again. 'She went shopping. With Ian? Is that what you're telling me?'

Lottie smiled and held her arms out to hug him. 'She is fine. Ian met her after breakfast and they're on the way to the gallery now. Ten minutes' walk away at most.

'You can stop panicking, Rob.'

But instead of embracing her and letting her ease away his anxiety and concern, Rob turned back to the railing and his fingers clasped around the back of the patio chair so fiercely that his knuckles were almost white under the pressure.

'She is not fine. Has Ian any idea of what I've just been

through?' Each word was almost spat out into the air through his clenched teeth.

'Hey.' Lottie tried to smile but failed. 'It was good of him to be so considerate.'

'Considerate? Is that what you call it? How about calling me first? Now, that would have been considerate.'

'Well, he might have done if he had your phone number. But seeing as he didn't and Adele couldn't remember it, he phoned me instead and then was going to call the gallery to let them know they were going to be delayed. I happen to think that is very considerate.'

'Do you, indeed?' Rob nodded and blew out hard. 'Then you don't have the faintest idea what you're talking about. Because I have been down this road before.'

Then he stepped back and dropped his head. 'A few years ago my mum had planned to hold an exhibition in New York with a few friends. Private gallery, exclusive, serious pieces from some of the finest contemporary artists. She was so looking forward to it that she insisted I take time out to have a holiday with Sean and my dad and the whole extended family in the new Beresford Miami. Have a real break for once.'

A hard, low laugh shook his shoulders and Rob lifted his head and looked at Lottie. 'The gallery was broken into the night before the exhibition and they took everything. Three years' work—gone, stolen. Can you imagine how destroyed she was? Of course, I offered to try and help with the police reports and the whole mess. But no. She insisted that I leave it to the police to deal with. My family holiday was far more important.'

Rob started to pace up and down the hard wooden flooring. 'When I got back to the penthouse in New York she had moved out. Just gone, no messages, no notes. No clue as to where she was. Do you understand what that felt like?

It took me three frantic days to track her down. She had gone to the Hamptons to be alone because she didn't want anyone to see her in the dark days of a big depression that could last for weeks.'

His eyes closed for a second and when they opened again some of her Rob was back.

So that when he reached out and took her hands in his she wanted to fall into his arms and tell him that she was sorry and that it would work out if he gave them a chance.

But he whipped that moment away from her before she even opened her lips.

'I am sorry, Lottie. But this is yet another reason why it's time that we should be going. And soon.'

'Going? What do you mean "going"?'

'I need to get back to California. That's where my work is, and I'm taking my mother with me. I am so sorry, Lottie, I really am.'

Lottie folded her arms. 'California? You're leaving, just like that. Exactly who do you think you are talking to? I'm not Debra. You can't mess me around like this, Rob. It's not fair.'

He whirled around to face her with a look of total fury.

Rob stomped forward and leant towards Lottie until she could feel his hot, bitter breath on her face. 'That's where you're wrong. You're precisely the same as Debra. And don't you dare say that I didn't tell you the rules.'

She shook her head and her gaze scanned his wrecked and tragic face.

'Stay. You owe me two more lessons, remember? And don't shake your head like that. We're clever people—we can work this out.'

'I have to be the one who's walking away, before that day comes when I'm forced to decide who to put first. Because that isn't fair on either of us. I'm sorry. I truly am.'

His arms tightened, drawing her to him, and he held her there against his chest as though it was the last time they would share this precious connection.

Tears welled in her eyes at the very idea that he was walking out on her for the best reason in the world.

No, this could not be happening. Not when they had only just found one another.

It took all of her strength but she slowly pushed Rob away so that she slid out of his arms. She yearned for his touch but she knew what had to be done.

'No, Rob, no. I'm not going to let you do this to yourself. You asked me to take a chance on you. Well, now it's my turn. Change the rules. Find the love you need, right here.'

'Every time I take a chance on love it's snatched from me one way or another. That's why I need to move on before you create a hole in my heart and my soul that nothing else can fill. I'm not taking the risk, for both of our sakes.'

He instinctively stepped forwards to hold her but she pressed hard against his solid chest.

'Move on? Oh, Rob, I saw my parents waste the best years of their lives living in quiet desperation, living a lie and denying their love in case the sadness and despair seeped out between the cracks. My mother had three precious months with the love of her life before giving him up. Why? Because she was too afraid of hurting the other people in her life. And do you know what? She regretted it from the moment she got back to London. And no matter how hard she tried and how much effort she made, it did not make one bit of difference.'

Lottie caressed Rob's face with her fingertip and saw his eyelids flutter at her touch.

'That's not good enough, Rob. I want more than three months with the man I care about. I want a lifetime, and we can have that. No! Hear me out. Adele is real and honest and true. She doesn't live a lie. She never has. She is one of the bravest people that I have ever met. Just like her son. Talk to her—talk to her today.'

'Lottie, it has to be this way.'

'I don't agree. I care about you and want to be with you.'

Then she slid her hands down his chest until only her fingertips were in contact with his body.

'Go! Go and do what you have to do. But only come back to me if you are prepared to go the whole way. I feel that I've only just started to get to know the real Robert Beresford, but you need to open up and give me everything of yourself, not just the part that you want other people to see. And if you're not prepared to do that, then perhaps you should go. And not come back.'

The words caught in her throat but she managed to squeeze them out before turning to the balcony so that she did not have to see him leave in silence.

Each of his footsteps on the wooden stair drove a stake into her heart, but it was only when the kitchen door slammed shut that she finally let go of the railing and slipped back into the bedroom. That way, Rob could not see her collapsed onto the floor, overwhemed by floods of bitter tears for the empty space he had created in her life.

CHAPTER TWELVE

ROB WALKED SLOWLY through the newly refurbished Beresford Richmond dining room and mentally checked off his list of essential must-haves. Simple, clean lines blended with pale polished wood and cream-and-biscuit shades in the decor and furnishings to create a warm, welcoming ambience. No fussy red velvet or snootiness here.

His mother's connections to wonderful artists had helped the Beresford hotel group to collect a fine art collection that perfectly matched the contemporary styling.

The whole room had been created with one purpose in mind.

To allow the guests to relax and enjoy sumptuous food and wine in a comfortable and luxurious setting without old-school formality. This was all about the diners and the food.

And it worked. The awards and food-critic plaudits were flooding in.

He should be proud of what they had achieved.

Instead, his mind had been a blur of uncertainty and doubt from the minute Lottie had told him to leave.

He didn't blame her.

Rob ran one hand over his face and blinked himself awake.

Sleep had come in fits and starts and every dreaming

moment was filled with the memory of how he had held Lottie in his arms and the way her long hair flowed out onto the pillow when asleep.

Damn. He had it bad.

But he had made the right decision. For both of them.

'Hey, I thought you were heading back today.'

Sean strolled out from the kitchens with his fingers wrapped around a napkin.

'Hey yourself. I am going today. And don't get crumbs on my floor.'

Sean replied with a snort and took one last bite of the new range of savoury pastries. 'These choux buns—' he smiled between swallows '—are amazing. Three kinds of cheese. Hint of paprika. Our white-wine aficionados are going to be in heaven.'

Rob shook his head and tried to smile back but his mouth was too tight with tension as he remembered the moment that had inspired that recipe. Cheesy bites at an art gallery.

'Was that the only reason you called me down here this morning?'

'Nope, I have news. I had a very long X-rated chat with my one true love, Miss Dee Flynn, last evening, and we have finally set a date for our wedding. What are you doing last week in September—apart from being my best man?'

Rob roared with laughter and slapped Sean on the back so hard it almost sent him flying.

'That's wonderful news. Congratulations. You're a lucky man.'

'I know it. You're doing the meal. Seven-course extravaganza. Best food you ever came up with in your life, right? And you've got to have these cheese things as canapés.'

'Damn right.' Rob grinned then man-slapped Sean again. 'The best of the best, I guarantee it.'

'Ah. But it gets even better. The lovely Charlotte Rosemount is the chief bridesmaid and creator of the wedding cake.'

'Lottie is making your wedding cake? What about me?'

'Bride gets to choose. But you, my friend, have the pleasure of slow dancing with Lottie at my wedding. Now that I want to see.'

Rob sucked in a long breath, then narrowed his eyes. He remembered only too clearly what had happened the last time he danced with Lottie.

'Have I just been set up?'

'By experts,' Sean replied, and rubbed the palms of his hands together.

'This is how it works. I know Adele and Ian are more than just friends and that's great. So great that I've already told Adele that she can stay in this hotel as long as she wants.'

'No, I've got that covered,' Rob tried to interrupt but Sean stopped him.

'Not this time, matey. You're stuck with a family who does not let one of their own deal with their problems alone, especially when you're the only one around here who seems to be blind to the fact that you're walking away from one of the best things that ever happened to you.'

Sean rapped Rob hard in the centre of his forehead. 'Lottie is good for you. Deal with it.'

'Me, in a long-term relationship? That would be a first.'

'Then we have something else in common. I adore Dee and it breaks me when we are apart but I am so crazy in love with that girl that nothing in my life comes close. You deserve some of that happiness, Rob. You've kept your promise to Adele and paid in advance for some time to enjoy your life. And why are you shaking your head like that?'

'Lottie needs someone who can make her happy and love her the way she deserves. She wants one hundred per cent of who they are. That's not me. I'm like Mum, always looking for the next rush where each relationship has an expiry date. I'm not built for the long term.'

'What are you saying? That Lottie's not worth fighting for? That she's not good enough for you?'

'Don't say that. Don't you dare ever say that! She is the best woman I've ever met. If there's a problem, it's with me. Stop looking at me like that. It's freaky.'

'That's because I've never seen the mighty Rob Beresford in love before. Yes, there you go. I used the *L* word and your name in the same sentence. Actually, come to think of it, that is a little freaky. And it's certainly going to take some getting used to. But I think I am up to it.'

Sean crumpled the napkin into a ball and crushed it in his fist.

'Your call, brother. You can stay on the same track you're on now and end up as cranky old Uncle Rob to the stunningly gorgeous and talented children that Dee and I plan to produce in the near future, or, and here's a thought, you'd better grab Lottie before some other lucky man snaps her up on the rebound.'

'Lottie, you have a visitor.' Gloria rolled her eyes towards the front door and bared her teeth in a wide-mouthed scream before shaking her fingers out and blowing on the tips.

'Who is it? Not that hot bloke who wanted to join the Bake and Bitch club so that he could pick up women?'

'Well, that sounds like fun. Where do I sign up?'

Rob!

Lottie refused to turn around and give him the satisfaction of seeing her flushed face and neck. Instead she had a full-frontal view as the women gathered around the table clutched at one another, open-mouthed, and started a chain of whispers between staring at Rob in disbelief.

'Ladies, it's a huge pleasure to meet you all. Lottie has told me so much about you. I hope you don't mind but I brought along a stack of signed recipe books, which I hope you find useful. I think there should be enough for everyone. There you are. Enjoy.'

A large box slid onto the table on her left side and before she could say anything the girls flung open the lid and attacked the contents, pulling out book after book with huge squeals of glee and delight.

The next thing Lottie knew, Rob had sneaked closer and she could feel his warm breath on her neck as he whispered into her ear. 'Can you spare me five minutes? I need to talk about Dee and Sean.'

'Hello, I am running a Bake and Bitch club here. Sorry, way too busy.'

'Ladies, I'm so sorry to interrupt but I need to steal Lottie away for a short time. Ladies?'

Not one reply. The girls were having far too much fun taking photos of Rob with their smartphones and diving into the pages of the recipe book, oohing and whistling at the full-colour photographs of the baked extravaganzas.

Traitors!

'Five minutes. But that's it.'

Lottie whirled around away from the man whose very presence was making her heart sing, marched into the main part of the tea rooms, and sat down at the table closest to the entrance, her hands neatly folded in her lap.

'Five minutes. Say what you have to say, then on your way. Time starts now.'

Focusing on the pattern on the tiled floor, Lottie heard and felt Rob pull out a chair and sit down opposite her.

She desperately wanted to look at him but her mind was

too busy trying to process the tsunami of feelings that just sitting in the same room had washed over her. It staggered her that one human being could be responsible for sending her senses into such stomach-clenching, mind-reeling chaos.

'Lottie. Nice to see you again.'

'I thought you'd already left for California, so you can imagine my surprise at seeing you this evening.'

A muscular arm extended across the table towards her. It was covered in a dark grey silky fabric and she knew that the tip of the tattoo that peeked out from below the pristine pale grey shirt ended in a curving blade design across his left shoulder where her fingers had caressed his skin only a few days earlier.

And her heart broke so badly at the memory that she had to blink away the sharp sting of tears.

She wanted to hold him close and relive those precious moments in his arms and feel the heat of his mouth on hers once more before they were finally separated by thousands of miles of ocean.

Instead she had to lift her chin and pretend that she was uninterested and cool to the point of ice.

'Work. Sean needed some help at the hotel. I could have phoned and made an appointment but I had a sneaky suspicion that you would have put the phone down on me so here I am, in person, ready to take it in the chest. So fire away, Lottie. Let me have it with both barrels. Because the sooner we get this over with and start working together, the better.'

'Working together!' Lottie shot up out of her chair, fingers tented on the table, and stared at him, wide-eyed with disbelief. 'What gives you that idea?'

'Apparently my brother is marrying the magnificent Miss Dervla Flynn. I am in charge of the reception but you, my lovely, are making the wedding cake for one of the most prestigious weddings that the Beresford clan have ever seen. You and me, rocking the food. It's going to be outstanding.'

Somebody in the Bake and Bitch club laughed out loud, probably Gloria, and the sound of the London traffic echoed through the glass and made the floor shake a little. But Lottie did not hear a thing. She was way too busy trying to process what she had just heard. And failing.

'Dee wants me to make her wedding cake?' Lottie asked.

'She's ringing you tonight from Beijing.'

'Beijing. Right. Oh, my.'

Suddenly her legs felt like jelly and Lottie sat back down in her chair.

Rob pulled his chair around a little closer to hers and stretched out his arms so that his fingers were only inches from hers.

'What do you say, Lottie?' There was just enough hesitation in his voice to make her pay attention. 'Do you think you could put up with me for a few weeks while we work out how to make this wedding the best it can be?'

He tilted his head and smiled one of those sweet, heart-breaking smiles.

'Sean is important to me and I know that Dee thinks the world of you. It wouldn't surprise me in the least if you already know what kind of wedding cake she wants for her big day. Was that a nod?'

'Two stacks of individual cakes with the name of each guest piped on. Every one different and totally, totally delicious. It's going to be the most important order of my life.'

She exhaled slowly and swallowed down an egg-sized lump of emotion. 'They're really getting married?' she whispered.

Rob nodded his head up and down. Very slowly. 'They really are. According to Sean I'm his best man and you are the head bridesmaid. Full details to follow the minute she gets back.'

'Wow,' Lottie choked and lifted one hand. 'I'm going to need a moment here. And what's in that cake box?'

'I made a courting cake. For you. It's a bit of a northern tradition but I thought I would give it a twist.'

'A courting cake? You march away from me in the middle of an argument just to prove a point and then you have the nerve to turn up with a *courting* cake? What are you trying to say, Rob? That you expect me to forgive you for treating me as a poor second best when it comes to deciding where your priorities lie? Well, newsflash. I've had enough of being told what to do and what to say and being generally lied to and pushed around as though my feelings don't matter. I'm not putting up with any of that behaviour. Not any more, and especially not from you. So you can take your cake and give it to someone who has such a low opinion of herself that she's willing to put up with you. And good luck to her because she's going to need it. Goodbye and goodnight.'

'Finished yet?' he asked in a semi-serious voice.

She took a couple of breaths. 'Yes, I think so.'

'Good,' Rob replied and slid the cake box across the table in front of her. 'Because it sounds to me like you need some sugar. Try the cake. You might even like it.'

Lottie reached for the box and then whipped her hand back.

'Wait a minute. If I eat this cake it means that we are officially dating! You scoundrel! Keep that cake well away from me. No way. You heard what I said the other day.'

Rob grinned, opened up the lid, and wafted the box under Lottie's nose, pushed it even closer and then sat back in his chair.

'It's lemon drizzle.'

She pushed it back towards him. 'You cheat. That's wicked.'

'I know.' And he pushed it towards her again. 'But my mum suggested you might like it. Right after she told me in no uncertain terms that she had been taking her medication since the last painting was complete and that Ian has asked her to dinner and she has said yes. Don't look at me like that. I like him and Ian is a remarkable photographer. He would love California and my mum cannot wait to show it to him. On her own. Apparently three is a crowd.'

'Ian and Adele? Oh, I'm so pleased.' Lottie grinned and reached out to take Rob's hand and then pulled it back again. 'Are you going to sabotage them?'

'No. He cares about her. Good and bad days don't matter. I think they will be happy together. In fact, I am relying on it. You see, my mother fired me. I am now officially redundant. My services as a full-time minder are no longer required. Apparently I have looked out for her long enough and it's time for me to start enjoying myself in a totally selfish manner.'

'Wow. How are you coping with that?' Lottie whispered. And it was her Rob who grinned back in reply. 'I'm getting used to the idea that it would break her heart if I let my chance of love pass me by. Just because I'm too scared of letting a woman see me for the man that I have become.'

Tears pricked the backs of Lottie's eyes as she watched in astonishment as Rob Beresford slid off his chair and onto his knees in front of her on the floor of the cake shop.

And her heart felt as though it was going to explode with happiness.

He didn't care that the girls from the Bake and Bitch club had sneaked out and were peeking at them from behind the counter, or that a lady with a toddler in her arms was staring at them in disbelief from the back of the tea rooms.

'That's why I stayed up last night working on this recipe. Just for you, only for you. Always and for ever, my love. I know I don't deserve you, but if you give me a chance I'll show you what real love is like. Will you take a chance, Lottie? Will you take a chance on us?'

The whole room went completely silent. No one moved, not even the toddler. Lottie felt that every eye followed the movement of her hand as she slowly picked up a spoon, waved it in the air for a millisecond.

And then plunged it into the lemon drizzle courting cake, picked up a huge piece from the very centre and brought it to her lips.

Rob was smiling at her all the way as she carefully closed her mouth around the spoon and slid the moist, succulent cake onto her tongue.

An explosion of flavour made her groan out loud and her eyelids fluttered closed as she savoured every morsel. It was the most delicous thing that she had ever eaten. No way was Rob going to make this cake for any other girl. A huge round of applause and cheering burst out in the room and when she opened her eyes the first thing she saw was the expression in Rob's eyes.

And in that instant she knew what it felt like to be the most beautiful woman in the room. She was loved and loved in return.

'Good cake.' She grinned. 'You can get up now. Because my answer is yes, yes, yes.' And she fell into his arms, laughing and crying and laughing again, and knew that her heart had found the only home she would ever want.

There was a lot to be said for the perfect recipe for seduction.

* * * * *

HOW TO GET
OVER YOUR EX

NIKKI LOGAN

Nikki Logan lives next to a string of protected wetlands in Western Australia, with her long-suffering partner and a menagerie of furred, feathered and scaly mates. She studied film and theatre at university, and worked for years in advertising and film distribution before finally settling down in the wildlife industry. Her romance with nature goes way back, and she considers her life charmed, given she works with wildlife by day and writes fiction by night—the perfect way to combine her two loves. Nikki believes that the passion and risk of falling in love are perfectly mirrored in the danger and beauty of wild places. Every romance she writes contains an element of nature, and if readers catch a waft of rich earth or the spray of wild ocean between the pages she knows her job is done.

CHAPTER ONE

Valentine's Day 2012

Close. Please just close.

A dozen curious eyes followed Georgia Stone into Radio EROS' stylish elevator, craning over computer monitors or sliding on plastic floor mats back into the corridor just slightly, not even trying to disguise their curiosity. She couldn't stand staring at the back of the elevator for ever, so she turned, lifted her chin…

…and silently begged the doors to close. To put her out of her misery for just a few blessed moments.

Do. Not. Cry.

Not yet.

The numbness of shock was rapidly wearing off and leaving the deep, awful ache of pain behind it. With a humiliation chaser. She'd managed to thank the dumbfounded drive-time announcers—*God, she was so British*—before stumbling out of their studio, knowing that the radio station's output was broadcast in every office on every floor via a system of loudspeakers.

Hence all the badly disguised glances.

The whole place knew what had just happened to her. Because of her. That their much-lauded Leap Year Valentine's proposal had just gone spectacularly, horribly, excruciatingly, publicly wrong.

She'd asked. Daniel had declined.

As nicely as he could, under the circumstances, but his urgently whispered, "Is this a joke, George?" was still a no whichever way you looked at it and, in case she hadn't got the message, he'd spelled it out.

We weren't heading for marriage. I thought you knew that…

Actually no, or she wouldn't have asked.

That's what made our thing so perfect…

Oh. Right. *That* was what made it perfect? She'd known they were drifting in a slow, connected eddy like the leaves in Wakehurst's Black Pond but she'd thought that even drifting *eventually* got you somewhere. Obviously not.

'For God's sake, will you close?'

She wasn't usually one to talk to inanimate objects—even under her breath—but somehow, on some level, the elevator must have heard her because its shiny chrome doors started to slide together obligingly.

'Hold the lift!' a voice shouted.

She didn't move. Her stomach plunged. Just as they'd nearly closed…

A hand slid into the sliver of space between the doors and curled around one of them, arresting and then reversing its slide. They reopened, long-suffering and apologetic.

'You mustn't have heard me,' the dark-haired man said, throwing her only the briefest and tersest of glances, his lips tight. He turned, faced the front, and permitted them to close this time, giving her a fabulous view of the square cut of the back of his expensive suit.

No, you *mustn't have heard* me. *Making a total idiot of myself in front of all of London.* If he had, he'd have given her a much longer look. Something told her everyone would be looking at her for much longer now. Starting with all her and Daniel's workmates.

She groaned.

He looked back over his shoulder. 'Sorry?'

She forced burning eyes to his. If she blinked just once she was going to unleash the tears she could feel jockeying for expression just behind her lids. But she didn't have the heart for speech. She shook her head.

He returned his focus to the front of the elevator. She stared at the lights slowly descending toward 'G' for ground floor. Then at the one marked 'B', below that—the one he'd pressed.

'Excuse me…' She cleared her throat to reduce the tight choke. He turned again, looked down great cheekbones at her. 'Can you get to the street from B?'

He studied her. Didn't ask what she meant. 'The basement has electronic gate control.'

Her heart sank. So much for hoping to make a subtle getaway. Looked as if the universe really wanted her to pay for today's disaster.

Crowded reception it was, then.

She nodded just once. 'Thank you.'

He didn't turn back around, but his grey eyes narrowed. 'I'll be driving out through the gates. You're welcome to slip out behind me.'

Slip out. Was that just a figure of speech or did he know? 'Thank you. Yes, please.'

He turned back to the front, then, a heartbeat later, he turned back again. 'Step behind me.'

She dragged stinging eyes back up to him. 'What?'

'The door's going to open at Reception first. It will be full of people. I can screen you.'

Suddenly the front-line of the small army of tears waiting for a chance to get out surged forward. She fought them back furiously, totally futile.

Kindness. That was worse than blinking. And it meant that he definitely knew.

But since he was playing pretend-I-don't, she could, too. She stepped to her left just as the doors obediently opened onto the station's reception. Light and noise filled the elevator but she stood, private and protected behind the stranger, his big body as good as a locked door. She sighed. Privacy and someone to protect her—two things she'd just blown out of her life for good, she suspected.

'Mr Rush…' someone said, out in the foyer.

The big man just nodded. 'Alice. Going down?'

'No, up.'

He shrugged. 'I won't be long.'

And the doors closed, leaving just the two of them, again. Georgia sagged and swiped at the single, determined tear that had slipped down her cheek. He didn't turn back around. It took only a moment longer for the elevator to reach the basement. He walked out the moment the doors opened and reached back to hold them wide for her. The frigid outdoor air hit her instantly.

'Thank you,' she repeated and stepped out into the darkened parking floor. She'd left her coat upstairs, hanging on the back of a chair in the studio, but she would gladly freeze rather than set foot in that building ever again.

He didn't make eye contact again. Or smile. 'Wait by the gate,' he simply said and then turned to stride towards a charcoal Jaguar.

She walked a dead straight line towards the exit gate. The fastest, most direct route she could. She only reached it a moment or two before the luxury car. She stood, rubbing her prickling flesh.

He must have activated the gate from inside his vehicle, and the large, steel lattice began to rattle along rollers towards her. He nudged his car forward, lowered his window, and peered out across his empty passenger seat.

She ducked to look at him. For moments. One of them really needed to say something. Might as well be her.

'Thanks again.' *For sanctuary in the elevator. For spiriting her away, now.*

His eyes darkened and he slid designer sunglasses up onto the bridge of his nose. 'Good luck' was all he said. Then he shifted his Jag into gear and drove forward out of the still-widening gate.

She stared after him.

It seemed an odd thing to say in lieu of goodbye but maybe he knew something she didn't.

Maybe he knew how much she was going to need that luck.

Hell.

That was the longest elevator ride of Zander's life. Trapped in two square metres of double-thickness steel with a sobbing woman. Except she hadn't been sobbing—not outwardly—but she was hurting inwardly; pain was coming off her in waves. Totally tangible.

The waves had hit him the moment he nudged his way into her elevator, but it was too late, then, to step back and let her go down without him. Not without making her feel worse.

He knew who she was. He just hadn't known it was her standing in the elevator he ran for or he wouldn't have launched himself at the closing doors.

She must have bolted straight from the studio to the exit the moment they threw to the first track out of the Valentine's segment. Lord knew he did; he wanted to get across town to the network head offices before they screamed for him to come in.

Proactive instead of reactive. He never wanted someone higher up his food chain to call him and find him just sitting there waiting for their call. He wouldn't give them the satisfaction. Or the power.

By the time he got across London's peak-hour gridlock he'd have the right spin for the on-air balls-up. Turning a negative into a positive. Oiling the waters. The kind of problem-solving he was famous—and employed—for.

The kind of problem-solving he loathed.

He blew out a steady breath and took an orange light just as it was turning red in order to keep moving. None of them had expected the guy to say no. Who said no to a proposal, live on air? You said yes live and then you backed out of it later if it wasn't what you wanted. That was what ninety-five per cent of Londoners would do.

Apparently this guy was Mr Five Per Cent.

Then again, who asked a man to marry her live on radio if she wasn't already confident of the answer? Or maybe she thought she was? She wouldn't be the first to find out she was wrong...the hard way.

Empathy curled his fingers tight on the expensive leather of his steering wheel. Who was he to cast stones?

He'd recognised that expression immediately. The one where you'd happily agree for the elevator to plunge eight storeys rather than have to step out and face the world. At least his own humiliation had been limited to just his family and friends.

Just *two hundred* of his and Lara's nearest and dearest.

Georgia Stone's would be all over the city today and all over the world by tomorrow.

He was counting on it. Though he'd have preferred it not to be on the back of someone's pain and humiliation. He hadn't got that bad...yet.

He eased his foot onto the brake as the traffic ground to a halt around him and resisted the urge to lean on his horn.

Not that he imagined a girl like that would suffer for long. Tall and pale and pretty with that tangle of dark, short curls. She'd dressed for her proposal—that was a sweet and unexpected touch in the casual world of radio. Half his on-air staff would come to work in their pyjamas if they had the option. But Georgia Stone had worn a simple, pale pink, thin-strapped dress for the big moment—almost a wedding dress itself. If one got married on a beach in Barbados. Way too light for February so maybe public proposals weren't the only thing the pretty Miss Stone didn't think through?

Or maybe he was just looking for ways that this wasn't his fault.

He'd approved the Valentine's promotion in the first place. And the cheesy 'does your man just need a shove?' angle. But EROS' listeners were—on the whole—a fairly cheesy bunch so it had been one of their most successful promotions.

Which had made the lift ride all the more painful.

Something about her pale, wide-eyed courtesy. Even as her heart ruptured quietly in its cavity.

Thank you.

She'd said it four times in half the minutes. As though he were a guy just helping her out instead of the guy that put her in that position in the first place. It was his contract she'd signed. It was his station's promotion she'd put her hand up for.

Her life was now in shreds around her feet but still she thanked him.

That was one well-brought-up young woman. Youngish; he had to have at least fifteen years on her, though it was hard to know. He reached for his dash and activated the voice automation.

'Call the office,' he told his car.

It listened. 'EROS, Home of Great Music, Mr Rush's office. This is Casey, can I help you?'

Christ, he really had to have their company-wide phone greeting shortened.

'It's me,' he announced to his empty vehicle. 'I need you to pull up the contract with the Valentine's girl.'

'Just a tick,' his assistant murmured, not taking offence at his lack of acknowledgement. She knew life was too short for pleasantries. 'OK, got it. What do you need, Zander?'

'Age?'

Her silence said she was scanning the document. 'Twenty-eight.'

OK, so he had nine years on her. And her skin was amazing, then. He would have said twenty-two or -three, max. 'Duration of contract?'

Again a brief pause. 'Twelve months. To conclude with a follow-up next February fourteenth.'

Twelve months of their lives. That was supposed to include engagement party, fully paid wedding, honeymoon. All on EROS. That was the fifty-thousand-pound carrot. Why else would anyone want to make the most private, special moment of their lives so incredibly public?

The carrot was cheap in international broadcast terms, for the kind of global exposure he suspected this promo would get. Even more so now, given it had probably already gone viral. Exposure brought listeners, listeners brought advertisers, and advertisers brought revenue.

Except that follow-up twelve months from now wasn't going to make great radio. At all. His mind went straight to the weakest link.

'Casey, can you send that contract to my phone and then call Rod's assistant and let her know I'm about half an hour away?'

'Yes, sir.'

He rang off without a farewell. Life was too short for that as well.

A year was a long time to manufacture content, but if they played their cards right they could salvage something that would last longer than just the next few days. Really make that fifty thousand pounds work for them. He still expected EROS to directly benefit from the viral exposure—maybe even more now—but that contract locked them in for the next year as much as her.

A black cab cut in close to his bonnet and he gave voice to his frustration—his guilt—finally leaning on the horn the way he'd been wanting to for twenty minutes.

He spent the second half of his drive across town formulating a plan. So much so that when he walked into his network's

headquarters he had it all figured out. A way forward. A way
to salvage something of today's mess.

'Zander...' Rod's assistant caught his ear as he breezed past
into her boss's office. He paused, turned. 'He has Nigel in
there.'

Nigel Westerly. Network owner. That wasn't a good sign.
'Thanks, Claire.'

Suddenly even his salvage plan looked shaky. Nigel Westerly hadn't amassed one of the country's biggest fortunes by
being easily led. He was tough. And ruthless.

Zander straightened his back.

Oh, well, if he had to be fired, he'd rather it be by one of the
men he admired most in England. He certainly wasn't going to
quail and wonder when the axe was going to fall. He pushed
open the double doors to his director's office with flair and
announced himself.

'Gentlemen...'

CHAPTER TWO

THANK goodness for seeds. And quiet lab rooms. And high-security access passes.

Georgia's whole National Trust building was so light and bright and...optimistic. None of which she could stomach right now. Her little X-ray lab had adjustable lighting so it was dim and gloomy and could look as if she were out even when she wasn't.

Perfect.

She'd called in sick the day after Valentine's—unable to crawl out of bed was a kind of sick, right?—but she'd gone tiptoeing back to work, her Thursday and Friday an awful trial in carefully neutral smiles and colleagues avoiding eye contact and a very necessary and very belated inter-departmental email to Kew's carnivorous-plant department.

It was also very short.

I'm so very sorry, Daniel. I'll miss you.

She knew they were done. Even if Dan hadn't concurred—which he had, once he'd cooled down enough to speak to her—she couldn't spend another moment in a relationship that just drifted in small, endless circles. Not after what she'd done. Conveniently, it also meant she didn't have to explain herself, explain something she barely understood—at least not for a while. And she was nothing if not a master procrastinator. She'd see Dan eventually, apologise in person, pick up her few things from his place. But this way they were both out of their misery.

Relationship euthanasia.

You know, except for the whole intensive public interest thing...

And now it was Saturday afternoon. And work was as good a place as any to hide out from all those messages and emails from astounded friends and family. Better, probably, because there were so few staff here with her and because she worked alone in her little X-ray lab behind two levels of carded access restrictions. The world wasn't exactly interested enough in her botched proposal to have teams of paparazzi on her trail but it was certainly interested enough to still be talking about it— everywhere—a few days later. She didn't dare check her social media accounts or listen to the radio or pick up a paper in case The Valentine's Girl was still the topic de jour.

London was divided. Grand Final kind of division. Half the city had taken up arms in her defence and the other half were backing poor, beleaguered Dan. Hard to know which was worse: the flak he was copping for being the reject*or* or the abject pity she was fielding for being the reject*ee*.

Didn't she know what a stupid thing it was to have done? some said.

Yes, thanks. She had a pretty good idea. But it wasn't as if she just woke up one morning and wanted her face all over the papers. She'd thought he'd say yes, or she wouldn't have asked. It just turned out her inside information was about as reliable as a racing tip from some random bag lady in an alleyway.

Why do it live on air? her detractors cried.

Because she woke up the morning after Kelly's stunning pronouncement that her brother was ready for more and the 'Give him a Nudge' leap year promotion was all over the radio station she brushed her teeth to. And rode to work to. And did her work to. All day. The universe was practically screaming at her to throw her name into the hat.

She rubbed her throbbing temples.

Their names.

Dan was in it up to his neck, too, but because she wasn't about to out her best friend—for Dan's sake and for his sister's—she was still struggling with exactly what her answer would be when he eventually turned those all-seeing eyes to her and asked, *'Why, George?'*

She loaded another dish of carefully laid-out seeds into the holder and slid it into the irradiator, then secured it and moved to her computer monitor to start the X-ray. It took just moments to get a clear image. Not a bad batch; a few incompetents, like all batches, but otherwise a pretty good sample.

She typed a quick summary report of her findings, noted the low unviable percentage, and attached it to the computerised sample scan to go back to the seed checkers.

Incompetents. It was hard not to empathise with them, the pods that had rotten-out interiors or the husks that formed absent of the seeds they were supposed to protect. Incompetent seeds disappeared amongst the thousands of others on the plant and just never came to fruition. Their very specific genetic line simply…vanished when they failed to reproduce.

In nature, that was the end of it for them.

Incompetent seeds didn't have to justify themselves and their failure to thrive constantly to their competent mothers. Didn't have to watch their competent friends' competent families take shape and help them move out to their competent outer-city suburbs.

'Ugh…' Georgia retrieved the small sample from the irradiator, repackaged it to quarantine standards and placed it back in its storage unit. Then she reached for the next one.

Twenty-five-thousand seed species in the bank and someone had to test samples of each for viability. Lucky for the National Trust she had weeks and even months of hiding out ahead of

her. Looked as if they were going to be the immediate benefi-
ciaries of her weekends and evenings in exile.

Across the desk, her phone rang.

'Georgia Stone,' she answered, before remembering what
day it was. Why was someone calling her on a weekend?

'Ms Stone, it's Tyrone at Security. I have a visitor here for
you.'

No. He really didn't. 'I'm not expecting anyone. I would
have left a name.'

'That's what I told him, but he insisted.'

Him. Was it Daniel? Immediately, new guilt piled on top of
the old that she'd not been brave enough to face him personally yet. 'Wh…who is it?' she risked.

Pause.

'Alekzander Rush. With a *K* and a *Z*, he says.'

As if that helped her in the slightest; although some neuron
deep in her mind started firing.

'Now he says he's not a journalist.' Tyrone sounded annoyed
at being forced into the role of interpreter. His job was just to
check the ID of visitors passing through his station, not deal
with presumptuous callers.

'OK, send him through. I'll meet him in the visitor centre.
Thank you, Tyrone,' she added before he disconnected.

It took her about seven minutes to finish what she was doing,
sanitise, and work her way through three buildings to the public
visitor centre. It was teeming with weekend visitors to Wakehurst all checking out the work of her department while they
were here seeing the main house and gardens.

She glanced around and saw him. Tall, dark, and casually
but warmly dressed, with something draped over his arm. The
guy from the elevator at the radio station. Possibly the last
person in the world she expected to see. Relief that he wasn't
some crazy out to find The Valentine's Girl crashed into curiosity about why he would be here. She ignored two speculative glances sent her way by total strangers. Probably trying

to work out why she looked familiar. Hopefully, she'd be back in her office by the time the light bulb blinked on over their heads and they remembered whatever social media site they'd seen her on.

She walked up next to him as he stared into one of the public displays reading the labels and spoke quietly. 'Alekzander with a *K* and a *Z*, I assume?'

He turned. His eyes widened as he took in her labcoat and jeans. That was OK; he looked pretty different without his pinstripe on, too.

'Zander,' he said, thrusting his free hand forward. She took it on instinct; it was warm and strong and certain. Everything hers wasn't. 'Zander Rush. Station Manager for Radio EROS.'

Oh. That wasn't good.

He lifted his arm with something familiar and beige draped across it. 'You left your coat in the studio.'

The manager of one of London's top radio stations drove fifty kilometres to bring her a coat? No way.

'I considered that a small price to pay for getting the heck out of there,' she hedged. She hadn't really let herself think about the signed document on radio network letterhead sitting on her desk at home, but she was thinking about it now. And, she guessed, so was he.

The couple standing nearby suddenly twigged as to who she was. Their eyes lit up with recognition and the girl turned to the man and whispered.

Zander didn't miss it. 'Is there somewhere more private we can speak?'

'You have more to say?' It was worth a try.

His eyes shot around the room. 'I do. It won't take long.'

'This is a secure building. I can't take you inside. Let's walk.'

Conveniently, she had a coat. She shrugged into it and caught him as he was about to head back out through the giant open doors of the visitor centre.

'Back door,' she simply said.

Her ID opened the secure rear entrance and deposited them just a brisk walk from Bethlehem Wood. About as private as they were going to get out here on a Saturday. It got weekend traffic, too, but nothing like the rest of Wakehurst. Anyone else might have worried about setting off into a secluded wood with a stranger, but all Georgia could see was the strong, steady shape of his back as he'd sheltered her from prying eyes back in the elevator as her world imploded.

He wasn't here to hurt her.

'How did you find me?' she asked.

'Your work number was amongst the other contacts on our files. I called yesterday and realised where it was.'

'You were taking a chance, coming here on a Saturday.'

'I went to your apartment, first. You weren't there.'

So he drove all this way on a chance? He was certainly going to a lot of trouble to find her. 'A phone call wouldn't suffice?'

'I've left three messages.'

Oh.

'Yes, I…' What could she say that wouldn't sound pathetic? Nothing. 'I'm working my way up to my phone messages.'

He grunted. 'I figured the personal approach would serve me better.'

Maybe so; she was here, wasn't she? But her patience wasn't good at the best of times. 'What can I do for you, Mr Rush?'

'Zander.' He glanced at her sideways. Then, 'How are you doing, anyway?'

What a question. Rejected. Humiliated. Talked about by eight million strangers. 'I'm great. Never been better.'

His neat five o'clock shadow twisted with his lips. 'That's the spirit.'

Well, wasn't this nice? A walk in the forest with a total stranger, making small talk. Her feet pressed to a halt. 'I'm so sorry to be blunt, Mr Rush, but what do you want?'

He stopped and stared down at her, his eyes creasing. 'That's you being blunt?'

She shifted uncomfortably. But stayed silent. Silence was her friend.

'OK, let me get to the point…' He started off again. 'I'm here in an official capacity. There is a contract issue to discuss.'

She knew it.

'He said *no*, Mr Rush. That makes the contract rather hard to fulfil, don't you think? For both of us.' She hated how raw her voice sounded.

'I understand—'

'Do you? How many different ways do you hear your personal business being discussed each day? On social media, on the radio, on the bus, at the sandwich shop? I can't get away from it.'

'Have you thought about using it, rather than avoiding it?'

Was he serious? 'I don't want to use it.'

'You were happy enough to use it for an all-expenses-paid wedding.'

Of course that was what he thought. In some ways she'd prefer people thought she was doing it for the money. That was at least less pathetic than the truth. 'You're here for your pound of flesh—I get that. Why not just tell me what you want me to do?'

Not that she would automatically be saying yes. But it bought her time to think.

Grey eyes slid sideways as his gloveless hands slid into his pockets. 'I have a proposition for you. A way of addressing the contract. One that will be…mutually beneficial.'

'Does it involve a time machine so that I can go back a month and never sign the stupid thing?'

Never give in to her mother's pressure. Or her own desperate need for security.

His head dropped. 'No. It doesn't change the past. But it could change your future.'

She lifted her curiosity to him. 'What?'

He paused at an ornate timber bench and waited for her to sit. *Old-school gallantry.* Even Dan didn't do old school.

She sat. Curious.

'The media is hot for your story, Georgia. Your...situation has sparked something in them.'

'My rejection, you mean?'

He tilted his head. 'They'll be interested in everything you do. And if they're interested, then London will be interested. And if London is interested, then my network will want to exploit the existing contract however they can.'

Exploit? He was happy to use that word aloud? She tried not to let her surprise show.

'Georgia, under its terms they could still require you to come back for follow-up interviews.'

Her stomach crimped. 'To talk about how very much I'm not getting married? How I suddenly find myself alone with half my friends siding with my ex?' And the other half so determinedly *not* talking about it. 'Not exactly perky radio content.'

He shook his head. 'It's what they could ask. But I have a better idea. So that the benefit is not all one-way.'

She waited silently for his explanation. Mostly because she had no idea what to say.

'If you agree to seeing the year out, EROS is willing to redirect the funds from the engagement, wedding, and honeymoon to a different project. One that you might even enjoy.'

She frowned. 'What kind of project?'

He took a breath. 'Our listeners have connected with you—'

'You mean your listeners feel sorry for me.' Pity everywhere she looked.

'—and they want to see you bounce back from this disappointment. They want to follow you on your journey.'

She ignored that awful thought and glared at him. 'Really? You see into each of their hearts?'

His scoff vibrated through his whole body. 'We spend four million pounds a year on market research. We know how many sugars they each have in their coffee. Trust me. They want to know. You're like…them…to them.'

'And how is me working through my weekends in a lab going to make good radio? Because that's how I planned to get through this next year. Low profile and lots of work.'

'I'm asking you to flip that on its head. High profile and getting back out into the sunshine. Show them how you're bouncing back.'

Honesty made her ask in a tiny voice, 'What if I don't— bounce back? What then?'

Something flooded his eyes. Was it…compassion? 'We plan to keep you so busy you won't have time to wallow.'

Wallow? Anger rushed up and billowed under her coat. But she didn't let it out. Not directly. 'Busy with what?' she gritted.

'Makeovers. New clothes. Access to all the top clubs… You name it, we'll arrange it. EROS is making it our personal business to get you back on your feet. Total reinvention. And on your way to meeting Mr Right.'

She stared at him, aghast. 'Mr Right?'

'This is an opportunity to reinvent yourself and to find a new man to love.'

She just stared. There were no words.

It was only then he seemed to hesitate. 'I know it feels soon.' She blinked.

He frowned. Scowled. 'OK, I can see that you're not understanding—'

'I understand perfectly well. But I refuse. I have no interest in reinvention.' That wasn't entirely true—she'd often dreamed about the sorts of things she might have done if she'd grown up with money—but she certainly had no interest in a manufactured man-hunt.

'Why not?'

'Because there's nothing wrong with me, for a start.' *Hmm… defensive much?* 'I'm not in a hurry to have you tally up my apparently numerous deficiencies and broadcast them to the world.'

He stared at her. 'You're not deficient, Georgia. That's not the point of this.'

'Really? What is the point? Other than to tell women everywhere that being yourself is not sufficient to catch a good man.'

Something her gran had raised her never to believe. Something that was starting to look dangerously possible.

'OK, look… The point of this is ratings. That's all the network cares about. This promotion was mine and it went arse-up and so it's my mess to tidy. I just thought that we could spin it so that you can get something decent out of it. Something meaningful.' Sincerity blazed warm and intense from his eyes. 'This is an opportunity, Georgia. Fully paid. To do anything you want. For a year.'

She couldn't even be offended at having her life so summarily dismissed. *Arse-up* was a pretty apt description. She sighed. 'Why would you even care? I'm nobody to you.'

He glanced away. When he came back to her his eyes were carefully schooled. 'I feel a certain amount of responsibility. It was my promotion that ended your relationship. The least I can do is help you build a new one.'

'*I* ended my relationship,' she pressed. 'My decisions. I'm not looking to shift blame.'

'And so…?'

'I don't want to find someone to replace Dan. He wasn't just someone I picked up out of convenience.' Though, to her everlasting shame, she realised that maybe he was. And she'd almost made him her husband.

'So you're just going to hide out here for the next twelve months?'

Yes.

'No. I'm going to take a year off life to just get back to who I really am. To avoid men altogether and just remember what I liked about being by myself.' The idea blew across her mind like the leaves on the gravel path ahead of them. But it felt very right. 'It will be the year of Georgia.'

His eyes narrowed. 'The year of Georgia?'

'To please no one but me.' To find herself again. And see how she felt about herself when left alone in a room with no one else to fill the space.

'Well, then, think about how much you could do for yourself with a blank cheque behind you.'

It was a seductive image. All those things she'd always wanted to do—secretly—and never had the courage or the money to do. She could do them. At least some of them.

'What would you do,' he went on, sensing the shift in his fortune, 'if money was no object?'

Build that time machine... 'I don't know. Self-improvement, learn a language, swim the English Channel?'

That got his attention. 'The Channel, really?'

She shrugged. 'Well, I'd have to learn how to swim first...'

Suddenly he was laughing. 'The Year of Georgia. We could mix it up. Get a couple of experts to help us out with some ideas.' Grey eyes blazed into hers. 'Fifty thousand pounds, Georgia. All for you.'

She stared at him. For an age. 'Actually, I really just want all of this to go away. Can fifty grand buy that?'

The compassion returned. It flickered across his eyes and then disappeared. 'Not literally, but there's an extra-special level of feeding-frenzy that the public reserves for those not wanting the attention. Maybe fronting up to it will be a way to help end it?'

That made some sense. There was a seedy kind of fervour to the interest of the English public specifically because she and Dan were both trying so hard to avoid it. Maybe it tapped into the ancient predator parts of mankind, as if they were scenting a kill.

'You were willing to sell us your marriage before,' he summed up. 'Why not sell us your recovery? How is it different?'

'Sharing the happiest time of my life with the world would have been infinitely different.'

His eyes narrowed. 'Is that what you thought? That marrying him would make you happy?'

'Of course.' But then she stumbled. 'Happier. You know, *still* happy.'

It sounded lame even to her own ears.

'Clearly Bradford thought otherwise.' Then he took a breath. 'Why did you ask him if you weren't certain of his answer?'

Her brow folded. 'Because we'd been together for a year.'

'A year in which he thought you were both just enjoying each other's company.'

For a moment she'd forgotten—again—how very public her proposal was. And Dan's decline. Three million listeners had heard every excruciating word. She hid her shame by dropping her gaze to the path ahead of them.

'So…what? His twelve-month expiry date was approaching?'

She lifted her eyes again. 'It was your promotion, Mr Rush. "Give him a leap year nudge," you said in all your advertising.'

His eyes flicked away briefly. 'We didn't imagine anyone would take us literally.'

She stared at him as a small cluster of walkers passed by. Her friend's illness was none of his business. Nor was Kelly's eagerness to see a happy ever after for two people she loved. 'I misunderstood something someone close to him said,' she murmured.

Actually her mistake was in hearing what she wanted to hear. And letting her mother's expectations get to her. Her desperate desire to fill the void in her life with grandchildren. And then she'd awoken to EROS' promotion and decided it was some kind of sign.

And when she'd been shortlisted and then selected…well…

Clearly it was meant to be.

And exactly *none* of those was even close to being a good excuse.

'I accept full responsibility for my mistake, Mr Rush—'

'Zander.'

'—and I'll need to seek some legal advice before answering you about the contract.'

'Of course.' He fished a business card from his pocket and handed it to her. 'You'd be foolish not to.'

Which was a polite, corporate way of suggesting she'd been pretty foolish already.

It was hard to argue.

'I think you should do it,' Kelly said, distracted enough that Georgia could well imagine her stirring a pot full of alphabet spaghetti in one hand, ironing a small school uniform with the other, and with the phone wedged between her ear and shoulder.

A normal day in her household.

'I thought for sure you'd tell me where he could stick his offer,' she said.

Kelly laughed. 'If not for those magic words...'

Fifty thousand pounds.

'You say magic words and I hear magic beans. I think this has the potential to grow into something really all-consuming.'

'So? Did you have any other plans for the next twelve months?'

The fact it was true—and that Kelly didn't mean to be unkind—didn't stop it hurting all the same. No, she had no particular plans that twelve months of fully paid *stuff* would interrupt. Which was a bit sad.

'George, listen. I don't want to bore you again with my life-is-for-the-living speech, but I would take this in a heartbeat if someone offered it to me.'

'Why? There's nothing wrong with you. You don't need reinvention.'

'There's nothing wrong with *you*. This doesn't have to be about that. This is an opportunity to do all the things you've put aside your whole life while you've been working and saving so hard. To live a little.'

'You know why I work as hard as I do.'

'I know. The whole "as God is my witness, I'll never be hungry again" thing. But you are not your mother, George. You are more financially secure than most people your age. Isn't there any room in your grand plan for some fun?'

She blinked, wounded both by Kelly's too-accurate summation of her entire life's purpose and by the implication of her words. 'I'm fun.'

Kelly's gentle laugh only scored deeper. 'Oh, love. No, you're not. You're amazing and smart and very interesting to be around, but you're about as much fun as Dan is. That's what made you two so—'

Kelly sucked her careless words back in. 'What I'm saying is, you have nothing to lose. Take this man's fifty grand and spoil yourself. Consider it a consolation prize for not getting to marry my stupid brother.'

'He's not stupid, Kel,' she whispered. 'He just doesn't love me.'

In the silence that followed, two little boys shrieked and carried on in the background. 'Well, I love you, George, and as your friend I'm telling you to take the money and run. You won't get a chance like this again.'

Kelly dragged her mouth away from the phone but not well enough to save Georgia's ears as she bellowed at one of her boys. 'Cal, enough!' She came back to their conversation. 'I'm going to have to go. World War Three is erupting. Let me know what you decide.'

Moments later, Georgia thumbed the disconnect button on her mobile and dropped it onto her plump sofa.

No surprises there, really. Of course Kelly would take the money. And the opportunity. She'd come so close to being robbed of life—and her boys of a mother—she was fully in marrow-sucking mode. And she was right—there really was nothing else going on in Georgia's life that a bunch of new activities would interrupt.

Her objections lay, not with the time commitment, but with the implication that she was broken. Deficient.

About as much fun as Dan. Did Kelly know what an indictment that really was? Mr Serious?

So that was three for three in favour. Kelly and her gran both thought it would be good for her and her mother...well, what else would a woman incapable of managing her money or her impulses say?

Which was part of the problem. Truth be told, Georgia had nothing against the idea of a bit of self-development of the social kind. She wanted to be a well-rounded person and maybe she had gone a bit too hard down the other path these past years. But the pitch of her mother's excited squeal was directly and strikingly proportional to her level of discomfort at the idea of frittering away fifty thousand perfectly good pounds—no matter how free—on meaningless, fluffy activity.

Her mother would have spent it in a week. Just as she spent every penny they ever had. They'd bounced through seven public houses before her gran called a halt and took a thirteen-year-old Georgia in with her.

And then it would be gone, with nothing to show for it but a fuller wardrobe, a liver in need of detox and a sleep debt the size of Wales.

She stretched out and pulled the well-thumbed EROS contract into her lap. It had her lawyer's recommendation paper-clipped to the front.

Sign, he said. And attached his invoice.

So that was four for four. Five if you counted the handsome and persuasive Zander Rush.

And only one against.

CHAPTER THREE

March

ZANDER'S assistant made an appointment right at the end of his day for her to sign the contract and so walking back into EROS was only *half* as intimidating as it might have been if it were full of staff.

An oblivious night-guard had just sat down at Reception instead of the two gossipy girls she'd met there the first time she visited, and most of the workstations in the communal area were closed down for the evening. Georgia clutched a printout of Zander's new contract in her hand and quietly trailed his assistant past the handful of people still beavering away at their desks. Most of them didn't raise their heads.

Maybe she was yesterday's news already.

Or maybe public interest had just swung around to Dan, instead, now that the calendar had flipped over to March. *Drop Dead Dan*. Apparently, he was fielding a heap of interest from the women's magazines and the tabloids, all determined to find him a match more acceptable than she. More worthy. London now thought he was too good for her. Not that *he'd* put it like that—or ever would have—but she could read between the lines. She didn't dare read the actual lines.

She shifted in her seat outside Zander's office.

Behind the frosted-glass doors, an elevated voice protested

strenuously. There was a low murmur where the shouted response should have been and then a final, higher-pitch burst. Moments later one of the two doors flung open and a man emerged—flushed, rushed—and stormed past her. He glanced her way.

'A lamb to the bloody slaughter,' he murmured, a bit too loud to have been accidental, before storming down the corridor and into one of the studios off to one side. She followed his entire progress.

'Georgia.' A smooth voice dragged her focus back to the doors.

She straightened, stood. Reached out her hand. The tiniest of frowns crossed Zander's face before he enclosed her hand in his and shook it. His fingers were as warm and lingering as last time. And still pleasingly firm. 'I was beginning to think we'd never see you again.'

'I had to think it over.' And over. Looking for any reasonable way out. And avoiding the whole thing, really.

'And?'

She sighed. 'And here I am.'

He stood back and signalled at his assistant, who was politely keeping her eyes averted, but not so much that she didn't immediately decode and acknowledge his signal. Did that little finger-twiddle mean, *Hold my calls*? *Bring us coffee*? Or maybe, *If she's not out in five minutes interrupt me with something fake but important.*

Perhaps the latter if the furrows above his brow were any indication. He didn't look all that pleased to see her. So maybe she really had taken too long with the contract.

'I needed to be sure I understood what you were asking.' Ugh, way too defensive.

His eyes finally found hers and they didn't carry a hint of judgement. 'And do you?'

She waved the sheaf of papers. 'All signed.'

A disproportional amount of relief washed across his face. He sat back in his expensive chair.

She tipped her head. 'You weren't expecting that?' She hated the thought that maybe there'd been more room for negotiation after all. She hated being played.

'I've learned never to try and anticipate the actions of people.' His eyes drifted to the door where the man had just stormed out.

'I had one question…'

The relief vanished and was replaced by speculation. 'Sure.'

'It's about the interviews. Is that really necessary? It seems very formal.'

'We just need an idea of who you are, so we know what we're starting with.'

'By filling out a questionnaire? I thought maybe if I had coffee with your assistant, told her a bit about myself—'

'Not Casey. She's not subjective enough.'

'Because she's a woman?'

'Because she's a card-carrying member of Team Georgia.'

Oh. How nice to have at least one person in her corner.

'Unless you were angling for a free lunch?'

She glared at him. 'Yes. Because all of this would be totally worth it if only I could get a free bowl of soup out of you.'

His scowl moderated into a half-smile.

'What about one of your other minions,' she tried.

His eyebrows shot up. 'Minions?'

'You have an assistant to do your bidding. And that man leaving just now didn't look like a man who enjoyed fair and equal status in his workplace.'

His frown deepened. 'I don't have minions. I do have staff.'

'Then any one of your staff.'

He studied her across the desk. 'No. Not one of my staff.'

She sighed. 'I'd really rather not do a questionnaire, Zander. It's too impersonal.' And a little bit insulting. As though a computer could tell her what was missing in her life when she was still struggling to work that out.

'Not one of my staff and not a form.'

'Then what?'

'Me.'

'You what?'

'I'll interview you.' He reached for a pen.

'N-now?' she stammered.

The half-smile graduated. 'No. I'm just making a couple of notes for Casey for tomorrow.'

She swivelled in her chair. 'She's gone?'

'Yes. Why?'

'I thought you… Didn't you signal for her to do something for you just now?'

'Yes, I told her to go home. Just because I keep long hours doesn't mean she has to. She's got a young family to get home to.'

So they were…alone? Why on earth did that make her pulse spike? Just once. She'd walked in a secluded wood with him. Being alone in an office wasn't all that scandalous. Except that it was *his* office, full of *his* comfy, oversized furniture and all of a sudden she felt a lot like an outclassed Goldilocks.

She pushed half out of her chair. 'I should go.'

'What about the interview? I thought we could go and grab a drink, talk. I can get what I need.'

For a bright woman, an astonishing amount of nothing filled her head just then. He prowled to the front of his desk and stood by her chair so that she had no choice but to stand and let him shepherd her out of his office.

'The contract…' she breathed.

He relieved her of the pages, flicked to the back one and signed it, unread. She pressed her lips together. 'I should have gifted myself a luxury car in small print.'

His lips parted, revealing smooth, white, even teeth. 'Where would you drive a luxury car?'

'You never know. Maybe that's something I'd like to get experience with—I've never driven anything flashier than a Vauxhall.'

His eyes softened as they alighted on her. Then he reached deep into his trouser pocket and tossed her a bundle of keys. They were still warm from his body heat. Toasty warm. She lifted her eyes to his.

'Never too early to get started. Consider this the first Year of Georgia activity. Driving a luxury car.'

'Not your Jag?' she gasped.

'Not flashy enough for you?'

Excitement tangled with dread. 'What if I scratch it? Or dent it?' Or drive it into the Thames in her excitement?

'You strike me as a careful driver.'

He ushered her out of the door, keys still lying limp and unwelcome on her palm. She closed her fingers around them.

'Besides,' he said, 'I have outstanding insurance.'

Why would you even care?

Her words had haunted him ever since she'd uttered them, wide-eyed and confused, when he'd first hit her with his counter-proposal. He did care—very much—on a personal level that even he barely understood, so he'd been shoving the echo of her words way down deep every time it bubbled to the surface.

Rod and Nigel were already celebrating a ratings coup— even bad PR was good PR in the communications industry— but they'd left the details of what the coming year would entail up to him. As long as Zander got her on board, that was all they cared about. Locking down the contract and making the best use of the publicity windfall.

This desperate attempt to make sure she got something back for her troubles, that was all him. It just didn't seem right to screw a girl at the most vulnerable moment of her life.

And he knew all about that moment. He'd lived it. He knew how it shaped his life.

It was stupid; he could hardly say that he'd bonded with Georgia the moment he decided to shield her from the prying eyes waiting in Reception. Back in the elevator. But he had. She'd lingered somewhere in the back of his mind from the moment she'd fallen so gratefully on the gesture, and then she'd popped up, unsolicited, when he wasn't armed.

In the middle of important meetings.

Late at night.

Out on the roads as he thudded one foot in front of the other.

'You seem to be dealing with this quite well,' he murmured as the waiter topped up both their glasses in his favourite Hampstead bar. 'Given how you felt about the whole idea last time we met.'

She took a long, steady breath. 'It seems I'm the only one of a longish list of people who doesn't think there's room for improvement with Georgia Version-Two.'

'Give yourself some credit,' he murmured, saluting her with his glass before taking a sip. 'You're more together than you think.'

'Based on what?'

'My observations.'

'During one quick walk in the woods?'

'I'm paid to pay attention to first impressions.'

Her eyes narrowed. 'The elevator?'

'That was a tough few minutes for you and you handled them well.'

She snorted. 'Weeping while your back was turned?'

He smiled. 'How someone reacts under extreme pressure tells you a lot about them. You were unfailingly courteous even as you were dying inside.'

Uncertainty flooded her dark eyes. 'You saw that?'

'But you didn't let it have you. You stayed in control.'

'You didn't see what happened to me once I got home,' she murmured.

He chuckled. 'I said you were strong, not a machine.'

He glanced down to her twisting fingers. Elegant, sensibly manicured hands. He wondered how much else Georgia Stone was sensible about. And what secret things she wasn't.

And he shut that curiosity down as fast as it came.

'So. Have you given any thought to the kinds of things you might like to do with the Year of Georgia?'

'No.'

A lie, for sure. She was human. Who wouldn't start thinking about how to spend that kind of money?

'Top restaurants? Boats? A-list parties? A taste of how the other half live.'

She shrugged. 'I can see how they live. It doesn't interest me, particularly.'

'Why not?'

'Because it's…frivolous.'

Wow. 'That's rather judgemental, don't you think?'

She leaned forward. 'More cars than one person can drive and glamorous houses and wardrobes bulging with unworn clothes?'

'Where'd you get that impression? Television?' She frowned. 'I have more cars than I can drive at once. A nice house and enough suits for two weeks without laundering.' As he knew from experience. 'But I wouldn't call myself frivolous. Maybe there's more to it than you imagine.'

And he wouldn't flatter himself that this was about him. This was an older prejudice at work.

She dropped her eyes briefly. 'Perhaps. But I'm still not interested enough to try. I like my own world.'

'Science and beautiful gardens? What else?'

She stared him down. 'Classical music. Rowing. Old movies. History.'

He blew out a breath. One part of him sighed at the image

of a life filled with those things. Quiet, solitary, gentle things. But the station manager in him baulked. 'Getting our listeners excited about rowing and classical music is going to be a hard sell.' Along with the rest.

She sat up straighter. 'Not my problem.'

The first real emotion she'd shown him. Shame it was offence. 'It kind of is, Georgia. You have a signed contract to honour. We need to find a way forward in this.'

Her astute eyes pinned him. 'As long as it also works for your listeners?'

'There must be things that they'll enjoy that you will, too.'

She stared at him. 'I won't do it if it's portrayed as me trying to find a man. Or to improve myself enough to find one.'

'Just the Year of Georgia, then. The Valentine's Girl getting back on her feet. You really cared for Daniel, our listeners will buy that.' God… Could he hear himself? He sounded just like Rod. Always an angle. Always a carrot. 'We'll assign someone from the station to—'

'No. I don't want one of them with me.'

'One of who?'

'One of the people who were there for the proposal. I don't want them coming with me.'

She didn't trust them. And he understood why. Though what she didn't understand was that the whole sodding mess was *his* fault. Not theirs.

'OK, I'll hire someone esp—'

'No strangers, either.' Her face pinched in several places.

'Georgia, if I can't use one of my team and I can't hire someone, who am I going to get to do it?'

'You do it. I know you.'

His laugh was as loud as it was immediate. 'Do you know what I get paid an hour?'

'Too much to actually get paid by the hour, I'm sure. But that is my condition.' She did her best to look adamant. Even that was moderated by a faintly apologetic sheen to her steady gaze. 'Take it or leave it.'

She had no idea how to negotiate. The innocence was insanely refreshing. 'You've already signed the contract,' he pointed out gently.

But even as the words came out of his mouth his brain ticked over, furiously. His assistant would jump at the chance for some extra responsibility, so he could offload some lower-end tasks to Casey. And if this was what it would take to get Georgia fully on board...

But he held his assent back, in case it had more power a few moments later.

His entire life was about holding things back until they had the most advantage.

'My days are packed out from dawn until dusk.'

Georgia shrugged. 'I have a job, too, so they're going to be evening and weekend things anyway, I imagine.'

It was hard not to admire her for sticking to her guns. Not too many people made a habit of saying no to him these days. He had them all too scared.

'I have things I like to do on my weekends,' he argued. But not very convincingly. Hard-to-get was all part of the game.

One dark, well-shaped eyebrow lifted. 'How badly do you want these ratings?'

A stain of colour came to her cheeks. Either she was shocked at her own audacity or she was enjoying giving him some stick. He used the time she thought he was thinking about her offer to study her features instead. She had a right-hand-side dimple that totally belied the determination of those set lips, and she had a chin built for protesting.

That was probably long enough. He hissed as if he hadn't made his decision sixty seconds ago. 'Fine. I'll do it.'

Her triumph was so brief. It only took her a heartbeat to realise that his commitment had fully sealed hers. And her next twelve months.

'One more condition,' she hurried as a pair of drink menus arrived. It was his turn to lift a brow. 'No one mentions Dan. No one. You will leave him completely alone.'

Loyalty blazed from her chocolate eyes.

Somewhere down deep where constancy used to live in him, he admired her for continuing to protect the man she'd injured. A man she still cared for even though he'd also hurt her horribly. It said she might have been impetuous and naïve but she was faithful. And that was a rare commodity in his world. Her hurt and anger were very clearly directed at herself. In fact, the most notable thing about her manner was the absence of the flat, lifeless lack of interest that he associated so closely with heartbreak—and knew so intimately.

He wondered if she'd even realised yet that her heart wasn't broken.

'OK, Daniel is out of it.'

'And get the media to lay off him.'

He snorted. Whoever taught Georgia about manners forgot to teach her about pushing her luck. 'No one can halt that train now that it's moving, Georgia. I can promise EROS won't use him, but there's nothing I can do about him being London's most wanted. He's a big boy. He'll be fine.'

Besides, judging by what he heard on the broadcast, Daniel Bradford could look after himself.

He leaned forward and locked his eyes on hers. 'You've played this well—' *for a civilian* '—but I've bent about as far as I'm going to go. I'll have an amendment to the contract drawn up and ready for your signature next week.'

She nodded and sank back in her side of the booth.

'How about some dinner?'

She just blinked at him.

'You do eat dinner?'

'Um, yes. Though not usually out. Except for special occasions.'

She truly hadn't begun to imagine ways of spending her

huge windfall? He tried one last time to prove that she was like everyone else. 'Don't tell me you're another mad-keen home chef?'

Her laugh was automatic. 'No, definitely not.'

'You don't cook?'

'I prepare food. But it's not really cooking. The latest in a number of reasons it was probably just as well Dan declined my proposal.'

She certainly was taking her failed marriage-bid a hell of a lot better than he'd taken his. Did that say more about her or Bradford?

Or him?

He fired up his tablet and tapped a few keys. 'I think we just found your first official Year of Georgia idea.'

'Eating out in every restaurant in London?'

'Culinary school.' He chuckled.

She stared. 'I hated home economics at school. What makes you think I'll enjoy it now?'

'Half the women on my staff are right into those social cooking classes. Wine, conversation, cooking techniques from the experts. The sessions must have something going for them.'

Her lips tightened. 'I'm not sure I'd want to go where your staff—'

'God, no.' He pushed his chair back and stood. 'That's the last thing I want, too.'

'You?'

'I'll be coming along. Or have you changed your mind?'

Her delicate brows folded closer together. 'It's not me doing it for me if I'm doing it with you. The dynamic would be all wrong.'

Dynamic. That sounded almost credible. What was she really worried about?

'I need to be there to record your progress, but…you have a point. We'll do it together, but separate. Like we don't know each other. I'll just shadow you. Watch.'

A streak of colour ran up her jaw. 'Won't that be weird?'

He pushed his glass away and leaned in closer. 'Georgia, I'm going to have a solution for any hurdle you put up. You've signed the contract. How about working with me on this instead of against?'

She sighed. Stared at him with those unreadable eyes. 'OK. Sorry.' She took a sip of white wine. 'What did you have in mind?'

'That's a long list.' Georgia stretched and read the upside-down sheet in front of Zander.

'A year is a long time. But we don't have to go with all of these. Plus things might come up along the way so we need to leave room for those. If you had to shortlist, which ones would you enjoy the most?'

He spun the paper around to her and passed her his fancy pen. She asterisked Wimbledon, cooking classes—which she agreed to because he'd indicated his listeners would love it, not because she actually wanted to know the difference between flambé and sauté—cocktail-making class, truffle-making, and a makeover. That last one because she got the sense he really thought it was important. She tugged her sensible shirt down further over her sensible trousers.

'I really want to do this one.' She circled one down near the bottom, taking a risk. It wasn't what he'd be expecting at all. And unlike some of the others this one actually did interest and intrigue her.

'Ice carving?'

'How amazing would that be? Ooh, and this one…' Another asterisk.

'Spy school?'

She lifted excited eyes. 'Can you imagine?'

He shook his head. 'I don't need to imagine. I'm going to find out.'

She sipped her wine.

'What about travel?' he asked.

'What about it?'

'Not interested in the thought of a holiday?'

Flying to a whole other country seemed a lot to ask. Besides, she didn't have a passport. Just the idea of applying for one got her blood thrumming.

'Where could I go?' she breathed.

His smile was almost indulgent. If it weren't also so confused. Had he never met anyone whose gratification went so far beyond delayed it was non-existent?

'Anywhere you want,' he said.

As she holidayed in her apartment as a rule, anything further afield than Brighton just didn't occur to her. 'Where would be good for your listeners?'

Zander shrugged. 'New York? Ibiza?'

Her breath caught... *Ankara?* She'd wanted to go to Turkey since seeing a documentary on its ancient history.

But no, that seemed too much. Fanciful. She wrote down *Ibiza* on the bottom of the list. That seemed like the kind of place EROS listeners would like to hear about. The party capital of Europe. Fast-pour bars and twenty-four-hour clubs and duelling dance arenas and swollen feet and ringing ears.

Oh, yay.

'I might add some things, as we go along. Things that occur to me.' Things she'd like to do but didn't want Zander knowing about. Though of course they wouldn't stay secret for long.

'That's fine. Just hook them up with Casey. I'll just go where she sends me.'

'That's very accommodating of you. Compliance won't do much for your reputation as a fearsome boss,' she said.

One eye twitched. 'I'm not fearsome; I just want them to think that I am.'

'Why?' That was no way to enjoy your work.

'Because it gets things done. I'm not there to be their friend.'

She thought of her own boss. A whacky, brilliant man whom

she absolutely adored. 'You don't think people would work just as hard with respect and admiration as their motivation?'

He lifted his gaze. 'I'd like to think they respect me. I just don't need them to like me.'

Or want them to? Something in his demeanour whispered that. But there wasn't much else she could say about that without offending him. Besides, last time she checked he was the most successful person she knew. And she didn't know him at all.

Silence fell. 'What do you do on your weekends?' she finally asked.

'What?'

'You said you had things to do on your weekend. What kinds of things?'

He regarded her steadily. 'Weekend stuff.'

She lifted both her eyebrows.

'I train.' He frowned.

Lord. Blood from a stone! 'For…?'

'For events.'

She took a stab. 'Showjumping? Clay shooting? Oh!' She drained the last of her wine. 'Ice dancing.'

A reluctant smile crept onto his face. 'Endurance running. I compete in marathons.'

'Truly?'

He chuckled. 'Yes.'

'What sort of distances?'

'Forty or fifty kilometres. It depends.'

'A *weekend*?' Her half-shriek drew glances from around the noisy bar.

His lips twisted. 'A day.'

A day! 'Well, that explains the body—'

Horror sucked the words back in, but not fast enough. *Oh, God!* She quietly pushed her nearly empty glass far away from her.

'I have to keep my fitness up, so I run every morning and I do long runs or hikes every weekend.'

'Every weekend?'

'Pretty much.'

Wow. 'Just running. For hours on end?'

'Or hard hiking. That's why it's called endurance.'

'Sounds lonely.' But also kind of…zen. Kind of what she did when she wandered deep into the dark heart of forests.

'I don't mind the solitude,' he murmured.

'Is that why you do it?'

His answer was fast. As if he'd defended himself on that point often. 'I do it for the challenge. Because I can. And I do my best thinking out there.'

Fifty kilometres. That was a lot of thinking time.

'Just…wow. I'm impressed.'

'Don't get too excited. In competition we can do that in under four hours.'

Georgia shook her head. 'Put marathon running on the list.'

He looked up sharply. 'You want to run a marathon?'

'God, no. I have two left feet. But I've never seen one. I can just watch you. Help you train.'

Intense discomfort flooded his face.

Once again she'd managed to misread a man. This wasn't a friendship. They weren't bonding. This was a business arrangement with the sole purpose of tracking *her* activity. Why on earth would he want her around during his private time? He probably had a raft of friends actually of his choosing to hang out with—and many of them women.

'I…uh…'

She'd stuffed up big enough to actually make a man stammer. World class.

'You know what?' she breezed, not feeling the slightest bit breezy. 'I've changed my mind. Me watching you run would make *terrible* radio. Scratch that off the list.' Was she a convincing liar? They'd find out. His pen was still frozen over the page and so there was nothing to scratch out, so she said the only other thing that came into her head.

'Another drink?'

The list grew as long as the evening. They hit the Internet for ideas of cool things for her to do in London. Pretty soon they had learn-to-dance classes, movie premieres, and a royal polo match.

'Aquasphering!' she said, a little bit too loud. 'Whatever that is.'

'Really? That's your kind of thing?'

'None of it is my thing—isn't that the point? Pushing myself out of my comfort zone.' *Wa-a-ay* out of it.

'Can we afford a seat on a commercial spaceflight?' she blurted, tapping the tablet's glossy screen. 'That would be exciting.'

He smiled. 'No. We can't. And we don't really have the time for it to become more mainstream.'

'Pff. You suck.'

Zander stared at her. Assessing. 'I think I need to get some food into you.'

'I told you I didn't do this for the soup.'

'I was thinking of something a little more solid than soup.'

Judgement stung, low and sharp. She sat up straighter. 'I'm not drunk.'

'No, you're not. But you will be if you keep going like this.'

'Maybe the new me drinks more often.'

He gathered up their papers and his tablet and returned them to his briefcase. 'Really? This is how you want to start the Year of Georgia? By getting hammered?'

She stared at him. Thought about that. 'Have we started?'

'First day.'

'Then we should leave.' Because, no, she didn't want to start that way.

'Let me feed you. I have somewhere in mind. We can walk. Clear your head.'

'Why isn't your head fuzzy? You've been matching me drink for drink.'

He shrugged. 'Body mass?'

She relaxed back into the booth and smiled happily. 'That's so unfair.' Then she sat bolt upright again, her fingers reaching for her phone before her mind was even engaged. 'I should ring Dan. I need to explain.'

Zander caught her hand before it could do more than curl around her phone. 'No. Let's not do that on an empty stomach. Let's go get some food.'

He was right. She needed to talk to Dan face to face, not over the phone. She stood. 'OK. What are we having?'

'We could start your cooking lesson tonight. Something informal.'

'I live miles from here.'

He smiled. 'I don't.'

And just like that—*bam!*—she was sober. Zander Rush was taking her back to his place. To feed her. To teach her to make food. Something about that seemed so…intimate.

'You know what?' she lied. 'I have some things to do tonight before work tomorrow. I think maybe I should just head home.'

'What about food?'

If she was clear-headed enough to lie she was clear-headed enough to catch the tube. 'We're one block from the station.'

His smile grew indulgent. 'I know. You drove us here.'

'It's on the same line as Kew Gardens. I used to catch it home all the time.' So she knew it well.

'At least let me walk you to the station, then.'

She shot to her feet. 'That would be lovely, thank you.'

He shook his head. 'Still so courteous.'

She shrugged. 'Old-school upbringing.'

'Traditional parents?'

Her laugh was more of a bark. 'Definitely not. My gran

raised me mostly. To give me some stability. My mother really wasn't...well adapted...to parenting.'

He threw her a sideways look. 'I'm the youngest of six to older parents so maybe we were raised by a similar generation?'

It took just a few minutes to walk down to the station and something in her speech or her steady forward movement or her riveting, non-stop chatter about her childhood must have convinced him she was fine to be left alone because he didn't try and stop her again.

He paused by the white entry gate. 'Well...'

'You'll be in touch?'

'Casey will. My assistant.'

Of course. He had minions.

'She'll pull together a schedule for the next few months, to get us started.'

'So...I guess I'll see you at the first one, then.'

'Remember, we'll be strangers as far as anyone else is concerned. I'm just your shadow. I won't even acknowledge you when I arrive.'

Weird. But better. If they were doing these things together she'd just get too comfortable. And that wasn't a good idea, judging by how comfortable she'd been for the past few hours. 'I'll remember. See you then.'

She stepped towards the ticket gate, then turned back and smiled. 'Thanks for letting me drive the Jag.'

'Any time.'

Georgia waved again and then disappeared into the station. Zander turned and jogged across the pedestrian crossing, then ducked down the commercial lane that led to the back of the garden of his nearby house where they'd parked the Jag. Except she thought they just got lucky with a street park convenient to his favourite bar, not parking in front of his house.

He was really out of practice. Who took a woman to a bar, then drank so that he couldn't drive her home? Who let a woman ride the tube alone at night?

A man who was trying really hard not to feel as if he was on a date, that was who.

He'd first caught himself back at his office when she'd thrust her hand out so professionally and he'd felt a stab of disappointment. What did he expect, a kiss on each cheek? Of course she was all business. This was…business.

And this was just an after-hours work meeting. He'd almost sabotaged himself by inviting her back to his house to eat, but it had just tumbled from his lips. The old Zander never would have let so many hours pass without taking care to make sure they'd both eaten. It had been a long time since the new Zander came along. This Zander had perfectly defined business muscle but it had come at the expense of social niceties.

Any muscle would atrophy without use.

And then the coup de grâce. *Any time*. He could have said 'you're welcome' or 'think nothing of it' but he went with 'any time'. As though there'd be a repeat performance.

He pushed through the gate to his property and started down the long, winding path between the extensive gardens to the conservatory.

Clearly something of the old him still existed. Something that responded to Georgia's easy company and complete failure to engage with him the way others did. She just didn't care who he was or that he was the only thing standing between her and a lawsuit. Or maybe she just didn't recognise it.

She stared up at him with those big brown eyes and treated him exactly like everyone else.

No one did that any more. Even Casey—the closest thing he had to a friend at work—was always super careful never to cross a line, to always stop just short of the point where familiarity became contempt. Even she was sensitive to how much of her future rested in his hands.

Because he was so thorough in reminding them all. Regularly.

His minions.

He smiled. The irony was he didn't think that way at all. Not deep down. He believed in the power of teams and much preferred collaborative working groups to the way he did things now. They'd served him well back in the day when every programme he'd produced had been the product of a handful of hard-working people. But there was no getting around the fact that EROS really did run better with a clear, controlled gulf between himself and the people who worked for him. And he didn't mind the gulf; it meant no complications between friendships and workplace relationships.

And driving Georgia home would have been a complication.

Having her here, in his house, would have been a complication.

He had a signed contract; the time for courting The Valentine's Girl, professionally, was over. He should have just given her a list of activities that the station was prepared to send her to and been done with it. Instead of being a sap. Instead of reacting to an event fifteen years old and letting it colour his better judgement.

Instead of empathising.

Just because he'd been exactly where Georgia was; on the arse-end of a declined proposal. Only in his case, he got all the way down the aisle before realising his fiancée wasn't coming down behind him because she was on her way to Heathrow with her supportive bridesmaids. What followed was a horrible half-hour of shouting and recriminations before the priest managed to clear the church. Lara's family and friends all went wildly on the defensive—as you would if it was someone *you* loved that had done something so shocking. His side of the church rallied around him so stoically, which only inflamed Lara's family more because they knew—*knew*—that there were a hundred better ways to not proceed with a marriage than just not turning up. Less destructive ways. But she'd gone with the one that would cause her the least pain.

And, chump that he was, he actually preferred that. He

wasn't in the business of wishing pain on people he loved back then.

The heartbreak was bad enough, slumped in the front row of the rioting church, but he'd had to endure the public humiliation in front of everyone he cared about. Their whispers. Their pity. Their side-taking. Worse, their determined, well-meant support. Every bit as excruciating and public as Georgia's turn-down live on air. Just more contained.

Like atomic fusion.

But the after-effects rippled out for a decade and a half.

He jogged up the stairs and headed straight for his study. The most important room in his house. The work he got done there was the difference between just-hanging-on in the network and excelling. No one excelled on forty hours a week. He was putting in eighty, easy.

It was the one thing he could thank Lara for.

Setting him up for the kind of success that gave him a luxurious study in a big house in Hampstead Heath and had him rubbing shoulders with some of the most powerful people in the country.

And just like that he was thinking of Georgia again. Her crack about big houses and unworn clothes and crowded garages. There was a reason he parked the Jag on the street. Because both the cars in his garage were worth more. He liked his life. Excessive though it might be at times. He barely drove the Lotus or the Phantom but he could if he wanted to. And he could look at them whenever he wanted. But they represented something to him. As did the suits and the house and the title on his business card.

They represented the fact that no one would ever pity him again.

And, God help him, no one would ever come to his emotional aid as they'd had to in that church. Not family. Not friends. He would never allow himself to be in that kind of vulnerable position twice.

Money made sure of that.

Success made sure of that.

The corporate world might be a brutal mistress but it was constant. And if you were going to get screwed you'd always see it coming.

He'd never be hijacked again.

How pathetic that she needed a good excuse to go to Kew and *accidentally* see Dan. If she'd found the courage to face the truth about her reasons for proposing, could she really not face Dan himself? The man who'd been such an important and steady part of her life for the past year. Even longer if you counted their friendship before that.

She did need to speak to him face to face. Six weeks was long enough to take the sting out of everything for both of them.

And she had seeds to deliver to his colleagues for identification.

She dropped them to the propagation department and then hit the pathways across Kew to the behind-the-scenes greenhouses. That was where Dan spent most of his time—cultivating the carnivores, he called it—as popular with him as they were with the public.

She knew these paths like the freckles on her body. Long before she knew Dan.

Huh. Look at that. Life before Dan. She'd almost forgotten what that felt like.

Determined not to cut corners—even turf deserved not to be trampled—she followed the path the long way around to the plain glasshouse where Dan primarily worked. Her pulse began to thump.

As she approached it the doors opened and a woman emerged.

'Oh, excuse me!' Georgia exclaimed, her hand to her chest. She had crazy blonde curls, and the serviceable work-coats that everyone wore here. But she had a tight pink dress beneath it, bright, manicured nails, three inch heels and flawless make-up.

Not like everyone else here.

'Nearly got you.' The woman smiled, stepping back to hold the door.

That was perfect, too. Her eyes dropped briefly to the woman's ID tag and, just like that, all Georgia's carefully constructed excuses about why she didn't have better clothes and better hair vanished in a puff of perfume. This woman was an orchid specialist—she worked with dirt all day. Yet she could do that and still look like this.

What excuse did she herself have?

'Can I help you?' the woman said.

'I'm looking for Daniel Bradford.'

'He's out in the display house tending to a struggling *Nepenthes tentaculata*. Can I give him a message?' The slightest hint of curiosity filled her eyes.

It was pure luck that she hadn't run into someone she knew, someone much more familiar with the past relationship between she and Daniel. She wasn't going to blow the opportunity for anonymity.

'No, I know the way. I'll chase him down there. Thank you.' Georgia stepped back from the entrance.

The woman stepped away from the doors, smiling, and they swung shut behind her. 'You're welcome.'

She turned left, Georgia turned right. But she watched the woman walk away from her. Heels. They did something very special to a walk, even on gravel and grass. Pity she didn't have a single pair above a serviceable inch.

Maybe that was something she could put on her Year of Georgia list.

Learn to walk in heels.

And not because men liked them—though the distracted glances of two groundsmen passing the woman confirmed that they did—but because heels were a side of herself that she just never indulged.

Heels and pole dancing. They could go on the side-list she was quietly developing.

Though both could easily break her neck.

It took nearly ten minutes to cross out into the public area and work her way around to the carnivorous-plants exhibit. The doors were perpetually closed to keep the ambient temperature inside right but, unlike the clunky ones behind the scenes, these opened and closed whisper quiet.

She took a breath. 'Dan?'

The silence stayed silent, but somehow it changed. Grew loaded. And Georgia knew she'd been heard.

'I know you're here, Dan.'

'Hey.' He stepped out from behind a large sign. Confused. Wary. 'I didn't know you were coming.'

'I was dropping down some stock for identification. Thought I'd come and say hi.'

Oh, so horribly bright and false.

He nodded. 'Hi.'

Silence. Maybe six weeks weren't enough. 'How are you doing?' she risked.

'OK. Managing.'

The intense scrutiny. Right. 'It's not getting better?'

His lips thinned. 'Not really.'

She nodded. More silence. 'So…I've come to say I'm sorry. Again.'

'Your emails and messages not enough?'

'I didn't want… Not without at least seeing you.' God. How could it be this hard breaking up with someone when you were already broken up?

He shrugged. 'Fodder for the paparazzi.'

She spun around, expecting to see flashes of cameras behind her. 'Oh, God, I didn't even think of that…'

'That's starting to sound familiar.'

The unkind words cut but she knew they were more than deserved. And short of ratting out Kelly to her brother, she couldn't enlighten him otherwise. She sighed. 'Look, Dan, if I could undo it I would. I know you didn't ask for any of this.'

'Done is done.'

Well… 'Not quite, actually.'

His shaggy head tipped. But his hazel eyes darkened with warning. 'Georgia…'

'I'm… I signed a contract with the radio station, for the whole…' She couldn't even use the word *proposal*. 'I have to see it through.'

'I hope you mean "I" and not "we".'

'Not we. I made it a condition that you weren't involved at all.' Something she should have thought about originally, perhaps. 'It's not about us, it's about me. Me getting myself all fixed up.'

God love him, he frowned. 'You weren't broken, George. It was just a really stupid thing to have done.'

'I know. But for me that's symptomatic of being broken. I don't do stupid things. I'm supposed to be rock-solid and reliable and never-changing like you.' It was why she'd allowed herself to think they might make a life together at all.

His scowl deepened.

Say what you have to say and get out. 'So I really just wanted to make sure you were OK and to tell you why you'll be hearing more from me on the station.'

'Are you kidding?' He snorted. 'I'll never listen to them again.'

Oh, right.

'You realise it will just stir things up again every time you go on there?' he huffed.

'Zander thinks that it will help draw attention away from you. Keep it on me.' Where it belonged.

'Zander?'

'He's the station manager. It was his promotion.'

The scowl returned. 'Forgive me if I don't put a lot of faith in the opinion of anyone who would think up a promotion like that.'

The intense desire to defend Zander burbled up out of nowhere. 'This is my responsibility, Dan. I'm trying to fix it as best I can.'

His brilliant mind ticked over behind carefully shielded eyes. 'I know. Sorry. You do whatever you need to, George.' He took a breath. 'And I'll do whatever I need to, to stay out of it.'

Intriguingly cryptic but fair enough. 'OK.'

They both shuffled awkwardly. 'So…I'll let you get back to your sick pitcher plant.'

His eyes narrowed. 'How did you know what I'm working on?'

'One of your colleagues told me.' And for no good reason at all she expanded. 'Blonde hair, flashy dresser.'

Cripes, Georgia, you might as well just ask him outright. 'Why wasn't I good enough for you?'

His eyes grew even more guarded. 'Right. Yes, she's new.'

'Pretty.' Pretty different from everyone round here, that was. Because actually she was gorgeous.

He shrugged. 'I guess.'

OK, he wasn't going to play. She should have known. 'Well, I should get going.' It hit her then that she would quite possibly never see him again. She frowned. 'I don't quite know how to say goodbye to you for the last time ever. It feels really wrong.'

But that was all, she realised. Just intensely awkward. It didn't really hurt.

Huh.

He walked forward, wiped the earth from his hand and then took hers. 'Bye, George. Don't be too hard on yourself. No one died, here.'

No. Except the part of her that used to be happy with herself. She squeezed his fingers. 'Take care, Dan.'

'Maybe I'll see you round.'

She turned. Left. And then it was done. That entire chapter of her life closed as silently and gently as the hydraulic doors of the greenhouse.

And still, no hurt. Just sadness. Like losing a good friend.

Did Dan feel the same? Was that why he'd never wanted their relationship to be more? His sister had always hinted at something big in his past, but he'd never shared and she'd never felt she could ask. Kind of symptomatic of why they weren't right for each other, really. He didn't want more because he didn't have more in him to give. And maybe neither did she. How long might they have gone on like that if she hadn't brought their non-relationship to a startling and public end?

She'd had no trouble at all imagining herself as Mrs Bradford, obligatory kids hanging off her skirts. As if it were just the natural extension of the life they'd had. She enjoyed his conversation, she liked to share activities with him, the sex was as good as she figured she would ever get. He was bomb-proof and reliable and she'd been drawn to the qualities in him that screamed *stability*. Because she'd had so little of it in her past. But she'd never gone breathless waiting to walk into Dan's office. She'd never felt as cherished with him as she had standing behind a perfect stranger in an elevator as he protected her from prying eyes.

Zander.

About as unsuitable for her as any man could be, yet he'd stirred more emotion in her in a few meetings than had the man she'd been planning on marrying.

All outstanding reasons to keep her distance, emotionally.

This was the Year of Georgia. Not the year of panting after sexy, rich, unavailable men. She'd made enough bad decisions in the interests of what her friends or the rest of the world was doing; she needed to have a good look inside and see what *she* wanted to do.

Even if she was a bit scared that she'd look deep inside and find nothing left.

CHAPTER FOUR

April

THE buzz in the perfume-rich room hushed but intensified as Zander walked into it. Georgia saw him from the corner of her eye but made a concerted effort *not* to see him. Every other woman in the place did the same but for totally different reasons.

'*Dieu merci!* The testosterone balance in the room just doubled,' the male chef joked and drew even more anti-attention to Zander's arrival. He smiled thinly.

Georgia had quickly realised that attending alone was a mistake. Every other woman there was paired up with a girlfriend, so, quite apart from whether there were any men in the room, she felt like a failure already. Learning to love doing things solo was going to be a much bigger challenge than just growing accustomed to doing things without a man by her side. Hard enough to be doing things that weren't in her comfort zone, but to be doing them alone...

Effectively alone. Her eyes snuck to Zander again, briefly.

'*Alors.*' Chef clapped his chopping board onto the bench top a few times to call the unruly crowd to order. 'Places.'

What did that mean? Her first reaction was to watch Zander but if he was any wiser he wasn't giving anything away, so she took her cues from the other participants instead. They each dragged a tall stool along one edge of the oversized kitchen bench as Chef laid out a generous wine glass in front of each place from the other side. Two women practically turned an ankle vying for the spot closest to Zander who—wisely—took up the seat right at the end so that he only had to negotiate one interested feminine neighbour.

Georgia waited until last and found herself in the space furthest from him. She filled her glass with water before anyone could put anything more ill-advised in it from the rapidly emptying bottle of chardonnay doing the rounds.

Getting tipsy in front of Zander once was bad enough.

'First point of the evening to the woman down the end. What's your name, *petite fleur*?'

All eyes snapped her way, including Zander's.

Every awful moment of her school career came rushing back with the unexpected attention. It never paid to be the brightest—and poorest—at secondary school. It led to all kinds of unwanted attention. 'Georgia.'

'Well, Miss Georgia,' Chef improvised in ever-thickening French, 'while wine is *perfection* for enjoying the consumption of a meal, water is, without question, the best choice for preparing one. Until you know what you're doing, of course. You want your tastebuds unassailed. You want your nose and palate unconflicted and clear-headed as you *assemblé* the ingredients you'll need...'

'An unconflicted palate. Score one for me,' she murmured.

Their prosaic teacher was fully underway by now and his continental theatrics and charm managed to recapture the focus of the women in the room. But Zander still stared at her, eyes lightly creased.

Stop smiling, her eyes urged him. *We're supposed to be strangers*. Though there was something just slightly breath-stealing about the game they were playing. Pretending to be strangers. Hiding a secret from the whole room.

It was vaguely...kinky.

Which said a lot about how very not kinky her life usually was.

She forced her attention back to Chef. Did her best to listen and understand what he was saying and not pay any further attention to Zander perched at the end of the bench, deftly deflecting the interest of the two women closest to him and studying everything that was happening in the room. Parts of what the chef was saying really resonated for the scientist in her—the parts about the chemistry of food and how ingredients worked together—but they were totally overshadowed by his try-hard vocabulary and his staged theatrics, which really *didn't* work for her. She caught herself smiling more than once at something ridiculous he said or the way he gushed over his rapt female audience. She was fairly certain he wasn't actually French.

'Excuse me, Chef?' she interrupted when he paused for a rare breath and before she could change her mind. 'Will we get to cook something tonight?'

'So *enthousiaste*,' he fawned, and she groaned. '*Non*, you won't get hands-on until week six. In Chef André Carlson's class we first develop *appréciation* for the art of the food, then we progress to *construction* of the food.'

And clearly much drinking of the wine, despite his own protestations.

She nodded, politely, and started counting the endless minutes until her first class was over. How would Zander feel about her dumping the first thing he'd sent her to? She glanced up. He had a resigned nothing plastered to his face. It hit her then that she was wasting two people's time on this terrible class.

'Excuse me, Chef?' This time he looked more irritated to have been interrupted mid-fake-French-stream. 'I have a terrible migraine. I'm going to have to leave.'

Much clucking of concern and old fake-French remedies for migraines later and she had her handbag over her shoulder and her feet pointing towards the door. No one cared.

'You'll need someone to walk you to your car,' Zander volunteered and then excused himself from the woman next to him. That got their attention, but he reassured them, 'I'll be right back.'

No, he wouldn't. Not if he was as dumbstruck by that class's awfulness as she was.

They practically bolted down the hall for the street door, together.

'You were going to leave me there!' he accused as they fell out into the street.

She laughed as she skipped down the steps to the footpath. 'Sorry. Every man for himself on the culinary Titanic.'

'That was awful,' he gritted. 'Why would anyone put themselves through that?'

'They looked like they were having a good enough time.'

'I can't imagine anyone coming away from that actually *appreciating* food more.'

Her laugh redoubled. 'No.'

'I take it the migraine was fake?'

'As fake as his accent. I think we should just cut our losses.'

He halted her with a warm hand to her arm. 'No. You came here tonight wanting to discover what's so special about cuisine.'

God, was he warming back up to another invitation to see his etchings?

'Let me just make a call...'

He made it. Brief and murmured, his back half to her. Then he turned and smiled at her. 'OK, all arranged.'

'What is?'

'We have a job for the night.'

'A job?'

'In a commercial kitchen. That's where you'll see what cooking is really all about.'

'I can't cook in a commercial kitchen!' She could barely boil water in her own home.

'Trust me, Georgia.' He slid his hand around behind her back and smiled. 'We won't be cooking.'

He wasn't kidding. Within fifteen minutes they were installed up to the elbows in suds in the back of the busy kitchen of an Italian restaurant and they'd washed more dishes in less time than she'd even dirtied in her whole life. But she didn't even notice.

The owner of the restaurant where Zander had called in his favour elevated the usual dishwashers to kitchen assistants for the night and had one of his demi-chefs explain everything happening in the kitchen for their benefit.

She and Zander eavesdropped on every word between suds.

And his digital recorder—totally approved by the owner—captured it for EROS' segment.

The kitchen ran like a ballet. Every item on the menu choreographed; every technique a combination of hard-learned steps. Every resulting dish a work of art, never the same twice.

The chef—a real, proper chef this time, with a real accent—yelled at everyone just enough to keep them moving, and didn't hesitate to yell at his trainee dishwashers if she and Zander fell behind. She felt more welcome being yelled at in this kitchen than being fawned over in the last one. The clunk and clatter of knives and pots and whisks merged with the hiss of frying fat and draining pasta pots to create a symphony of experience that had so much more excitement and interest than just how to cook a good cordon bleu.

And such language! The night was an education for more reasons than one. She loved even that. Though she knew Zander's editors would be busy with the bleep button.

The symphony and ballet went on for hours. She grew transfixed trying to take it all in even as her feet started first to ache, then protest and finally give up and just burn. But her sore feet were the least of their worries. A whole dish went wrong and sent the kitchen into desperate chaos catching back up and she felt the adrenaline of the race, the thrill of contributing, the deep satisfaction of getting the replacement meals out in time. Even if her role was only keeping the clean cutlery coming.

And now the night was nearly over. The last customers were on their desserts and only one big pot bubbled away in the half-empty kitchen. The promoted-for-a-night assistants were more than happy to cook something simple for the people who'd triggered their unexpected elevation, and Georgia and her sore feet were more than happy to be cooked for by them.

Who knew, maybe the two men would get to do it more often now that they'd been ripped out of their sudsy pigeonhole.

She'd watched them make it from scratch. Pasta. Carefully mixed, rolled, strung, cooked. And the leftover sauce from the night's bolognese. The owner-chef passed through and plated up for both of them, a modest bowl for Georgia and an enormous mound for Zander. With a barrage of hasty Italian between.

'Are you pregnant?' she joked, settling her heat-wrinkled fingers around one of the forks she'd washed herself.

He chuckled. 'I'm carb-loading.'

'Which is what for the uninitiated?' She curled a dozen strands of beautifully shaped pasta around her fork.

'The day before a big run you load your body up on carbohydrates and water to ensure it's full of energy.'

'Energy you burn off running fifty kilometres?'

'Exactly.'

'Where will you run tomorrow?'

He hesitated answering. She didn't let her sigh show. 'You don't like to talk about it much.'

'I'm unaccustomed to anyone asking. It's usually just my thing.'

That rankled just a tiny bit. 'I'm not going to invite myself along again if that's what you're worried about.'

'I know,' he replied as she slid a fully loaded fork into her mouth.

Oh, my God... She liked spaghetti. She'd even been excited enough once or twice to make her own lumpy Napolitano sauce in her slow cooker. But this...*this*! The combination of home-cooked bolognese and minutes-old, fresh pasta on top of the bone weariness, hollow stomach and flat-footed agony of having stood doing dishes for hours...

'This is amazing, Zander!'

'One of my favourite bolt holes.'

She glanced up at him. His choice of words struck her. 'Where do you bolt from?'

How could a shrug be so tense? 'Life. Work. Everything.'

She could understand that, if the man bursting out of his office was a regular occurrence.

'We could both do worse than running our workplaces the way Chef ran this kitchen,' she said softly.

'What do you mean?'

'Firm. High expectations. But fair. And everyone here was working with him, not despite him.'

Zander looked around the near-empty kitchen. The two assistants had already removed any hint of evidence that their meal had ever existed. The way they were demolishing their pasta, it very soon wouldn't.

'What makes you think it's not like that already?' he asked.

'Something one of your staff said when I was in your office.' She'd been there a few times over the weeks finalising the list with Casey, so that was suitably broad. He wouldn't know who amongst his team it was. 'They said I was a lamb to the slaughter.'

He blinked at her, then recommended eating his meal. But his brows remained low.

'Not saying I agree with them. You've been nothing but nice to me.' If one had a liberal definition of *nice*. 'But, you know, clearly they thought you were going to make things hard for me.'

He thought about that some more. 'It's what they would expect.'

'Why?'

'Because it's what they know.'

Sadness washed across his expression and then vanished. 'Why do you make things hard for them?'

'Because I'm their boss. The network delivers the good news and I deliver and implement the bad. It's what I get paid for.'

'That's a miserable kind of job. Why do you do it?'

He laughed. 'You've seen where I live.' One of London's better suburbs.

'And you've seen where I live. So what? That's not who we are.'

His eyes grew assessing. 'Really? Your apartment exterior is modest and plain, but well kept. Someone cares for that building. I'd hazard a guess that the inside would be the same. Everything in its place, nothing unessential. Isn't that exactly as you are?'

She stared at her near-empty bowl. 'Is that how I strike you? Orderly and dull?'

'You strike me as someone who's stuck in a rut. Maybe who has been for some time.'

She lifted her chin. 'Ruts come in all shapes and suburbs. Besides, you shouldn't judge a book by its cover.'

He lifted his chin to match hers. 'Really? Care to put your money where your mouth is?'

'You want to bet on it?' She frowned.

'I want to see it.'

Oh.

'When?'

'How about now?'

'It's not tidy—'

'Yes, it is.'

Yes...it is. She sighed. 'You have a race in the morning.'

His eyes grew serious. 'I'm not proposing sleeping over, Georgia, just a quick look.'

Heat flared up the back of her neck and she worked hard to keep it from flooding around to the front. She *had* made the immediate assumption that this was some kind of line. Zander Rush was a fit and sexy man. And so of course it wasn't a come-on. Not for her.

'I just meant…it's late.'

'I don't run until noon. And it's too late for you to be taking the tube.'

It wasn't, but she didn't mind the idea of a comfortable Jag ride home. She wasn't ready for their first night to be over.

The first night. Not *their* first night.

'OK, I'll take the lift.' And show him the inside of her flat for a minute or two. And then he and his fascination would be gone. 'Thank you.'

They rinsed their dishes in the cooling water, thanked the chef who was enjoying a drink with his team out in the now-empty restaurant, and headed out into the dark.

'You want to drive?' he asked.

No. She wanted him to drive. Inexplicably. So of course, she said, 'Yes, please.'

He pulled his coat collar up as high as possible against the cool April weather. 'One of these days you'll stop being so courteous and I'll know we're finally getting somewhere.'

The drive took about twenty minutes. Conversation was light between them but not because they had nothing to say. She just didn't feel the need to say anything. And besides, the scrumptious dinner was kicking in and metabolising down into a warm goo that leached through her veins. She worked hard to keep her focus sharp while driving Zander's land-yacht.

'Who else lives here?' he murmured quietly as they crossed into the shared entry hall of her apartment building.

She ran her fingers along the four letterboxes by the door.

'Two students, a long-term resident...' She traced the last box; its lettering was cool and smooth under her touch. 'And me.'

She led him through to the back of the entry hall where her door was.

If Mr Lawler came out for one of his late-night cigarettes now he'd be in for quite a surprise. Not that she'd never had a man here before, but not like this...tiptoeing in late at night. All clandestine and exciting...

She turned her key, wiggled it, put her shoulder to the door, and popped it quietly open. It swung inwards into the darkened apartment. 'Acquired touch,' she whispered.

Why was she so breathless? Was it just because she was walking into her home with a virtual stranger? Or was it because she loved her apartment? It was so...her. So if he judged it, he judged her.

She flicked on the light.

His eyes scanned the room, giving nothing away. 'This is...'

Crazy and shambolic? Nothing like the outside? She saw it how a stranger must, the explosions of random colour, the stacks of books and home-beautiful magazines. Trailing plants everywhere.

He touched the nearest green frond. 'How do you get them to look like this inside?'

She crossed to the double doors opening onto her small courtyard and pulled back the blind. 'I rotate them every day. One day in, three days out.'

His eyes swung to her. 'How many do you have?'

It was too dark to see outside, too dark for him to discover the full extent of her guilty pleasure. 'I'm kind of the crazy cat-lady of trailing ferns.'

He looked around him again, then found her eyes. 'It's not what I expected.'

That could mean anything, but she chose to interpret it positively. 'Surprise!'

His focus fell onto the stack of brightly packaged CDs

stacked up on her corner desk. He crossed to them. 'Are you studying?'

'Espionage through history. I'm getting ready for the spy class.'

He flipped one of the CDs over and read the description of the lectures. 'You're doing homework before the class?'

'I like to be prepared. And I'm really looking forward to the spy classes.'

One brow quirked. 'As distinct from the others?'

Heat rose and consumed her in the tiny apartment. 'I listen to them when I'm gardening. On the bus to and from work. Or when I'm walking.'

'You walk?'

'Regularly.'

'Where?'

What was this, the Inquisition? 'Anywhere I haven't been before. Deep in some wood somewhere.'

His nod was distracted. He suddenly looked intensely uncomfortable.

'I bought these with my own money.' In case that was what was putting that deep frown on his face.

'Why?'

'Because your money is for things that interest your listeners.'

He turned towards her. 'You don't have to hide things from me. If there's something you want to do, do it. The money is for you.'

It wasn't him she was hiding from. She took the CDs out of his hands. 'It's not… I feel like these are normal me, not new improved me. Besides, you've already indicated that the things I'm interested in aren't that…exciting.' She cleared her throat. 'For your listeners.'

His eyes fell on her heavily. Searching and conflicted.

'Coffee?' she asked just to break the silence.

He broke free of her gaze, bustling towards the door as

though this were all the most terrible inconvenience. 'No. I should get going.'

And suddenly she was feeling self-conscious for agreeing to *his* request. She followed him back out into the hall. 'Thanks for the lift.'

'No problem.'

He had to stop at the door to the street to negotiate the intricate series of locks. If not for that, she wondered if he might have just flown down the stairs and path and been gone. She opened it for him and stood below the arch.

'And for the restaurant. It was fantastic to see.'

'We'll find you new cooking classes. You don't have to go back to the French guy.'

'The not-French guy...'

'Right.' He practically squirmed on her doorstep. Confusion milled around them both. This *had* been his idea? Or had she just misunderstood?

'Well, see you next time, then,' she said quietly.

'OK. 'Night, Georgia.'

And then he was gone. Not quite running as she'd imagined, but certainly making good time on those long, marathon legs. Into his car and away. Expensive tail lights glowing until they turned onto the high street in the distance.

And still she stood there.

OK. That was just weird. Their whole night had been genial enough, the silence in the ride over here mutual and comfortable. Or so she'd thought. She'd only offered him coffee, not exactly controversial.

Modest, plain but well kept. Was that what he'd been expecting her place to be like? She resecured the front door and turned off the porch light, then crossed back to her gaping apartment door, assessing the inside critically. Shambolic but not unclean. She had nothing to be particularly embarrassed about.

Maybe he had a plant phobia.

She sighed. Maybe this was a Year of Georgia test. See how she was going with the judgement of others. Not well, apparently.

She cared what people thought. She didn't run her life by it, but criticism did impact on her. Especially someone like Zander Rush. Rich, powerful men might not particularly matter to her professional life, but this one mattered to her personal life. She had a year ahead of her with Zander, they were going to be in each other's faces a reasonable amount. She'd really rather not have that time be tense and awkward.

And below that, somewhere deeper that she only peeled a corner back on, lay her secret fear: that the same *lack* that made Daniel not interested in marrying her might have occurred to Zander as he stood here in her little apartment. Some undefined deficiency. Was she too geeky? Too dull? Was she so left-of-normal that even a man whose connection to her was only professional felt the need to run for the hills? If so, he was in for a disappointing year.

There was only so much that reinvention was going to fix.

Zander tossed his keys and wallet into the shallow dish by his bed and then took himself off for a shower. As hot as he could stand it. Desperate to scald himself clean of the sudden tingle of awareness he'd experienced standing in Georgia's apartment just half an hour before. He'd learned to live with the perpetual hum of sensual responsiveness that resonated whenever she was around, but this was different, this was…

Interest.

The prickle of intrigue and the glow of connection. So much more than just sexual. Unexpected, unwanted, and unacceptable. And the slither of empathy, that his words made her doubt herself, made her so defensive.

He stood under the hot, thumping water and let it stream over his head.

The crazy cat-lady of trailing ferns.

Of all the things to suddenly bring this *burbling* inside him to the surface…that little touch of self-deprecation, her modesty about her lived-in, loved-in apartment, her raw defence of a place that was clearly special to her. That was clearly *her*. She defended her property and herself with a gentle kind of resignation. As though she knew full well that she didn't fit the conventional moulds and was reconciled with that.

And he was there telling her that her mould wasn't interesting enough for his listeners.

Then showering himself raw just half an hour later because of how interesting it *was* to him.

Hypocrite.

His life was so laden with false, socially aggressive people, all hungry to climb ladders that they had to jostle for. So full of noise and gloss and professional veneer. He did his best to limit his exposure to it to his working hours, running from it—literally—on weekends, but when you worked as much as he did it had a way of just dominating your consciousness.

Until you stood in the middle of someone's small, packed greenhouse of an apartment and felt as if you'd just walked into some kind of emotional resort. Far from everything and everyone.

Until you breathed in for the first time in fifteen years.

Zander shut off the water, towelled off, and stepped out into his bedroom. Carefully styled by the owner before him, all beige and tones of brown and harmless neutrals he'd never bothered to change. Then he walked out of the hall, into every room one by one, growing increasingly incredulous.

Not one single plant, anywhere? Seriously?

He kept looking, kept not finding one. Until he did. A small cactus in a pot that Casey had given him before she'd twigged to the fact that gifts between them weren't going to do anything but make their relationship more awkward. He'd plonked it on his kitchen window sill and never given it another thought. It survived only on the steam issued by his coffee maker. And maybe the dishwasher.

But it survived.

The similarity to his thorny, parched heart was ironic.

He flicked a switch and lit up the entire length of his rambling back garden. Did it even count if you paid someone to tend it for you? If the most you did was cut roses to take to your aging mother and the only time you walked through it was on a shortcut back from the local coffee house?

The fun Georgia would have if let loose in there...

He killed the lights, plunging the whole garden and that train of thought back to darkness.

There would be no letting loose. There'd be no more curious visits to her apartment. He'd only gone to assure himself that her home would have been as lacking in personality on the inside as the exterior. As some kind of ward against finding her interesting.

Well, that had bitten him well and truly in the arse.

He couldn't blame his complicated mess of interest and appreciation and affection on her botched proposal any longer. Georgia Stone might have started out as the embodiment of every professional and ethical compromise he'd made on his meteoric corporate trajectory—and he still felt the cuts every time someone praised him for the sensational PR surrounding her proposal—but she was rapidly morphing into something else.

A living, breathing, *haunting* reminder of the man he used to be. Before the heartbreak of being jilted by Lara. Before the humiliation that drove him headlong into his intense professional life, and the professional life that drove him headlong into his insane training regime just to balance out all the noise. Before all of those things left no room for an actual life. He missed life. And moments like tonight didn't help him to keep that longing safely tucked away where it couldn't gnaw at him.

But work did. And running did. And he had plenty of both to be getting on with this weekend.

Neither of which were served by flashes of the sheer contentedness in Georgia's face as she stood in the midst of her meagre worldly possessions, richer than he could possibly conceive.

CHAPTER FIVE

May

WEDNESDAY night salsa dancing was an education—a great way to discover she had three left feet and not just two. Georgia danced with a raft of partners of various coordination—some more patient than others—but never Zander. He was always careful to share the love around with strangers, favouring the much older or much younger and discouraging the interest of anyone in the middle.

Her, most especially.

She'd only made the mistake of asking him once.

We're here to work, he'd said.

Right.

This was the side of him his staff saw. Officious. Distant. Work-centric. That other side of him that she'd glimpsed only lasted as long as it took him to tire of the novelty of following her to endless courses and classes and experiences. The more they did together, the less civil he became.

So maybe she'd been demoted to minion in his mind?

The only blessing was that the segments he was producing from their time together in class didn't reflect any of his impatience and ennui. She'd moved past her instinctive cringe at hearing herself as others heard her and let herself enjoy reliving the classes through Zander's eyes. His ears. His art. Because while they were commercial by necessity, they were also pretty good. Floating out across the airwaves once a month.

And she'd busied herself finding things to do in class that didn't amplify this awkward...blech...between them.

Thursday night was Michelin-starred restaurants night and she'd become adept at pretending she didn't know the handsome man at the next table. And at eating alone. There was a certain loveliness that London's service staff reserved for a woman taking a meal by herself. At first she worried that it was pity, but then she realised they just wanted to make her solo experience as nice as possible. She got twice the smiles and extra free bread that Zander did. That pleased her to an unnaturally high degree.

Friday night wine appreciation was at least a blessing because it meant their minds and mouths were both fully occupied and so conversation between herself and Zander really wasn't an option, anyway. But at least the wine class provided quality alternatives in the shape of other men to talk to. And women—but they never got much of a rise from Zander. It was the men that really got up his nose, presumably because it was impacting on the quality of their Year of Georgia project.

She wasn't supposed to be on the hunt. She was supposed to be discovering who she was. And it was working; it turned out she was a woman who liked to goad surly, silent executive types.

She turned to Eric on her left and laughed loudly at something he said. Even he looked surprised to have been that amusing. He developed software apps for a living and he and his techie-mate Russell, on her right, had decided their circle of friends really needed to include someone other than the pair of them. And preferably with the X chromosome.

Hence the wine appreciation.

The three of them developed a healthy symbiosis—they honed their flirting skills on her and she let them. It felt good being appreciated by someone and not just tolerated by Zander. Buoyed by their company, she sniffed and she sipped and she spat and she was careful never to quaff in front of Zander. And, it turned out, she had a pretty good nose and palate for identifying wine types. Unlike cooking, which she'd still not really mastered at all. Though, she wasn't above quietly taking the mickey.

She agitated the wine in her hand until it made large circles in the balloon glass and its aroma climbed. She waved the whole lot under her nose.

'Truculent. With undertones of—' she looked around for inspiration and her eyes fell on the earrings of the woman across from her '—amber and—' she searched again and her eyes fell on Zander '—oak moss.'

Because that was what he always smelled like to her. One of her forests.

Russell's eyes narrowed. 'Really?'

Eric just laughed. 'She's lying.'

She leaned closer to both of them. 'Truly, it just smells like good red wine.' She tossed her sample back. 'Yep. Good.'

All three of them laughed and she turned to place her empty glass onto the cleaning tray, but as she did so she lifted her eyes and encountered Zander's, intense and assessing.

As usual.

Class wound up not long after and she farewelled her friends happily. They always asked her out with them after class. She always declined.

'You can go,' Zander said, suddenly close behind her as Eric and Russell left. 'You're off the clock.'

She bit down her retort. How typical that about the only thing he'd said to her all evening was boorish. 'If I wanted to go I would go. I wasn't waiting for permission.'

'It's Friday night.'

'And this class is my Friday night activity.' Poor effort though it was. She slid her coat more firmly on and headed onto the street.

He stuck to her heels. 'They're going to go off you if you don't give them something.'

She turned and glared. 'Something? A bit of leg? A flash of cleavage?'

'Not what I meant.' He glowered.

'I know what you meant. I'm not interested in anything beyond their company in class.' And—just quietly—the impact it had on Zander. Getting his blood up was at least better than stony silence. 'This isn't about dating, remember.'

'I was wondering if you did.'

She spun and huffed in equal measures. 'I have to talk to someone. You're the only person I know and we're strangers here.' And increasingly everywhere. 'Some of them are going to be men. It's not dating strategy.'

He just grunted. 'This is my Friday night, too, you know.'

She stared. 'I do know.'

'So it would just be useful to keep everything professional. On mission.'

On mission? 'I'm not allowed to have a good time, at all? Doesn't that defeat the purpose?'

'The purpose is you getting back on track. Learning new things. Reinventing.'

A month of standoffishness took its toll. 'I'm not sure that you appreciate how hard some of this is for me. Walking alone into a room full of people I don't know. Striking up friendships. I would so much rather be at home curled up with a good book.'

His eyes clouded over. Was he thinking? Or just bored? 'How hard?'

'It's…difficult. I'm not social, like you. I like to meet people, find out about them, but I'm just not really good at it. It's work.' And developing those skills was part of her twelve-month plan but it was a case of chicken and egg. She needed the skills to be able to walk into any social situation, but she wasn't going to develop the skills unless she kept walking into those situations.

He looked truly astonished. 'I didn't realise. You make it look so easy.'

Was he kidding? 'It's exhausting.'

'Would it be easier to have a friend along?'

'Yes.'

'Let's do that, then. This isn't supposed to be punishment. We can tweak the budget.'

It felt like it some nights. She let out a long breath and added yet another humiliation to her very many. 'I don't have anyone to bring. Not every week.' She could probably get any one of her friends away from their parenting responsibilities once, maybe twice. But weekly? Sometimes twice weekly? Not a prayer. This was the sort of thing she used to rely on Dan for.

Her social handbag.

The great mess that was them struck her again. *Imagine if he'd said yes...*

'I'm here anyway,' he said. 'I'll do it.'

Her heart flipped like a fish. 'You wanted to remain impartial.'

'The situation has changed.'

'You know you'll have to speak to me. Not just interview me or record me talking to others.'

Impatience leaked out of him. 'I've been trying to keep things professional.'

'What's unprofessional about having the occasional conversation?'

'If you're talking to me then you're not talking to everyone else.'

It was a valid point. She was just as likely to talk to him all night given half a chance. But it didn't make it feel any better. 'I promise to multitask. If you promise not to scowl at me the whole time.'

'I don't scowl.'

'You're doing it now. That's just going to scare away anyone that comes close enough to talk to.'

'They'll just assume I'm one of many dates who are there under sufferance.'

'A date with a digital recorder?' He'd started bringing them along to the second and third sessions of each activity. The first was pure reconnaissance.

'That reminds me. I'm going to start recording next week. We have permission.'

'Make sure you get Eric and Russell. Maybe a bit of fame will increase their chances with the ladies.'

He grunted. 'I don't think anything will increase their chances.'

'They're nice men.'

'They try too hard.'

'Doing this *is* hard. For a lot of people coming to one of these things is either last resort or a kind of admission of failure. That you can't be cultured and interesting without help.'

His eyes narrowed. 'Is that how you feel?'

She studied him, wondering if she could trust him. She would have told Zander off a month ago, no problem. But corporate Zander wasn't anywhere near as approachable. Then again, the Year of Georgia was all about taking risks.

'I'm smart, I have a good job, excellent work ethic, property. I'm passable-looking. So what's wrong with me?'

Zander opened his mouth but she barrelled onwards. 'Maybe he would have liked me more if I was sportier, wittier, prettier. Maybe there's a whole range of things that other women out there can do that I can't.'

'This is about Daniel?'

'No. Daniel is Everyman, he's just a symbol. But he was a man so like me I thought we were a perfect fit, so to not even be good enough for him...'

'I thought you were doing this for you. The Year of Georgia.'

She glared at him. 'First—as you've so carefully pointed out—I'm doing this for you. Because your contract says I have to. But right behind that *is* me. And part of me is wondering why I'm not more popular with men. Or with other women. Why I don't have more friends. Or a family yet. Or a better job. Or why my life isn't like other people's.'

He shook his head. 'What do you imagine happens in other people's lives that's so special and different?'

'I don't know. Cool stuff. Busy, interesting, challenging stuff?'

'That's just dressing. Most people's lives are exactly the same underneath. The same worries about finances, their careers, the same family dramas. Only the outer coating changes.'

'What about you—rich, popular, respected, in demand, powerful? You can do whatever you want and go wherever you want whenever you want. That's not the same as everyone else.'

He stopped again and faced her. 'I haven't had a holiday in five years because the network believes the station will collapse if I walk away from it for a moment. I have a big, expensive house that someone else decorated and I can go weeks without even going into rooms that aren't my bedroom, bathroom, and study. I have parents who live in a perpetual state of warfare. That power you covet means people either shy away from me or suck up to me. So my life is riddled with its own hassles but I don't dwell on it and I certainly don't voice it. I just get on with it.'

Such a confession, after weeks of standoffish Zander, struck her deep. Was that really how he felt about his life? Maybe the trappings of success and popularity really were just that.

'Are you saying I should just suck it up?' And shut up.

Maybe that was exactly what she needed to hear? Perhaps her self-reflection was just self-indulgence in disguise.

'I'm saying all the classes in the world aren't going to make your life better, because life isn't something you apply like make-up. It's something you grow and tend. Like a garden.'

Her present life would make a pretty straggly, restricted garden. But a life filled with makeovers and clubbing and movie premieres wasn't all that brilliant, either, unless you happened to discover a new passion. They were just flashy statues amongst the weeds.

She blinked. Thought. Smiled. 'That's kind of profound. We should have recorded that.'

'I have my moments.'

'So am I wasting my time?' Because she certainly hadn't discovered a hidden passion for anything they'd done so far.

'Not if they're things you've always wanted to do.'

They weren't, really. They were things she thought she *should* do. Things EROS' listeners might like. Things that she felt Zander might have expected her to do.

'How locked in is the schedule?'

He squinted one eye. 'Some of them are all booked and paid, some transferable. Why?'

'I think I need to tweak them. To be more…me.'

He smiled. 'OK. Just talk to Casey.'

Just like that? How strange that she felt so uncomfortable asking for what she wanted. When it was so straightforward.

They walked on.

'So, how come you don't fix your life, then?' Her words came out as mist on the cool air. 'Make changes? If you believe so much in the garden of life.'

He shrugged. 'Not everyone wants a garden. Or the hassle of tending it. Sometimes a single focus is just easier.'

His work. Of course. 'But you love running. Your weekends are always full. That's at least a small garden *bed*, surely.'

'I don't do it because I'm passionate about it.'

'Why then?'

'For the silence.'

Hours and hours of silence as his machine of a body put foot in front of foot. 'Just you and the voices in your head, huh?'

He smiled. 'Right. That's all the company I need.'

Suddenly she felt very self-conscious to be standing here taking up his silence. Although she suspected he'd only be working anyway. Fortunately, a tube entrance loomed.

'Well, I guess I should—'

'I have a garden,' he blurted. 'An actual one, I mean.'

She figured that the big house in Hampstead Heath came with a big plot of land. 'OK.'

'I'd like you to see it.'

'Why?'

He paused before answering. 'Because it's lovely. It should be appreciated.'

The man who didn't even use the rooms in his house? She couldn't picture him getting out in the garden. But maybe this whole contract arrangement had some kind of implied reciprocity that she hadn't considered.

Or maybe this was some kind of peace overture. If it was, she'd take it.

'Sure. I'd like to see it.'

'Maybe you can give me some tips on what to do with it.'

'I'm not a landscaper—'

'I'm not looking for shape, I'm looking for soul.' Surprise flooded his face, as if he'd never considered that before.

'A soulful garden. Well, I'm sure I can at least give you some tips.'

'Don't underrate yourself. Look at what you do in your back yard. The life you've invested that three square metres with.'

She considered that. 'When do you want me to come by?'

'How about next Saturday?'

'Aren't you running?'

'I'm doing a night run. I have all day free.'

All day? 'Just how big is this garden?'

He smiled and ushered her onto the tube steps. 'You'll see.'

Enormous was the answer. Gi-flipping-gantic. At least four times the size of the house sitting like a stone sentry on its western edge and that was already very big.

Georgia turned a slow three-sixty from her spot in the middle of the garden's first chamber and surveyed the extraordinary, neglected space. Not physically neglected—the turf was mowed and the pruning regular. But Zander was right: this garden lacked any kind of soul.

'This is amazing.' She looked at him. 'Do you truly not use it?'

'I shortcut through it from the main street.'

Sacrilege. To have a garden like this, to have it be all your own and then never use it.

'There's a lot you could do here.'

'I have brown thumbs.'

'You have something better. Deep pockets. You could hire a team.'

'I don't want a team. I want you.'

She glanced at him.

'Someone like you,' he rushed on. 'Someone with passion for it. To look after it.'

The awkwardness of the moment flailed around between them. *I want you.* She'd practically given herself whiplash snapping her head around to look at him.

'I don't think you'll have any trouble finding someone to do more than just mow and prune. I could give you some names if you like.'

Hers would have been at the top of the list for anyone but him. What she wouldn't give to get to tinker in this garden.

'That would be great.'

She basked in the heat coming off him in the cool mid-morning air. Maybe carb-loading turned you into a furnace. Whatever the cause, she caught herself swaying towards his warmth.

She turned the unintentional move into a full body spin before he noticed it and looked again at the magnificent potential all around her.

'I have hedgehogs,' he murmured.

Her eyes fluttered shut. Of course he did. That was just the final nail in the coffin. 'This is wasted on you,' she said, bleak.

But her soft groan must have communicated her affinity for the space because he didn't take offence.

'Because I don't use it?'

'Because you don't love it. This garden—' she turned back to the west '—this stunning house… These should be in the hands of someone who worked hard their whole life to have it. Not someone who only uses the garden for short cuts and who uses just two of the rooms.' Yet paid a premium for them. 'Why do you stay?'

She'd asked him before but he hadn't answered.

'Come on in,' he hedged. 'I'll show you inside.'

Maybe she'd been rude to say it like that—out loud, to his face—but she truly didn't understand how someone could have all this and not want to spend every waking moment in it.

Inside was the carefully styled twin of outside. Perfectly maintained, but utterly soulless. Like a short-term executive rental.

'Where's your study?' She could hardly ask to see his bedroom, but she was desperate to get a sense of him. Of who Zander Rush really was.

He led her up a sweeping, curved staircase to the upper floor and along a spotless landing. It struck her then that he'd be better off closing off the unused rooms and throwing cloths over all the furniture. She suggested it.

'No. I don't want to live like that. It doesn't take my cleaner long to dust and vacuum. This way it's ready if people come over unexpectedly.'

She slid her eyes sideways. 'Does that happen often?'

Something told her it didn't. She had the strangest feeling she was one of only a few people this house ever saw.

Again, criminal.

A house like this should be seen. By someone.

He paused outside a door and looked at her. 'Welcome to the inner sanctum.'

It felt like that. Privileged. Rare. Something about the air that whooshed out as he swung opened the big timber door. She thought to see some kind of expansive library with ladders and a massive antique desk and dead animal heads lining the wall. Something as grand as the house. She couldn't have been more wrong. It was small but not tiny. Opulently carpeted, tasteful timber desk at the far end, and an array of antique bookcases of all different sizes and shapes and filled with books.

It was charming. And warm. And personal.

And such an unexpected thing given the rest of the house.

She stepped forward and trailed her fingers along the various surfaces. He watched her silently.

'It's lovely,' she said, conscious that he seemed to expect some kind of verdict. 'And comfortable; I can see why you spend a lot of time in here.'

Not as much as the garden, if this were her house and not his. She'd build a nest in the conservatory and hibernate in there.

'I get much more done here at home than at the station.'

'I'm surprised you don't work from home more.'

'There's only so much alone time a man can take.' He smiled. 'Even me.'

She couldn't imagine a busier or noisier Monday to Friday than working in a crowded radio station. She crossed around behind his desk and studied the carved bust by the window. 'A relative? Some famous broadcasting type?'

He shook his head. 'It was in the house when I bought it. I had it moved in here because it seemed a fitting sort of decoration for a study.'

How sad. A beautiful house full of someone else's memories. She turned and skimmed her eyes over the paperwork scattered around a closed laptop on his desk. None of it interested her, but a colourful mini-poster pressed to the surface of the desk by a chunk of granite did.

His next event notice. Hadrian's Wall, Gilsland to Bowness.

The following weekend. She'd never seen a marathon in progress. And it was a public event…

She conveniently ignored the fact that she'd promised him she wouldn't ask to go to one of his events. And that not telling him was just plain creepy.

'Do you cook in your kitchen?' she blurted, steering her focus—and his—away from the notice on his desk.

'With fifteen restaurants in walking distance there's little need, but yes, I have used the oven.'

'I was thinking more about the kettle. I'd love a coffee while I make that list of landscapers.'

And get a better feel for the man himself, and what might have happened to him in his life to make him such an under-committed, over-achieving workaholic.

'Best. Course. Ever!' Georgia said as she hunkered down on the opposite side of a half-destroyed door, chest heaving and brandishing her heavy artillery up near her face.

Zander chuckled from the darkness beyond the flimsy doorway. 'I don't believe it. Have we finally found something you'd have done if you had free choice?'

'Totally! Who knew I'd be so fast at assembling a gun?' She tightened the harness crossing her chest until it was snug again.

'Or cracking a code.'

She leaned back into the artfully decorated set designed to look like a shelled-out building. Less shabby-chic and more… Afghanistan-ic. 'Makes up for being such a lousy femme fatale, I guess.'

'Not everyone's cut out for seduction,' he threw away in the brief moment he peered his head around the doorway to assess the enemy location.

Some of the joy sucked out of her day. Believing it herself was different from having it pointed out by a man. By this man.

'Ready?' he checked.

She shook her doubts free and readied her weapon. 'Locked and loaded.'

'On my count...'

God, this was fun. She braced herself against the wall and waited for 'three'. When it came she surged to her feet and sprinted across the open courtyard, as damaged and rubble-strewn as the rest of the set, with Zander hard up behind her. Halfway across, one of the yellow team popped up out of no-where and aimed right at them both. Georgia dived to her left, crashing into a fake rubbish skip and sliding around behind it only to come face to face with one of her instructors, kitted out in the garb of the yellow team.

'Bang,' he said, popping the barrel of his fake gun hard up to her laser-tag and firing. The lights came on in the arena. He gave her his hand. 'The good news is, you were the last of your team to die. If that's any consolation.'

Yay for her! Last woman standing.

'What happened to Zander?' she puffed.

'The big guy? He got hit by the shot you dodged.'

Her breath caught. *Whoops.*

Sure enough, the look Zander threw her as she stepped out from behind the skip was incredulous. 'I can't believe you let me take that hit!' he accused.

She lifted her weapon and unclipped her body harness. 'I would have died.'

'But I'm your superior.'

She tipped her head back and threw him her sweetest smile. 'Superior at dying, maybe...'

He snagged her arms and pinned them behind her, stepping in hard against her body and glaring down on her. 'Isn't that just like a woman?'

The hardness of his body—all strapped up in military chest plate and pressed up so firmly against hers—stole what little breath she'd managed to recover. 'The sarcasm or the faith-lessness?' she whispered.

He tightened her hands and his eyes bored down into her soul. 'Both.'

'Just because I wouldn't die for you? Is that what you expect of people?'

A shadow crossed his features and he let her hands go. 'Is a little loyalty too much to ask?'

He was taking this very seriously for a game. 'We're highly trained agents. Loyal to no one but Queen and country.'

He grunted.

'Besides,' she breathed, 'just think how guilty you'd have felt for the rest of your military career, letting a woman die for you. It would eat you up and you'd find yourself a hermit, living in a mountain, loving no one and letting nobody in. All bitter and twisted. Useless to MI6. I saved you from a fate worse than death, Agent Rush.'

Although it occurred to her that the description wasn't all that *unlike* the real him. Minus the mountain.

His eyes narrowed. 'Also just like a woman, spinning it so I should somehow be grateful.'

'All right, people,' the instructor shouted over the din, and she stepped away from Zander's warmth, reluctantly. 'Great to see that a full day of spy training has taught you all absolutely nothing about field survival...'

Georgia laughed along with everyone else and glanced at Zander. How long had it been since she'd felt this...light? He took her weapon for her and just held it. As though it were her hand.

Of course it wasn't.

'Next week we'll be looking at surveillance gear,' the instructor continued, 'and having a go at planting a bug on someone.'

She rounded on Zander, eyes wide, and mouthed, *Yay!*

He shook his scraggy head, laughing, and stood back to let her pass in front of him back to the classroom. They stripped off their borrowed military accoutrements—very reluctantly on Georgia's part because she'd been having herself a nice little fantasy about Zander doing that for her—and collected up their belongings.

'Would you truly have wanted me to take that hit for you?' she queried as they walked back towards his Jag a little later.

'It's nice to think someone would.'

She lifted her eyes to his.

'Isn't that what anyone wants?' he said. 'Someone to sacrifice all for them.'

'You don't seem the type,' she murmured, sliding into the passenger seat next to him.

'I'm as susceptible as anyone to grand gestures.'

She laughed as they pulled away from the kerb. 'And you wonder why your staff are frightened of you.' And then, at his frown, 'If death is the only way they can get in your good books. Even metaphorically.'

He stared ahead at the road, letting that sink in.

'You value loyalty that highly?' she risked.

He took a moment answering, but when he did it wasn't with the same light tone that they'd been firing back and forth since the war-games ended. 'I've not had a lot of it in my life.'

'Who from?'

But of course he wasn't going to answer that. And no matter how many hours of fun they'd just had, it didn't give her much of a right to ask.

Instead he turned to her, brightly, and said, 'Want to grab something to eat on the way?'

No. But she wasn't ready to go home alone, either. Maybe she could wheedle some clues out of his assistant, Casey. Now that she was a super spy and all. Then again, Casey probably hadn't stayed as an assistant to a man as exacting as Zander Rush for as long as she had by chatting casually about his private business.

She'd have to be smarter than that.

She matched the brightness of his smile. And the fakeness.

'Sure.'

CHAPTER SIX

June

'IT's a good ten kilometres longer than a regular marathon,' the spectator perched next to Georgia on a fold-out chair said, his eyes firmly on the bend in the road they were sitting by. 'But it's only a club-training day so it doesn't count as an ultra-marathon. It's just a good run.'

Georgia chuckled. Calling a fifty-three-kilometre run 'good' was like calling her drive up from London in her gran's borrowed car 'brief'. Though getting herself to the starting point up towards the Scottish border reminded her just how long it had been since she'd taken herself right out of London.

Too long.

So even if this was the craziest and most spontaneous of bad ideas, it at least had the rather pleasant silver lining of getting her out into fresh, brisk, northern air.

The event didn't run adjacent or even near to the actual Hadrian's Wall remains; disappointing but understandable. The past two thousand years hadn't been kind to them already, the last thing they needed was forty sweaty runners and their support crews plodding along their length. But the route trundled along paved roads and tracks and along a river in one place, and so Georgia was able to drive ahead, park, and set herself up at strategic locations with the other spectators to watch them go by.

She quickly realised that Zander would be in the front half of the pack, though not right at the front. Those spaces were occupied by the elite professional runners and their support crews. But he wasn't too far behind, sans support crew. Last stop she'd practically hidden in the shrubbery as the pack ran by, keen for Zander not to spot her on the side of the road. But as she'd watched him steadily plod past she realised he wasn't paying the slightest bit of attention to the spectators. He was just lost in a zone of his own. The zone that got this tough job done.

She'd had a good poke around a Roman ruin and Hadrian's Wall itself and still been ready at this next vantage point twelve kilometres along for the moment he came jogging along the track.

'Here they come,' the man said in his thick accent, standing. He readied himself with squeeze-bottles of energy drink and a pair of bananas and stepped up to the road edge in case his runner needed supplies. Georgia stepped back into his considerable shadow so that she was partially screened from the runners.

Just in case.

Zander stood out in the field, both for his height and also his electric-green vest top. So she watched for that. Only about a dozen runners passed her before she saw the flash of lime and she tucked back even further into her companion's wake. As before, Zander was totally focused on the path ahead and, not expecting anyone to be out here for him, he wasn't looking for anyone. That meant his eyes were locked forward, determination all over his face, and he sucked air in and blew it out steadily between the thud of his sturdy runners on the track.

A slick gloss of sweat covered most of the exposed areas of his body but instead of making him look hot and miserable, it just made him look...hot. Some men really did sweaty well and apparently buttoned-up Zander was one of them. The all-over sheen defined the contours of muscles that flexed taut with effort and made her imagine other ways he might get that sweaty. And that taut.

She shut down that thought hard as he ran past.

'Is that your guy?' the man next to her asked, his eyes still on the bend in the road up ahead, his bananas and energy drink still outstretched.

'No, he's just a friend,' she laughed. Way too brightly.

The man glanced at her quizzically, as if she'd answered a totally different question from the one he asked. 'I meant is he the one you're here cheering on?'

Heat surged into her face. 'Oh, yes.'

He turned his eyes back to the bend and waited for sight of *his* guy. Or girl. That was how little attention she'd paid to anyone but Zander. 'Next stop you're welcome to one of my squeeze-bottles if you want.'

'Thank you, no,' she said, dragging her eyes back off Zander's disappearing form. 'I'm just watching.'

She picked up her fold-a-chair.

'Well, I'll see you at the King's Arms,' the affable fellow said. 'We'll all have earned a brew by then.'

She hadn't planned on waiting at the end, she'd only thought to watch him for a bit, get a feel for this sport that he loved, and then drive the many hours back to London. But while the idea of sitting waiting to surprise him in a pub didn't appeal, the thought that what she was actually doing was tantamount to stalking appealed even less.

'Yes,' she suddenly decided. 'I'll see you there.'

Late night be damned.

She clambered her way back across the farmer's field to where her car was pulled off the road heading west—the same direction as the pack of runners.

As the afternoon wore on, Zander's form remained steady but the exertion showed in the lines around his mouth and the cords that became more pronounced in his neck and calves.

So even with all his heavy training this wasn't an easy run. The front of the pack certainly made it seem so and she was always gone by the time the rest of the pack went through. But Zander went from the front-runner in the second cluster of runners to the rear-runner in the front group with a brief, lonely stint by himself as he transitioned the ever-stretching gap between them.

Most of the other spectators went to the final checkpoint to cheer their runners across the line but Georgia headed straight for the small pub on the main street. There was no guarantee that Zander would even go there; if he valued his solitude enough he might just clamber back into his Jag and head straight back to London all puffing and sweaty.

And she'd be sitting here for nothing.

But she stayed. She wanted him to know she'd come—even if he might not be all that happy about it. She wanted him to know how much she admired his dogged determination. She wanted to know what time he'd run. Those long waits on the side of the road were great for getting a feel from the regulars on what was a good time, what the stages in the pack meant and why long-run competitors did what they did.

Curiosity and a real sense of anticipation hung with her.

She wanted him to have done well. For his sake.

The front-runners started to appear amid the small crowd in the pub. She recognised some of them since they were the ones she'd been looking at all afternoon. Their arrival at the Arms was a mini-version of the race order. Clearly there was a procedure followed by most competitors—finish, shower, pub.

Her eyes drifted to the door yet again.

The crowd grew too thick in the small pub for her to see the moment Zander actually came through the door, but they spotted each other at virtually the same moment as he turned from the bar. She sucked in a small breath, held it, and smiled.

As casual as you like. As though this were her local and he'd just happened into it. As though she weren't three hundred miles from her local. Sitting on the border of a whole other country.

'Georgia?' His confusion reached her before he did.

She stood. 'Congratulations. That was quite a run.'

'What are you doing here?' It wasn't unfriendly, but it wasn't joyous, either. Had she expected pleased?

She took a deep breath. 'I thought I'd watch you compete. I just wanted to say hello before I headed off.' *Let you know I'm not a stalker.* She reached for her handbag, realising what a desperately bad idea this all was. Not only was she not invited, but she'd intruded on his privacy. Presumed her way into his own space and sporting circle. The least she could do was keep it short.

She threaded the straps of her handbag in her fingers. 'How did you do?'

He shook his head, still trying to come to terms with her presence. 'Good. Personal best for the distance.'

She nodded. 'I saw you make that big break between the chase group and the lead,' she babbled. 'That was exciting.'

He frowned.

'I had lots of time to talk to the spectators,' she confessed, flushing. 'Ask me anything about marathon running now...'

She laughed. He didn't.

Oh, God... 'OK. Well, congratulations. I'm going to go.'

She didn't wait for a farewell, but started weaving her way immediately through the assembled throng. She got to the door before a hand on her shoulder stopped her.

'Georgia...'

She turned. Forced a bright smile to her face. She was getting quite good at swallowing humiliation now.

'I'm sorry,' he said. 'You being here really threw me. I'm not...' He frowned again and looked around at everyone else's support teams laughing and sharing stories. 'I'm not used to having someone here for me. Stay for a while longer?'

One foot was, literally, out of the door. It would be so easy to make an excuse about the sinking sun, the long drive home, and flee. But there was Zander, all freshly showered and apologetic and great-smelling, standing in a room full of excited buzz, inviting her to stay in it. To enjoy everyone else's post-run high. To vacation in his world for just a short while.

She scanned his face for signs of being humoured. 'Maybe for a bit, then. If you're sure you don't mind.'

'Stay. We can chalk this up to a Year of Georgia project.'

The radio promotion. Of course. Everything came back to that.

They returned to the place she'd been seated but someone had taken quick advantage of the vacant seat and slid into it. Zander turned and shepherded her through to an area behind the bar. Still busy but quieter. A small table-for-one in the far corner was empty. It didn't take him long to find a spare chair.

'I'm sorry I didn't see you out on the road,' he started, sinking onto one of the seats.

She waved away the apology. His job was to stay focused on the run, not glance at spectators in case one of them was for him. 'How do you feel after the run?'

'Always the same. Exhilarated. Drained, yet like I could do it all again. I'll feel like a conqueror for a few hours yet.'

'How many recovery days do you have?'

His lips parted in a smile and in this private little corner of the bar it was all for her. 'You really are a quick study.'

Heat filled her cheeks. 'They were quite long roadside vigils.' And lots of listening so that she didn't have to talk too much to strangers.

A genuine smile lit up his face. 'Sorry. I should have run faster.'

They chatted more about the race, the pastime, the rules, and the challenges, and Georgia found herself sinking into his obvious engagement.

'You look totally different,' she blurted.

'In civvies?'

'No. When you talk about running your entire face changes. You become so animated.'

'How do I normally look?'

She gestured to his frown. 'More like that. When you're talking about work. This Zander is...very human.'

His eyebrows shot up. 'Wow. I'm not even human in London?'

What the hell? She'd intruded on his space, she might as well go the whole way. He was a puzzle she wanted to solve. 'You're so guarded in London.'

He shrugged—totally guarded—and she regretted raising it. 'I'm in work mode when I see you. It's not London's fault.'

'Are you saying you're not yourself when you're in work mode?'

'A different part of myself.'

'So which is more you—this Zander or London Zander?'

He squinted as he thought about it. 'I work eighty hours a week so, statistically, being like this is less common. But scarcity just makes me enjoy it more.'

So he liked this side of him as much as she did.

Around them a few people stood, as if on cue. He noticed, too.

'Come on,' he said. 'We have a tradition when we run the wall.'

She followed him out of the King's Arms, feeling very comfortable and welcome in this crowd—with Zander—even though she knew how out of place she was. Such a fraud. A line of them trooped, beers in hand, down to the banks of the tidal flat that had been halfway out when she'd arrived earlier. Now water lapped right up to the banks. The groups split down into small pairs and threes and spread out along the length of the foreshore. It practically glowed with rich, dusk light.

'Solway Firth,' Zander said, taking his cue from a pair of nearby cows and sinking onto the grass. 'Best sunsets in England.'

'And Scotland,' she said, dropping down next to him and looking across the narrow expanse of water that separated the two countries. She wondered what Scots might be sitting on the opposite banks looking at England and sharing the sunset. Then she looked inland. 'What town is that down there?'

Lights twinkled where the tidal flats became a river as the sun lowered.

'Gretna Green.'

'Convenient if we were eloping.' She laughed.

But the mention of marriage dented the relaxed companionship that had blossomed between them since they sat back down at the pub.

'Have you never wanted to get married?' she asked, without thinking about how he might construe such a question. In such a context. With Gretna Green an hour's stroll away.

His answer was more of a stammer.

'Not that I'm volunteering,' she hurried. 'One misguided proposal a year is my limit. I'm just curious. You'd be quite the catch, I'd have thought.'

Understatement.

He took his time answering that. Or deciding how to. 'What self-respecting woman would want me and my insane schedule?'

OK, they were going with flippant, then. 'I think you'd find your postal code and credit limit would be sufficient compensation for many people.' Not to mention the body.

'Many? But not you?'

She blew a breath slowly out and stared into the orange glow of the sunset. 'I would actually be quite choosy about who I married,' she started.

'Despite all evidence to the contrary,' he murmured.

She looked at him. 'It's not like I picked Dan out of a Proposals-R-Us catalogue. I'd known him a while. I really like him as a person. He's bright and dedicated and he has really good family values.'

Would he notice the complete absence of the L-word?

'You two wanted kids?'

She snorted. 'We never discussed a week into the future, let alone years.' Which only made her proposal even more misguided. 'But he'd been looking after his sick sister and her kids for a while. So I got to see it in action. The potential.'

'Family's important to you?'

She frowned, thought about it. 'The values are important. The capacity to love and nurture something to adulthood.'

'Like plants?'

She chuckled. 'Exactly. Kids can't possibly be any fussier than ferns.'

'And that's more important to you than money or an address? Values?'

She looked at him. 'You've seen how I live. Do I strike you as someone who cares much about money or the trappings of wealth?' Or threw them around needlessly?

'Not having it is not necessarily synonymous with not wanting it,' he said. 'I used to have none and I definitely wanted it.'

'Some things are more important than money.'

'So what was the leap year promotion all about?' he asked suddenly. 'If not for the fifty grand. Why put yourself and Bradford through that?'

The sun touched the horizon. 'Did you know that sunsets are only a mirage? By the time we're seeing it touch water, the sun has already dropped below the horizon. Something to do with the curvature of the earth.'

He turned to look. And it wasn't until then that she realised how closely he'd been watching her before. But then he brought his eyes back around. 'I didn't know that. But I do recognise a subject change when I hear one.'

'It's not… I'm not comfortable talking about it.'

'Why? You think I'm going to judge you?'

'I think it might end up in the radio show.'

His face changed, then, in an instant. Back to London Zander. 'Right.'

'Zander…' Her eyes fell shut to block out his offence, but she forced them open again. 'I could barely admit to Dan why I'd done it. I can't tell the whole country.'

I can't tell you. Not without having to ask herself why Zander's good impression mattered more to her than Dan's.

He stared. 'Off the record.'

She dropped her eyes and plucked at the long blades of the estuary bank. 'Do you know what I do for a job?'

'You study seeds.'

'I X-ray seeds. Day in, day out, to find the ones that are incompetent. The ones that aren't viable. The ones that aren't normal. It makes a person quite proficient at spotting the signs of irregularities in others. Or in yourself.'

He stayed silent. Waited for her to connect the dots.

'Everyone I know has paired off. Started families. I felt like I was falling behind.'

There was no judgement, just curiosity. 'Is it a race?'

'No.' She had years of optimum childrearing ahead of her. 'But?'

She lifted her eyes. But the clock was ticking. 'It's hard, being with them and not being able to contribute, to understand. They all have that shared experience in common. They've become so much closer.'

'You were going to get married and have kids just to ensure you could contribute to conversation? That seems extreme.'

Put like that it sounded as ridiculous as it probably was. 'I want what they have.'

'School debt and early grey hair?'

She went to stand. 'I shouldn't expect you to understand. You have so much—'

His fingers caught her wildly flapping ones. Tugged her back down. 'George, sorry. Go on. What do they have that you want so much?'

She stared at where his long fingers held hers. Not releasing them. 'Everything. The package. A man and children to love them. A nice house in the country. Security and someone to celebrate joys with. To be wanted enough for someone to give up their freedom for.' All the things she didn't have growing up. 'Someone to fill all the holes inside me.'

'So Daniel was your gap-filler?'

She stared. Swallowed. Dropped her head with shame. 'Poor Dan. That's awful.'

'Give yourself a break. Everyone fills their gaps with something.'

'What fills yours?'

His answer was immediate. 'Work. Running.'

The only two things he did. They couldn't both be gap fillers, surely? 'What are you filling?'

He stared. 'A whole lot of empty.'

Wow. That was quite a mouthful. There was nothing to say to that. They just stared at each other as the sun fully set. Its sinking took with it some of the magic of the cusp of night and day, breaking the spell she'd been under.

How else could she excuse her revelations of the last few minutes?

She let her eyes refocus over his shoulder.

'It's gone,' she whispered.

'It'll be back tomorrow.'

She nodded. But still they didn't move.

'Why are we here, Zander?' she breathed into the fading light.

He stared at her in the rapidly cooling, darkening evening. 'Because you followed me up here?'

Half of her was terrified he'd just shrug and blame tradition. That this *thing* between them wasn't mutual. But she wasn't about to be put off so easily. 'Here, by the twinkling water as the sun sets.'

'Do you want to leave?' he murmured, eyes locked on hers.

She should. 'No.'

'Do you want to feel?'

Her lungs locked up. Suddenly the grass and cows and water around them seemed to grow as if the two of them had just hauled themselves over the top of a beanstalk, forcing them closer together and making the scant distance separating them into something negligible.

Her pulse began to hammer in earnest.

Zander raised his hand and slipped it behind her head, lowering his forehead to rest on hers. His heat radiated outwards. His eyes drifted shut.

She hesitated for only a moment, then turned her face to rub her jaw along his, twisting inwards, seeking out the lips that hunted for hers. The full lips she'd been wanting to taste since she'd seen them stained with bolognese sauce and a smile in the restaurant kitchen.

Was that how long she'd been wanting it for?

Her breath came heavy and fast and mingled with his. Then she turned inwards, drawn by the plaintive breath that was her name on his lips. Their mouths touched. Sensation sparked between them and birthed a flame, hot and raw. Zander pressed their lips more firmly together, leaned into her. Curled his fingers into the hair at her nape. Georgia pressed a hand to the damp, cool earth and used it to lever herself closer to him, to hold the connection fast. To explore and taste and experience. His breath became hers. Her breath sustained them both. She kissed him harder. Greedy for his taste.

Desire raged up around them as though the setting sun had boiled the waters of the firth and they'd spilled over to the banks where they lay.

And, yes, it was *lay*. Somehow, between one desperate breath and the next, they'd sunk down to the grass and Zander twisted half over her. She couldn't remember getting there. Her entire consciousness was consumed with the press of his mouth against hers and the weight of his body on hers. He leaned on his elbows, both hands free to tangle in her hair, his mouth free to roam wherever it pleased.

And, boy, did it please.

Her head spun, her chest squeezed, her insides squirmed. Every cell in her body cried out to just merge with his. As though they recognised their chemical equal.

It wasn't until his thigh slid down between hers that reality intruded.

For both of them.

She twisted her face away from his and sucked in a breath of fresh coastal air. Sweeter and colder than anything they got in London. It helped to clear her muddled head, just a little.

Zander lifted his lips and stared down at her. Speechless.

'Um…' What more could she say?

Where the hell had that come from?

One minute they were talking and the next she was crawling down his throat, hungry for more of the best kiss she'd ever had.

He pressed back up, grinding closer where it really counted and sending a new wave of heat to her cheeks. He twisted sideways and his heavy, sexy weight lifted off her.

She missed him instantly.

She sat up and blew air slowly through swollen lips.

'Georgia, I—' He cut himself off to clear his throat.

She couldn't bear to hear him apologise, or declare it a mistake or express remorse. Not for a kiss like that. Not him. So she jumped in before he could start again, laughing lightly. Faking heavily. 'Chalk it up to your post-race high? All those conquering impulses?'

He'd conquered her all right—like a Viking. And that thought triggered a rush of new images and sensations. God, how she'd love to just lie back and concede defeat.

Weighing up his choices showed in his face, even in the dim light. 'We could say that.'

She took a breath.

'Or we could acknowledge the chemistry that's been between us since we met.'

Acknowledge it sounded a lot like forgiving it. Releasing it.
Ignoring it.

'Since we met?' Though she still remembered the spark as
he'd handed her the coat out at Wakehurst.

'It had to come to a head at some time.'

'You ignored me for so many weeks.'

'I was trying to ignore *it*. Not you. Our relationship was a
professional one.'

Past tense? 'And now?'

'Now it's going to be even harder keeping things professional.'

'Back in London?' Back in the real world. Where adrenaline-
fuelled kisses and dramatic sunsets didn't happen.

'It would be inappropriate for me to start something with
you.'

'Inappropriate?' She sat up and tucked her knees to her
chest. How politically correct.

He followed her upright. 'I'm the manager of the station
running your promotion. I sign the cheques that pay for your
classes.'

And would do for months yet.

'And it's not fair to you, either. You're not equipped for
something like this.'

She sat back, hard. Shook her head. 'Like what?'

'Something happening between us.'

Not everyone's cut out for seduction, he'd joked back at
spy school, though maybe it hadn't been entirely a joke. She
had failed abysmally at flirting her way to information from
a stranger in class, though Zander's eyes had remained glued
to her the whole time. But that was…you know…a stranger.
And this was Zander.

Totally different situation.

Though maybe not for him. How cruel to kiss her half to

death, to make her feel so desirable, and then to back-pedal so very obviously.

He rambled on. 'This was—'

Fantastic? Overdue?

'—an aberration.'

Pain sliced through her. Could he have found an uglier way of saying it was a mistake? She stared across at Scotland, and would have given anything to spontaneously teleport over to the far bank.

'I should have had more control,' he said. 'This is my fault.'

Oh, please. 'I came up here willingly.'

'Not expecting that, I'm sure.'

No. Definitely not expecting that. She just wanted to get to know him a little bit. But she'd discovered a whole other Zander hidden inside the first one. 'So now what? We just go back to how it was?'

He looked at her.

Did he need it spelled out? 'You ignoring me?'

'I won't ignore you, George. I couldn't, now.'

George. The same nickname her friends used for her. The irony bit hard. 'So then business as usual?'

Silence was nod enough.

She pushed to her feet. 'OK, then. Well, my first order of business is to get back to London before dawn.'

'I'm staying at the Arms. Maybe they'll have a second room?'

Was he joking? Stay anywhere near him and not want to be with him? While he found her so...ill-equipped?

'I have a prep session for the personal makeover tomorrow morning. Measuring and stuff.' Never mind that she'd never felt less like doing anything. Despite—apparently—needing all the help she could get. She grasped her excuses as she found them.

'I'll walk you to your car,' Zander said.

For a guy who had protested so vehemently about her catching the underground home after a couple of wines, he was sure very willing to let her drive a deadly weapon half way across the country with still-scattered wits.

Maybe he wanted her gone as much as she needed to be there?

They walked, in silence, back up the road to her vehicle. The rapid journey from body-against-body and lips-against-lips to this awful, careful distance was jarring, but the cold night breeze helped her to blow the final wisps of desire from her mind like fog from shore.

It was for the better. Almost certainly.

She turned and faced him, a bright smile on her face. 'See you Wednesday night, then?'

Salsa class.

She held her breath. If he was going to pull out of his pledge to go with her, now was the moment it would happen.

He stared down at her, leaned forward as if to kiss her again, but pulled on the handle of the car door behind her instead. 'See you Wednesday.'

Him being chivalrous with the door went exactly no way to making her feel any better about what an ass he'd just been back on the bank of the firth. She grunted her thanks, slipped into her front seat, and slammed the door shut on his parting words.

Drive safely.

CHAPTER SEVEN

THE best run of his life turned into the worst night of his life.

Not the evening—the evening touched on one of the most special moments he'd ever had. But the night, after Georgia drove off so quickly down Bowness's quiet main street… He barely slept that night despite his exhaustion and even Sunday was pretty much a write-off.

He spent the whole time trying to offload the kiss he had stolen from her like a fence trying to move appropriated diamonds. Failing abysmally.

After all these months—even after the stern talking to he'd given himself after getting all touchy feely with her at spy school—why had he let himself slip to quite that degree?

Kissing her. Touching her.

Torturing himself with what he couldn't have.

There were endless numbers of women back in London that he could kiss. And touch. And sleep with if he wanted. Bold, casual, riskless women. Georgia Stone was not one of them. She wasn't made of the same stuff as any of them. She wasn't bold or casual. And Lord knew not without risk.

But then she'd walked into his world, the only woman— the only person—ever to watch him race, to wait with a cold drink and a proud smile at the finish line, and he'd let himself buy into the fantasy. Just for a moment. Then one fantasy had led to another until they were lying in the long, cool grass, tongues and feet tangling.

He'd let himself slip further than any time since Lara.

Worse, to *trust*. And he didn't do trust.

Ever.

He'd finally tumbled into an exhausted sleep Sunday night, but his mood was no better today.

As evidenced by the way his staff were tiptoeing around him extra carefully. Even Casey, who usually only gave the most cursory of knocks before walking into his office, actually stood, waiting, until he gave her permission to enter.

'Zander,' she started, lips tight. She looked as if she'd rather be calling him Mr Rush.

'What is it, Casey?'

'I wanted to…' She changed tack. 'Georgia just emailed these instructions, and I thought I'd better run them past you.'

That got his attention. Not just because the sentence had the word *Georgia* in it, but because his assistant and their resident scientist were thick as thieves, so Casey ratting her out meant something big was going on.

She stood across the desk from him. 'She's made some changes to the programme.'

No big news—Georgia changed things around regularly. He was getting used to it. He stared and waited for more from Casey.

'Big changes.' She held out a sheaf of papers.

'How big?' But as he ran his eyes over them he could see instantly. 'Ankara? Are you kidding me?' He eyeballed his assistant. She took half a step back. 'Ibiza's already booked isn't it?' Their flights to Spain were in a few weeks. Georgia's big holiday. Now she wanted it to be Turkey?

'Actually I can still make changes—'

Not what he wanted to hear.

Casey's mouth clicked shut. She started backing out of the room. 'I'll leave you to read the—'

'Stay!' he barked, though deep down he regretted commanding her like a trained dog. None of this was her fault.

All of it was his. He'd been stupid to give into his baser instincts and kiss her. As though either of them could go back from that.

He flipped to the next page. Georgia had ditched the cocktail-making class in favour of life drawing. She'd dumped aquasphering on the Thames to go on some underground tour of old London. She'd dropped out of salsa and replaced it with belly dancing, for heaven's sake.

'I see spy lessons made the cut,' he snorted.

'Yeah, she loves those—' Again, Casey's jaw clicked shut. As if she suddenly realised she was siding with the enemy.

'Get her on the phone for me.'

'I tried, Zander. She's not answering.'

Right. 'I'll take care of it tonight.' At salsa.

Assuming she went at all.

'I wasn't convinced you'd be here,' he said as Georgia slipped through the dance studio door, quietly, and joined him on the benches. She smiled and nodded at some of their fellow dance regulars. Twice as big as the paltry smile she'd offered him.

'I wasn't sure if the change got approved, so I didn't want to leave them with uneven numbers.'

'What's with the swap to belly dancing?'

She shrugged and glanced around the room. Zander tried again. 'I had no idea you were such a fan of all things eastern. First belly dancing, then Ankara…'

She brought her eyes back to his. Surprised at his snark, perhaps. 'You helped me to see that my list was built out of things I thought I should be doing more than things I actually wanted to do.'

'Come on, Georgia. You actually want to belly dance?'

She kicked her chin up. He might as well have waved a red flag. 'It interests me. It's beautiful.'

Uh-huh. It couldn't have anything to do with the fact that belly dancing was a solo occupation and she wouldn't have to touch him again. 'And what's in Ankara that's of so much more interest than Ibiza?'

Other than less alcohol, less noise, less crowds.

'Cappadocia.'

'And what's that?'

'A region full of amazing remnants of a Bronze-Aged civilisation. You can fly over it in balloons.'

He just stared. 'And that's what you want to do?'

Her hands crept up to her hips. 'Yes.'

'Why the sudden change of heart on all your activities?'

'It's not all that sudden. I don't want expensive makeovers or hot stone massages or guidance on how to wear clothes I'll never be able to afford to buy.'

The dance instructor clapped them to attention.

'Is this about the cost?' Zander whispered furiously. Hoping it really was.

'This is about me. Doing things that matter to me.'

It was her money—her year—to spend however she liked. And it was his job to make even the wackiest list sound like something all EROS' listeners could relate to. But it was becoming increasingly important that it helped Georgia to find her way back to feeling whole. He wanted her whole.

He just didn't know why.

'Partners!' the dance instructor called.

They knew the drill. They'd done weeks of this. He'd gone a little bit crazy getting all the audio he needed, grabs from Georgia, the dance instructor. That should have been heaps. But he'd interviewed just about everyone else, there, too. Every single one of them had an interesting story, their own personal reasons for learning to dance at seventy, or despite being widowed recently or coming alone. And for every single one of them it wasn't about dance at all.

It was about living.

There were thirty interesting stories in this room. But he was only paid to tell one of them.

The instructor clapped his hands again. He and Georgia were supposed to partner up. She was supposed to step into his arms, assume the salsa start position. But the stance they were supposed to assume was the vertical version of the one they'd found themselves in a few nights ago: lying there in the long grass as the sun extinguished in the ocean.

A little bit too familiar.

A little bit too real.

She hovered indecisively. And again, this was his mess to sort out. He was the one who'd failed to control his wandering thoughts and hands that night. He was the one who'd lacked discipline. Folded to his barely acknowledged need for human contact.

He stepped closer to her, kept his body as formal and stiff as he could. Raised his hands. 'Georgia...?'

Her smile was tight, but she stepped into his hold carefully, and stood—just as stiff, just as formal—close to his body. As the music began he did his best not to brush against her unless essential—out of respect for her and a general aversion to self-torture—and they stepped as they'd been taught, though nowhere near as fluid as it had been in the past.

It was as clunky as them, together, now.

But it was functional.

The instructor drifted around correcting posture, demonstrating steps, voicing words of encouragement, but when he got to the two of them he took one look at their total disconnect, his lips pursed and he said in his thick accent, 'Not every day is magic. Sometimes this happens. You will have the magic again next week.'

No. There would be no magic next week. There would be no salsa next week. And the guilt in Georgia's eyes confirmed exactly what he'd suspected. This sudden change to belly dancing was about *him*.

'I could have just stopped coming,' he gritted as she moved close enough to hear his murmur.

She drifted away again. But he knew the steps would bring her right back. He tried to read her face and see if she was going to feign innocence or not.

'I wanted something that didn't force us to dance together,' she breathed, her total honesty pleasing him on some deep level. A level deep beneath the one where he hated what she was suggesting. 'The only other solo option was pole dancing. Belly dancing seemed like a decent compromise.'

And suddenly his mind was filled with poles and Georgia and seedy, darkened venues. He forced his focus back onto the key issue.

'What about the segment?'

'You've got more than enough for a salsa segment. In fact, why do you have so much? You'll never use all of that in a two-minute piece.'

Prime-time air was too expensive to dedicate more than two minutes a month to the Year of Georgia. So why had he spent all that time recording everyone else in the session as well? 'The laws of documentary-making,' he hedged. 'Get ten times more than you think you'll need.'

'This isn't a documentary,' she reminded him, her breath coming faster with the dancing. 'It's a stupid commercial promotion.'

Stupid. Nice.

But he was too distracted remembering the last time she'd been this breathless to argue.

He yanked her towards him as the funky music crescendoed. As usual the whole room was slightly out of synch so what was supposed to be a passionate crash of body against body always looked like a vaguely geriatric Mexican wave.

She pressed against his chest, staring up at him, angry colour staining her cheeks. 'I've changed my mind.'

'About what?'

'My reluctance to have a stranger come along with me. You can go back to your paperwork and give me the work-experience kid as far as I'm concerned.'

'You think our schedules are that elastic? That I can just make a change like that with no warning? Disrupt everyone's plans every time you change your mind?'

'It's called dynamism, Zander,' she gritted. 'Maybe your station could use some.'

OK, now she was just picking a fight.

He stopped when he should have twirled her into open position. She stumbled at his misstep. Then he curled his hand around hers and hauled her back towards the door. A few eyes followed them, including the speculative ones of the instructor.

'Next week!' he shouted at their backs. 'Magic!'

She shook free as soon as they hit the cool June air. 'What are you doing?'

'What's going on, Georgia?'

'Nothing's going on. I just realised that I needed to be true to myself or this whole thing is a crock.'

'Which part is being true to yourself? The part where you start switching all our plans around or the part where you'll do just about anything not to get too close to me.'

'*Aberration,*' she parroted back to him. 'That was your word, Zander. You wanted things back on a professional footing.'

'Not at the expense of any civility at all between us.'

Her breath hissed out of her. 'The changes I'm making are trying to keep things civil. So they don't end up like this every night.'

Boundaries. She was stacking them up and he kept knocking them down. Why? He should be thanking her. He took two deep, long breaths. 'We just kissed, Georgia. Heat of the moment, influence of the sunset, romance of the wall. Whatever you want to call it.'

He had to call it something, otherwise he was just a jerk for hitting on her while she was still vulnerable from her breakup with Bradford.

'Who are you trying to convince, Zander? Me or yourself?'

That was a damned fine question. 'It doesn't have to change anything. We just agree to let it go.'

'Just like that?'

Sure. He was a master at denial. 'I have a job to do and you have money to spend. Let's just focus on that.'

'You don't object to any of the changes?'

'I don't care what you do with the money, I just want you to be—' he caught himself a half-breath before saying *happy* '—comfortable with it.'

'I'm hoping I'll be more comfortable this way. Forcing myself to do things way outside of my usual interests was probably a mistake. I was trying to be someone I'm not.'

'Why?'

'Because I thought it was what was expected. What your listeners would expect. What you wanted.'

Her eyes flicked away and he struggled with the deep satisfaction that she'd done any of it for him. 'Listeners are the first to spot falsity on air. If it's not of interest to you it's going to show in the segments.'

She nodded. 'Well, hopefully we've taken care of that now.'

We. He liked her accidental use of the collective. For the same reason he liked coming along to these crazy classes even though he had much more efficient things to be doing with that time. It legitimised his being with Georgia. He could play at relationships without actually being in one. Enjoy her company without the commitment. She was generous with her wonder and excitement doing new things and he could live off that for a whole week back in the soul-destroying environment of the station.

If he spaced it out right.

Kisses… Those he could live off for a year.

She chewed her lip. 'Should we go back in?'

Her reasons for changing classes were valid. The more he had to put his hands on her, the harder it was going to be taking them off. 'No. Let's just call it a night.'

'Sure.'

Courteous but cool. It bothered him enough to glance down the street for the nearest coffee shop. He saw the blinking LED sign a few blocks down. So much safer than having her in his house. So much safer than a bar with a few drinks under his belt. So much safer than the back of a black taxi, pressed together for twenty minutes.

'Let's grab a coffee,' he said and turned her west.

Georgia did her best not to flinch at the feel of Zander's hand at her lower back. It was just a courteous gesture. Unconscious. It didn't mean a thing. Even if it did feel more intimate and personal than the salsa clinch they'd been in just moments before. Something about the way it failed to entirely disengage even once she was fully moving...

It took a few silent minutes to get to the Tudor-style coffee shop. Then a few more to get seated and settled and their drinks ordered.

She struggled to not be distracted by his long fingers tapping on the tabletop—fingers that had traced her skin so beautifully just nights ago and curled so strongly in her hair. But if she looked at his face she'd either drown in his eyes or start obsessing about his lips.

All of which were entirely off limits to her now. Despite the torment of the taste-test after the marathon.

So she fluctuated between looking at the place where a lock of his hair fell across his forehead, a spot of fluff on his collar and glancing around the room at the other patrons.

'Tell me about Ankara.'

That managed to bring her eyes back to his. 'Now?'

'I know nothing about it and I'm going to be going with you. Why is it so special?'

'Cappadocia.' Amongst other wonders.

He shrugged. 'Old cities and ballooning. That's it?'

She pressed forwards against the table. 'Seriously? You can't understand why someone would want to float high above a city where houses and chapels are carved into the rockfaces? Where entire communities used to live underground to hide from invaders two thousand years ago? Cities that were founded twenty centuries before Jesus?'

He just stared. 'You're serious?'

Excited warmth warmed her cheeks. 'Where else could you do it? It's so intriguing...'

'It's not to put me off?'

'It's not about you at all.' *Lies!* 'It's something I'd like to do. I saw it in a documentary years ago and I've never forgotten it.' And if Zander came along, bonus. Good things happened to them when they got out of London. Things just tended to go south when they were back in it.

His eyes burned into hers. Deciding. He slid his recorder up onto the table. 'OK. Tell me more.'

She did. For the next hour and a half. All about Göreme, where she wanted to stay, all about Cappadocia's extraordinary ancient lunar-scapes and traditional villages and the amazing peoples that had lived there for forty centuries. All about how it had wheedled its way under her skin all those years ago.

'And you can stay in these underground buildings?'

'They carve them out of the side of enormous rock faces. And they've been modernised. Electricity, water. They even have Wi-Fi. So you won't be slumming it.'

He'd been smiling for the last five or six minutes straight, though she knew she wasn't saying anything funny. His eyes practically glittered looking at her.

'What?'

'You just...' He struggled for the right words. And he turned the recorder off. 'You *love* life, don't you?'

Generally, she just endured life. But maybe that was because she'd been missing the best of it. 'I love the possibilities.

I love that you've given me this opportunity and I'm going to do something I've always wanted to. I couldn't do this without you.'

'Without the station,' he clarified.

Right. Just in case she was thinking he was doing this for *her.* 'Without help.'

'You might have got there by yourself. Eventually.'

'Maybe not. I was this close—' she pinched her fingers '—to consigning myself to the role of wife and mother. That would have meant a lot less flexibility and freedom for a really long time.'

He shrugged. 'A different kind of adventure, perhaps?'

His words sank in. If marriage was an adventure, then shouldn't you enter into it with someone that you'd want to be adventurous with? Discover new worlds with? Fly across a lunar landscape with. Her breath tightened up. She said the first thing that came into her head in order to stop anything more inappropriate appearing there.

'Is that what you think marriage is? An adventure?'

'I used to.' He pressed his lips together the moment those few tiny words voiced.

The unexpected glimpse into his past was tantalising. She wanted more immediately. 'Is that why you created the Valentine's promo?' she fished. 'To celebrate marriage?'

His answer was fifty-per-cent snort. 'Definitely not. I created the promo to cash in on the leap year commercialisation. Nothing more.'

Well, that was depressingly cynical. 'You don't think matrimony is worth celebrating?'

'On the whole I think marriage is highly overrated.'

She stared at him. 'I guess that shouldn't surprise me. Otherwise you'd have been snapped up ages ago.'

One expressive eyebrow lifted. 'You don't think I'd have done the snapping?'

'You strike me as a man who gets what he wants. If you

wanted a wife in that big lonely house of yours there'd be one there now.'

He drained the last of his second coffee. 'You have a very high opinion of my desirability. Not everyone would agree with you.'

His staff perhaps? 'Maybe you work too hard keeping people at a distance…'

'You're here.' He tossed it out like a challenge. 'I can't seem to shake you at all.'

His light words filleted her neatly along her ribs. Although, she could see he wasn't saying them to be cruel. In fact, if anything, he looked more engaged and more intent than ever. And positively mystified.

'I'm particularly uncaring about societal niceties,' she murmured. 'I'm sure there's been a hundred not-so-subtle hints I should have been taking.'

If she weren't so busy looking for hints that he might be more interested than he was letting on. Maybe than he even knew, himself. But for every sultry look, for every gentle touch, for every unexpected waterside kiss there was a frown, pressed lips, words like *professional* and *aberration*. And *ill-equipped*.

They kind of cancelled each other out.

'Besides,' she braved on, 'I'm not your target market.'

His eyes narrowed. 'Really? Who is?'

She looked around. A lone woman sat reading a thick book in the far corner. Her perfectly manicured nails were the exact same shade as her shoes. 'Her. Maybe…' She looked around for someone else. 'Maybe her?'

Two glamour queens in one coffee shop. Convenient.

Zander looked around far more subtly than she had. 'They're both very attractive.'

Of course that would be the first thing he noticed.

'And stylish,' he went on.

'And well educated.' She nodded to the woman with the thick hardback. 'She's reading Ayn Rand.'

'And that's who you think my target market is? Stylish intellectuals?'

'I can see either one of them in your house very easily.' Much as it galled her to admit it.

His grey eyes pierced her. 'Can you see them sitting on the side of a weather-beaten old track for an hour making conversation with the locals while waiting to hand me an energy drink?'

She just stared. Because, no, she couldn't.

'So maybe my target market isn't as clear-cut as you think?' His chin rested on his steepled fingers and he lifted it enough to tilt his head.

Maybe not.

'It's a moot point, anyway,' she breezed. 'If you're not actually *in* the market.'

He started to answer that but then changed his mind. His mouth gently closed again without making a sound.

'So three weeks before the underground cities?' he hedged, after a moment.

'And two dance classes before then.'

'What about my garden?'

She studied him. This man was more baffling than any of the complex scientific mysteries she'd studied at university. His garden had sat there, untouched, for years. Now suddenly he wanted it to progress immediately? 'What about it?'

'Don't you want to see how it's progressing?'

Did she want to see what some other lucky sod got to create with? 'When it's done.'

It was never too late to implement some self-restraint.

That triggered a couple of lines between his brows. 'Guess I should trade in my dancing shoes and get onto a visa for Turkey, then.'

'Ten minutes and ten pounds at Heathrow.' She nodded. 'I checked.'

He considered her. Then smiled. 'You're really excited.'

There was something looming on her horizon and every

cell in her body told her it had something to do with Turkey. It had been swaying her away from Ibiza almost the moment she agreed to Spain. Making her look east. Agitating subconsciously for her to change her mind. And then, the moment she'd made her decision, this odd kind of emotional hum had commenced and it had been slowly building ever since.

Ankara. Cappadocia.

Something was going to happen there. Something life-changing. Something that felt almost fated. Briefly she wondered how she ever would have found her way there if not for the disaster that was her botched proposal, if she hadn't met Dan before that. And suddenly everything started to feel very…

Meant.

Excited? About standing on the edge of something so huge and new?

'You have no idea,' she breathed.

Georgia stood at the door to the curtained-off change area in the dance studio and hovered awkwardly in the doorway. Possibly she hadn't thought this through as thoroughly as she might have.

Imagine that.

'Off you go…' the woman behind her nudged. Emma. A friendly, motherly sort. A total born-again about belly dancing, given she'd only been coming a few weeks herself.

Georgia took a deep breath to quell her nerves. Maybe belly dancing wasn't the best choice to get away from the close body contact with Zander, the brushing and heated touching. Salsa was, at least, a partnered thing. It wasn't Zander sitting on a seat in the corner watching her wiggle and jiggle and cavort around semi-naked.

Even if it was very prettily semi-naked.

Turned out one of the things this class loved the best was a newcomer. A newcomer who turned up in the middle of a semester and in a tracksuit. The lesson of the day went on hold and all the women helped rifle through the dress-up box of spare belly-dancing bits to put a full costume together—educating her the whole time about each piece's name, purpose, and heritage—then they thrust them at Georgia and thrust her into the change room.

Zander sent his digital recorder in with one of the ladies to capture the sounds of the excited chaos and was cooling his heels out in the dance area, getting the necessary permission forms all ready for their return.

Georgia glanced in the mirror. Her full, beaded skirt fell from her hips down to brush the floor and the matching top-piece they'd selected for her was equally modest—no worse than the vest tops she often wore at home in summer—cupping her small breasts and cascading stringed coins down in a V to point at her exposed belly button. She'd never before mourned her slim build—in fact her curvier friends had envied her for it—but standing here amongst the luscious curves and gener-ous breasts and gorgeous outfits of the other women in the class she'd never wished more to be curvier. Rounded instead of flat.

And Zander was about to get an eyeful of all that flatness.

Emma pinned Georgia's face veil up behind her ear and gave her a shove.

'Out you go, love. Get it over with.'

Then they all rushed out, ankle bells ringing, dragging her along in their bright, jangly wake.

Zander's eyes locked on her the moment she stepped out. How he spotted her amongst so many disguised, Technicolor women was a mystery. Unless he was just looking for the only boyish figure in the room.

She shrivelled up inside, instantly. This had to be her most foolish of fool-moments…

The woman he'd given his digital recorder to returned it to him with a flirty smile, and he flirted right back. In fact, from that moment on he seemed to become entranced by every other woman in the room and—God love them—they enjoyed his presence just as much. Far from being shy about the presence of a strange man in this heavily female environment, the room full of housewives, teachers, and bank clerks dressed in little more than sexy pyjamas lapped it up, escaping into their dance personas and focusing their attention on the only man in the room.

They weren't gratuitous—they seemed respectful of the awkwardness of Zander's position—but they were thorough. They zeroed their efforts on him and unleashed the full force of the moves for his benefit.

He grinned his way through the whole thing.

But avoided looking at her at all.

Small mercy, perhaps, given how hot she flamed and how stumbling her movements were. But she'd signed up here for a reason—actually two reasons—and she wasn't in a hurry to go back to the close, breathy, partnered clinch of salsa nor to be doomed for ever to being *not cut out for seduction*.

She lifted her chin, willing to bet that every woman in this room turned up in a tracksuit the first time and had to ease their way into the rhythmic gyrations they were currently exorcising on an indulgent Zander. And every one of them must have felt exactly as out of place and outclassed as she now did.

But had they ever felt as invisible? Despite the raunchy outfit?

Or was she deluded in thinking the draped fabrics and accenting jewels were attractive? Maybe where she saw rich, sensual colour, he saw tacky, flashy glitz.

She turned back for the change rooms.

'Not yet, love,' the instructor called, leaving Zander to fend for himself against the barrage of oestrogen and turning Georgia away from the gaggle that shielded her from his *non*-gaze towards the large mirrors lining the wall.

She forced her focus on the instructor, keeping one eye on the professional moves and the other on her own reflection, mimicking the basic choreography, taking correction, and trying to repeat the positions and sequences of the more experienced dancers.

Keeping her eyes steadfastly off the man in the background the whole time.

Belly dancing wasn't about sex, the instructor told her, correcting Georgia's too-jerky hips. It was about empowerment. But right now she felt pretty darned sexy. And that wasn't something she could remember feeling in the past.

Pleasure, sure. But not sexy. Not…sensual.

The fluidity of the moves started to come more naturally, and the way the soft fabric brushing against her bare skin accentuated and teased her senses. It made her feel so…alive.

Between the concentration, the keeping of her arms above her head, and the surprising amount of effort required to gyrate everything that needed to be gyrating, her colour and her breath were up in no time. And with rows of dancers between her and the only distraction in the room she was able to concentrate better, forcing the embarrassment away with her focus and determination. It took no time at all to realise that every woman here wore a mask, something they slipped on with the beautiful fabrics. She might not be naturally seductive but, by God, she'd learn to fake it. Under her veil, she could be anyone she wanted. Sexier, smarter, stronger, more fun, more delightful—everything Zander and Kelly and Dan and her mother thought she apparently should be.

She twisted and twirled and undulated to the throng of the music and kept her eyes firmly locked on her own reflection in the mirror. She took a few more risks. She turned and twirled and kept only half an eye on what Zander was doing as he wandered the room, recording the music and the vocalisations of the women who danced for—and around—him.

He seemed totally uninterested in her presence.

Anger fuelled her moves, turned them more defiant.

Really, Zander? Even this isn't enough…?

She spun back to the mirror, tired of trying to be what other people wanted and failing. Tired of making her decisions based on priorities that weren't her own. She was going to be wild and sexy and beautiful just because she could. Here, in this place and in these clothes, she could.

Zander could go jump.

She slowly raised already-aching arms above her head, her concentration focused on the serpentine movements of her hands, the slow twists, the way the dozens of borrowed bracelets jangled and spun on her undulating wrists. She swayed and rolled and let her head fall back, her eyes close, and just felt the music, felt the movement of the women around her.

And she danced purely for the pleasure of it.

And then she lowered her gaze back to the mirror, back to her own flushed reflection and sparkling eyes.

Straight into Zander's.

Everyone else in the room danced on, the instructor dissolved tactfully back into the throng and the odd person danced across the gap between them. But it did nothing to shake Georgia's gaze free of Zander's.

Every part of *old* Georgia screamed to stop. Still. On the spot.

Yet her body kept moving. Fluid, teasing. Flirting.

And just like that she felt the empowerment kick in.

Two hours ago she wouldn't have been able to brush up against him without feeling self-conscious, but behind the veil she could do anything. Be anyone. She could look at him as she'd so desperately been wanting.

She danced on. His recorder hung, ignored, by his side.

Around them, the music faded slowly, the chat-level rose. A door opened on the far side and someone's husband tiptoed in with a small boy in tow, both of them dressed in football colours. The balance between make-believe and real-world started to shift back.

Georgia lowered her arms, and her eyes. And she turned.

Zander still watched her, though his own expression was as guarded as hers must have been.

'That was fun,' she said, still breathing out the exertion. Not ready to lose the rush of empowerment.

He looked around them. A few covert glances looked back. 'For everyone, it seems.'

'Great workout.' But all that did was draw his eyes to the heaving rise and fall of her tiny, beaded top. And he didn't speak, just nodded his agreement.

'I'll just get changed. Won't be a minute.' She knew what came next. He always liked to interview her right after the first class, to capture her first impressions. She wasn't sufficiently clothed or her breath sufficiently recovered to do that just yet. She followed a couple of other women into the change area. Most went home exactly as they were so it was just the few of them, all newer participants, returning to street wear.

They chatted excitedly as they stripped off the layers of magic and mystery and slid themselves back into their clothes. Just one hour ago being in her underwear in front of strangers was excruciating. Now they were sisters. Lumps, bumps, big, small. The thing that had shifted inside her wasn't switching back.

The three others had only been coming weeks and were curious whether she'd enjoyed it, whether she'd be back. She knew, without question, that she would.

'I hope you're bringing *him* every week,' Emma said. 'Way to change the dynamic!'

They all laughed.

'No one means any offence by dancing for your man,' another said. 'It's just the novelty.'

'He's not my man,' Georgia was fast to correct, though low so that Zander wouldn't hear them through the flimsy fabric walls.

That caused more hilarity. 'Oh, love,' Emma whispered, 'if he's not I think he soon will be. We all saw his face while you were dancing. He's wound as tight as a drum. It would be a shame if no one was to benefit from all our good work tonight.'

Georgia stopped one leg halfway into her tracksuit bottoms and stared at the women. They laughed wildly again. She understood exactly. A weird kind of adrenaline was still coursing through her body, too. She would have joined their laughter if the suggestion hadn't thrown her into such a breathless stupor. And an unshakeable vision of her *benefitting* from tonight's endeavours.

She tidied her hair, carefully folded her borrowed costume items, and placed them in the washing pile, and then dawdled a moment longer. Delaying the inevitable. She wasn't sure she could walk out there and see Zander if the women with all their speculation were still around.

The longer she took, the fewer people would be in the room.

But eventually she couldn't delay any longer. He needed his interview. She rolled the waistband of her running pants down to be more like the beautiful women she saw at the gym, more like the low-hung skirt that had just caressed her legs. More casual. As if this weren't an enormous deal. She took a deep breath and stepped out of the change area into the dance space. Only a handful lingered. None of them was male. After the events of the evening she couldn't really blame Zander for stepping outside so that he didn't have to face his unexpected seductresses in the full fluorescent light of indoors.

She thanked the instructor warmly and whole-heartedly, assured her she would be back the following week and stepped out into the cool night air.

She looked left.

She looked right.

She looked across the road in case he was leaning on the lamppost, waiting.

Her stomach clenched. Nothing. No Zander anywhere.

They'd arrived separately but she saw him pull up so she knew where his Jag was. Tucking her crossed hands under her armpits, she hurried down the road a way in case he was waiting in his car. But there was just a dry rectangle on the otherwise rain-dampened road where his Jag had been.

Gone.

Her jaw tightened. Maybe he'd gone for a drink with one of the other participants in the class. Maybe he'd formed a connection with someone in particular while she was so busy ignoring how he was ignoring her. But that seemed both unlikely and unfair to Zander—he wasn't a complete jerk. His absence didn't automatically mean he'd scarpered with some hot, bejewelled stranger. It just meant he hadn't stayed to see her.

That probably should have made her feel better.

But it didn't.

All that power, the erotic blast, the sensual costume…the out and out *risk* she'd taken forcing herself to let those secret feelings show on the outside. All that had done was sent Zander running. So embarrassed by her display that he couldn't even stick around to face her.

She'd thought maybe he was being tactful, keeping his eyes averted, trying to make a difficult class that bit easier for her. That maybe he was more affected than he was letting on. She'd thought that burning, blazing moment in the mirror might have been sensual desire pumping back at her.

But what if it was anger? Or discomfort.

A tight ball settled high in her chest. Maybe he was just plain embarrassed. Just because he'd admitted to there being some chemistry between them didn't mean he wanted it there. Or wanted to do anything about it beyond the kiss they'd shared—some lousy accident of adrenaline.

She hooked her thumbs under the curled waist of her pants and let them unravel back to their usually modest position. She flattened them down with unsteady fingers as deep sorrow washed through her.

That was it.

She was done.

If who she was just wasn't enough for the high standards of Alekzander Rush, then so be it. She liked Georgia Stone. Lots of people did. And not because she was a carbon copy of everyone else spilling out of London's entertainment district, but because she was *her*: loyal and bookish and fond of long, quiet walks in ancient forests and lazy afternoons with girl-friends tucking into a steaming ale pie.

She'd set out on the Year of Georgia to find out who she really was and—surprise, surprise—she'd been there all along. And it only took her half a year.

She turned and walked the block back to her car.

And if Zander didn't like the Georgia she'd uncovered, well…his loss.

CHAPTER EIGHT

August

THERE really weren't enough showers cold enough or long enough to get the haunting, hot mirror scene out of Zander's mind. It was all too easy to cop out when you were the boss, when you had staff to do things for you.

Minions.

He'd never felt the distinction so clearly until he had Casey ring Georgia up and let her know he wouldn't be coming to belly-dancing classes with her any more. That she was OK to go to them solo. That he got what he needed that first night. It wasn't hard to find an excuse. Salsa was on a Wednesday night. Belly dancing was on a Tuesday. He had network meetings until late on a Tuesday.

Not so late that he couldn't get across town to the dance studio, in fact, but it was too convenient an excuse to pass up. There was no way on this green earth that he was setting foot back in there while Georgia was around.

He'd already been back to see the instructor, to get from her the interview he'd been too much of a coward to get from Georgia right after her first class had finished. It was only the fact that her borrowed car was parked virtually outside the door to the dance studio that made it even remotely OK that he'd just bolted on her. Left her there alone.

What a class act.

She hadn't called him on it. Or emailed. Or even asked Casey what was up with her coward of a boss. And that said a lot about how she was feeling about his disappearing act. Defiant. Irritated.

Possibly hurt.

But getting hands-on with her was no better an idea now than it had been up at Hadrian's Wall. And so walking out of there seemed like the most prudent action at the time. He'd spent a lot of time and energy avoiding emotional entanglements, focusing on his career; this was really no different. If spending time around Georgia was making it too hard to keep her at arm's length, then there was really only one solution.

Getting Casey to do his dirty work for him—well, there was no excuse for that. He'd just needed some space from the mirror scene before they headed off into the wilds of Turkey together.

But that was only effective if he could exorcise the memory branded into his brain.

And three hours in the air and three more in a car—no matter how luxurious—was a lot of nothing to try and fill with other thoughts.

Another cowardly act. Getting Casey to shift his flights so that they weren't travelling together. That bought him precious more hours to build up his reserves against Georgia. To get through the weekend in Turkey. Both of them had jobs to be back for come Monday morning so this was the most fleeting of Turkish experiences. But he'd re-routed through Istanbul whereas Georgia was touching down in Ankara. Again, precious hours for last-minute fortification.

'Göreme.'

His driver slowed on the limits of a village. At first glance it looked much like the extraordinary landscape they'd been driving through for some time: gorgeous, golden rock faces, enormous jutting spurs of sandstone. But as they got closer Zander started to notice the details. Square edges, dark windows, balconies, a layer-cake of dwellings carved into the rock face. They drove more fully into town and it looked much like any other, people milling around stone storefronts with brightly painted signs on them, cars angle-parked in front for the convenience of shoppers. But behind it—towering high behind it—a rock face filled with homes.

And hotels. Like the one he was heading for.

They pulled around a corner and the whole city unfolded before him. A mix of enormous stone monoliths surrounded by carved homes. And nearly a dozen bright colourful balloons drifting silently overhead. The sharp protrusions of the rocks contrasted with the square edges of the façades of the cave-houses and the bulbous curves of the hot-air balloons, which dropped insanely low to give their passengers a good look at one of Cappadocia's underground cities.

The whole thing was bathed in a golden, afternoon light.

Zander wound his window down and breathed in the air—sweet, fresh and carrying a distinctive tang. Was it apples?

He asked his driver.

'Shisha,' he said simply. The apple-flavoured tobacco smoked by the locals.

The car stopped in front of a stone hotel that reflected the shapes of the entire city. Square edges of the block construction of the fascia of the hotel, the rolling curves of the darkened archways that led deep into the rock face, and the sharp, zig-zagging stairways that led up the mountain face to the dwellings higher up. But the closer he looked, the more detail he saw.

Intricate carved patterns around the doors and windows. Niches everywhere filled with bright intriguing ornaments, and potted colour spilling from every available surface.

Clearly the Cappadocians loved their plants as much as Georgia did.

Georgia.

He looked up the length of the building, at some of the balconies carved into the rock face, as if she'd be standing there waiting for him. A beautiful smile on her face. Bouncing on her toes the way she did when she got excited.

He forced the image away. That kind of thinking was barred, too.

It took a few minutes to register in the small, cool interior of the hotel reception. From where he stood he could see five possible exits. A set of stairs going up, another set twisting Escher-style around to the left and down, a small archway and a larger one to its right and the view behind him after his climb to the hotel's entrance. A balcony wall dotted with pot plants and with an old shingled sign saying *Reception*. A ginger kitten rubbed its cheek contentedly on the sign while another slept curled around the base of the plant in the pot. And behind them, the extraordinary expanse of the city.

'This is amazing,' he murmured to himself.

'Welcome to Göreme,' the young girl said in confident English. Better than his driver's. And certainly better than his own Turkish. 'This way.'

He followed her through the labyrinthine interior of the hotel, instantly feeling the heat of the desert afternoon drop off as the earth's insulation did its job. The walls, windows and stairs of the hotel were all carved from the surrounding mountain.

'I hope you will be comfortable here,' the girl said, pausing at a landing with a timber door. She pushed it open. The room inside was enormous and open-plan. Carved entirely out of the ancient limestone, its walls streaked with eons of stratification. On one side, a large window faced the bobbing hot-air balloons outside, streaming golden light in from the west.

Polished timber floors stretched out underfoot and carved archways led off in two directions. One to an external balcony niche and one to the natural flagstone floor of a luxury bathroom deeper in the rock face. The whole place was filled with plump, bright furniture, and traditional rugs and light fixtures.

Comfortable? 'I can't see how I could be anything but.'

Truly the most amazing thing he'd ever seen.

He thanked the girl and closed the door after her, then set about exploring, following his nose to a new extraordinary smell. His balcony had its own large niche built into it off to the side of his room. Off the side of the rockface. It had an expansive daybed complete with rich linens and a small, low circular fire on the stone floor, on which hot Turkish coffee bubbled away on a piece of roasting hot slate. A ubiquitous hookah was set up ready to go next to it preloaded with fragrant tobacco.

He poured himself a cup of dark, strong coffee immediately. Then he turned and stared at the view down to the hustle and bustle a dozen flights of steps below and out across the valley of houses to the ones lining the hill on the other side.

All so ancient.

Traditionally built. Yet peppered with solar panels, satellite dishes, and modern conveniences as carefully meshed as the hot water, Wi-Fi, and television in his room.

A muffled knock drew his eye back across the room. It took him only a moment to cross to it and open it, expecting the girl that had just left.

'I asked them to let me know when you arrived,' Georgia said, standing on the threshold of this amazing place dressed in a light, cotton-weave dress in the style of the locals, her hair peppered with tiny flowers. She breezed past him into his cave.

'Wow. Yours is much bigger than mine. Oh, you have a window.'

'You don't?'

'I have a skylight. Carved out of the top of the room. My whole room is one big arch, it's very medieval. But beautiful. And so comfortable.'

'When did you arrive?' he hedged, knowing full well because he'd taken such care not to travel with her.

'This morning. I flew in overnight and slept in the car on the way out here. You wait until you see Göreme bathed in morning light. Stunning.'

She spoke as if she'd been living here for years and he had no trouble believing it. There was something very right about the way she fitted into the natural setting. Like a local come to show him around. She set about poking around every corner of his room and checking out the balcony. 'Oh! A daybed,' she exclaimed. 'I'm thinking Casey's looked after you this trip.'

He didn't doubt it. He'd been like a bear with a sore head the past ten days so his assistant probably thought a dud room would be more than her life was worth.

'Oh, my God. Definitely the executive suite.' That came from his bathroom. He followed the sighs. She trailed her hand over every surface of a room about half the size of the open-room area again, gouged into the rock face. An enormous ornate stone bath filled the corner and he had sudden visions of slaves filling it with buckets of scented rosewater for some Turkish overlord. Or princess. Georgia peered into the void. Then turned and glared at him. 'It's a spa!' she accused.

'You're welcome to borrow it.' He laughed. Given he was only here for two nights it wasn't exactly going to see a lot of use, otherwise.

He followed her back out into the main room and onto the balcony beyond. To the front of the niche with the coffee and daybed in it was a low timber table and two old traditionally upholstered armchairs. Completely exposed to the outside air.

'Clearly Göreme doesn't get a lot of rain,' Georgia said, sinking into one of the armchairs

His lips twisted. 'Make yourself at home.'

She peered up at him and sighed. 'That's exactly what it feels like. But I've only been here a couple of hours.'

'Hospitality is obviously a traditional trade here.' Their customer service and presentation was faultless. He felt ridiculous standing over her, still dressed in his Londonwear, while she lounged there looking so comfortable and fresh and assimilated and...Turkish. 'I'm just going to change. Give me ten.'

'I'll order some drinks,' she called to his back.

The shower in that old stone bath worked as if it was brand new and it rinsed the travel grime off him no time. He pulled on a deep red T-shirt and a pair of brown shorts. As he crossed back out to Georgia he noticed he now matched the floor rug.

His own kind of assimilation.

Weeks of tension started to dissipate.

On the balcony, a different girl from the one he'd checked in with finished placing out two tall glasses of something and then she smiled at him as she ducked around the far side of the daybed niche. Yet another exit. He could well imagine spending his two days in Turkey trying to find his way out of his room. Or back to it.

Georgia leaned on the balustrade in the corner of the balcony, potted colour either side of her legs. The golden late-afternoon light blazed against her white cotton dress, making it partly translucent and thrusting a graphic reminder of the body he'd tried so hard not to ogle in the dance studio back to the forefront of his mind.

He was used to admiring Georgia's quick wit and her ready opinions and her passion for all things green. He was used to staving off the speculative zing when he brushed up against her or touched her. Or kissed her. But he was neither prepared nor sufficiently armed to manage the explosion of sexual interest that had hit him when she did that little private dance for herself in the mirror back in London. All that rippling and writhing. Nothing different from what the other women had done much more gratuitously for him but somehow so much better.

So much worse.

If she turned around right here and now and started to undulate that body he could see the shape of below her dress it wouldn't be the slightest bit out of place with the ancient curiosity of Turkey stretched out behind her. And he wouldn't be able to do a thing about standing, transfixed.

Or possibly about sweeping her up and falling down with her onto that luxury daybed just metres away.

He cleared his throat. 'Are you about to accuse me of having a better view than yours?'

She turned, smiling. 'No. The view is the same. I'm just the next level down.' She pointed down and across to a small balcony with a single chair on it. He liked the idea that he could watch her without her knowing. A small shape on the chair below caught his eye.

'You have a cat,' he said, expunging such inappropriate thoughts from his mind.

'I do. Sweet thing.'

'I think I saw its kittens at Reception.'

She smiled and it was like that breath of apple-scented air he'd taken after the long drive. 'I'm guessing there's a lot of cats in Göreme.'

He nodded. 'I'll have to get onto Casey. I seem to be missing mine.'

Her eyes glowed half with the rich light of the evening and half with a rich light all their own. 'I'll trade you cat-time for spa-time.'

He breathed her in. 'Done.'

For moments neither of them spoke, they just stood lost in each other. 'Want to go for a walk?'

No. He wanted to haul her behind him into that big, comfortable, wasted bed and not come out till morning. But that wasn't going to happen. Not outside his head. And if he was smart he wouldn't let it happen inside his head, either.

No complications.

No risk.

No Georgia.

'Sure. Show me the town.'

There was a lot to see in Göreme. They roamed all over the maze of paths and stairs and twisted byways, sometimes emerging accidentally in the private areas of people's homes and then retreating, embarrassed, despite the friendly and unsurprised response of those intruded upon. Clearly, they weren't the first tourists to end up in someone's living room. They hiked out on foot a half-hour from the town and spent the last two hours of light poring over the ancient rock-hewn world-heritage monasteries with their immaculate and stunning frescoes. A local kindly showed them back through the warren of now-dark dwellings after the sun plunged unexpectedly quickly below the horizon. Orange light glowed from almost all of them but it didn't help them a bit with their orientation.

'Thank you,' Georgia gushed as the pleased-as-punch man deposited them on the doorstep of their hotel and then waved his farewell. She wasn't totally sure Zander would find his way back to his room without assistance—she'd needed two attempts the first time for her own room—so she followed him up.

'Left,' she dropped in just at the last moment.

He turned and looked at her. 'Not right?'

'Not right.'

Left it was. One more corridor and they were at his door. 'What about dinner?' he asked.

She groaned. 'That would have been good to mention back at the entrance. We'll have to retrace our steps.'

'Hang on, I'll just get a jacket.'

He was back in moments with a light jacket over his T-shirt. Whether it was for the evening cool or whether he wasn't used to going to dinner in a T-shirt, it didn't matter. He always looked extra good in a collar so the stylish jacket was very welcome from her point of view. He'd morphed back into casual Zander as the afternoon wore on. The same man she'd spent so much time staring at and smiling at back in the King's Arms.

That was a slight analgesic against the dull ache of his rejection the past fortnight.

Discovering the city with him was a joy. His inquisitive mind and her gentle probing drew fascinating information from the locals. Twice he'd bemoaned not bringing his recorder with him on their walk to capture the lyricism and beauty of the language and the particular sound of voices as they soaked into the ancient limestone. He wouldn't make that mistake again.

The hotel had a small outdoor balcony restaurant on its roof and a serve-yourself arrangement inside. Georgia laughed at Zander's bemused expression.

'When was the last time you ate at a buffet?' she said. Though this was no ordinary buffet. Colourful fruits she'd never seen before spread out on one table and dishes of aromatic mysteries on another. She loaded a little bit of each onto a large plate and planned to round off her day of Turkish discovery here.

Some of it was odd, some of it was tasty, and two things were just plain amazing. She went back for seconds of those. They talked about the flight, the drive out, their impending early start for the balloon trip; anything they could think of that wasn't about London.

As if by agreement.

Here, they could be two totally different people. She didn't have her purposeless life or her humiliating proposal to deal with. He didn't have his work or his marathons to distract and absorb. And they didn't have the Year of Georgia between them.

Or the kiss, and what it meant.

Or his running from the dance studio. And what that meant.

She knew that she never would have achieved this amazing experience if not for the shove that Zander's radio promotion had led to. She would have drifted along in her rut for who knew how long before eventually bumping to shore and clambering out, miles off track.

'It's hard not to sit up here and feel that anything is possible,' she murmured out over the night lights of Göreme.

'Anything *is* possible.'

She laughed. 'Spoken like a true executive. For most people a lot of things are impossible. Financially, socially, time-wise.'

'You just have to get your priorities in order.' He shrugged.

She stared at him. They could make small talk or she could ask him something meaningful. 'Do you prioritise activities over personal things?'

He looked up. Cocked his head.

She sank back into her over-stuffed chair, stomach full and single drink warming her from the inside out. 'You keep yourself closed off from people, yet you're so busy and active all the time. That must be a conscious choice. It would take quite a bit of work, I would have thought, to be around people all the time but not really interact with them on a meaningful level. It must be exhausting.'

Wary eyes considered her. 'Are we talking about my staff again?'

'No. But that's a good place to start. Why do you work so hard to keep them at a distance?'

He thought about not answering. She could see it in his expression. But something tipped him the other way. 'Because I'm their manager. I don't want to be friends with them.'

'Is it that you don't know *how* to be friends with them?' Or maybe anyone.

'Pay them more and give them half-day Friday off and I'm sure they'd feel more friendly.'

'You don't buy friendship.'

'I bought yours. At fifty grand to be exact.'

That stung. Not because it wasn't true that it was his money funding her fabulous year of self-revelation, but because it cheapened what she would gladly have given him for free.

'You don't think I'd have chosen to be your friend without the Year of Georgia?'

'We never would have met without it.'

That was true. If she'd run out of his radio station a few moments earlier or later she might have been sitting here alone. Or not at all. So much of who she was finding deep inside was because of Zander's prompting. His goading.

She sat up straighter. Tired of the subterfuge. 'If we'd met in a coffee shop and I'd got to know you I would have wanted to be your friend.' Though she'd never have worked up the courage to speak to him. She'd have considered him way out of her league.

Her sub-conscious use of the past tense suddenly became remarkably apparent. Exactly when did she decide that Zander Rush was in her league?

'Is that what we are? Friends?'

'That's what I think we are. Though I know you wouldn't call it that.'

'What would I call it?'

'Acquaintance? Contact? Obligation?'

'You're not an obligation, George.'

But she *was* just an acquaintance? 'I'm sure you're not going to tell me what a great time you have trailing me all over London for my classes. Not when you bailed on the belly dancing at the first decent opportunity.'

He studied the way the dark liquid swirled in his glass. 'I owe you an explanation about that…'

'Is there even a Tuesday night network meeting?'

His eyes lifted. 'There is. That's real. But I did use it to get out of the dance class.'

She just stared.

'I wasn't…' He paused and tried again. 'I wasn't comfortable there.'

Her jaw tightened. 'Was it me or everyone else?'

He didn't answer. Her stomach sank.

So it was her.

'It's a very confronting form of dance when you're on the receiving end,' he said.

'You didn't look too confronted.' Until he'd looked at her. 'I was just enjoying exploring the art form.'

The intense need to justify why she'd let herself get carried away with the sensuousness of the dance washed through her.

And hot on its heels was the blazing knowledge that she owed him no apologies.

'And you should enjoy it. It's your thing,' he said.

'You're not up to spectating on a bit of sexy dancing? You didn't mind the salsa.'

'Sexy would be fine. It's just that it's...'

Colour started to show low on his jaw. Given how dim it was under the shade-sail on the hotel roof, the fact that she could see it meant it had to be a reasonable amount. Was he blushing?

'It's what?' she risked.

Embarrassing? Pathetic? Something that really shouldn't be done in public?

His eyes lifted to hers, heated. 'It's erotic.'

Her breath halted. She sagged back in her seat, dumbstruck, and crossed her hands demurely in her lap. Studying them. Then she looked out into the orange glow of the city lights far below. Then the candle of the table next to them. Taking the time to decide what to say. Taking the time to remember how to speak.

She cleared her throat and had a go. 'Erotic?'

Didn't that suggest some kind of attraction? More than just a kiss by the sea kind of attraction? More than just chemistry.

'It was very seductive.'

A sense of the same empowerment she'd felt dancing there in front of the mirror came back to her now. Dancing in front of the mirror had felt good because it was good, maybe? 'It's supposed to be seductive.'

'We don't have that kind of relationship.'

Polite Georgia burned to take the hint. To change the subject. But she was tired of being polite. Of doing what everyone expected her to. She kicked her chin up. 'You don't have that kind of relationship with the other women there, either, but you weren't running a mile from them.'

Just her.

The light came on in her mind as slow and golden as the lights of Göreme had glowed to life. But just as certain.

Just her.

She took a breath and whispered, 'You liked it.'

He didn't look away. But he didn't speak. He let her three words hang out there over the city, unanswered, for eternity. But finally he spoke.

'I loved it. And I shouldn't have.'

Heat to match his flared up her throat. Her gut tightened way down low. He'd loved her sensual display. 'Why?'

'Because we don't have that kind of relationship,' he repeated, his frustrated hiss more at himself than her.

She took a breath. Took a chance. 'Why don't we?'

He stared. 'What?'

'Why don't we have that relationship?'

'I'm… You're… We're doing business.'

'Why can't it be more?'

Those all-seeing eyes suddenly darted everywhere but her. 'I don't do relationships. Not of that kind.'

It was true. In the months she'd known him he never once said he couldn't do a class because he had a date. Never once mentioned anyone in his life. 'What kind do you do?'

His eyes flicked up. 'I have…encounters. Short and sharp. Over before they start.'

'One-night stands, you mean?'

'Sometimes more. But never much more.'

'Why?'

His eyes shadowed over.

'Don't you get lonely?' she breathed.

'There are worse things than being lonely.'

Like what? Being hurt? Making a wrong choice? She wondered again about what had happened to him in the past to give him that view. And what had changed in her that she was about to suggest what she was about to suggest even though she didn't feel she could ask him about his past.

'An encounter, then.' Picking up where they left off that night at Hadrian's Wall.

She'd never, ever propositioned someone so directly in her life. Even with Dan, their first time was an awkward kind of inevitable. But this didn't feel wrong. Or loose. It felt exactly as she'd felt dancing in front of that mirror.

Strong. And fated.

'Right here in Göreme. We have two nights.' Her own daring made her breathless. Was there a faster way to screw things up between them than to...well...?

'George—'

'If you're not interested, that's OK.' Knowing without a doubt that he was interested made it OK. 'But we're in a fantasy world for the next two days. We might as well get the most out of it.'

She kept her eyes on his, but it was the hardest thing she'd ever done.

'Is this a Year of Georgia thing?' he grated.

'No. This is just a Georgia thing.' She filled her lungs. 'I think we should go back downstairs.'

'What about dessert?' he asked, and it smacked of desperation.

'Do you want dessert?' she breathed, still locked onto his cautious eyes.

As she watched the caution cleared, the relief filled them, then desire. And that— finally—was what made her pulse hammer. After all the newfound confidence of the last few surreal minutes, the old doubts crept back in. Dancing in front of a mirror was one thing. Getting down and dirty—and naked— with a man like Zander was almost completely overwhelming in principle. Let alone practice.

She imagined the light cotton of her dress was the caress of sheer silk. And that helped. She imagined the respectful scarf she still wore from their explorations of the city was a face veil covering all but her eyes. She imagined the expression in Zander's gaze was the same as the one she'd caught in the mirror.

Only she didn't have to imagine that because it was. Identical. Only this one was far less repressed and infinitely more terrifying.

And exciting.

They stumbled to their feet.

'Which room?' he asked as he stood back to let her out.

Was he kidding? 'Yours. That spa is wasted on you.'

His hand burned where it pressed into her back, shepherding but also keeping a gentle contact as he urged her down the carved corridor towards the stairs. A teasing kind of torture. A perfect kind of bliss.

He bent to murmur into her ear, 'It's wasted on *just* me, maybe.'

And suddenly her mind was filled with images of the two of them tangled together in the hot opulence of the old stone bath, and her breath just about gave out. It was all she could do to keep her feet moving, but she knew if she stumbled Zander would just sweep her into his arms and carry her down the three levels to his enormous suite with its enormous bathroom and that enormous, luxurious bed.

Just like the conqueror he'd once spoken of.

He stopped at his door, turned her until the timber was at her back, and pressed into her. Peered down on her. 'Are you sure?' he murmured.

She didn't waste breath on words. Instead she pressed up onto her toes and kissed him. Showed him how sure she was. Even though this was totally out of character for her, even though she had to block thoughts of anything more future than Sunday night from her mind.

She was sure about the next two days.

This was *her* reinvention, and Zander Rush was an integral part of the new Georgia Stone. She'd never felt more certain about anything.

He hemmed her against the door with his body, his heat, and brought his hands to her face so that he could seal her acquiescence in. His tongue and his lips worked a magic just like this entire city as the cool of the earth soaked into her back.

She shivered. From delight.

'Hot bath,' he murmured, misunderstanding, and she wondered how long a big tub like the one he had inside would take to fill.

'Or hot blankets,' she whispered, but thought of the blanket of his scorching body on hers would do just fine.

He reached out with one hand, turned the doorhandle, and they fell through into the fantasy interior.

CHAPTER NINE

THEY never made it to the bed, as it turned out. And the hot bath came quite a bit later. They got about as far as the sumptuous pillow-filled conversation niche off to the side of the room before passion got the better of them and, there, Zander made the kind of love to her that she'd never experienced before. And would never forget.

Worship.

There was no other word for it. He took the sort of care of her body—with it—that she'd only ever dreamed might happen. Measured and thorough and poignantly careful. Not tentative—she had enough aches and stretched muscles to know that he'd challenged and pushed her to be the Georgia she'd never let herself be, never needed to be, before. To roam far, far out of her comfort zone. Safe in his embrace.

She lay on her back on the daybed in the balcony niche, her head hanging back over the edge, and stared at the dark sky. Only it wasn't quite the deep black it had been when they'd first come out here, wrapped in traditionally woven blankets, wrapped in each other. It was a deep blue now, with hints of regular blue at the edges.

'Remind me to get more sleep before having sex with a marathon runner,' she murmured. Stamina? Oh, my God... 'It's nearly dawn.'

Across her legs, the heavy heat of him stirred. 'Don't we have somewhere to be at dawn?'

The balloon.

They'd come all this way to do the Cappadocian balloon experience. Could she really justify skipping it to stay here in heaven with Zander?

She sighed. Almost.

'Come on... You don't want to miss it.' He slapped her thigh gently and pushed himself into a sitting position. Dark or not, there was nothing but sky to look in on them high up on the mountain face, but within the hour the sun would be up and hot-air balloons would be rising over Göreme filled with curious, binocular-holding tourists.

And they were supposed to be in one of them.

That was the only thing that got her moving. *They.* The fact that Zander would be with her. If he wasn't booked she'd have blown the whole thing off—dream or no dream.

She padded in silence into the room with him.

What exactly did one say after a night of no-holds-barred sensual exploration?

'Let's get ready,' he said, 'and we'll get moving.'

Huh. As good as anything, she supposed.

But he tempered the banality of the words by swooping down behind her and latching onto her throat with his lips. For a bare heartbeat. Then he was gone again, gathering up his scattered clothes and rummaging in his suitcase.

She thought about running back to her room to change but, really, when you'd been awake the whole time it qualified as the same day, so slipping back into her day clothes felt acceptable.

Plenty of time to change later.

Though her eyes roamed back to Zander's big beckoning bath. She really hadn't had much chance to get clean while they were in there. Quite the opposite, in fact. She did her best to wrestle her secret, satisfied smile into submission.

It wasn't dignified to gloat.

The rush and bustle of getting out to Göreme's airfield in the still-dark of morning did a fine job of distracting her from thought, just as Zander's talented lips had done all night. Whether kissing her or murmuring conversation. It hadn't all been lascivious. They'd lain, tangled together and curled in blankets, and talked about anything that came to mind until one or other of them—or the conversation—had turned sensual again and then there was no talking for quite some time.

On arrival at the open balloon fields, four enormous bulbs glowed in the dim morning light. They lay, powerless, on their sides, and the roaring gas fires slowly filled them upright. The palest of the four lit up like its own sunrise.

'That's ours,' Zander said, coming back to her side, his digital recorder in hand.

They crossed to the enormous basket that was tethered to the ground and Georgia said a quick whisper of thanks for its size. They might look tiny in the sky but on the ground they were enormous.

She was entirely distracted and romanced by the lumbering bulbs taking shape along the roadway. Looked as if their dawn flight would be a balloon convoy. But while groups of ten and more waited for the other baskets theirs was just the two of them and their pilot.

Nice work, Casey.

'Are you my private?' A uniformed American woman stepped forward.

'EROS radio station,' Zander confirmed.

'That's you. Come on aboard and I'll give you the pre-flight information.'

By agreement, Zander recorded the whole safety presentation and the pilot put on an extra-thorough show for the media. But by the end of it Georgia certainly felt very sure about what to do if the balloon failed, and absolutely certain that it would not. The whole thing was far more regimented and controlled than she'd expected.

'I get motion-sick,' she volunteered out of nowhere and Zander looked up, surprised.

'We have bags,' the unfazed pilot said 'but you won't need them. You'll see. It's as though the planet is moving and we'll be standing still.'

Zander threaded his fingers through hers and the gentle gesture filled her with the same golden glow that kept their balloon aloft. She tightened her fingers around his as the pilot closed the door.

'Ten minutes before sun-up,' the pilot announced. 'Let's get you guys in the air.'

Zander curled Georgia into his body and stood behind her against the basket edge in the centre of the basket. She felt both sheltered and protected.

The balloon didn't rise straight up as she imagined it would when the ground crew dropped their tethers—then again her entire experience of hot-air balloons was from *The Wizard of Oz*. Instead, it skirted along, centimetres above the ground, and slowly those centimetres became meters and then Georgia got a sense of what the pilot had promised. As soon as they had some height, it suddenly felt as if the earth had started to treadmill below them and they were stationary, just hanging there in space.

The pilot gave the gas its voice and the entire balloon inhaled the burst of flame, long and steady. It rose again. Then she killed the flame and silence resumed; the only sounds were the clinking of guy ropes and the distant squeals of the passengers in the balloon ascending behind them.

Theirs breathed enormous gulps between long silent stretches and climbed and climbed in pace with the sunrise.

'Do you want to describe what you see?' Zander murmured against her neck, crossing his strong arms around her and holding the running digital recorder below her chin.

Golden light fingered out from the horizon and the deep blonde colour of the earth began to glow with a vibrancy and a gentle kind of fire. Georgia described the stunning scene, punctuated by the occasional breath of the balloon, and full of words like *God* and *heaven* and *other-worldly*. And *whole* and *healing* and *soul-breath*.

Zander and the pilot remained silent, letting her speak.

They flew over Göreme and then left it far behind as they floated over the lunar-like deserts. A distant mesa grew bigger and bigger as they approached but the pilot kept the balloon level though the others in their convoy all lifted. Georgia's adrenaline spiked and Zander's arms tightened around her, but at the last moment the pilot fired the lungs hard and their balloon soared up and over the lip of the mesa and the vast plains of Anatolia were revealed before them.

Tears filled Georgia's eyes.

Zander recorded the balloon's respiration as they drifted over great clefts in the earth and the rolling, twisting, ancient tortures of the granite and sandstone crust. He interviewed the pilot and got some close-up sounds of the clanking guy ropes and a passing flotilla of geese, generally capturing the atmosphere of this amazing experience for his listeners.

Though of course that was completely impossible to do.

This was as close to angel flight as she was going to get.

'What are you thinking about?' he murmured, back by her side and pocketing the recorder.

She spoke before she thought. 'Dying.'

He twisted around to look at her face. She laughed. 'I mean what it might be like after you die. Ascension. I'm thinking it would be like this. So…gentle and supported. No fear.'

'I didn't know you were so religious,' he murmured.

'I'm not, generally. But it's tough to be up here and not wonder…'

They fell to silence, but Zander eventually broke it.

'I remember wondering… I thought when I was young with so many people queuing up for communion there must be something in it.'

She tipped her head half back and contacted the strength of his chest. 'You're Catholic?'

'Sufficiently Catholic to have had mass at my wedding, but not to get up early every Sunday for one.'

He was close enough and smart enough to interpret the total stillness of her body—as still as the balloon felt in space—correctly.

'You're married?' she whispered.

The pilot shifted away to the far corner of the basket. If she could have climbed out to check the rigging at the crest of the balloon Georgia thought she would have.

Zander was as stiff as she was now. 'No.'

Part of her sagged with relief, but she didn't let it show. 'But you were married?'

That was a hell of a thing to be finding out now.

'Actually no.'

She turned her back on the spectacular view and looked up at him. 'But you had a wedding mass?'

His face tightened. 'We had one scheduled.'

'It didn't go ahead?' This was too important a moment to be playing word games.

'No. It was… The wedding was cancelled.'

Oh. 'You broke it off?'

His brows dropped. 'Why would you assume it was me?'

Because no woman in their right mind would jilt a demi-god? 'I don't know. Only that you're not very pro wedding.'

Though suddenly that particular prejudice made perfect sense if he'd had a broken engagement in his past.

The gas flame belched and they rose slightly.

She tried again. 'Was it mutual?'

Zander looked out to the now blazing dawn horizon. 'No.'

Empathy washed through her. If anyone could understand the awfulness of being rejected, she could. Though she knew now that she'd never loved Dan. And Zander had clearly loved his fiancée. So how much more would that have hurt. 'I'm sorry.'

What else could she say? Better to know now than find out later? Just because she considered Dan's rejection of her proposal a dodged bullet didn't mean that was how Zander felt. And judging by the tightness of his expression and his general close-mouthedness on the subject of marriage...

Would it ever have come up if not for his slip up?

'Did she tell you why?'

'No. She and her bridesmaids fled England while the ushers were doing the friend-of-the-bride/friend-of-the-groom thing.'

Georgia's jaw dropped. 'She left you at the altar?' Didn't that only happen in movies?

He nodded. 'Even her parents weren't aware.'

Oh, my God. 'Zander, I don't know what to say.' Not about how awful that must have been for him. Not about the raging anger towards a woman she'd never met for hurting him so badly. Or the raging jealousy that was suddenly surging through her for some stranger he'd loved enough to marry.

'There's nothing to say.' He shrugged, but it was the least casual thing she could imagine. 'It's ancient history.'

'When was this?'

'Right out of uni.'

Fifteen years wasn't ancient. 'You were young.'

'And stupid as it turns out.'

She slid over to stand beside him so they could both look out at the beautiful, healing landscape below. 'It's not stupid to want to spend your life with someone. It's brave.'

And that was an odd word to have chosen.

He digested that for a moment. 'I wasn't brave. I think I did it because it was the right thing to do.'

'How long were you together?'

'Four years. Since final year at school. We both enrolled at Lincoln.'

Excellent. High-school sweetheart, too. 'You must have loved her a lot.' Maybe he still did? It would explain a lot.

He thought about that. 'I think it was one of those break-up-or-get-married moments. So I proposed.'

'And she broke up.'

'Pretty much.'

'In the worst imaginable way.'

He slid his eyes down to her. 'Strength of character wasn't one of her strong suits. She had very dominant parents.'

That wasn't a woman she could imagine him admiring. 'Hurting you was easier than facing them?'

Dark brows folded. 'Seems so.'

Cappadocia whizzed by beneath them.

'Well, I guess now I understand your cynicism about marriage. And your reaction after the promo went so wrong.'

He looked at her for the first time in minutes. 'I had to face two hundred of our family, friends, and neighbours, and tell them Lara wasn't coming. The idea that I'd set someone else up for the same public humiliation...' He shook his head.

That stole her breath every bit as much as the moment the balloon had played chicken with the sharp slope of the mesa. Her stomach lurched the same, too. In crystal-clear replay she saw the moment in the elevator all those months ago that he'd seen her distress, turned and shielded her from prying eyes with his body, and then helped her slink, unseen, from the parking garage. That was a foundation moment for her. And for him it had all been about sympathy.

'Is that what the whole Year of Georgia thing is about?' *Pity?*

'If I could have started my life over, back then, I would have. Gladly. So I was happy to be able to give you the chance.'

She stepped away, just slightly, and pretended to admire the view. But she was as taut inside as the ropes holding the two parts of their aircraft together. 'So this is your restitution?'

His voice dropped low. 'Somewhat. Making sure you got something out of it.'

Right.

Then he stepped up behind her. 'But not all of it. I can see where you're going, Georgia. Working your way to assuming I slept with you out of guilt.'

'Didn't you?'

'No. I slept with you because it was inevitable. I've been wanting to since we met.'

She slanted a look back up at him. 'It's not some twisted Year of Georgia loyalty-programme bonus class?'

His smile rivalled the sunrise. And his chuckle warmed her from the inside out. Even as she fought it. 'No. Though that suggests you learned a thing or two.'

She blew at the curl that hung over her eyes. 'You have no idea.'

He nodded slowly. She felt it against her back. 'Me, too.'

Well…this was awkward.

'So, the fifty grand was about guilt, but the sex is about… sex?'

It was stupid to hope for more. But it wouldn't be the first time her heart and her head had operated in opposition. The secret, foolish desire that she would be the one woman who he wanted more from.

His eyes shadowed over briefly. 'The fifty grand was about keeping us both out of court for breach of contract.'

And the nine hours of intensive loving…?

He lowered his voice, given the proximity of the pilot. 'Last night was about you and me and this amazing place,' he went on. 'And the attraction that's been distracting me so much for the better part of half a year.'

That sounded a lot like… 'Scratching an itch?' It sounded as awful as it felt.

He sighed heavy and hard behind her. 'Medicating a burn.'

If she needed any clue that they'd be going back to their

London lives—separately—on Monday morning, that was it. You only medicated something you wanted healed over.

Zander hadn't promised her more. She'd made her decision last night despite knowing that. So she had no grounds for complaint.

'Up ahead,' the pilot said with the best timing.

They both forced their eyes onto something other than each other and Georgia gasped as they descended amongst a field of giant, jagged pillars that stretched skywards, strong and masculine and potent.

Just like the man behind her.

'This is extraordinary,' Zander breathed, his eyes fixated on the ancient geology as their balloon bobbed amongst others over the natural wonder.

This whole weekend had been extraordinary. Living her dream just being here in Turkey, then, overnight, immersed in heaven with Zander.

But extraordinary in a bad way, too. Unravelling the origin of his anti-marriage sentiment and discovering firsthand how that was going to impact on her. No wonder he wasn't interested in risking himself again.

Zander Rush liked to take holidays from reality. But they were only mini-breaks.

First Hadrian's Wall and now Göreme. Every time they got away from London he was like a different man; he let himself indulge the attraction between them and be someone totally different from everyday Zander. Someone who communicated. Someone who laughed. Someone who loved.

Except it wasn't love. It was *medication*.

As though his connection to her was something he needed to be cured of. A temporary ailment.

Back in the real world, Zander took care to pack himself carefully away—in his big empty house, on his epic, solo marathons, in his expansive plush office. He kept everyone at arm's length. Absolutely by design.

Georgia stared out, letting the verbal spiel of the pilot wash over her: about the people of Cappadocia, about the heritage. She could hear it later on Zander's recorder. It was hard to be in this prehistoric place that had seen war and famine and death and entire civilisations come and go and worry about one man's feelings for one woman.

It seemed so trivial.

But she was that woman. This was her life. And so it wasn't trivial at all. The Year of Georgia was supposed to have taught her who she was. It was supposed to have given her a taste of what was possible and highlighted the deficiencies in her life. And it had worked.

She was Georgia Stone. For better or for worse.

Weirdly obsessed with plants, content to walk alone amongst Roman ruins, uninterested in cooking or wine appreciation or shoes, but a crack shot with a blank-pistol and the fastest code-cracker the spy school had ever seen. Terrible at the contrived sexy steps of salsa but a natural at the private undulations of belly dancing. A decent rower but a terrible swimmer. She was a lab rat and a loyal and ethical employee.

And she had a heart as protected and hidden as any of the seeds she X-rayed. But at least now she knew, without a doubt, that it was competent. That *she* was competent.

She was Georgia Stone. She would find her way.

And though she'd enjoyed the detour of the past few months, it dawned on her in realisation as blazing as Cappadocia's sunrise that *her way* just wouldn't include Zander Rush. He'd come into her life bearing the gifts she needed to find herself again. Perhaps his cosmic role was now complete and the last twenty-four hours were just the most amazing swansong.

This conversation, this day, was her marker. He wasn't sorry about what they'd done but he wasn't interested in more and he certainly wasn't interested in for ever.

And she was.

It hit her every bit as dramatically as the Cappadocian landscape had. She wanted a for ever someone. Dan hadn't just been about keeping up with her friends. He'd been about trying to build something lasting for herself.

She wanted someone to share her life with. To explore with. To commiserate with. She was tired of being alone.

But just anyone would not do. She'd had a taste of something spectacular—someone spectacular. That was going to be very hard to go back from. And holding out for someone worthy didn't seem as scary after the six months she'd just had.

Her heart buoyed just like the envelope bobbing above their heads.

He was out there. She would find him.

But then, with the same sinking feeling that came with shutting off the gas, she accepted another hard truth.

She just wouldn't find him in this balloon.

Stalling the inevitable was easy to start with.

First, there was the business of getting the balloon back down to earth, onto the back of the pickup truck, the air out of the envelope, and the glossy fabric rolled up and stowed in the gondola. Then, there were too many ears in the bus that drove them back to Göreme to do more than smile politely at each other. Once back in the hotel, the exhaustion of twenty-four sleepless hours had claimed them both and it wasn't too hard to convince Zander that she wanted the comfort of her own room and shower for a very necessary few hours of shut-eye.

When all she wanted to do was curl up and sleep in the circle of his arms.

But now it was late afternoon and Zander stood at her door, an optimistic bottle of wine in his hand.

'Right now?' He gaped.

'My flight leaves in three hours. A car's coming for me soon.'

The wine sagged towards the stone floor. 'Why?'

'Emergency at work,' she lied.

He lifted one brow. 'A seed emergency?'

Defensiveness made her rash. 'I don't remember signing anything that gave you say over what I do with my private time.'

He didn't bite, though he did glance around him in the dim hallway. 'May I come in?'

'I'm packing.' Truth was she was already packed because, even though she desperately needed it, sleep had evaded her. But her suitcase lay conveniently open on her luxurious, plump bed. She stood back so he could enter.

'What's going on, Georgia?'

'Nothing. I just have to get back.'

'Your seed emergency. Right.' He placed the wine on the table. 'What's really going on?'

He had to know. Surely.

She shrugged. 'We've done Göreme. We've done the ballooning. We're done.' In more ways than one.

'But you were so keen to see Cappadocia.'

'And I'm already planning on coming back for a longer stay.'

'This is about last night.' It wasn't a question.

'Last night was…' What did more cosmopolitan people say at this moment. Fun? Wild? Memorable? 'Last night was a one-off.'

The eyebrow quirked again. 'Really? And you felt the need to fly out of the country to avoid a repeat?'

'I didn't want to hurt your feelings.'

He snorted. 'Right. This is much easier on my feelings.'

His sarcasm triggered hers. 'I'm not really up on the protocols of dis-entanglement.'

He repeated the word, silently. 'Wow.'

'Zander—'

'For someone inexperienced in the art of casual sex you certainly are a quick study at the kiss-off part.'

'This isn't a—'

'Yeah, Georgia, it is. But what makes you so sure I was even offering a round two?'

'I...' That took the wind from her sails. 'You turned up with wine.'

He held the bottle up. The text was in Turkish but the image on the label was of a big balloon flying over Cappadocia. 'It was a keepsake. I got me one, too.'

Oh.

'If I hadn't knocked would you have even told me you were leaving?'

'Of course!' But not until the very last minute. And he seemed to know it.

'You don't have to leave, Georgia. If last night was a mistake for you, then fine. We can keep our distance until tomorrow. But this is your trip. You've wanted this for ages.'

'I can't—' *Be here. With you. And not be with you.* 'It's time to go.'

'You don't trust me.' Again, not a question.

'Of course I do.' She sighed. She didn't know anyone she trusted more. Dan included.

'So what's the problem?' Awareness blinked to light in his grey eyes. 'Unless you don't trust yourself.'

She just stared.

'That's it, isn't it? If you stay you don't trust yourself to stick to your own resolution.' Triumph glossed over his anger. He stepped closer. 'So if you want me,' he went on, 'why are you leaving?'

'I don't want you.' *I don't want to want you.*

'Liar.'

Yeah, she was. 'This was an aberration, remember?'

He frowned. Clearly he didn't remember saying it.

'Besides today, tomorrow, what does it matter when we finish it?' she asked. 'Or do you just like to control the use-by dates on your affairs?'

Lord. That word sounded both very grown up and very old-fashioned at the same time.

His lips thinned. 'I just want to understand it, Georgia. To understand you.'

Something made her ask. 'It would have finished tomorrow, wouldn't it, Zander?'

He tensed up.

'Because this isn't real. You said it yourself, you and me in this fantasy place. We would have ended the moment we touched down in London.' He didn't contradict her. 'So what's a few hours between friends?'

His eyes narrowed. 'Friends?'

'Unless I've misunderstood you,' she risked. 'If you wanted something more long-term, Zander, now's your chance. Just say.' Because she'd be up for it.

His lips pressed tighter together. His eyes roiled.

She held on longer than was good for her dignity, just in case. But still he stood silent. As expected.

'So, now that we're on the same page,' she said, heartsore, 'I'm exercising my right to choose. And I choose out.'

She sounded much calmer than she felt.

'I guess I should thank you,' he said after a long, silent age.

'What for?' Giving herself so wholeheartedly to him?

'At least this time I won't have to explain myself to two hundred people.'

Her heart sank. She hadn't even considered the similarities to his runaway bride. But the two situations were nothing alike. Were they?

'I'm not running out on you.' Yeah, she was. Avoiding the whole situation. 'I'll see you in London.'

'Business as usual.'

'Is there another way?'

She longed for him to say there was. She longed for him to say, *Stay and we can be a couple.* She longed for him to tell her she meant enough to him to break his work-only rules for.

But he wouldn't.

And they both knew it.

He scooped the wine up and placed it carefully in the centre of her open suitcase protected by her intimates. Then he turned back to her and spoke.

'See you in London.'

And then he was gone.

CHAPTER TEN

November

THWACK.

Her arrow hit the target, not quite as close as she was aiming but at least it found purchase. She lowered the bow.

Indoor archery—the latest on her list. Actually, it was supposed to be outdoor archery but it was the dying days of November and autumn had already dragged as interminably as her mood. The Year of Georgia was galloping by and would be over before there was any further warm weather, so indoors it was.

She and Zander were back to the early days of her Year of Georgia classes—politely civil. He came to exactly as few classes as he needed to get the monthly segments done and he seemed to have lost his enthusiasm for recording everything—much more sound than he needed. But the segments were proving unexpectedly popular with EROS' listeners and so he had to keep producing them, even when she thought he would probably have preferred to just let the whole thing go. Maybe buy out her contract personally to be rid of the hassle.

They'd had their promotional value well and truly. Twice over. Every time a segment aired people remembered Dan, too, and there was a flurry of general media attention about where he was. What he was doing.

Who he was doing.

He'd been seen around town with someone. A woman. The same woman. So at least one of them had managed to find their way out of the mire to a regular sort of relationship. Although as fast as the gossip had come that they were on, it seemed as if maybe they were off again.

For her part, she surprised herself by discovering that even being given everything money could buy got old. She was tired of the Year of Georgia. She was tired of smiling politely at Zander and speaking into his digital recorder and pretending everything was fine.

Everything was not fine.

He filled her consciousness when he was around and plagued her thoughts when he wasn't. She sat in life-drawing class looking at a phenomenally proportioned naked male model and all she could think about was Zander's proportions. The curve of his strong shoulder. The gentle undulation of his throat. If her drawings never looked like the man she was sketching it was because they generally looked more like Zander.

Having asked Casey to strip her schedule of anything resembling Egyptian stone therapy and deep muscle massage, she begged Zander's assistant to put them back in. If only to relieve the new tension she lived with these days.

They helped, but only for an hour or so each week. Then the lingering dissatisfaction and un-rightness returned and troubled her until the following week.

Float tanks, hypnosis, Bowen therapy—she tried something new every week for months. And nothing helped quite like the moment Zander walked into her class. The precious seconds before her brain reminded her not to get so excited. For those few breaths all the tension drained from her body.

She lived for those moments.

His garden was progressing, he'd told her one week, before passing her his phone to have a look at the design that flourished under the care of his landscaper. Irrational, blazing envy tormented her that she didn't get to prune it or mow it or love it herself.

But she just smiled and said, 'That's great,' and handed the phone back.

Another week he played her the completed Cappadocia segment and her heart squeezed both for the memories of Turkey and for the sublimely neutral expression on his face. Totally untroubled.

She equally envied and grew infuriated by his lack of concern.

Turning it off like that was a gift. Just not a very nice one.

'Nice shot,' Zander murmured, off to one side as a helper ran in and pried her arrow from the target.

Nice condescension, she thought. But aloud she only thanked him. She lined up another arrow. The Amazons must have had some serious upper-body muscles because doing this just once a week had given her a perpetual muscle ache in her chest.

Unless that was just her heart.

'To the left,' he murmured from her right side. She ignored him. 'Your left, not my left.'

She lowered her bow and turned. 'Seriously, Zander? You're going to back-seat drive?'

'Here…'

He stepped in behind her and told her to assume the firing position. Then he slid one hand along her extended bow arm and curled the other around her pulled back firing arm. And he reoriented her the tiniest bit to the left.

'Just a smidge.'

'Is that a professional archery measure?' she muttered through tight teeth.

His laugh was a puff of warm air against her ear and her whole neck broke out in gooseflesh.

'Yes, it is.'

'You know this because of your many years of competition in the sport.' At the very last second she realised he *could* have archery experience. It was a solo enough sport to be right up his alley.

'I miss you,' he said, as though that was exactly what they'd just been talking about. And maybe they had.

'You miss the sex.'

'No. I could get that anywhere.' *Charming.* 'I miss you. I miss your conversation and your snark. I just wanted to feel you. Just for a moment.'

She stood stiff and unyielding in his arms. It was the hardest thing she'd ever had to do. Even her eyes didn't waver from the target across the room. 'And have you had your fill of feeling me up?'

'George—'

The way he said her name…it caused her bow arm to tremble. She forced it to stillness.

'—do you have to drag it down to such a level?'

'What level should it be at? You're not interested in a relationship but you're not above a bit of casual sport at my expense?'

His arms dropped. Not scorched, but definitely not relaxed. 'I hate this.'

'Not my fault. You set the rules.'

'I don't recall making any rules.'

'By implication.' She lowered her bow. There was no way it was safe to fire an arrow while she was this distracted. But she didn't turn around. 'Or have you changed your mind about relationships?'

'Why can't we just…feel our way?'

She turned. 'Are you asking me on a date?'

Instantly he stiffened. 'I'm… No. Aren't we a bit beyond dates?'

'So you're asking me just to sleep with you at your request?'

His brow folded. 'No. George—'

'You're offering me sex with no commitment, Zander,' she pointed out. 'And that can't work.'

And, astonishingly, she saw clearly for the first time why.

But he couldn't. 'Why not?'

An insane kind of lightness flooded her. 'Because I know who I am, now. And I know why I proposed to Dan.' Even though it had been unconscious. To bring his lack of commitment to a head. And sure enough the very next relationship she walked into was the same. Worse.

'What's Dan got to do with this?'

'Nothing. And everything. Dan had a dozen little ways of keeping me at emotional arm's length. You have a hundred.'

He lowered his head.

'I don't want to beg and scrounge for scraps of emotional intimacy,' she said. 'I'm worth more than that.'

'No one's going to promise you a ring before you even begin exploring who you are as a couple, George.'

His words cut deep. But she stayed strong. 'You've ruled a commitment out right from the start. Why would I set myself up for that?'

'Because of what we have?'

'What do we have? Cracking chemistry? Intellectual compatibility?' She started packing up her gear. 'You're either condemning me to still be waiting for you to throw me a bone when I'm eighty or a courteous breakup in two years when you tire of me. Either way I lose.'

'You're losing now.'

It wasn't conceit. She absolutely *was* losing. 'I'm cutting my losses.'

'So that's it? New improved Georgia wants all or nothing?'

'No.' She looked up at him. 'I definitely want it all. But I'll choose nothing if I have to.'

He stared, thinking. 'Maybe I'll change my mind?'

'Really, Zander? Based on what? Give me some criteria for what will mean you can get over what happened to you in the past.'

His lips thinned.

'Because otherwise you're expecting me to just limp along hoping I'm being the kind of girlfriend that a man like you changes his mind for. That I'm saying the right things, doing the right things, wearing the right things. Dying a thousand deaths every time I find that maybe I'm not.'

'George—'

'I'm not negotiating, Zander, I'm explaining. I'm telling you why I'm choosing nothing, because everything is not on the cards with you.'

He hissed his displeasure.

She took a long breath. 'I'll come back for the Valentine's show but you should have enough audio to carry you through Christmas and January. I'm done rediscovering myself. I'm done with classes.'

'You still have twenty thousand left—'

'You can keep the change.'

In more ways than one.

'Wait…' But he had nothing to say after that.

She took a breath. Took a chance. Exhausted from holding it in. And lying to herself. 'I love you, Zander. I love your dedication to your sport, I love your hermit ways, I love your big, pointless garden, and the joy I saw on your face in Turkey. I want it all with you. What are you going to do about it?'

His eyes flared. He stared.

But said nothing.

Her heart crumpled inwards as if it were vacuum sealed. 'And there we go.'

She picked up her bag and moved to the door. He stopped her with a hand on her arm. Gentle. Uncertain.

'So that's it? I'm not going to see you again?'

'Isn't that how you prefer your life? As empty as your house? Surely it must be easier to keep yourself from forming relationships that way.' She curled her fingers around his. 'This isn't judgement, Zander. This is my choice.'

He stared, then dropped his eyes to her fingers as she used them to unclasp his from her arm.

'Goodbye, Zander. Good luck.'

And then she walked out. Straight. Steady.

Just as an arrow through the heart should be.

CHAPTER ELEVEN

February

THERE was only so much thermal a man could wear and still run comfortably. February meant he moved most of his outdoor exploits indoors. He hit the treadmill instead of the highways, and he did endless laps of his grand staircase and reacquainted himself with his friendly neighbourhood indoor-climbing facility in lieu of hiking.

It kept his event fitness up and his time occupied. In body if not in spirit.

'Mr Rush,' the guy belaying his stack said. He'd been coming here every winter for the last six years but still he was Mr Rush to them all. He'd never invited them to call him anything else.

*It's Zander…*he imagined saying.

How hard could that be to say? Just a few short syllables. But the words were an overture for something else, something he wasn't in a hurry to have. Acquaintances. God forbid, *friends*. You told a guy your Christian name one week and you were helping him move house the next.

Georgia had accused him of having a hundred ways of keeping her at an emotional distance. Maybe that kind of thinking was just one of them. Most people would be too polite to push past that kind of passive resistance. And only some people had what it took to sneak past it.

Georgia had it. Straight in under his skin. Between his ribs. Into his thoracic cavity where his heart hung out.

He'd never imagined that having all his time back just for himself would be such a burden. He'd whinged long and hard to Casey about Georgia's endless classes, the impost on his time, and she'd tutted and said all the things a boss liked to hear—*Yes, Mr Rush. I'll see to it, Mr Rush*—yet, somehow they'd snuck up on him and started to feel normal. So that when they were gone he felt...

Bereft.

As if a part of him were missing. Yet it was much bigger than the sum total of the hours he'd put in at class.

He smiled at his spotter as he finished fixing his rigging. 'Thanks, Roger.'

See...Roger. How hard was that? But still he didn't say it. *Call me Zander.*

He forced his mind off his bloody social skills and onto the stack ahead of him. Newcomers climbed the left—hard but civilised—regulars got the fierce alignment. A good brutal climb was definitely in order.

It worked for about six minutes. People thought the point of indoor climbing was to spider monkey up the fastest, like some kind of country-fair attraction. For a free stuffed elephant. To him, the point of indoor climbing was stamina and endurance. Taking it slow and making it hard. Making it hurt.

Pain had a way of putting everything else into perspective.

Except today. Today it wasn't working.

Isn't that how you prefer your life? she'd said. *As empty as your house?*

No, actually it wasn't. He liked it quiet. He liked it predictable and undemanding. But he didn't actually choose empty. Empty chose him. When you worked as hard and as long as he did, when you had the kind of responsibility the network had entrusted him with and the kind of income they offered, then there really wasn't a lot of room for anything *but* empty.

Of course Georgia would have called those excuses. She would have asked him what he really wanted to do with his life and then challenged him to do it. No matter what.

Which kind of relied on him knowing what he wanted to do. And he had no idea.

He just knew what he was doing now definitely wasn't it.

His hand slipped on a misplaced transfer and he slammed hard against the wall, braced only on one foot peg, two fingers taking his entire weight.

Now wasn't it. The network wasn't it. EROS wasn't it.

The enormous gulf those missing classes had left started to make some sense. He'd enjoyed those. A lot. Recording the experiences, capturing people's stories. He'd exercised creative muscles that he'd let wither over the past corporate decade. He'd plucked remembered strands from something he'd been passionate about before the network. Before Lara.

His roots.

And audio production was a thousand miles from what he was doing now. What he'd grown rich and famous on.

What he'd grown empty on.

He tried not to imagine his big empty house, because every time he did the same thing happened. He saw it full of life, and colour.

And Georgia.

She'd planted the seeds of herself as surely in his imagination as she did plants in her garden. And she'd grown there, like some kind of invasive creeper vine. Tangling. Binding.

Bonding.

Until he could barely separate the reality of what he was left with from the fantasy of his imagination.

'Bloody hell.'

A grunt to his left drew him out of his self-obsessed focus. How long had he been hanging here, not moving? Roger knew him too well to think he was in difficulty, but while he was off absorbed in fanciful thoughts another climber had managed to get fully rigged and halfway up the wall. Albeit the easier configuration.

He turned to look at the new guy and nearly lost his finger hold again.

Bradford.

No question. He'd been in enough newspaper articles and on enough gossip sites to be recognisable anywhere. Even sweaty and bulging on a rockface. However simulated.

An insane rage overcame him.

This man had rejected Georgia. She gifted him her unique heart—she risked and exposed herself—and this guy thought himself too good for her. He hadn't fought for her when she ended it and he'd wasted no time in picking up with someone new once he was free to.

Bradford glanced at him, frowning, and then very purposefully climbed ahead.

Every hormone in Zander's body urged him to speak. To demand Bradford justify himself. Explain in what universe hurting the most gentle, courageous woman on the planet was acceptable. Except then he remembered that he'd done effectively the same thing and much more recently.

Rejected her.

Returned the gift of her love. Unopened.

Let her go without a fight.

And he realised that Bradford was no more suited to for ever with a woman like Georgia than he was. And no more worthy.

He signalled Roger, below, leaned back, and zipped to the floor. He fumbled his way out of the climbing gear in his haste and left it where it lay.

And he got the hell out of there before he asked Bradford the only thing he really wanted to know.

How did you get over her?

* * *

A year.

An entire year had gone past since she'd last sat in EROS' broadcast studios. Actually, it wasn't the same studio, it was a twin, the mirror image of the one through the tinted glass that she'd first sprinted from twelve months ago when Dan turned her proposal down.

Back then she'd thought that nothing could be worse than standing in the elevator with the aghast curiosity of the station's entire staff directed at her, begging the doors to close.

But coming back in here, today, was infinitely worse.

Back into Zander's territory.

The man she hadn't seen for over two months. A man she'd longed for over Christmas and cried for at New Year and absolutely dreaded seeing as Valentine's Day approached.

A day of love and celebration.

Ugh.

'Can I offer you a coffee?' the segment producer said.

Yes. A warm drink would take the February chill from her fingers even if it couldn't do anything for the one in her heart. She knew because she'd been trying these past months. 'Tea, please?'

The producer shot a look at the teenaged girl by her side and she scarpered off to make Georgia's tea, flushing.

'Work experience,' the producer grunted, tossing her hair.

Dogsbody, Georgia thought and instantly sided with the kid.

'Have a seat,' the woman said, and then, as Georgia sat, she added, 'So you were sent the questions?'

'Yes.' And she had notes for her answers. 'What was the best activity? What will I be keeping up after today? What did I learn from my year?'

'If there's anything off-script you'd like to add, you can go for it.'

Anything about Dan, she meant. The station was as good as their word—he'd not been mentioned since she first signed the contract.

'If it comes up,' she agreed. But nothing more. She wasn't going to be pressured on her last moments under EROS' power.

'I've heard Zander's final segment,' the producer said. 'It's good.'

Georgia tried not to stiffen at the mere mention of his name.

'Speak of the devil...' one of the announcers murmured without the slightest change in facial expression and she did stiffen, then. Fully. But turning to look would have been too obvious.

The producer also pretended not to notice his arrival in the studio next to theirs, but her eyes flicked briefly to the darkened glass behind Georgia. 'Great. Nothing like being watched to improve performance,' she muttered while slightly diverting her face.

The announcer laughed.

The disrespect at Zander's expense irked Georgia. She might have cut all ties with him but this was their boss they were sniggering about. A decent—if complicated—man, with a tough job to do.

'Don't worry,' the producer said, misreading her face and leaning in to pretend to adjust Georgia's headset. 'He can't hear us until I press the button. Soundproof.'

'Then you'd better hope he can't lip-read,' she murmured.

Defending him was strangely pleasurable. Was she that desperate for a connection between them? Walking in here today was fifty per cent pain and fifty per cent anticipation that she might find him standing in the hallway.

Where she'd first seen him.

But no, he'd been predictably absent.

Until now.

'Guess he's more interested than usual because they're his segments.' The producer tried to cover her gaffe.

Or he just wanted to see her without being seen.

Hopeless optimist.

'Have I got time to go to the Ladies'?' Georgia asked, out of nowhere, then tried to add veracity to her lie. 'Nervous pee.'

The producer huffed. They'd just got her settled and all wired up. 'If you're quick.'

She scooted up out of her seat and crossed to the door without paying the tinted glass the slightest attention. Outside she turned right and walked in the opposite direction to the staff toilets.

She opened the next door without knocking.

'Zander...'

He spun by the tinted glass in the half shadows. The studio on the other side was fully lit and much easier to see than he had been in reverse. She did her best to stay back in the shadows, out of view of gossipy eyes.

'Georgia.' He swallowed. 'How are you?'

'I'm good. And you?'

'Good.'

Excellent. That meant they were both crap. 'I wanted to ask you about the cheque.'

'That money is yours. You shouldn't be penalised for your thrift.'

Thrift. That made her sound about as exciting as a dusty old book. 'Twenty thousand pounds, though?'

He shrugged. 'You earned it. What will you do with it?'

She hadn't let herself think. 'Maybe back to Turkey?'

'You should. See it properly.'

'There's so many options once you have actual money in your hands,' she breathed.

'You can do whatever you want. I hope you enjoy it.'

His sincerity struck her. And why not? She wouldn't have fallen in love with a man who wasn't genuinely lovely.

'Why are you hiding in here?' she asked.

'I'm not hiding, I'm monitoring.'

'That seems to have upset your staff.'

He smiled, not the slightest bit sorry. 'I'm sure. Some of them are big on fame and short on accountability.'

Silence fell. Next door the work-experience girl reappeared with her cuppa and glanced around anxiously.

Georgia pushed away from the wall. 'Well, I should go.'

'Are you nervous?' he asked.

Yes, and not just because she was going on air. 'A bit. This is going to be hard for me.'

'I've been very clear on the limitations. Anyone who mentions Bradford will be collecting unemployment next week.'

The kindness touched her. And his total obliviousness hurt her lungs. 'Thank you.'

'I heard about his new girlfriend,' Zander risked. 'How do you feel about that?'

Feel? 'I'm happy for him.'

'I worried for you. That you might—'

'Take it personally?'

He dropped his eyes.

'I'm not going to say I loved the implication of him finding someone so soon. That it must have been me that made the two of us a bad fit.'

'That's not how it works.'

'Yeah, it does. Finding someone you can spend your life with is rare enough so the chances of both people finding that someone in each other...' She left the rest unsaid. 'Truly,' she reassured. 'He seems really content. It's been a tough year for him but he's found his reward.'

Zander stared. Breathed out slowly. 'You're a good person, Georgia Stone.'

She lifted her chin. 'I know. I'd be my friend if I wasn't already me.'

His lips parted in a classic Zander chuckle.

'I'd better go. Your producer's taking my absence out on your work-experience girl.'

He looked into the bright booth and she turned for the

door. His voice stopped her just as she reached for the handle. 'Georgia…'

She turned.

'You're looking good.'

No, she looked pretty much the same as she always did. With the exception of the grey smudges under her eyes that she'd worked hard to disguise. 'Thank you.'

'And you're sounding good.'

She could easily have said something flippant, but these might be the last words they ever exchanged. She wanted them to count. 'I am good. I'm finally doing what makes me happy. Regardless of what everyone else expects. It's very…healthy.'

'Healthy.' He turned the word over on his lips. 'It's very compelling.'

Her chest tightened. Two minutes before going live on air was not the time to mess with a woman's head. 'See you later, Zander.'

Though, no, she wouldn't. Not after today.

Today was the end.

She stepped back out into the full fluoro-brightness of the radio station and crossed back to her own studio. She smiled at the young girl who passed her a cup of tea as she walked in and let the producer set her up with her headphones and mic, again. And she did a cracking job of ignoring Zander's presence. Even though she could barely see him now in the darkened studio next door, she felt his every breath.

The two announcers ran through a barrage of vocal warm-ups, which she figured were mostly for show, and she gave the young girl now inside the control box two thumbs up for a great cuppa.

Amazingly the hot drink did help, just slightly.

'Thirty seconds,' the producer announced over the studio loudspeaker, and the sudden sound of commercials filled the room. The announcers sat, smiled at her, and readied themselves.

Georgia took a deep breath and forced her mind off the man whose gaze burned into her back.

'You're listening to EROS: all the best music all the time. We're back with The Valentine Girl, Georgia Stone, who has just finished the most amazing year of self-discovery. Georgia—' the announcer was gifted at sounding as if he hadn't used the last song break to go over in detail what they were about to say '—what was the highlight of your year?'

She leaned a little more into the microphone and did her best to imagine she was speaking only to her gran, not to three million Londoners. 'There was a moment, just a heartbeat really, high above Cappadocia in the balloon, when everything in my life just—' she struggled for the right word, then found it '—reconciled.'

'Reconciled?' the younger announcer said.

'Everything just clicked. Into place. And I knew that I'd found what I was looking for.'

'What were you looking for?'

She forced herself not to even flinch in Zander's direction. 'Myself, mostly.'

'That sounds very Zen.' The second announcer giggled, dubiously.

Introspection. Broadcasting death, Zander had warned her all those months ago. She closed her eyes and gave in. 'And spy school was pretty cool, too.'

And they were off…asking with enormous relief how she'd felt firing a gun and what it was about numerical codes that made her such a natural at solving them.

Empowered and *no idea* were the respective answers.

'An empowered woman with a gun in her hands, look out!' the male announcer said.

Georgia didn't even bother laughing out of courtesy.

The man's eyes flicked up to the control booth window where the producer was making uninterpretable hand signals.

'We're going to take some of your calls now…' the announcer said. He glanced at his computer monitor. 'Lucinda from Epping, go ahead.'

Lucinda from Epping wanted to wax lyrical about belly dancing and how much she enjoyed it since starting it on Georgia's recommendation. She was easy to enthuse with because the belly dancing was something she'd kept up even after the necessity to go had ended. It was somewhere she could escape back to Göreme in her mind. Back to Zander.

And back to the way he'd made her feel when his arms were around her.

Russell from Orpington wanted to complain about his girlfriend and her high standards and how impossible it was for an ordinary man to meet the expectations of empowered women.

'Just try, Russell,' she murmured. 'None of us are looking for perfection. Just a decent effort.'

That even birthed a knowing smirk between the surly producer and her teenaged slave.

'Alex from Hampstead. You've had your own—' the young announcer stared at his computer screen and did his best to pronounce what was obviously an unfamiliar word '—epiphany?'

'That's Alek,' the quiet voice said, and Georgia tightened up like a barrel bolt. 'With a *K*.'

The announcer rolled his eyes. 'Clock's ticking, mate.'

Could they not hear it? She glanced between them all and none of them seemed to have the vaguest idea that it was their boss on the line. Her chest started to rise and fall. She forced herself not to turn around but her inner eye was focused squarely on the glass of the mirrored studio behind her.

'I've had exactly the same moment,' Zander murmured down the line. 'That moment where everything just falls into place and works. Effortless.'

'It's a great feeling,' Georgia pressed past her dry throat. Was he talking about his engagement fifteen years ago?

'And once you've had it and then you lose it it's…intolerable. Worse than never having it at all.'

Yeah, he was. Her chest tightened up.

'But once you've had it,' she whispered, 'then you at least know what to strive for. You know what your bar is.'

'True.'

And she didn't meet his bar the way every man out there would struggle to meet Zander's.

The announcer glanced at his producer for assistance; clearly this wasn't his idea of riveting radio.

'What if you fear you'll never reach it again?' Zander said, low and personal.

His voice, in her earphones, was like lying on that daybed in Göreme with him. Intimate. Breathless. She closed her eyes, pressed the ear pads harder to her head to keep him close. To keep it private.

'If you reached it once,' she whispered, 'then you know you *can* reach it again.'

Even though he was talking about his fiancée, she hated the pain she heard in his voice. She loved him; she didn't want him suffering. The way she was.

'Is that what you believe?' he murmured.

'I have to. Or I'd go crazy wondering if I let the best thing in my world go.'

The announcer suddenly saw an in. 'And someone else has snapped him up now,' he said.

Georgia's eyes flew open and her stomach heaved. Had Zander moved on already? 'What?'

'Your ex. He's spoken for.'

Relief and anger pulsed under her skin in equal measures. Daniel. Not Zander.

The producer's lips formed a string of swearwords clear enough to be readable even by her. The announcer seemed to remember he wasn't supposed to mention Dan. He flushed to his roots. And then paled.

She wondered if Zander hadn't exaggerated how stern a warning he'd given them all.

Silence screamed live on air. She was so conscious that she had to say something. 'I still adore Dan.' She picked her way carefully to an answer. 'But, no, I wasn't talking about him.'

'Aren't you going to ask me where it was?' Zander murmured down the line.

The announcer circled his finger above his head, signalling his producer to wind up the call. She moved to disconnect the call.

'No!' Georgia said out loud and stilled the announcer's gyrofinger and the producer's steps.

'No?' The husky voice grew amused.

'Not you, *Alek*,' she corrected, matching the warmth. 'So go ahead. Where did you have this epiphany?'

How could she be alone in the dark with Zander when three million people were listening? Yet she just didn't care.

'There's a tiny town up near the Scottish border. Great for viewing sunsets.'

Her breath caught.

The radio staff threw up their hands in silent protest as their segment started to unravel before their eyes.

'I kissed a woman there and it changed my life.'

The blood rushed from her face. 'A kiss can't change your life. Only you can do that.'

'I'm beginning to understand that.'

Both announcers and the producer all snapped their focus behind her and their mouths gaped open. She turned and saw the studio lights now fully blazing next door. Illuminating Zander leaning casually up against the glass, his mobile phone to his ear.

'You taught me that,' he said.

Georgia stared, lost in the fixed focus of his eyes. 'I did?'

'I watched you week after week, plunging into situations that you weren't comfortable with, taking the best parts out of them. Always positive. Always interested in the people you met. You only had to do the minimum but you didn't, you applied yourself fully to it.'

'I wanted to fix myself.'

'You weren't broken. You never were. You're perfect the way you are.'

'Perfectly crazy?' She smiled through her tears.

'Perfectly competent.' He tipped his head. 'I want to be competent, too.'

'You are.'

'No. I'm not. I do a job I hate because someone once told me I was good at it. I live a life I hate because someone once convinced me I wasn't worthy of better.'

Lara.

She stood and tugged her headphones and mic with her. They were her lifeline. An umbilical cord to Zander. She crossed to the glass. '*She* was never worthy of *you*.'

'I believe that now. It's taken a long time. She didn't have your courage. Your character.'

No, she didn't. 'What life would you lead, if you could choose?' This moment was too important to care whether EROS' listeners were interested. They might have gone to a commercial for all she knew.

'I want to go back to my roots. Making audio documentaries for syndication. It's what I always wanted to do.'

She thought about all those unnecessary hours of additional sound he'd recorded. 'Is there a market for that?'

'I'll make a market. My house would make a great studio.'

She smiled. His optimism was so infectious.

She placed her small hand on the glass, over his large one where he leaned on it. His eyes glowed down into hers. 'What else?' she whispered.

'I'm going to travel more. See amazing things. Record amazing things. My world has grown way too tiny.'

'You won't be able to travel.' She laughed, though it was more of a cry. 'You'll be poor.'

'You forget, I run marathons. I'll run the world on foot if I have to.'

He would, too, this new Zander. The best of the two Zanders. A tear streaked down her face. She curled her fingers on the glass and wished she could touch his.

'What else?'

'I'm going to get a new gardener.'

The rapid change in direction threw her. 'What happened to Tony?'

He shrugged and smiled, but it was nervous. 'Tony won't live in.'

'You want a live-in gardener?' He might not be able to afford that, either.

He nodded. 'If you're free.'

Behind her, the announcers gasped, as one. And it saved her the trouble.

She had to swallow twice to get the words out. 'You want me to be your gardener?'

He curled his fingers to match hers. 'I want you to have the garden. And you're going to need to tend to it every day.'

'You want me to live in your house?' she whispered.

'For ever, George. With me.'

'But you don't want to get married? You told me.'

He shook his head. 'I didn't want to get hurt. But that hasn't worked. I hurt every day because I'm not with you. So I'm cutting my losses.'

All over London women probably gasped, but Georgia knew exactly what that meant.

'Ever the romantic, Alek,' an announcer said in both their ears.

Zander didn't laugh. Neither did she.

'I love you, Georgia,' he whispered through the glass, down the line and out of three million radio speakers. 'I thought I was managing the rest of my life but the moments with you were like a blazing beacon and they spilled light on just how dull the rest of my existence has become.' He took a breath. 'It's lucrative but it's nothing without you. Totally empty.'

Tears clogged her throat. She struggled to clear them.

'Are you proposing, Alek?' the second announcer prompted, scenting a ratings slaughter.

'Marriage? No,' he breathed, and her heart lurched. 'When I do that I'll do it somewhere infinitely more special than my workplace.' He tucked his phone to his ear and pressed a second hand up against the glass. 'But I am proposing a future. A life together. A second chance for both of us.'

Georgia stared at him through the glass, speechless. Then she ripped her headphones and mic off and turned for the door.

The announcers went into panic mode but she didn't care. They'd talk their way out of it; they always did. They could earn their enormous pay. She threw her gratitude to the young work-experience girl, grinning from ear to ear, who held the studio door open for her so that she could practically run through it.

Outside, the whole office stood, transfixed, staring at the studio doors. She ignored them. Except for Casey who bounced on two feet, tears streaming down her face, both hands pressed to her excited mouth.

Zander met her the moment she burst through the door. Swept her up and locked her to his strong body, turning slowly, eyes squeezed shut.

'I'm so sorry,' he murmured over and over.

'For what?' she gasped, lifting her face from the crook of his neck. 'Practically proposing on air?'

'For letting you go. For making you go.'

'I needed to stand alone. I needed to find that part of myself and know I could survive it.'

He sighed. 'Your courage shamed me.'

'No…'

'But it inspired me, too. To be authentic. To risk everything.'

'Did you think I'd say no?'

'I wasn't thinking. I wasn't planning on calling in when I went into that studio. I just saw you and you were so radiant and...*fine*...it boiled my blood.'

She tipped her head. 'It made you angry that I was doing well?'

'It made me angry that I wasn't. I *so* wasn't. And I realised why the moment you walked back out of this studio. You took all the light with you.'

'And you want me to live in your house?'

'I want us to be together. I think I've been sitting in that house just waiting for it to populate itself with a family. A family I didn't want. But, truthfully, I don't care where we live. In fact, I'd be really happy to go back to Göreme and grow old underground with you. Whatever you want.'

Heat filled her cheeks. 'I really want your garden.'

His lips turned up slightly at the corners. 'Just the garden?'

'No,' she breathed. 'I really want you.'

She lifted her lips and Zander pulled her up closer in his arms to help close the distance. They clung together, sealing their promise in flesh.

On the other side of the glass the two announcers were exploding with mute action, like a pair of mime race-callers. Georgia feared for exactly what was being said but, after the year they'd had, really, how bad could it be?

'I'm sorry we're not going to be rich,' he whispered against her lips.

'I don't want to be rich.'

'I wanted to give you the world.'

She traced his jawline with her finger. 'You already have. Besides,' she said, breathless, 'I'm only cash-poor.'

He frowned. 'But your flat...'

'It's one of four in the complex,' she reminded him. And he nodded. So she broke the news. 'I own them all.'

He just gaped.

'Well, technically the bank owns them all but, you said yourself, I'm thrifty. When all my friends were out clubbing, I was paying the world's biggest mortgage. Determined never to have to beg for somewhere to live again. Between my neighbours' rent and my own repayments and the area booming I have more than seventy per cent equity. So maybe we'll end up closer to equal?'

'You were so scathing about my money.'

She shrugged. 'It was so fun do to. That's the real me. You may want to reconsider...'

'I wouldn't want to do this with anyone else.'

That raised the tiny ghost of the past. 'You did want to do this with someone else, once.'

He considered her seriously. 'It took me a really long time to get to the place where I could be objective about Lara. About the whole sorry mess. But our relationship was always about me making allowances for her, and she loved *that*, she didn't love me. She did me the biggest favour in getting out before it was too late.'

Just as Dan had. 'I understand.'

'Yes. I think you do.'

They kissed again, stepping back out of the view of the viewing window between studios.

'You were so right about how I treat people at work. To keep them at a distance. And my running. All designed to stop me from having to interact with anyone emotionally. And then you came along.'

'And bullied my way in?'

'And looked deep inside me and accepted who I was.'

She beamed up at him. 'Well, aren't we a pair of lucky-to-have-found-each-others?'

He smiled. 'Yeah. We really are.'

'Mr Rush?' The producer's voice boomed out over the studio PA system. Georgia could hear music in the background and knew the segment was over.

She was free.

Free to love the best man in the world.

Zander crossed to the panel and pressed a blue button. 'Yes?'

Just as fearsome as ever, despite the monumental scene he'd just made in front of his whole staff. His tone must have worked because she spoke to him with more courtesy than Georgia had heard from her all afternoon.

'*Nigel Westerly* is on line two, Mr Rush.'

She said it with the same awe she would have used if the Queen of England had picked up the phone.

Zander glanced down at the flashing light on the console, then back at Georgia. He pressed the blue button.

'Tell Westerly I'm busy.'

And then he stepped away from the panel, towards her. The last thing she saw as his head swooped back down for another kiss was the gaping dread on the face of the producer at having to tell the head of the entire network he wasn't going to get his way. And the secret smile on the face of the work-experience kid.

'That was terrible,' she whispered up at him between kisses.

'God, it felt good, though. Never did like her.'

'They aren't all bad.'

'No, they're not. I'm thinking of taking Casey with me, in fact. I'll need a bomb-proof business partner.'

'You think she'll come?'

'I have a way with women.'

'Cocky.'

'I got you, didn't I?'

'Yeah,' she breathed against his lips. 'You absolutely did.'

* * * * *

BEHIND THE FILM STAR'S SMILE

KATE HARDY

For Daisy Cummins, with love and thanks for letting me grill her about film – making!

Kate Hardy lives in Norwich, in the east of England, with her husband, two young children, one bouncy spaniel and too many books to count! When she's not busy writing romance or researching local history, she helps out at her children's schools. She also loves cooking—spot the recipes sneaked into her books! (They're also on her website, along with extracts and stories behind the books.)

Writing for Mills & Boon has been a dream come true for Kate—something she wanted to do ever since she was twelve. She's been writing Medical Romances for over ten years now. She says it's the best of both worlds, because she gets to learn lots of new things when she's researching the background to a book: add a touch of passion, drama and danger, a new gorgeous hero every time, and it's the perfect job!

Kate's always delighted to hear from readers, so do drop in to her website at www.katehardy.com

CHAPTER ONE

OMG. LUKE *MCKENZIE*.

When Jess had taken the assignment from the temp agency to work as a production assistant for a film company, she'd expected it to be a low-budget affair with actors she'd never heard of. Not Luke McKenzie, who'd been named as the most beautiful man in the world for three years running. Luke McKenzie, the favourite actor of both her sister and her best friend, and whose films they dragged her to see at the cinema, even though Jess would rather watch a decent sci-fi movie than sit through a rom-com for the umpteenth time.

Luke McKenzie, who right now didn't look very happy.

Neither did the chocolate Labrador who was sitting beside him, radiating guilt.

Well, this was none of her business. She was meant to be sorting out some paperwork, not gawking at an A-list movie star or listening in to her boss's conversation.

'Jess, can you come here a second, please?' Ayesha Milan, the production manager, called.

'Sure,' Jess said, expecting to be sent on an errand.

'Can you look after Mr McKenzie's dog today?'

Jess froze.

Look after a dog.

That was precisely why she'd left the career she loved and had become a temp. So she'd never have to look after another dog again.

'I...'

'She doesn't bite,' Luke said, rolling his eyes. 'Just steals things and chews them. She seems to have a particular taste for Louboutins.'

Expensive designer shoes. Well, that would explain why he didn't look too happy—the owner of said shoes had probably had a mammoth hissy fit on him when she'd discovered the damage, and replacing them would be far from cheap.

'Jess, are you scared of dogs?' Ayesha asked.

'No-o,' Jess said hesitantly. She wasn't scared of dogs. She was scared of bonding with them. Of having her heart shredded again. It had taken her more than a year to get to where she was now. The thought of having to look after a dog was bringing everything right back to her.

'Then can you take charge of...?' Ayesha looked at Luke to prompt him for the dog's name.

'Baloo.'

'Baloo,' Ayesha finished, looking straight at Jess.

Oh, help.

As a production assistant, Jess was basically meant to do anything she was asked to do. Saying no would be tantamount to cancelling her contract. Even though she'd worked for the temp agency for nearly a year now, it would still make her look unreliable if she walked out of this job less than an hour after she'd started it, leaving the client in a mess. Which meant they'd be less likely to give her any more assignments, and she couldn't afford to lose her job.

But saying yes meant putting herself back in a vulnerable position. Something she really didn't want to do.

'I've got to get back to the set. I don't have time for this. Here,' Luke said, and handed her the dog's lead.

Before Jess could process what was happening, he'd stomped off.

Leaving her with the dog.

'I—look, don't I have other stuff to do for you?' she asked Ayesha, inwardly panicking. Please let her not have to do this. Please.

Ayesha spread her hands. 'The big thing is to keep the stars happy. We have to tiptoe round them.' She sighed. 'I expected Mimi to be the difficult one, not him.'

'Why did he bring the dog on set? Especially if he knows that she chews things?'

Ayesha shrugged. 'I have no idea.'

'He could've brought a crate with him. Where the dog would've felt safe instead of worried by all the people round her, and—' Jess stopped, aware that Ayesha was looking curious.

'You sound as if you know about dogs.'

A degree in animal behaviour and working as a police dog trainer for most of her career had taught Jess a lot. 'A bit,' Jess mumbled.

'Then you'll be the perfect person to look after Baloo,' Ayesha said brightly.

No, she wasn't. She was the last person to look after the dog. Why hadn't she lied and said that she was scared of dogs, or allergic to them? And she was furious at the way the actor had behaved. This was as bad as the socialites who carried a little dog around with them as an accessory. 'If you haven't got time to look after a dog properly, you shouldn't have one,' Jess said. 'I don't care if he's the star of the film. This isn't how you treat dogs.' She frowned. 'My sister and my best friend think he's wonderful. I didn't think he'd be like—well, like *that*, in real life.' Grouchy. Demanding. Whatever the male equivalent of a diva was.

'He never used to be,' Ayesha said. 'I worked on a film with him a couple of years ago, and he was a total sweetheart—he remembered everyone's name, thanked anyone who ran an errand for him, and I think every female member of the crew and cast fell in love with him. Including me, and I'm used to actors being charming. With him, it wasn't acting. He meant it.' She shrugged. 'But he's had a pretty hard time the last year. I think it's changed him.'

Jess remembered seeing the stories about the break-up of Luke McKenzie's marriage in the press. A divorce must be hard enough to deal with, but having the press zooming in on every detail must make it so much worse. And even Carly and Shannon—her sister and her best friend—had admitted that Luke's last film hadn't been quite as good as the previous ones. Not surprising, really: when your life imploded, it was pretty hard to concentrate on your job and do your best. Which was why Jess was focusing on doing something completely different from her old life. 'Even so, you don't just dump your dog on the nearest stranger.'

The dog licked her hand, as if glad that someone was batting her corner, and Jess felt something crack in the region of her heart.

No.

She couldn't do this. She couldn't make herself that vulnerable and open again.

'Wouldn't it be better if she went to the animal handling department?' Jess asked, hoping she didn't sound quite as desperate as she felt.

'They work part-time and they're only on set when we actually need them.' Ayesha looked at her schedule. 'Which isn't today.'

So she had no choice?

'Jess, if you could look after the dog, I'd be really grateful,' Ayesha said. 'I need to keep everything running as smoothly as possible. And if we say we can't do it and give the dog back to him, it's going to affect rehearsals. We start filming this week, so we can't afford any setbacks. The dog chewed Mimi's shoes. I've already had a message from the director to get another pair delivered here by lunchtime. I get the impression that if we refuse to look after her and the dog goes back with Luke, then Mimi's going to walk off set. And it'll take an awful lot to unruffle her feathers and persuade her to come back.'

'Artistic temperament?' Jess asked.

'Let's just say she lives up to her name.'

Mimi—me, me, me, me. Jess got it instantly.

Ayesha blew out a breath. 'Though I'd appreciate it if you didn't repeat any of that.'

Jess remembered what the production manager had told her right from the start: set rules were non-negotiable. What happened on set, stayed on set. No photographs, no social media, no mobile phones, no leaks. Everything within the bounds of the set was to remain a completely separate world. 'Of course not.'

'And if you can get those call sheets for tomorrow sorted while you're looking after the dog, that'd be good.' Ayesha smiled at her.

Dismissed, but nicely so. It looked as if she didn't

have a choice in the matter, then. 'OK,' Jess said, and took the dog over to her own desk.

Luke McKenzie hadn't bothered to bring a water bowl with him, or give any information about the dog's feeding schedule. And she had no idea when the movie star planned to come and collect the dog. He hadn't bothered to tell them that, either.

Jess wasn't sure what made her angriest: the fact that Luke had dumped his dog, or the fact that he'd put her in an impossible position. She didn't want to look after his dog, but she had no way to refuse. Not without explanations she didn't want to make, because she'd had enough of people pitying her.

'He needs a lesson in manners,' she said to the dog. 'And a lot of lessons in how to look after you. You haven't even got any toys to keep you busy.'

The dog shifted closer to Jess and put her head on Jess's knee.

Jess had to fight back the tears. It'd been so long since she'd worked at a desk with a dog cuddled up close to her. And the spaniel-shaped hole in her life felt as if it had just opened up again.

She dragged in a breath. 'Let's see what we can sort out for you, sweetie.' A word with the catering department netted her a plastic bowl for water, and a word with the props department gained her a tennis ball. 'It's a bit sketchy, but it's better than nothing,' she said. 'We'll work round this.'

And she wouldn't bond with the dog in just one day. Would she?

That, Luke thought as he headed for the temporary building of the production office, was possibly one of the worst days he'd ever spent in his entire career as a film actor. A co-star who wanted to be treated as if she were the empress of the entire universe, a ridiculous bill for replacing a pair of shoes that said co-star could barely walk in, and now he had to go back and collect the dog that had been dumped on him. The dog he didn't want. The dog who'd wrecked both his house and his sleep over the last two days.

The icing on the misery cake now would be another of those snide little articles asking if Luke McKenzie was in the process of making another box office flop. He was pretty sure that the last couple had been written by one of his ex-wife's cronies, but calling them both on it would just result in yet more bad publicity for him. Say nothing, and he was a wimp. Protest, and he was a spiteful bastard who was trying to get revenge on his ex. Whatever he did, he lost.

'Just grin and bear it,' he told himself. Fleur would get over the guilt eventually, and she'd stop trying to paint him as the bad guy in an attempt to make herself feel better about what she'd done.

He hoped.

There was *one* way Luke could turn the tables on her and get all the sympathy, but he wasn't prepared to do that. Particularly as he knew how quickly the press could put the opposite spin on a story to get more mileage from it. That part of his life was private, and it was staying that way.

OK. He only had to put up with the dog until Thursday. Just another three days. Then his aunt would be back in London to find the dog a permanent home; and he could get back to concentrating on his career. And on making damn sure that this movie was a huge success so Fleur and her cronies wouldn't be able to say another word.

Luke walked into the office, expecting to see Ayesha Milan, but the only person he saw was the new assistant. He hadn't actually caught her name this morning. He really regretted that; he'd always sworn that he wouldn't be one of the stuck-up stars who forgot what it was like to be at the bottom of the heap. He usually made a point of making sure that anyone who worked with him knew that he appreciated what they did and he didn't take them for granted. Today, he'd slipped up. Badly.

'Mr McKenzie,' she said, her mouth thinning. 'Come to collect your dog?'

'Yes.'

He was about to apologise for the way he'd dumped the dog on her that morning, but she didn't give him the chance. 'I don't care if you're Mr Big Shot Actor, and I don't care if you complain to Ayesha and get me fired for this, but what you did this morning is most definitely *not* the way to treat a dog. You dumped her on us—without any water, any food, any bedding, any toys—and that's just not good enough.'

OK. He already knew that.

She wasn't finished. 'My sister and my best friend think you're the greatest as a movie star.'

Implying, he thought, that *she* didn't.

'But, let me tell you, you totally suck as a dog owner.'

He couldn't deny that. She was speaking the truth.

'Absolutely. I know nothing about dogs.' He paused. 'And Baloo isn't mine.'

That seemed to take the wind out of her sails. 'She's not yours?'

'I'm looking after her—not that I had any choice—until my aunt gets back from America in three days' time.'

'Oh.' She paused, frowning. 'Why didn't you have a choice?'

'Doesn't matter. I'll take her off your hands, now.' Not that he was going to make a good job of it. The next seventy-two hours or so were going to stretch him to the limit. It didn't help that the dog had chewed his script, too. The damned dog chewed *everything*. Worse still, how could he remain angry with an animal who leaped around in joy and wagged her tail madly when she saw him, and right now was sitting at his feet, looking up at him with what was definitely the canine equivalent of a dopey welcoming smile?

'Why didn't you have a choice?' The assistant's voice was softer, now. Kinder.

God, how easy it would be to let himself respond. But he couldn't afford to do that. He needed to keep his focus.

'Your aunt must've known you're working this week. She could've booked Baloo into kennels.'

'She's not my aunt's dog, either.' The words slipped out before he could stop them.

She raised an eyebrow. 'So how come your aunt asked you to look after Baloo?'

It was a long, long story.

Diversion was the best tactic here. He smiled at her. 'I'm sorry; I didn't catch your name earlier.'

'Jess Greenacre.'

'Jess.' Short for Jessica? A staccato name, clipped and a little harsh. How she'd been with him when he'd walked in. But now he looked at her—Jess. Softer. Sweeter. She wasn't wearing a scrap of make-up, not even mascara to enhance those amazing green eyes.

And what the hell was he doing, letting himself no-tice that? He shook himself. Even if he was in a position to think about another relationship, it sure as hell wouldn't be with anyone remotely connected to the movie business. Been there, done that, and been vilified by the press for it. Which really rankled, considering that he hadn't been the one who'd cheated and broken up the marriage.

Though he *had* lied. About one tiny little fact. And if that ever got out...

He shook himself. 'Jess. I was pretty short with you this morning. Rude, even. I'm sorry. This is your first day on set, isn't it?'

She looked surprised that he'd noticed. 'Yes, it is, Mr McKenzie.'

'Call me Luke. And welcome to the team,' he said.

She folded her arms. 'OK, you get points for good manners. Even though I suspect you might be acting your socks off, right now.'

To his surprise, he found himself laughing.

When was the last time he'd really laughed like that? Really been amused?

And when was the last time someone had called him on his behaviour instead of tiptoeing round him? Probably not since before the break-up of his marriage.

Jess Greenacre was refreshing. And she was the first person in a long while to intrigue him. She looked older than the average production assistant, so this probably wasn't her first job. So why was she in such a junior role?

None of his business, he reminded himself.

'I'm not acting right now,' he said. 'And I'm not usually—well, like I was this morning.'

'But your dog had just chewed your co-star's shoes, there were some feathers that needed unruffling, and time was tight. You were under too much pressure, and you snapped.'

She'd worked all that out? Bright as well as refreshing, then. Apart from the one thing she just hadn't seemed to grasp. 'Baloo's not my dog, but otherwise yes,' he admitted. 'My co-star didn't want a doggy audience at rehearsals. I did put Baloo in a crate but then she howled the place down and the director wasn't too pleased. I thought she'd be OK if I let her out. She sat really nicely and just watched. I thought it would be fine.' He sighed. 'I wasn't prepared for her to sneak off when my back was turned and steal some shoes to chew. Even though she's pretty much destroyed my house, the last two days.'

'Destroyed your house?' Jess asked.

'I left her for ten minutes on Saturday morning to get some croissants and a newspaper. She opened every cupboard in the kitchen while I was gone and shredded every bag and box she could find. You wouldn't believe how much mess rice, pasta, oatmeal and a bag of flour can make. Or how long it takes to clear up.'

Jess raised an eyebrow. 'You didn't leave her with any toys?'

'She didn't come with toys.' He sighed. 'She's gutted three cushions, shredded two newspapers, chewed my script—and she can undo doors, so she won't stay on her own bed at night and then insists on having more than half of mine.'

This time, Jess laughed. 'I think Baloo needs something to keep her mind busy. Like those balls you can stuff with treats, and the dog has to work hard to get the treats out.'

Jess sounded as if she actually knew what she was talking about. 'You know stuff about dogs?' he checked.

She looked wary. 'A bit.'

'Jess, I need help. I know *nothing* about dogs. I've never had one.'

'So why did your aunt ask you to look after her?'

'It's a long story.' He looked at her. 'You've probably been in here since the crack of dawn, and you'll be expected in at the same time tomorrow. I can't hold you up any longer. That's not fair. I'll take the dog and let you get on.'

She looked surprised, as if she hadn't expected him to notice the kind of hours the production team worked. And he could hardly blame her. She'd accused him of acting like Mr Big Shot Actor.

Which, admittedly, he had.

'I'm not usually this much of an idiot,' he said. 'Without a good support team, no matter how many awards the cast has won between them, a film just won't happen. You need the whole crew to work together, whether they're in front of the camera or behind the scenes.'

'Right.' She looked thoughtfully at him. 'I can stay a bit longer. How about I make us a cup of tea and you tell me about Baloo?'

'How about,' he said, '*I* make the tea?'

'But you're—'

'Part of the team,' he cut in, not wanting to hear her repeat that he was Mr Big Shot Actor. 'If you're going to tell me things that can help me deal with a shoe-stealing dog who chews anything she can get her paws on, then making you a cup of tea is the very least I can do.'

Was he still acting? Jess wondered.

Then again, Ayesha had said that Luke used to be a total sweetheart, but he'd had a hard time over the last year and it seemed to have changed him.

Maybe this man was the real Luke McKenzie, rather than the arrogant, grumpy man she'd met this morning.

And everyone deserved a second chance.

Well, *nearly* everyone. There were a couple of people that Jess hoped would stay in prison for the rest of their lives. Though now wasn't the time to think about that.

'Thank you, Mr McKenzie.'

'Luke,' he reminded her.

This was surreal. Since when would an A-list movie star ask you to call him by his first name? She pinched herself surreptitiously, just in case this was some weirdly realistic dream. It hurt. Not a dream, then. 'Luke,' she repeated. 'I like my tea very weak and milky.'

'So the tea bag says hello to the water and disappears again? That's utterly gross,' Luke said, 'but OK, if that's how you want it. Sugar?'

'No, thanks. Tell me about Baloo.'

'My aunt volunteers at a home for abandoned dogs,' he said. 'Baloo was—um—oh, just cover her ears for a second, will you?'

Cover the dog's ears? Jess didn't get it, but she did as he asked.

'She was on death row. Monica—my aunt—smuggled her out. The problem was, Monica had to be at the airport six hours after that, and all the kennels were full.'

Jess smelt a rat. A very, very big one. *'All* the kennels were full?'

'According to Monica, yes. She didn't actually tell me why Baloo was on death row, but I'm guessing it's to do with the stealing and chewing.'

'Normally it's because they're an older dog who's been abandoned, or because the owners can't look after them any more—' Jess forced herself not to think *because they'd died* '—and none of their friends or family has room for a pet. She's young and healthy.' She shrugged and stopped covering Baloo's ears. 'You're probably right about the chewing. I'd guess it's separation anxiety, especially as she wanted to be with you and she doesn't cope with being left alone. But your aunt must've realised you know nothing about dogs.'

'Yeah. Half the time, I'm not even in London; having a pet wouldn't be fair because it would spend half its time in kennels.'

'But you still agreed to look after Baloo.'

'Temporarily. We're rehearsing this week, and Monica's back the day we start shooting.' He raked a hand through his hair. 'I had no idea that looking after a dog would be this hard.'

'A dog who's been kicked out of at least one home, to be on dea—well, in the position she was,' Jess amended. 'A dog with special needs. Not the easiest starter dog for a rookie owner.'

'You know about dogs.' It was a statement, not a question.

A lie would be too obvious. 'Yes.'

'Can you help me?' he asked. 'Please? I know you're a virtual stranger and I have no right to ask you for help, but apart from my aunt you're about the only person I've met who knows anything at all about dogs.'

Which wasn't her problem. She could just walk away. This wasn't part of her job description. She didn't *have* to deal with the dog.

But Jess had never been the sort to walk away and refuse help when someone needed it. Saying no would be denying who she was.

'Please, Jess?' he asked again.

'You're the star of a movie, where I happen to be the production assistant and I'm supposed to do whatever I'm told. All you have to do is tell Ayesha you want me to jump, and she'll ask you how high,' Jess pointed out.

He winced. 'God. I always swore I'd never be like that. And I was horrible, this morning. Worse than Mi–' He stopped abruptly.

Jess could guess whose name he'd just cut off. Mimi, his co-star. Owner of expensive designer shoes, and clearly also hater of dogs.

'I'm sorry,' he finished.

She was pretty sure now that he wasn't acting. His eyes were almost silver in this light. And they were utterly sincere. 'Maybe you were having a bad day,' she suggested.

'A lot of bad days all in a row,' he said, wrinkling his nose. 'But that's still no excuse for treating people badly.'

Did he have any idea how cute it made him look when he wrinkled his nose like that?

Yes, of course he did. He must do, she thought. It was his job, after all. Hunky movie star. The job description no doubt included the line: *must look gorgeous and appealing to all women at all times*.

'Jess, can you help me? Please?' he asked again.

More charm. He'd made her a cup of tea, just the way she liked it. And she noticed how often he'd used her name—a trick she'd been taught at work, too. It made people have confidence in you if you used their name. It made them feel that you were on their side. It made whatever you said feel *personal*.

No.

She ought to say no.

She didn't want to get involved with another dog.

Not after losing Comet. The whole point of working as a freelancer was that she wouldn't get time to bond with any of her colleagues—not like her days with the police, when she knew every single dog in her team and every single handler she trained. When they were friends as well as colleagues. When she'd known most of the dogs from the moment they were born.

Being that close to everyone had left her life in tatters, and she just couldn't let that happen all over again.

'Please, Jess?' he asked softly. 'I can't hold up rehearsals until my aunt gets back. We're on a tight schedule and a tight budget as it is. And I definitely can't take Baloo back to the dogs' home. You know what will happen if I do.'

The dog would be put down.

And Jess had had enough death in her life, this last year or so. She couldn't bear the idea of a young, healthy dog being put down just because she hadn't been trained and was a bit boisterous.

'She needs training. Which means a lot of time and hard work and patience,' Jess warned.

'I guess that'll be Monica's job. Or maybe when she gets back she'll find the right home for her, with someone who can do the training. But for now Baloo's with me. And I haven't got the time to train her or give her the attention she needs.' He stooped to scratch the back of the dog's head, and the dog rubbed her face against his knee.

Not his dog, hmm? From Jess's point of view, that looked like some serious bonding going on. He'd made a fuss of the dog without even realising he was doing it. And the dog was looking adoringly back at him. As far as Baloo was concerned, she'd found the person she wanted to live with for the rest of her days; Jess had a feeling that Luke might not have quite as much say in the matter as he thought he did.

'So can you help us, Jess? Please?'

Say yes, and open herself up to the risk of getting involved and being hurt.

Or do the sensible thing and say no, sorry, she couldn't.

Except that would mean refusing to help a dog who was already in trouble and had nobody to speak up for her. How could Jess possibly do that?

'Can't you find a dog-sitting service?' she asked in a last-ditch effort.

'Dump her on someone else, you mean?' He grimaced. 'Monica trusted me with her, and I've already messed up once. I feel Baloo ought to stay near me.'

'Even though you keep telling me she's not your dog?' She couldn't help calling him on the inconsistency.

'Fair point.' He sighed. 'Look, Monica's my favourite aunt. And she's batted my corner more than once. This is my chance to do something for her. I just need someone to help me get through the next three days.'

Three days.

Knowing that she was probably doing totally the wrong thing, but not being able to steel her heart enough to be sensible, Jess said, 'OK. I'll help. Provided it's OK with Ayesha.'

'Thank you, Jess. I really appreciate this.'

When Luke shook her hand, it made Jess feel all funny. Tingly. Weird. Like nothing she'd ever experienced before.

Then again, Luke McKenzie was a movie star. He had stage presence—no, *screen* presence—and this was a straightforward case of being faced with that for the first time. After a couple of weeks of working on the set, no doubt she'd be completely immune to it.

'No problem, Mr McKenzie,' she mumbled.

He gave her another of those knee-melting smiles. 'I meant it when I said to call me Luke.'

Oh, that smile. On the big screen, his smile was stunning. In real life, it was a hundred times better. No wonder he had a ton of female fans willing to fall at his feet and do just about anything for him. Jess was horribly aware that she'd just joined their ranks and she understood now for the first time why her sister and her best friend had always raved about him so much.

Because Luke McKenzie really was something else.

'So, where do we start?' he asked. 'What time are you in tomorrow?'

'Half past seven.'

'You'll need time to get stuff sorted, first. Shall I meet you here at half past eight?' he asked.

Again, Jess's whole body felt tingly and weird. Which was crazy. Luke McKenzie wasn't asking her out on a date and arranging when and where to meet her. Of course a movie star wouldn't ask an ordinary person on a date. He just wanted her to help him train his dog. This was business.

'If it's OK with Ayesha,' she said again.

'If what's OK with me?' the production manager said, walking back into the office and clearly overhearing the end of Jess's words.

'I need help with the dog,' Luke said. 'So she doesn't steal anything else from Mimi and chew it to pieces. It's only for three days. And I'm more than happy to pay for a temp to fill in for Jess.'

'Baloo wasn't any trouble today,' Jess said. 'I don't

need anyone to fill in for me. I can still do what I need to do here and have her with me.'

'Are you sure?' Luke asked.

She nodded.

'If the actors are happy, then I'm happy,' Ayesha said. 'OK, Mr McKenzie. Jess can help with your dog.'

He grimaced. 'We were on first-name terms when we worked on *A Forever Kind of Love*, a couple of years back. Or would you prefer me to call you Ms Milan now?'

Ayesha winced. 'This film isn't the same as that one.'

'You mean, *I'm* not the same,' he said softly. 'I'm sorry. I shouldn't take my personal life out on my colleagues. You're right—I haven't been my normal self on set for a while now, and that isn't fair to the rest of the crew. Let me know if I've upset anyone here, and I'll have a quiet word with them and apologise tomorrow.'

Ayesha nodded. 'Thank you, Luke. That makes things a bit easier.'

'And I'll try not to be such an idiot in future.'

That earned him a lick on his hand from Baloo, and Jess couldn't help smiling.

Maybe she wasn't doing the wrong thing, agreeing to help.

Maybe this was going to be just fine.

And maybe, she thought, Baloo was going to do them both a favour. Help them both move on from a difficult situation in the past.

'Half past eight,' he said to Jess.

She nodded. 'Bring her water bowl, food bowl and whatever she eats during the day, a bed and some toys.'

'Toys?'

'Baloo, you need to take him shopping,' Jess told the dog. 'Something to chew is top priority.'

'Not squeaky,' Ayesha called over, 'or you'll drive me potty.'

Jess laughed. 'There you go, Luke. Your mission, should you choose to accept it…'

He laughed back. 'That's about right. OK. Doggy toy shop it is, then. Come on, Baloo.'

CHAPTER TWO

AT HALF PAST seven the next morning, Jess was in the production office, running errands for Ayesha and sorting out all the things that needed to be done before rehearsals for the day started.

It still didn't feel real that she was meeting Luke McKenzie this morning.

And she still wasn't quite sure whether he was a genuinely nice guy who was struggling through a tough time, or arrogant, selfish and just playing Mr Nice Guy in order to get her to dog-sit for him.

Either way, she needed her head examining. Spending a day with a dog was the last thing she needed.

But at least today she was prepared. And she had every intention of making Luke McKenzie do some of the work.

At twenty-five past eight, he turned up with the dog and several bags. 'Morning, Ayesha. Morning, Jess,' he said as he walked through the door.

'Morning, Luke,' Ayesha said.

'Good morning, Luke,' Jess echoed. 'And hello to you, Baloo.'

The dog wagged her tail madly and strained on her lead, pulling Luke along the length of the office to get to Jess, and then put her paws on Jess's knee and licked her face.

'Get down, you bad hound,' Jess said, but her tone was very far from scolding.

She'd missed this so much, having a dog around.

But she knew she had to compartmentalise. This was a job.

Three days.

No bonding.

'I've just ticked the last thing off your list. Is it OK for me to go and help train the dog for an hour or so, Ayesha?' Jess asked.

The production manager looked up from her desk. 'Sure.' She smiled. 'I'll have another list waiting when you get back.'

'That's fine,' Jess said.

Luke produced a box of expensive-looking chocolates and handed them to Ayesha. 'Thank you for lending me your assistant. She'll be back with you as soon as we start rehearsing.'

Ayesha went pink with pleasure. 'Dark chocolates. How lovely.'

'I hope I remembered right?' he checked.

'Oh, you did—dark chocolate's my absolute favourite.' She smiled at him. 'Thank you, Luke. See you both later.'

A showy gesture from a movie star? Jess wondered. Or a heartfelt thanks, and he'd actually taken the trouble to remember the production manager's tastes? Or maybe it was a mixture of the two, because people were never quite that simple.

'Right. One bed, one water bowl, one food bowl, one doggy packed lunch, one non-squeaky bone to chew, one ball, one rope thing…' Luke handed Jess the contents of the large bag, one by one.

'What, did you buy up the whole pet shop?' she asked, amused.

'No. I stood in the doorway with Baloo and asked the assistant to get me stuff to keep a chocolate Labrador from chewing everything in sight. Oh, and I said it had to be stuff with no squeaks.'

Jess looked at the assortment of toys on her desk and grinned. 'I think you've just about got enough to keep her interested.'

'I hope so,' he said, sounding heartfelt. 'So what are we doing this morning?'

'We need a quiet corner to work in. No distractions for Madam, here,' Jess said, unable to resist scratching the dog behind her ears. Baloo closed her eyes in bliss.

'A quiet corner. Let me think for a second. OK.' Luke took them to a bit of the set Jess hadn't been to while running errands the previous day.

'The very basics are "sit" and "stay". I'd guess that Baloo's never been trained at all, so it might take her a while to pick it up,' Jess warned. 'Baloo, sit.'

The dog glanced at her blankly.

Jess gently stroked down the dog's back. 'Baloo, sit.'

The dog sat; Jess gave her a piece of chopped liver from her pocket and the dog wolfed it down before licking her hand in gratitude.

'Dog treats?' Luke guessed.

'Cooked chopped liver,' Jess enlightened him.

'And you keep it in your pocket?' Luke looked horrified.

'In a Ziplock bag. But, yes—if I left it all within her reach she'd scoff the lot within seconds and I wouldn't have any training treats left,' she pointed out.

He eyed her curiously. 'You've done this before, haven't you?'

There was no point in lying. 'Yes.'

'So, if you can train dogs, why are you working as a temporary production assistant?'

Because I can't handle doing my old job.

'It's a job.' Jess shrugged. And, to stop him asking any further questions, she said, 'Right, your turn.'

It took him a couple of goes, but Baloo sat for him.

'Now the treat.' Jess offered him the bag. Was he going to be all prissy about it and refuse to get his precious movie star fingers dirty?

But he took a piece of liver from the bag and gave it to the dog.

That was a good start, she thought. Maybe she could work with him.

'Next, we teach her to stay.' She got Baloo to sit. 'Stay,' she said, and walked a couple of steps away.

Baloo bounded straight over to her, clearly panicking that Jess was going to leave.

'No, sweetheart, I'm not going anywhere. But I need you to do what I tell you,' Jess said. She walked Baloo back to the spot and tried it again. On the fourth attempt, the dog got it. 'Good girl.' Jess made a fuss of her and gave her a treat.

'Your turn,' she said to Luke.

Again, it took a couple of tries, but eventually the dog did what he asked. 'Good girl,' he said, and made a fuss of her before giving her a treat.

Luke didn't seem to be so uptight today, Jess thought. He was definitely more relaxed than he'd been yesterday, and he was interacting with the dog instead of dumping her as fast as he could on someone else. Maybe it was because rehearsals hadn't started yet today, so he hadn't had to deal with his difficult co-star; or maybe the dog was helping him relax.

She so wanted it to be the latter.

They worked with the dog for a bit longer before the runner came over. 'Mr McKenzie, the director's ready for you now.'

'Sure,' he said with a smile. 'I'm coming now. Jess, thank you—and you're sure it's OK to look after Baloo today?'

No, she wasn't sure at all. 'Ayesha said it was OK.'

He pulled a wad of paper from the back of his jeans, ripped a corner off one piece and scribbled a number on the back. 'Any problems, this is my mobile phone.'

Luke McKenzie was giving her his mobile phone number?

Surreal.

It was a far cry from her old life.

She stopped the thought before it could grow any more. The past was the past, and she couldn't change it. There was no point in dwelling on it and wishing, because doing that hadn't made a scrap of difference in the last year. The shooting had still happened, the drug-dealers were all still in jail with life sentences, Matt and Comet were still buried under a carpet of flowering bulbs, and she still had nothing left but memories and wishes.

'I can hardly ring you in the middle of rehearsals. It'd mess everything up.'

'Text me, then. I'll leave my phone on silent,' he said. 'OK.'

Back in the production office, as promised, Ayesha had another list ready. Jess worked her way through it, either at her desk with Baloo snuggled in her bed next to Jess's desk, or with the dog by her side as she walked round the set, taking scripts to people and running errands.

'So what did you do to Luke McKenzie to make him human again?' Ayesha asked when Jess returned from the last errand on her list.

'I told him what I thought of him,' Jess confessed. 'Sorry.'

'That's a dangerous tactic, Jess. If he'd been a certain other member of the cast—one who cannot *possibly* be named—then you would've had to grovel publicly and you would still have been fired,' Ayesha said. She came over to make a fuss of the dog. 'But well done. It's nice to see Luke being more like his old self. Let's hope it lasts.' She looked at the dog. 'She's beautiful, isn't she? And she's the perfect match for him. Sexy movie star hero with the cute dog. How could any woman resist that combination?'

Good question. Well, Jess would have to, for her own peace of mind. She wasn't looking for a relationship. Even if she was, she knew that Luke McKenzie was from a different world—one where she wouldn't fit in. She was ordinary, and he lived his life in the glare of the spotlights.

'Time for your lunch break, I think. Though you'll need to take the dog with you.'

'Sure.' Jess smiled at her boss and then looked at Baloo. 'How about a run in the park opposite?' she asked Baloo.

The dog looked at her as if she was speaking Martian.

'Your owners didn't do that with you, did they?' She sighed. 'OK. Walkies?'

Baloo still looked blank.

'You're going to enjoy this, sweetie,' she said. 'But

I'd better let Luke know where we're going.' She didn't want to call him, in case he was in the middle of a scene; but she was pretty sure a text would be safe and he'd be able to pick up the message later.

She texted Luke to tell him she was taking Baloo to the park, put the dog's water bowl in a bag, then headed off the set.

When Jess took Baloo for a run, she realised how much she'd missed it. Working out on a treadmill in a featureless gym was nothing like running outside in the fresh air, with grass and trees all around, and the scent of spring blossom in the air. There really was nothing like running with a dog bounding along by your side. She swallowed hard. It wasn't the Labrador's fault that her head was still a bit messed up. But the memories made her catch her breath and she had to stop.

She filled the dog's water bowl from the bottle she carried with her, then bought another bottle of water from the kiosk in the park, along with a chicken wrap for her lunch.

Once she'd settled herself on a park bench and Baloo was sitting next to her, the dog looked hopefully at her. Or, rather, at her chicken wrap.

'You think I'm going to share this with you?' she asked.

The dog's expression was eloquent enough, and Jess laughed. 'OK. You can have some of the chicken, but I'm going to make you work for this, Baloo. Shake hands.'

To her surprise, the dog caught on very quickly. What a shame that her former owners hadn't seen her potential. And what a shame that Baloo was only going to have a temporary home with Luke McKenzie.

Maybe she could...

No. She stopped her thoughts before the temptation got too strong.

Her lease said no dogs—and that was one of the reasons why she'd chosen the flat in the first place. To make sure that she had a solid reason not to weaken and let another dog into her life. A dog she could lose, the way she'd lost Comet. She'd spent the last year putting the pieces of her life back together, and the only way to keep herself safe was to keep herself separate. She needed to remember that. She absolutely couldn't adopt Baloo. No matter how tempting the idea was.

Luke checked his phone during the scene break. There was a message from a number he didn't recognise; he assumed it was from Jess and flicked into it.

She was taking Baloo to the park?

That was definitely above and beyond the call of duty. He still felt a bit guilty about dumping the dog on her, but what else could he have done? He couldn't leave Baloo at home because he knew she'd trash the place and he didn't want the dog in a situation where she could get hurt. He couldn't take time off from rehearsals, because that wouldn't be fair to the rest of the cast. And, thanks to Mimi's tantrum after the shoe episode yesterday, he couldn't keep the dog on the set with him either.

And then there was Jess herself. Straight-talking, and not afraid to stick up for an unwanted dog even if it could mean she'd be fired.

Something about her drew him.

Which was ridiculous. Apart from the fact that Luke wasn't in a place where he was even looking for a relationship, for all he knew Jess could be happily married, or at least committed to someone. Even if she wasn't, who would want to date a man in the public eye and have her life stuck under the less than kind microscope of the press? And when Fleur's cronies found out he was dating her, they'd rip her to shreds in the press. He couldn't let that happen. And that meant keeping some distance between them. Not acting on the attraction.

He texted back:

Enjoy the park. Will be rehearsing until about five. Let me know if any problems. And thank you.

A few moments later, his phone beeped to signal an incoming message. Jess again.

All fine. Baloo v keen on chicken.

Uh-oh. Had the dog stolen her sandwich? Something else he'd have to replace.

He typed:

Sorry. Will reimburse you for anything Baloo steals or trashes.

The reply was a smiley face.

No need. Is training aid.

'Luke, we're ready to go again,' the director called.

Director wants me back to work. See you later.

He switched his phone off again when the message had been sent.

* * *

At quarter to six, Luke walked into the production office. 'Sorry I'm late. Rehearsals overran a bit.'

Jess looked up from her desk and smiled. 'No worries.'

At the sound of his voice, Baloo leaped up from her bed, woofed, and raced over to him.

'I think someone's missed you,' Ayesha said with a grin.

'Just tell me she didn't disgrace herself,' Luke said, rolling his eyes.

'She's been great,' Jess told him. 'Actually, Baloo has something she wants to show you. Stand in front of her and crouch down a bit. Baloo, shake hands,' she instructed.

The dog obliged by lifting her paw and shaking hands with Luke.

'Wow. I didn't know she could do that.' He looked impressed.

'She can now. She picks things up quickly and Labradors are very trainable—I think you could have a potential movie star dog here.'

He laughed. 'If I didn't know better, I'd say my aunt called you and recruited you to her campaign to get me a dog.'

'She adores you.'

'Because I'm her favourite nephew. Yeah, yeah.'

'I meant the dog adores you.' Jess couldn't help laughing. 'You're that used to people adoring you?'

'My aunt, yes.'

Interesting that he'd mentioned his aunt rather than his parents or grandparents. So did that mean he was closer to his aunt than to any other relative? Had he lost his parents young, maybe?

Not that it was any of her business. She was simply looking after his dog for three days, not becoming his best friend or anything even close to it. She needed to back off. Now. 'I, um, guess I'd better let you and Baloo get on,' she said. 'See you tomorrow.'

'OK. Want me to make you a cup of tea before I go?' he asked.

Ayesha coughed. 'How come you've managed to snag yourself a personal tea boy, Jess?'

Luke grinned. 'If I remember rightly, Ayesha, you hate tea and only drink espresso. Stronger than anyone else I know can take it, and that includes the Italians.'

'Actors and their memories. I swear they have elephant genes,' Ayesha teased.

'Well, there has to be some benefit to learning lines,' Luke said with a wink.

'Jess, you can go now, if you like,' Ayesha said. 'I'll finish up here.'

'Sure?' Jess asked.

'Sure,' Ayesha confirmed.

And somehow Jess found herself walking out of the office with Luke McKenzie.

'Can I take you for a drink to say thank you?' he asked.

Now she knew he was being polite. And she'd be polite back. 'Thanks, but no. I have a standing date on Tuesday evenings.'

'Uh-huh.'

'With my sister, my best friend and a pizza.' And why had she felt the need to explain that? she wondered, cross with herself. He wouldn't be interested. He was a movie star, for pity's sake, not a normal everyday guy.

'Enjoy,' he said. 'Maybe we can take a rain check on that drink.'

A permanent rain check, she thought. So they'd never actually go. 'Sure.'

'Seriously. Baloo and I owe you.'

A mad idea floated into her head. 'If you really want to say thank you, you could give me two signed photos.'

He looked taken aback. '*Two* signed photos?'

What, did he think she meant to sell them on eBay or something? 'For my sister and my best friend,' she explained. 'It'd make their day. They drag me off to see all your films.'

He grinned. 'Under duress, would that be?'

She winced. 'Sorry, that came out wrong. I like your films, too.'

'But rom-coms aren't your thing?'

'I like them,' she said, trying to be polite.

'But?'

'But I prefer action films,' she confessed. 'Especially sci-fi. I'm sorry. I don't mean to be rude.'

He laughed. 'No, it's refreshing. It's nice to have someone being honest instead of telling me that they've seen all my films twenty times and I'm the best actor in the world—which I know I'm not. Of course I'll give you a signed photo for your sister and your best friend. It's the least I can do. Come back with me and Baloo to my trailer and I'll get them now.'

'You have a trailer? And one of those chairs with your name on it?' She felt her eyes widen. Luke McKenzie was a huge international star, and he'd made her feel so at ease that she'd actually forgotten that.

He laughed again. 'Don't be expecting a huge palace with gold-plated taps or what have you. It's just an ordinary caravan. Somewhere to have some space to myself.' He scratched the top of the dog's head. 'Which

Madam here would chew up in a matter of seconds if I left her there.'

Baloo just gave him an innocent look.

Jess followed him back to the trailer. As he'd said, it was just a caravan, a place where he could make himself a drink and chill out. It was also incredibly tidy; either he was a neat freak, or one of the runners had to tidy it up for him every day. There was a dog cage, she noticed; obviously the one he'd talked about yesterday, from which the dog had escaped.

'Photos. OK. Give me a second.' He rummaged in a drawer and brought out two photographs and cardboard envelopes. 'Who do I sign them to?'

'Carly—she's my sister—and Shannon, my best friend, please.'

He took out a pen, signed the photographs with a flourish, and put them neatly in the envelopes.

'Thank you.' She smiled. 'You'll probably hear the shrieks of joy all the way across London when I hand them over tonight.'

'Pleasure.' He rubbed the dog's ears. 'Right, you. Home for dinner. And don't keep me awake tonight with your snoring.' He rolled his eyes. 'I had no idea that dogs snored. Or that they were pillow hogs.'

'Oh, they snore, all right. And they'll sneak onto the sofa between you if they think they can get away with it.'

He glanced at her left hand, and she realised what she'd just let slip. Cross with herself, she lapsed into silence.

It sounded very much to Luke as if Jess Greenacre had once had a dog, but didn't have one any more. And she'd also clearly been in a relationship, though she wasn't wearing a wedding ring.

So what had happened?

Had it been a bad break-up and her ex-partner had claimed custody of their dog? Was that why she'd been reluctant to look after Baloo, because it brought back memories of a dog she missed very badly?

She clearly didn't want to talk about it because she'd gone quiet on him and the laughter had gone from her green eyes.

Luke was shocked to realise that he wanted to make her smile again. Which was crazy; he didn't plan to get involved with anyone, ever again. Fleur had put him off relationships for life. Picking up the pieces when things went wrong was hard enough; to have to do it in the full glare of the media spotlight had been a nightmare.

But he couldn't leave it like this, with things so awkward between him and Jess. The best way he could think of to break the ice again was to ham it up. Entertain her. 'And she raided my shoe rack. She had one of every single pair in her bed yesterday, didn't you, Madam?'

The dog glanced up at him and looked as if butter wouldn't melt in her mouth.

Jess reached over to rub the top of the dog's head. 'That explains a lot.'

'Does it?' Luke was mystified.

'I think I can tell you her history now,' Jess said. 'She was left home alone a lot. Her owners probably weren't used to dogs and either didn't know how to train her or just couldn't make the time.' For a second, she looked angry—on Baloo's behalf, Luke thought. 'If they'd looked on the Internet, they could've found tips to help. Leaving the radio on, putting a blanket or an old towel in the laundry basket overnight and then putting it on her bed so it smelled of them and made her feel less alone, or giving her a special toy to distract her.'

Luke wouldn't have had a clue about any of that.

'She probably chewed the place down from a mixture of boredom and anxiety.' She sighed. 'Some people just shouldn't have dogs.'

Including me, Luke thought.

'She's really worried about being left alone, now, and she's going to need separation training.'

'That's what you said before. Is that difficult?' Stupid question. Especially as it would probably make Jess think that he wanted to learn how to do it so he could keep the dog himself. Which he couldn't.

'Not so much difficult as the fact that it takes time,' she said.

'Which I don't have.' He grimaced. 'Without you, we'd be totally stuck. And it's a relief not to have someone complaining about her all the time.'

'People whose shoes she chews?' Jess asked archly.

'I don't think Mimi minded so much about the shoes as, um, not getting time with me on her own.'

She flushed. 'Sorry. I didn't mean to get in the way of your date.'

'Trust me, I'm not dating Mimi, and I don't want to.'

'She's really that difficult?'

The look of shock on Jess's face told him that she hadn't meant to blurt out the question. 'She's really that difficult,' he confirmed wryly. 'I'm looking for an easy life right now.' Just so Jess knew he wasn't hitting on her.

'Look, I don't want to put my foot in it, but I, um, saw the papers last year.'

Hadn't everyone? Fleur had turned the end of their marriage into a total media circus.

'I get where you're coming from and, just so you know, I'm not going to turn into your Number One Fan and stalk you or anything,' Jess finished.

'I know.' He tried for lightness. 'Otherwise I'd set my dog on your shoe wardrobe.'

'Shoe wardrobe?' She looked surprised.

'Don't all women have them?' he asked. Fleur had needed a walk-in wardrobe to hold all her shoes—organised by colour and heel height. She'd had ten pairs of black court shoes with four-inch heels, and Luke hadn't been able to tell the difference between them.

'I have three pairs of shoes,' Jess said. 'No, *four*, if you count my running shoes.'

He laughed. 'I like you. You're refreshing.'

'Thank you. I think.' She smiled, and it sent a thrill all the way down his spine. Which was crazy. He and Jess came from different worlds. He barely knew her. He couldn't be reacting to her like this.

'Just for the record, I think I like you, too.' Then she grimaced. 'Sorry. You must hear that all the time, people coming up to you and telling you they love you.'

He smiled. 'It happens a bit, yes, but I'm not daft enough to think that they love *me*. They don't know me. They love the character I played in a movie, and there's a big difference between the two.' Which had been half the problem with Fleur. She'd loved who she thought he was, not who he really was. That, and the fact that he hadn't been able to give her what she really wanted.

'I suppose it's like the baddies in soap operas. People shout at them in the street because they confuse them with the character, and they might be incredibly sweet in real life instead of being mean,' she said thoughtfully. 'So you're not a handsome, charming and posh Englishman with floppy hair, who isn't very good at talking about his feelings?'

He laughed. 'Got it in one.' Though, actually, he knew it wasn't that far off the mark. He'd been typecast for a reason. 'Well—I'd better let you get on. Enjoy your evening with your sister and your best friend.'

'I will, and thanks again for the photos. Enjoy your evening, too.' She made a last fuss of the dog. 'And you, be good. We'll do some more training tomorrow. And go for another run.' She glanced at Luke. 'She likes running, by the way. And there's nothing like a good run with a dog at your side.'

'If that's your idea of a subtle hint,' he said, 'I'd hate to know what a heavy one's like.'

'You want a heavy hint?' She laughed. 'When you've had a day of dealing with people you have to be civil to, but really you want to shake them until their teeth rattle and tell them to grow up... That's when a good run with a dog at your side will definitely put the world to rights. Even if you do have to go out in public wearing dark glasses and a silly hat.'

'I do not wear dark glasses and a silly hat,' he said.

She folded her arms. 'My sister gets every magazine with your picture in it, so I know you're not telling the truth. You've got a silly hat. A beanie. I've seen it.'

'Busted,' he muttered, enjoying himself hugely. When had he last met someone he could have fun with like this?

'I think you should steal the hat, Baloo,' Jess said in a stage whisper. 'Chew it to pieces. Then he'll have to go and get a sensible one.'

Luke couldn't remember when he'd enjoyed banter-

ing with someone so much, it had been so long ago.
'What counts as sensible? Deerstalker? Fez? Top hat?'

She groaned. 'You're not Sherlock Holmes, Dr Who
or Fred Astaire.'

'Ah, but I'm an actor,' he said. 'So I *could* be. If you
wanted.' He did a little tap dance. 'See? I'm Fred.'

She grinned. 'Don't make me dare you.'

'Dare me,' he said softly, willing her to dare him to
kiss her. Because right at that moment, he really, *really*
wanted to kiss her.

But then panic flared in her eyes, as if she realised
that their flirting was starting to get a bit too intense.
A bit too close. 'I need to get going. See you tomorrow.
Bye, gorgeous.'

The way she made a last fuss of the dog made it
clear to Luke that the 'gorgeous' had been directed at
the Labrador, not at him.

Pity.

He was definitely attracted to her. He thought it
might even be mutual. But to act on that attraction
would be the most stupid thing either of them could
do. They were from different worlds. It would never
work. And if it turned out that she, like Fleur, wanted
something he most definitely couldn't provide…

Better not to start anything he couldn't finish. 'See
you tomorrow,' he said. And watched her walk away.

CHAPTER THREE

JESS'S ENTRY-PHONE rang at precisely seven-thirty. She buzzed her sister and best friend up, and met them at her front door with a hug.

'Pizza,' Shannon said, waving the box at her.

'Wine, strawberries and ice cream,' Carly added, handing over the pudding. 'And we want to know *everything*.'

'Food first.' Jess shepherded them into the kitchen, where the table was already set, and put the strawberries in the fridge and the ice cream in the freezer.

Carly poured the wine. 'So how was it?'

'Fine.'

'Brave face fine, or *really* fine?' Carly persisted.

'Really fine,' Jess reassured her with a smile.

'So tell us all about it. What's it like, working on a film set? Did you see anyone famous?' Carly asked.

'Set rules—everything's confidential. So I can't tell you that much about it,' Jess warned.

'Confidential. Just like your old job,' Shannon said wryly.

No. Because this time Jess wasn't getting involved. And nobody was going to get hurt. Working on a film set was nothing like being a police officer, apart from her work having to be confidential. There were no thugs with loaded guns to face, for starters. It wasn't life or death. 'Not quite. Everyone I worked with was nice.'

She couldn't tell Carly and Shannon everything about Luke McKenzie—if she told them about Baloo, she knew they'd both suggest immediately that she should move to a flat that allowed animals and give the Labrador a home. But she was looking forward to their reaction to her little surprise. 'As for anyone famous... You have to keep this totally confidential, OK?'

'Promise. Cross our hearts,' they chorused, following up with the actions.

'Good.' She fetched the cardboard envelopes and handed them over. 'These are for you.'

She watched the expressions on their faces as they opened the envelopes and took out the signed photographs. Surprise turned to disbelief and then delight—and then the pair of them hugged her half to death.

'Oh, my God. You met Luke McKenzie! I can't believe it. My little sister just met the most gorgeous man in the world. What's he like?' Carly asked.

'Complicated,' Jess said. 'When I first met him—well, he was being Mr Big Shot Actor.'

'But he's always so nice in interviews,' Shannon said, looking disappointed.

'He got a bit nicer as the day went on,' Jess said.

'Maybe he's just not a morning person and needs a ton of coffee before he's even halfway human,' Carly suggested. 'I still can't believe you actually met him.'

'Is he as beautiful in real life as he is on the screen?' Shannon asked.

More so. But Jess couldn't quite admit to that. It would be totally inappropriate to have a crush on Luke McKenzie. She was the most junior member of the film crew, and he was the headline actor. 'You wouldn't be disappointed,' she said.

'So you're actually working with him?' Shannon shook her head. 'Wow. I can't take this in.'

'He's not the only actor in the movie,' Jess said with a smile.

Carly laughed. 'You're talking to *us*. Of course he's the only actor in the movie!'

Jess laughed back. 'Come on—let's eat before the pizza gets cold, and I'll tell you as much as I can about today.'

At the end of the evening, Carly held her close. 'It's good to see you smile again, Jessie,' she said. 'I know you've had a really tough time of it, this last year, and it's been hell watching you go through it and knowing that I couldn't do anything to make things better for you. I would've given anything for a magic wand to fix things. I still wish I could bring Matt and Comet back. Well, not even have them in danger in the first place.'

'You were there for me, and just knowing that I could call you at stupid o'clock in the morning if I needed to helped a lot,' Jess reassured her.

'You never actually called me, though,' Carly pointed out. 'Because you're too stubborn.'

Jess gave her a rueful smile. 'I guess I just needed time to come to terms with things in my own way. I'm never going to stop missing Matt and Comet, but I'm finally learning to see the sunshine again.'

'I just wish you'd go back to working with dogs,' Shannon said. 'You loved your job so much. And working as a temp doesn't make you anywhere near as happy—even if you did get to meet the most gorgeous man in the world today.'

'I'm fine,' Jess said. She'd heard this argument countless times before. And she had the same answer: she wasn't ready to go back to working with dogs. She might not ever be ready. As a temp, she kept her days too full to think, and that suited her right now. 'See you both later. Text me to let me know you're home safely.'

'Of course,' they said, rolling their eyes.

She couldn't even use the excuse that she was a policewoman any more. She just wanted to know that they were safe. *Needed* to know.

'Stop worrying, sweetie,' Shannon said and hugged her. 'Everything's going to be just fine.'

On Wednesday morning, Jess spent an hour working through Ayesha's list, then had an hour of training with Luke and Baloo before his rehearsals. She was guiltily aware that her best friend was absolutely right about Jess being happiest when working with animals: despite her initial reservations, Jess was really enjoying training the dog. She loved seeing the Labrador blossom and become more confident as her training progressed. And she'd missed this.

Maybe she should consider going back to it. Not with the police—she knew she couldn't handle the idea of training people and their dogs to face the kind of situation Matt and Comet had faced—but maybe she could set up classes doing something like this. Or even working with the animal handling department of a film company.

'She's doing really well,' Luke said. 'I can't believe how quickly she's picking things up.'

'She's very trainable. And this will make her life easier.' Jess paused. 'And yours.'

'Baloo's not mine,' Luke reminded her.

Oh, yes, she most certainly is, Jess thought, but kept her counsel.

As the runner came up to tell Luke that the director was ready for him, Jess said, 'See you later. Break a leg—or is that only said for stage performances?'

He laughed. 'It's pretty much the same thing. Thanks, Jess. See you later.'

At lunchtime, Jess's phone rang.

'Hi. It's Luke,' he said.

As if she wouldn't recognise that voice—like melted chocolate, warm and rich and sensual. 'Hi.'

'I was wondering if you and Baloo would like to have lunch with me.'

'Baloo's very partial to chicken sandwiches,' she said. 'So if they're on the menu, our answer is yes.'

He laughed. 'I'll bear that in mind. See you at the catering tent in ten minutes, then?'

'Hang on, I'll just check with Ayesha.' When the production manager confirmed that it was fine for Jess to take her break, she told Luke, 'Yep. Ten minutes.'

And hopefully by the time she met him her common sense would be back in control. Along with her knees, which right now were doing a great impersonation of blancmange. Ridiculous. Luke McKenzie was a movie star. He was *supposed* to have that effect on women. It wasn't real.

They reached the catering tent at practically the same time.

'The team here is pretty good,' Luke said. 'I don't know if chicken sandwiches are on the menu today, but I can definitely recommend their BLTs.'

Baloo looked hopefully at him, and Jess laughed. 'Bacon is full of salt. Which is not good for dogs.'

Baloo hung her head and looked sorrowful.

Luke ruffled her fur. 'Did you train her to do that?'

'No. She's a natural.'

'Don't say it,' Luke warned, 'because it's not going to happen.'

Jess spread her hands. 'Not a word will pass my lips.' But she was thinking it, and she knew he knew it.

'So how was your pizza last night?' he asked as they walked over to the catering area.

'Good. I meant to say earlier, my sister and my best friend asked me to say thank you for the photos. They were thrilled.'

'My pleasure,' he said simply.

The bacon, lettuce and tomato sandwiches were as good as Luke had promised. Although Jess refused to let Baloo have any, she relented enough to let the dog have a treat from her pocket, and the dog settled between them both with a happy sigh.

'Care to indulge a nosey actor?' Luke asked.

Her heart skipped a beat. 'How?'

'Set rules,' he said. 'Were you a dog trainer before you did this job?'

Apart from the last year. But she wasn't going into that. 'Pretty much,' Jess said. 'I thought about being a vet when I was at school, but I realised I couldn't handle the tough side of it—situations where I couldn't make an animal better and had to put them down.' She grimaced. 'I was never allowed to watch Lassie films as a child because I'd always sob through them.'

'I was never allowed to watch them, either,' Luke said.

Jess had hoped he'd be soft-hearted when it came to animals. Good. Things were starting to look that much more hopeful for Baloo.

'So what made you think of being a trainer?' he asked.

'I took my dog to agility classes when I was twelve, and I loved it—I got chatting to the trainer, and she suggested it,' Jess explained. 'My parents were brilliant and supported me all the way. I did a degree in animal behaviour, then qualified as a dog trainer.' Luke didn't need to know that she'd become a police dog trainer and had spent two years as a police officer first.

'So what made you stop?'

My husband and my dog were shot and killed. That was a tricky one to broach. And she didn't want Luke to pity her and treat her like a special case. She grimaced. 'Right now, do you mind if we don't talk about it?'

'Sore spot?' he asked.

She nodded.

'Sorry.'

'Not your fault.' Taking the focus off herself, she asked, 'What about you? Did you always want to be an actor? Obviously, that's under set rules.'

'Sure.' He smiled. 'Actually, I read law at university,' he said, surprising her. 'I was meant to join my dad in the family firm.'

Clearly that hadn't happened, or they wouldn't be on the film set together right now.

'Then I joined Footlights,' he said.

She blinked as his words sank in. 'You were at Cambridge?' So he was super-bright as well as gorgeous.

He gave a self-deprecating shrug. 'I loved Footlights. I met some really nice people—people who are still close friends now—and found what I really wanted to do in life.'

But he'd just told her that his family had expected him to follow in his father's footsteps. Had they been disappointed when he hadn't? Or had they encouraged him to follow his dreams? Jess wished now that she'd paid attention whenever Carly or Shannon had thrust a magazine article about Luke McKenzie in front of her. It would be rude to ask him, and she could hardly grill her sister or her best friend—not without giving an explanation she wasn't ready to give. So she just smiled at him and hoped he'd take it as an invitation to continue talking.

'I had a deal with my parents that I'd take a year out after graduation. If I couldn't make it as an actor within that year, then I'd join the family firm and train as a barrister.'

'I think you'd have made a good barrister,' she said. 'You've got presence and that would show in court.'

'Thank you.' He looked at her, his eyes narrowed slightly. 'That sounds as if you're talking from experience.'

She backtracked fast. 'I know a couple of barristers,' she said, keeping it vague. He didn't need to know that she knew them professionally rather than socially. 'So obviously you made it as an actor.'

'By the skin of my teeth—half the time in that first year I was "resting" and working as a waiter,' he admitted. 'It got to the eleventh month in my year out and my parents were starting to put pressure on me—but then I got my lucky break. A director had seen me play Benedick in *Much Ado* and wanted me for the lead in her new film. It was a small-budget indie production, and it was pretty likely that it wasn't going to get anywhere, but I loved the script. So I thought I might as well end my acting career doing something I really loved.'

'Was that when you played Marcus Bailey?' It was the film her sister and best friend had first seen him in and fallen in love with him. Thousands of other women had clearly felt the same, because the independent film had taken the world by storm. 'That was the one.' He smiled. 'Which is why I'd work for free for Libby. Without her I would've been stuck in chambers. I mean, I could've done the job, and I would've put in enough effort to make sure I did it well—but I would always have regretted losing my dreams.'

Her own parents had always been so supportive, Jess thought. She'd been really lucky. Whereas Luke's parents had given him an ultimatum and put pressure on him not to follow his dreams. She wondered if his aunt Monica—the dog rescuer—had been the one to take his part. Though asking wouldn't be tactful. Instead, she turned the conversation to something much lighter, and by the time they'd finished their sandwiches his laughter was definitely genuine and showed in his eyes, rather than being faked to put her off the scent.

'Has anyone told you how restful you are?' Luke asked when they'd finished.

Jess looked surprised. 'How do you mean?'

'You don't need to fill all the silences.'

She shrugged. Probably because she was used to spending her time with animals. You needed to know when to shut up and let them get on with their job. 'Is that so unusual?' she prevaricated.

He laughed. 'I guess I hang around with too many actors. They're not so good at shutting up.'

'But you use silence in films—for comic timing and what have you.'

'That's scripted,' he said. 'Or your own interpretation of the script. That's different. I mean outside work. And it's so nice not having someone trying to set me up on a date.'

'Tell me about it,' she said, rolling her eyes. 'They've found absolutely the *perfect* partner for you, so all you have to do is go on a date with them and life will be fantastic again.'

'You, too?' he asked.

She wrinkled her nose and nodded, and Luke wondered if she knew how cute she looked.

Probably not.

There was nothing studied about Jess. What you saw was what you got. She wasn't like most of the women in his world, very aware of how every move and gesture could be interpreted.

'Not everyone tries to fix me up,' Jess said. 'My parents, my sister and my best friend know I'll date again when I'm ready.'

'And the others?'

'Have discovered that I'm not very available.' She wrinkled her nose again. 'Which is horrible of me. I know they mean well and they want me to be happy.'

'But you'd rather choose your own date.'

She nodded. 'You, too?'

'You're lucky that your family understands and doesn't push you,' he said feelingly. 'I've pretty much run out of excuses to avoid my mother's dinner parties.'

'Tut, and you an award-winning actor.'

Luke couldn't remember the last time he'd met someone with such a dry sense of humour. Someone who made him laugh for all the right reasons. He grinned. 'You have a point. If I can't act my way out of a dinner party, I shouldn't be doing this job.' He scratched behind Baloo's ears, and the dog sighed with happiness. 'Like you say, they mean well and they want you to be happy. But sometimes their idea of what makes you happy isn't the same as yours.'

'So you still miss Fleur?' She grimaced. 'Sorry, that was really nosey. I shouldn't have asked you. Ignore me.'

'It's OK.' Of course she'd be curious. And of course she'd know his ex-wife's name. The gossip pages had been full of their divorce, last year.

'No, it's not OK,' she said. 'You don't have to tell me.'

Luke was surprised to find that actually he did want to tell her. Some of it, anyway. Jess might be the one person who really understood how he felt. And he already knew he didn't have to remind her about set rules. What he said to Jess would stay with her and go no further.

'Sort of. I know I don't feel the same way about her as I did eighteen months ago. I don't love her any more.' He didn't hate her quite so much any more, either, so that was progress. Of sorts. 'I suppose I don't miss *her* so much as I miss being married,' he said. 'I miss the closeness.'

She nodded. 'Yeah. That's the hard part. Waking up in the middle of the night and the bed feels too big.'

She definitely knew what he was talking about, then. 'It's the stupid little things. Putting the kettle on to make tea and remembering that you only need one mug. Buying croissants for one at the deli on a Sunday morning.'

'Coming home, and there's nobody to tell about your day—because if you ring someone to talk about it then they'll know you're feeling lonely and miserable. Then they'll feel bad if they can't change their plans and come and see you; and you'll feel bad if they *do* come and see you, because you know you really ought to be able to cope with it on your own,' she said.

Oh, yes, he knew that one, too. 'Then, the next day,

they'll ring you and suggest joining them for dinner or a show at the theatre or the opening night of an exhibition, and you go along to discover they've also invited someone else—someone they think might stop you being lonely.'

'And you're polite, and you try to have a nice time, but it pushes you even further into that little box of loneliness,' she said.

'Absolutely.' He reached over and squeezed her hand. 'Thank you.' Her skin was soft and warm, and he had to resist the temptation to draw her hand up to his mouth and fold a kiss into her palm. Which would be insane, because that wasn't what either of them wanted. She was offering him friendship. Understanding. And that was exactly what he needed, right now. He loosened his hand from hers. 'You have no idea how good it feels to meet someone who understands that.'

'Me, too,' Jess said.

'I'm glad I met you.'

'And you.' She smiled. 'If anyone had told me six months ago I'd start to make friends with a movie star, I would've—' She spread her hands, laughing. 'Well, I don't move in those sort of circles.'

'You do now.'

She laughed again. 'I'm hardly Hollywood material. I don't think I'd fit in.'

He thought that Jess would fit in just about anywhere. But now wasn't the right time to say that. 'Hollywood's a lot of pressure.' He shrugged. 'And a lot of relationships can't take that. I thought Fleur and I would buck the Hollywood trend—that we'd be one of those strong marriages that can survive one of us working away for half the year. I loved her and I thought she loved me.' Except she hadn't loved him enough. She'd wanted something he hadn't been able to give her—at least, not something he could give her easily, and how he wished he'd been able to do it. But a simple childhood illness had put paid to that. Somehow they'd managed to keep that little bit of information out of the press. But the nasty little secret had been eating away at him ever since. Along with the fear that it would be leaked. And that it would change people's view of him—and in turn that would change directors' views of him, too, and mean that he wasn't considered for the role of romantic male lead any more. Actors in the Fifties had had to keep their sexuality under wraps for the same reason: public perception could close off huge areas of their career. Nowadays, it was acceptable for an actor to be gay. But Luke's problem was a little tricky.

'I'm sorry it didn't work out that way for you.'

'Me, too. But she's with someone else now.' Someone who *had* been able to give her what she wanted. Which was how he'd learned about her affair in the first place.

Jess reached over and squeezed his hand. 'Sorry. I didn't mean to bring back bad memories for you.'

'Not so much bad memories as regret,' he said. 'I wish things could've been different. But they're not, and I've pretty much learned to come to terms with it.' He blew out a breath. 'Thank you for not pitying me.'

'Pity's harsh.'

It sounded as if she was speaking from experience. He wanted to ask, but he didn't want her to go back into her shell. If she wanted him to know, she'd tell him. 'Yes, it is,' he said, leaving it up to her whether or not she wanted to talk.

'I hated it when people pitied me—or people crossed the street to avoid me because they didn't know what to say to me. They'd pretend later that they hadn't seen me, but I knew they had.'

'People always take sides in a breakup,' he said. 'You can't always choose your friends.'

'No.' She looked away.

'I'm not going to pry,' he said.

'Thank you.'

Her words sounded heartfelt. Clearly she still loved the guy who'd broken her heart. Maybe it hadn't been as long for her since the breakup as it had for him; he'd gradually trained himself to stop loving Fleur. Except he was aware that it had also made him keep an emotional distance from anyone he'd dated, too. Or maybe he just hadn't found the right person to help him to trust again.

Like Jess. And Baloo.

He pushed the thought away. He wasn't getting involved. End of story.

'That's me back on set,' he said regretfully when there was a call for his scene. 'I'll see you later. Have a nice afternoon.'

'You, too. Break the other leg,' Jess said. 'Baloo, wave goodbye.'

To his surprise, the Labrador sat and put her paw up, for all the world as if she were sketching a salute goodbye. 'Wow. You taught her that?'

She grinned. 'This morning, in a quiet moment in the office.'

'You,' Luke told the dog, ruffling her fur, 'are a very clever girl.' He looked up at Jess. 'And you might be a genius.'

'It's all her. Sweet-talk your director and get her a part in his next film,' Jess said with a saucy wink. 'See you later.'

That wink stayed in Luke's head all afternoon, to the point where it even distracted him from some of his lines. Which really wasn't good. He was a professional. He never let things put him off his stride at work.

This was crazy.

He couldn't be attracted to Jess Greenacre.

He didn't want a relationship. He was pretty sure that she was in the same position; she was guarded about her personal life, and something major had clearly happened in her last job to make her change direction so completely in her career. But the little that she had let slip made him think that she was recovering from a broken relationship and needed time to get her head together, too. She was the worst person he could get involved with.

Enough.

He had work to do.

He made it through the first scene without letting himself think about Jess. And the second. But, in the short break after the second scene, Mimi sashayed across to him. Wearing the expensive designer shoes Luke had replaced the day before.

'Hey, Luke.' She gave him a sultry look to accompany the equally sultry drawl.

'Hey, Mimi.' He forced himself to be charming. He was going to have to work with the woman for the next couple of months, and the last thing the rest of the cast needed was any awkwardness between the lead actor and the lead actress.

'I was thinking, maybe we could have dinner tonight.'

Her pout made it very clear that dinner wasn't all she planned to offer. Oh, help. Everyone knew he was single, which probably made him fair game in his world.

But even if he had been interested in a relationship, Mimi wasn't his type. Too mannered, too studied, too fake. Every move was calculated for maximum effect—and maximum PR. If he dated Mimi, the pictures would be plastered all over the gossip magazines, the very next day. And he'd had quite enough of his personal life being in the press, thanks to his ex-wife.

'Sorry, Mimi. I'm already promised elsewhere tonight,' he said, giving her an equally fake but absolutely charming smile, and hoping that would be enough.

'Tomorrow night, then. To celebrate the first day of shooting.'

'Sorry, no can do—my aunt's back tomorrow and she'll need a proper update on Baloo.'

Mimi's smile slipped just a fraction and her eyes went cold. 'The mutt.'

'Actually, Jess thinks she's a pure-bred Labrador.'

'Jess? Oh, yes. The *gofer*.' The actress made it sound as if Jess were the lowest of the low.

Shockingly, Luke found himself wanting to defend Jess. Which was crazy. She was perfectly capable of standing up for herself. Plus, if Mimi thought he was taking Jess's part over hers, she was capable of making life very difficult on set for Jess. Best to back off. Discretion being the better part of valour, and all that.

Though at that precise moment Luke thought he was as much of a coward as Shakespeare's rotund knight. Maybe the easy life wasn't necessarily the best life.

'You're sure you can't get out of your plans tonight?' Mimi asked, giving him another of her famed sultry looks. 'You can't throw a sickie?' She dipped her head and looked up at him, making her blue eyes seem huge and pleading. 'Not even for me?'

'Sorry, Mimi. No can do.' He knew he needed to

keep this polite and firm, without giving any explanations that could give her an excuse to prolong the conversation or try a different tack. 'I don't know about you, but I could really do with a coffee. Shall we join the others?'

To Luke's relief, the actress agreed. And George, the director, had clearly seen his predicament and taken pity on him, because he needed a quick chat with Luke alone about tweaks to the last scene.

'You know, Mimi usually dates her leading men,' George said quietly.

Yeah. Luke knew. But he didn't want to date her. 'I'm not in the market for dating, right now,' he said.

'Just one date, for a quiet life,' George suggested.

It would be the easy way out. But Luke couldn't face it. This wasn't a game he wanted to play.

And he was horribly aware that if Mimi was a different person—a gentle-voiced woman with intelligent green eyes, no make-up and a sharp sense of humour—then the situation would be very different.

'Maybe I can persuade her that I'm still not over Fleur,' he said.

'Well, you can try,' George said, his expression saying very clearly that he thought Luke would need to be very lucky indeed for it to work.

CHAPTER FOUR

LUKE TRIED TO ignore the noise, but the shrilling was insistent.

Then his groggy brain focused on the fact that it was the telephone.

In the middle of the night.

Nobody called him at this time of night. Not unless it was an emergency.

He groped for the receiver, his eyes still not accustomed to the low level of light in the room, and mumbled, 'Hello?'

'Lukey, it's me.'

He registered firstly that it was his aunt Monica, and secondly that her voice sounded gravelly, as if she'd been crying. And then he was wide awake. He switched the bedside light on, trying to dispel the flood of panic. 'Monica? What's happened? Are you OK?'

There was a quiet woof from the end of the bed, where Baloo had settled herself—Luke had given up trying to make her sleep in her crate in the kitchen.

'Not really.' She dragged in a breath. 'I can't believe I was so stupid. I've broken my leg in two places.'

'Where are you?'

'Hospital. Laura's with me.' She paused. 'Oh, no.

You were asleep, weren't you? I got the time difference wrong. I'm so sorry.'

She sounded very, very close to tears. 'It's fine, Mon,' he reassured her. 'You know you can always call me at stupid o'clock if you need me. That's what family's for.'

'Thank you, love.' She choked back a sob. 'They won't let me fly home tomorrow. And I promised I'd be back and I'd rehome the dog for you.'

There was another gentle woof from the end of the bed.

'Did I just hear her bark?' Monica asked.

'Uh, yeah.' He raked a hand through his hair. 'Let's just say Baloo's good at opening doors and I've given up trying to make her sleep downstairs.'

Monica gave a huff of laughter. 'That's the first thing I've heard all day to make me smile. It's been a rotten day, Lukey.'

'What happened?'

'We were hiking. We'd gone to see the falls. I slipped and landed awkwardly.' He could practically hear her inject a note of bravery into her voice. 'It's just one of those things.'

'You said you broke your leg in two places.' So it must've been a pretty nasty fall. And if she'd been out hiking... 'How did you get to hospital?'

'A combination of the mountain rescue team and an ambulance. Luckily I've got decent travel insurance,' Monica said lightly. 'And good painkillers.'

Considering that his aunt didn't even take paracetamol for a headache, that told him a lot. 'How long are you going to be in hospital?'

'I don't know. They want to make sure there aren't any complications, and the cast has to set. I don't know when I'll be able to fly. And—oh, Lukey, I've let you down. I'm supposed to be in London, not stuck in Portland.' She sounded anguished. 'Are you all right to keep Baloo until I get back?'

Keep the dog for an unspecified length of time— which could mean anything from a couple of days to a few weeks, depending on when his aunt was able to fly home again and how mobile she was.

No, he wasn't all right to keep the dog. He had a film to shoot. The deal was, he'd look after the dog until the end of rehearsals. Monica was supposed to pick up the dog on Thursday afternoon. *This* afternoon.

But his aunt was clearly in pain and upset. Luke wasn't mean-spirited enough to make her feel guilty about the change in plans on top of all that. 'It's fine,' he lied. And he just hoped that Jess would be able to help him out. He had no idea how long her contract was with the film company—a week, a month, the whole of the film—but she'd been a dog trainer. Maybe she knew someone else who could step in, if she couldn't do it.

'Mon, is Laura still with you?' he asked, not wanting to think that his aunt was alone and in pain.

'Yes. She's going to change her flight and stay here with me, at least until we know what's happening.'

'Good.' Though he knew he'd be happier if he saw his aunt for himself. Laura was one of Monica's closest friends, but there wasn't quite the same bond as there was with family. And Luke was the nearest Monica had to a child. If he was honest with himself, he was closer to his aunt than he was to his parents. 'Look, I can head to Heathrow now and get the next flight over. Tell me which hospital you're in and which ward, and I'll get a taxi from the airport when I land.'

'No, love. You're shooting the film this week. You haven't got time to fly halfway across the world.'

That was true. But family was more important. He'd find some way of sorting this. Maybe the director could shoot out of order and do some of the scenes Luke wasn't in, tomorrow. Half a day's filming—it could be done, he was sure. 'For you, I've got time.'

'Lukey, don't. I'll start crying.' She sniffed. 'Really, I'll be fine. Don't go to the airport. You'd better get back to sleep. You'll have bags under your eyes tomorrow and your director will want to strangle me.'

'No, he won't. The make-up team is pretty good,' he said with a smile. 'Don't worry. Do you have your mobile phone or is there another number I should use to call you?'

'There's a phone next to the bed. I think I'm meant to keep my mobile off. Do you have a pen?'

'Give me a second.' He grabbed a pen and scribbled the phone number on the back of his hand as she dictated it. 'I'll call you tomorrow morning.' He chuckled. 'That's tomorrow your time, I mean—it'll be afternoon here when I call.'

'I *am* sorry I woke you, Luke. I wasn't thinking straight. I just—' Her voice caught. 'I just wanted to talk to you.'

'Don't worry about it, Mon. It's not every day you break your leg.' And, although his aunt packed more into her life than anyone else he knew, she was a lot closer to sixty years old than to twenty. A fall and broken bones were bound to shake her up, and he knew that it would take her much longer to recover physically than if she'd been his age. 'Ask for anything you need and I'll pick up the bill, OK? Just remember that nothing's too much trouble or too expensive when it comes to my favourite aunt. Anything you need, you get it. I mean it.'

'Thank you, Luke.' She sounded close to tears again. 'I love you.'

'Love you, too, Mon. Get some rest and I'll call you tomorrow.' He put down the receiver. *I love you*. Monica was the only person in his life who said that to him and meant it. He blew out a breath. And how pathetic was he for minding? Anyone would think he was five years old again, not thirty-five. He'd minded then. He knew better now.

'Get a grip, McKenzie,' he told himself roughly. He was doing just fine. He had a good career, plenty of friends and a comfortable house. He didn't need anything else.

During the conversation, Baloo had moved further up the bed and had curled up by his knees.

'It looks as if you're going to be my house guest for a bit longer,' he said, stroking her head.

She licked his hand.

'It's still only temporary,' he warned her. 'Just until Monica's leg has healed. And then she'll find you a real home.'

Another lick.

'And we'd better hope that Jess can help us out. Otherwise you and I are going to be grovelling to Mimi for *weeks*. We're talking flowers every day, shoe-shaped chocolates, and more charm than I'm capable of.'

Baloo put a paw over her nose, and he laughed. 'I think Jess is right. You could be a showbiz dog.' He stroked her head. 'But I can't keep you. It wouldn't be fair to either of us.'

She just looked at him.

'I can't.' And he wasn't going to think about how

much he'd bonded with her in the few days he'd been looking after her—especially since he'd been working with Jess to train her. How much he was enjoying having company at home. How good it was to let himself care about someone again.

To Luke's relief, Jess was already in the production office when he and Baloo walked in the next morning.

And he was aware that it wasn't just relief that she'd kept her word about helping out with Baloo. Jess's sweet, shy smile made the world feel as if it was a brighter place. Which was crazy. He'd only known her since Monday. Less than a week. Although she was looking after his dog while he was rehearsing, they were still virtually strangers. He couldn't possibly start feeling this way about her. He didn't want a relationship with her—with *anyone*.

He made an effort to control his thoughts. 'Good morning, Jess.'

'Good morning, Luke.' She bent to make a fuss of Baloo. 'It's your last day with Baloo and the first day of shooting today, isn't it? Do you have time to do any training with her?'

'Yes and no.' He wrinkled his nose. It wouldn't be fair to let Jess look after Baloo all day and then drop the bombshell on her that he needed her help tomorrow as well—and probably for quite a few days after that. 'Can we have a quick chat in my trailer, first?'

She looked surprised, then a little wary, but nodded. 'Sure. What's up?'

'Tell you when we get there.' He didn't want to have this conversation on the open set and then have everyone gossiping about him. Been there, done that, and rather not rinse and repeat.

Once they were in the trailer, he unclipped Baloo's leash from her collar and the dog settled down on the rug. 'Can I get you a coffee or anything?' he asked.

'No, I'm good, thanks.' Jess frowned. 'What did you want to talk to me about?'

'My aunt called me in the middle of the night,' he said. 'From America. She's in hospital.'

Jess looked shocked. 'Oh, no. What happened?'

'She was out hiking when she had a fall. She broke her leg in two places, so they're keeping her in for a few days. She was meant to be arriving home this morning and picking up the dog this afternoon, but right now I have no idea when she's going to be allowed to fly home.' He grimaced. 'It might not even be until her leg is healed. Which could take weeks.'

'It depends on the length of the flight, her age, and how bad the break is,' Jess said, surprising him. 'Do you know how long the flight is?'

'She's in Portland—I think she said it was something like eleven hours between there and London.'

'So she'll need to get up and move around a few times during the flight, then. With a cast, she's more of a risk of developing DVT,' Jess said thoughtfully.

'How do you know this sort of thing?' Luke asked.

She shrugged. 'I used to know a few medics. It kind of rubs off.'

He was intrigued. Why would a dog trainer know medics? But he had a feeling that she'd clam up on him if he asked. Besides, he had a more pressing question.

'As I said, I don't know how long it's going to be before Monica comes back to London. But, even once she's home, she's not going to be able to look after Baloo with a broken leg,' Luke said. 'It's going to be hard for her even to let the dog out, and she definitely won't be able to take Baloo for walks.'

Baloo gave a soft woof, and he bent to stroke her head. 'I didn't mean now, you daft hound. She knows the W-word,' he told Jess ruefully. 'I can help out a bit, but not enough—not when I have full days shooting on set. And I can't pull out of the film this morning, not when they start shooting this afternoon. It wouldn't be fair to the team and I can't expect someone else to come in at ridiculously short notice and learn the part.' He shook his head. 'It just wouldn't be fair on anyone. A lot of people are relying on me. I can't let them down. But I can't let my aunt down, either.' He looked at her. 'Jess, I really need your help, and I'll understand if you can't do it, but if you could help me look after Baloo until Monica's properly back on her feet…'

Look after Baloo. With Luke. Spend time with both of them. *Get close to them.*

No. Jess knew that she should walk away, right now. That would be the sensible course of action. Walk away and don't get involved.

But she had a nasty feeling that it was already too late. She'd already started bonding with the dog. And she couldn't even begin to let herself think about what was happening with Luke himself. How she'd been looking forward so much to the mornings at work because it meant spending time with him as well as with Baloo.

She was an idiot. She should know better than this. Getting involved would be a bad, bad, *bad* idea. Especially with someone who was so very much in the public eye—someone who was way out of her league.

But Baloo was looking at her with pleading brown eyes. Luke was looking at her in exactly the same way.

And she was pretty sure that this was genuine, not just an actor excelling in a role.

They needed help.

From her.

Could she be mean-spirited enough to say no? Especially as working with Baloo had helped her to focus, move on to the point where she was able to think about maybe going back to her old career, albeit in a civil role rather than with the police force?

Jess took a deep breath. 'OK. I'll do it.'

Luke wrapped his arms round her and held her close. 'You're a lifesaver. Thank you so much.'

It was the first time in more than a year that a man had held Jess tightly like this, as if she were the most precious and most important thing in the world. The first time since Matt had been shot. Part of Jess wanted to bawl her eyes out, remembering how much she'd lost. Part of her wanted to hug Luke back. And a really crazy part of her wanted to tip her head back in invitation for a kiss.

Oh, help.

This was unfair to both of them. Luke had made it clear that he wasn't interested in a relationship, and neither was Jess. This had to stop right now. She needed to be sensible. Yes, the man was drop-dead gorgeous, but she was just being star-struck. This was a reaction to stage presence or whatever it was that actors had.

'You're going to be late for work,' she said.

'I guess.' He pulled away and took a step back. And there was a slash of colour across his cheekbones that she'd never seen before.

Oh.

So did he feel this weird pull of attraction, too? She'd

guess that he didn't particularly want to feel that way, either.

But they were both far from being teenagers. So they could deal with this like the adults they were. Couldn't they?

'I'll see you later,' she said.

He nodded. 'I'll call you when we break for lunch. And thank you, Jess. I really do appreciate this.'

'No problem,' she said. 'Come on, Baloo. We're going to the office. Walkies.'

The dog perked up and wagged her tail. 'See you later, Luke,' Jess said, clipped Baloo's leash onto her collar, and headed for the production office.

Normally, Luke loved his job. He liked the script for this film, he liked the director, and he liked most of his co-stars—Mimi, admittedly, he could do without, but he'd put up with her for the sake of the film.

But today he couldn't concentrate.

All he could think about was the fact that he'd be seeing more of Jess. And how she'd felt in his arms when he'd hugged her impulsively.

It should make him want to run a mile. After Fleur, he'd dated a lot, in a vain attempt to make himself feel better. But it hadn't worked, so he'd simply stopped dating and given himself a bit of space to get his head together. He'd managed to avoid most of the situations where well-meaning friends had tried to fix him up with someone they thought would be perfect for him.

But Jess Greenacre… Jess intrigued him. He wanted to know what made her tick. What made her laugh.

She was definitely a puzzle. A dog trainer who knew barristers and medics. Or maybe they were people she'd met at university, or friends of the family, and he was making too much of it.

He just about managed to focus on rehearsals until the lunchtime break. And then he discovered he wasn't actually getting a break—they needed to go straight into shooting.

'I need to make a couple of quick calls, first,' he told George, the director.

'They need to be really quick,' George warned.

'I'm calling Jess, to let her know that I need her to look after Baloo at lunchtime, and my aunt Monica, to see how she's doing this morning,' Luke explained.

And how stupid was it that he was disappointed not to get the chance to see Jess?

'No, it's fine. I understand,' Jess said when Luke explained the situation over the phone. 'You don't need to apologise. Now go, before you get into trouble.'

In the end, she took her lunch break with Baloo in the park opposite the set. Just for fun, she ran through a couple more training moves with the dog, and was impressed by the way the dog responded. 'You could have a real career in show business, sweetheart,' she said, scratching the top of the dog's head.

Baloo sighed and rested her head on Jess's knee.

'Enough for today, I think,' Jess said. 'Give me a wave goodbye for the park?'

Baloo woofed and lifted her paw.

'That's cool,' a voice said beside her.

Jess turned to see a little girl who looked as if she was six or seven. Alone in the park and talking to strangers? That wasn't good. She tried to keep the little girl talking while she scanned the park to see if a parent or carer was nearby. Failing that, she'd put a call in to the nearest police station and get someone to look after the little girl and keep her safe until her family or carer was found. 'What's cool? That my dog can wave?'

The little girl nodded. 'Does your dog dance?'

'I've never tried dancing with her,' Jess said. Where on earth was the child's mother? Was she one of the nearby women concentrating on a mobile phone call?

'There was a dancing dog on the telly on Saturday night. It was really good.' The little girl regarded Baloo solemnly. 'You should get her to dance.'

To Jess's relief, a woman came hurrying over to them. 'Aisling! You know you shouldn't go off and talk to strangers,' she scolded, then grimaced at Jess. 'I'm so sorry. My daughter does like to talk.'

'You were on the phone, Mum,' Aisling said.

Jess schooled her face into a neutral expression, though privately she agreed with the little girl. Her mum really should've concentrated on her rather than on the phone call. Children were precious—and Jess knew from her police work how easily things could go wrong. 'Aisling, maybe next time you should wait until your mum's said it's OK before you start talking to someone,' Jess said gently. 'Not everyone's nice.'

The little girl's lower lip wobbled. 'But you've got a *dog*. That means you're nice.'

Not always, Jess thought. And the dog wasn't actually hers.

'She's desperate for a dog,' Aisling's mother explained to Jess. 'Love, you know we can't have one. The landlord won't let us have dogs because they chew things.'

'This one definitely chews and she especially likes designer shoes, which gets her into a bit of trouble,' Jess said with a smile. 'Maybe wait until you're grown up, Aisling. Then, if you can't have a dog of your own, maybe you can work with animals—you could be a dog trainer.'

'Are you a dog trainer?' Aisling asked.

It was too complicated to explain. Jess simply smiled and nodded.

Aisling brightened. 'So you *could* teach your dog to dance…'

Jess smiled. 'Maybe one day.'

She thought about it when the child had gone. Baloo had responded so well to the training they'd done so far. Would she take to performing?

She took her MP3 player from her bag, found some music, and encouraged Baloo up on her hind legs. And she was surprised by how quickly the dog picked up the idea. Two steps forward, two steps back, head to one side…

'We could work out a routine,' she said thoughtfully as she rewarded the dog for her work. 'You're the perfect dog for Luke McKenzie. I'm with his aunt, on that. You could even be in show business with him.'

Baloo's answer was to lick Jess's face, and Jess laughed.

She headed back to the production office and spent the afternoon run off her feet. Luke texted her to let her know that shooting was running over and ask if it was OK to look after Baloo a bit longer. She texted back to say it was fine, and simply carried on at her desk until he came to collect the dog.

'How's your aunt doing?' she asked.

'Better, after a night's sleep. And I told her you were helping me with the dog, so everything's fine and all she has to worry about is getting back on her feet. She still doesn't know when she'll be allowed home, though.'

Jess looked sympathetic. 'That must be so frustrating for her.'

'Given that Monica lives her life at a hundred miles an hour…I'll give her a day before being stuck in bed drives her completely crazy and she's begging to be let out.' He sighed. 'At least her best friend is with her.'

'But you'll be happier once she's back in London and you can keep an eye on her?'

Luke smiled. 'I'm not sure that Monica would allow anyone to keep an eye on her. But something like that, yes. How was your day?'

'Good, thanks.' She paused. 'Dare I ask how it's going, or is that bad luck?'

He smiled. 'I'm not superstitious. It's going OK, thanks. I'm just sorry things overran. I feel as if I'm taking advantage of you.'

She shook her head. 'It's fine. Really.'

'Can I buy you dinner?' he asked. 'Just to say thanks?'

Making it very clear that it wasn't a date, she thought. 'It's fine. You really don't have to do that.'

'Would you accept it from Baloo?' he asked.

She smiled. 'I don't think dog treats count as legal currency.'

'I'll give her an advance on her pocket money,' he said. 'Have dinner with us. It's not going to be anything fancy—I mean, I think The Ivy might just say no if I ask them to reserve a table for two and a dog bowl. But we could have some take-out in my trailer.' He nudged the dog. 'Hey. This is your cue to do the big brown eyes bit and the sad face.'

Baloo immediately dropped to the floor and put her head on her paws, looking up at Jess.

Jess couldn't help smiling. 'You two are such a double act. OK. Take-out would be lovely.'

'And it also means we won't get papped,' he said softly. 'That's the one bit I hate about my job. I don't get much privacy. I mean, yes—the film business has been good to me, and I appreciate that. I never mind spending time talking to fans and signing autographs—without them, I wouldn't get to do the job I love. But sometimes living your life constantly in the spotlight feels like too high a price. I'd love to be able to take you for dinner at the nearest dog-friendly pub. But, if I did, there's a very good chance a photographer would be around, and then you'd find your picture in the gossip pages tomorrow morning and a lot of speculation to back it up.'

Which was the last thing she wanted. With a little bit of digging, any journalist would quickly find out that she was Matt's widow. The story would be dragged up all over again. And who knew what spin they'd use to talk about Luke?

'Agreed,' she said softly. 'At least here we're under set rules.'

'Thank you for being understanding,' he said. 'It's not that I'm ashamed to be seen with you. I mean, we're friends. And I'm not looking for a relationship right now.'

He couldn't make it clearer than that. Any secret thoughts she might've been harbouring about him—well, it wasn't going to happen. Besides, hadn't he already warned her about people who fell in love with the characters he played, which weren't necessarily anything like the man himself?

'Me, neither,' she said. Just to make sure he didn't

think that she was going to turn out to be a Kathy Bates-style 'number one fan' from the movies.

'But friends…I could use a friend,' he said.

'Me, too,' she said, and hoped her voice didn't sound as quivery as her knees felt when he smiled at her.

Luke found the menu from a local takeaway online, and between them they decided on a selection of dishes.

'Can I be horribly rude and sort out a couple of things for tomorrow's filming while we wait?' he asked.

'Sure. I'll take Baloo for a walk. See you in a quarter of an hour?' she asked.

'That'd be good.'

She took Baloo into the parkland surrounding the set, and they found a patch of evening sunshine to sit in.

'I need my head examining, Baloo,' she told the dog, and was rewarded by the dog putting her paws on Jess's shoulders and licking her face.

'Very helpful,' she said dryly, making a fuss of the dog. 'If you could talk, you'd tell me that you adore him, wouldn't you?'

Big brown eyes regarded her thoughtfully.

'I think he's a nice guy. Just his life's a bit of a mess, right now. I think he needs you,' she told the dog. 'Someone to teach him to love again. To trust.'

Ha. The same could be said of her. Though she wasn't single because of a betrayal by her partner. Trust didn't come into it. Her problem was fear.

'And I have no idea how I make the fear go away, Baloo,' she said softly. 'If I let someone close…what happens if I lose them, too, the way I lost Matt and Comet?' OK, so what had happened to them was outside the norm. Death wasn't usually the result of someone's intent. It was more likely to be a serious illness, or an accident. There were no guarantees that anyone in her life could cross the road safely every day for the next fifty years. Jess knew all that, intellectually. But knowing it emotionally was a different matter. And the fear kept her shut in that box of loneliness.

'Now I'm being maudlin.' She glanced at her watch. 'And we're due back at Luke's trailer.'

They arrived at the same time as their meal. Luke found some plates and Jess served up. And then Jess fed morsels of chicken surreptitiously under the table to Baloo.

'Are you feeding that dog under the table, Ms Green-acre?' he asked, catching Jess's eye.

'Busted.' She laughed. 'Sorry, I'm really not supposed to do that. It's a bad habit and it means she'll be a pain at the dinner table in the future, begging and expecting treats.'

'But those big brown eyes have suckered you in?'

'Yes,' she admitted.

Luke spread his hands. 'Well, she's looking for a good home. You could always adopt her.'

Jess shook her head. 'I can't have a dog where I live. Whereas I'd guess that you don't have a landlord who's banned dogs from the premises.'

He laughed back. 'Are you quite sure you haven't been talking to my aunt?'

'I'm sure.'

'Monica would like you,' he said thoughtfully. 'And you'd like her.'

'I already like what you've told me about her.' Jess ruffled Baloo's fur. 'And I like the fact that she rescued this one. Baloo's a great dog, Luke. She just gets a bit anxious when she's left, and a bit of training can sort that out. She won't always open your cupboards and chew things.'

'I guess,' he said. 'But my answer still has to be no.'

Maybe, Jess thought, he might change his mind when he realised that Baloo was most definitely a performer's dog.

And she'd do her best to convince him.

CHAPTER FIVE

ON FRIDAY, WHEN Luke came to collect Baloo, he said, 'Jess, I know you've probably had enough of both of us this week, but would you like to have dinner with us tonight?'

Another take-out in his trailer? 'Only if it's my shout,' she said, striving for a bit of independence. She didn't want Luke thinking that she saw him as a potential open wallet. He might be wealthy, but that didn't mean he should give everyone a free ride.

'Actually, I thought maybe I could cook for us,' he said diffidently.

She looked at him in surprise. 'You can cook?'

He lifted his chin, and she was pretty sure that he was deliberately hamming up the offended expression when he intoned, 'Of course I can cook!'

'Interesting.' She raised her eyebrows. 'Considering that all the food we've eaten together since I've known you has been made by someone else—even the sandwiches.'

'It's easier that way when I'm working, because I never know when I'm going to finish,' he said, 'but, seriously, when I'm not working I usually cook for myself. It relaxes me. Come and have dinner?'

It felt like a genuine offer rather than being polite.

And, given what he'd said last night, she was pretty sure he meant on a friendship only basis. 'OK, then. That would be nice.'

When the afternoon's shoot had finished, Luke drove them back to his place.

'I'm impressed that you have a crate in the back for Baloo,' she said.

'That was Monica's idea,' he admitted. 'And it's a lot easier driving her to work than dragging the poor dog across London on the Tube.'

As they drove into Bermondsey, Jess realised that they were heading towards the Thames. Did Luke actually live in a place overlooking the river?

They reached a block of modern three-storey mews houses, built from yellow brick with a line of red brick above the elegant white window frames. The ground floor of the building was painted white, to match the front door and garage doors; this was the kind of house, Jess thought, that would need a seriously large salary to support the mortgage.

Luke pressed a switch on his key fob and the garage door opened.

'Impressive,' she said. 'Parking where I live is on the street, with a permit.'

'There really isn't enough space to park on the street, here, so they built this block with integrated parking,' Luke said.

Once they were inside, he shut the garage door behind them, let Baloo out of the car, and unlocked the door to the house.

'I guess I should give you the guided tour, first,' he said, and gestured to the first two doors. 'Utility room and downstairs toilet.' He opened the third door. 'This room was meant to be a bedroom, really, but I use it as my office because of the view.'

It was incredibly neat and tidy, Jess thought. There was a very plain glass desk with a state-of-the-art desktop computer on top of it, a filing cabinet, a small sofa, and bookshelves that she itched to browse through—but she managed to stop herself, because she didn't want to appear rude and nosey.

He gestured to the French doors. 'Take a look.'

She glanced out. The room overlooked the garden and had an amazing view of the River Thames. 'Wow—you can actually see Tower Bridge from here,' she exclaimed.

'And the City of London skyline—there's a better view from the next two floors.' He smiled. 'The important thing here is the garden, from Baloo's point of view.'

Like his office, the garden was very neat; it was laid mainly to honey-coloured paving slabs, though there were stylishly arranged terracotta pots containing flowering shrubs.

'I'm not the best gardener,' he admitted. 'The garden's all thanks to my mother. It kind of keeps her happy.'

It was the first time Jess could remember him mentioning his mother; and it sounded as if the relationship was a little strained, because he'd spoken about his aunt with a great deal more affection.

Baloo pattered up the stairs and they followed her to the landing on the next floor. 'The top two floors are bedrooms and bathrooms,' he said, indicating the stairs. 'And this is the kitchen.' It was more than twice the size of Jess's own narrow galley-style kitchen, and it looked like something from a magazine showpiece, with light ash cabinets, shiny black worktops and a slate floor. There wasn't a river view, this time, as the room overlooked the street.

Again everything was very neat and tidy; there was no clutter of any description on the worktops, apart from a kettle and an expensive Italian coffee-maker. There weren't even any magnets holding photographs or notes to the fridge. It felt like more a place to live than a home, she thought.

Not that she had room to talk. She hadn't put up any of her framed photographs in her new place, and she'd lived there for almost a year now.

The next room was a huge reception room. Again, it looked fresh from the pages of a style magazine, with soft leather sofas, a state-of-the-art TV and sound system, and what looked like original oil paintings on the wall. The floors were polished wood—clearly real wood and not cheap veneer—and there were a couple of artfully placed silk kelims between the sofas. There was an area with a dining table and eight chairs, so obviously Luke was used to entertaining.

There were two more sets of French doors on the wall overlooking the river. Luke unlocked them, and she stepped onto the narrow balcony with its wrought iron bistro table and two chairs. The view of the waterfront was stunning, and she could pick out all the landmark buildings of the London skyline along with Tower Bridge; the Gherkin and the Shard were instantly recognisable. 'This is amazing,' she said, meaning it. 'I totally get why you love this house. You can sit on this balcony and watch the world go by. Well, on the river.'

'We get some amazing sunsets with the bridge in the background,' he said. 'There are fabulous views at night, too, when all the buildings are lit up.'

'I can imagine,' she said wistfully. This was another world. How the beautiful people lived. So far from her own life. 'I can see why you chose it.'

'I wanted to live on the river, but I didn't want another flat. I wanted a house, and I was really lucky when this one came on the market.' He smiled. 'I've always liked this area of London. It has a lot of connections with film—did you know they shot part of a James Bond movie here? As well as *Bridget Jones* and *Oliver*.' He spread his hands and gave her a disarming smile. 'I can get really boring about Dickens, so shut me up when I start.'

She couldn't imagine that Luke McKenzie could be boring about anything. He had one of those voices that could make a reading of the telephone directory sound interesting—deep, clear and slightly posh. She could listen to him for hours. But obviously he expected her to change the subject, so she did her best. 'Is that the Thames Path between your garden and the river?' she asked.

'Yes. It's based on the old towpaths that the barges used,' he confirmed.

'I always meant to walk part of it—well, obviously not the whole thing.' She knew the path was almost two hundred miles long, running between the source of the Thames in the Cotswolds and the Thames Barrier outside Greenwich. 'But I never quite got round to it.' And walking it on her own, without her partner and her dog, just hadn't felt right.

'Maybe some time you could come exploring with me and Baloo,' he suggested.

Of course he'd offer. Luke McKenzie had impeccable manners. She bit her lip. 'Sorry. I wasn't fishing for an invitation.'

'I know. But I was planning to do it anyway—and, if you come with us, then people aren't going to stare at me as if I'm this total lunatic talking to my dog.'

She laughed. 'Half the time they'll be talking to their own dogs. Besides, it's more likely that they'd be staring at you, working out if they dare come and ask you for an autograph.'

He shrugged. 'Well, the offer's there. I understand if you're busy. Baloo and I have already taken up a lot of your time this week.'

No pressure. And she appreciated that. 'I'm already doing something this weekend,' she said, 'but I'd love to come for a walk with you both some time. I don't really know the Docklands area.'

He smiled. 'I do. I've lived here for five years. Well, not this house—I moved here after the divorce. There were too many memories in my old place.'

She could understand that. She'd moved out of their house a month after Matt's death, even though everyone had said she should leave it for at least three months before making any major changes in her life. But she just hadn't been able to handle going into a room and expecting to see him and Comet there, then having to relive the loss all over again. She'd needed a fresh start. Somewhere with no memories. 'I know how that feels, too,' she said softly.

'Yeah.' He wrinkled his nose. 'Time for dinner. It's a nice evening, so do you want to eat on the balcony?'

'That'd be nice. What can I do to help?'

'Nothing, really. Except maybe feed Baloo.' He showed her where the dog food was kept, and the dog sat patiently while Jess filled her bowl.

'And now for dinner.' He produced a chef's hat, making her laugh.

'No way do you wear that to cook dinner every night.'

'Oh, but I do,' he said with a grin. 'Perfect for reheating a TV dinner in the microwave.'

She laughed back. 'So do you have a full collection of silly hats, then?'

He smiled. 'Busted. Actually, I borrowed this one from Wardrobe, earlier today. And they won't be happy if I get it messy.' He took off the hat and put it safely out of the way. 'I was bluffing about the TV dinners, too. I'm not quite that bad.'

Jess watched him cook. And she noticed that he used a container of ready-prepared vegetables, another container of ready-chopped chicken, and a sachet of ready-made stir-fry sauce.

She couldn't resist teasing him. 'I thought you said you were cooking?'

'I am.'

She coughed. 'You're just throwing ready-prepped stuff into a wok and sizzling it together. That's not *really* cooking.'

He laughed back. 'It's just a quick meal. So you're a gourmet cook, are you?'

'I like experimenting,' she said. Not that she'd bothered much since Matt's death. Since then, she'd barely noticed what she ate, so there hadn't been much point in spending time on preparation.

'I think I need a demonstration. Just to prove that you can walk the talk,' he said.

Was he teasing her back, or was he serious?

She decided to call his bluff. 'Sure. I'll cook for us next weekend.' Then her common sense kicked in. She paused. 'That is, if you're not already booked up.'

'At a glitzy showbiz party?' He rolled his eyes. 'Trust

me, they're not as frequent as the press like to make out. And they're even less fun.' He smiled. 'Baloo and I are free next weekend, and we'd love to accept your offer.'

Oh, help. He *had* been serious. 'Small problem,' she said. 'Not that I'm trying to chicken out. But my lease says I'm not allowed to have a dog, and one of my neighbours is a little bit…how can I put this, without being mean? I think he's lonely, so he takes a little bit too much interest in what other people do.'

'So he'll tell your landlord if you have a canine visitor, which will get you into hot water.'

She nodded. 'And you can't leave Baloo here on her own.'

The dog, hearing her name, looked up and woofed softly.

'So that lets you off the hook.'

Was that really disappointment in his expression, or was she just seeing what part of her secretly wanted to see? She decided to take a risk. 'Unless,' she said, 'you wouldn't mind me using your kitchen. Though it's a bit of a cheek to ask.'

'It's not a cheek, it's a workable solution,' he corrected. 'I'm not territorial. Though you'll have an audience when you're cooking. And we'll both expect treats for good behaviour, you know.'

She laughed. 'I love your sense of the ridiculous. Treats, hmm? I'll see what I can do.' She stroked Baloo's head. 'Talking of treats and audiences, we've been working on a little something. Would you like to see the premiere, after dinner?'

Jess Greenacre was turning out to be full of surprises. Away from the set, she was opening up more, and Luke liked the woman he was getting to know. She had a sense of fun. She teased him, and she let him tease her back. And she didn't treat him as if he were on a pedestal: she treated him like an ordinary man. Which was incredibly refreshing.

'I'd like that,' he said. 'Dinner's ready.'

He waited until she'd had the first mouthful. 'So? Cheat food, is it?'

'Yes. But it's nice. I'll give you that.'

He laughed, relaxing. And he appreciated the fact that Jess didn't have a desperate need to chatter. Silence with her was gentle, rather than awkward.

When they'd finished dinner, he let her carry her plate through to the kitchen, but refused to let her help clear up. 'That's what a dishwasher's for. I'll sort it later. You promised me a premiere.'

'I did indeed. Ready, Baloo?' she asked.

The dog gave a soft woof.

'OK. Then have a seat, sir, and enjoy the show.' She gestured to the sofa, and gave him a small bow, making him smile. Then she took her MP3 player from her handbag, flicked into a song, and set the player on his table.

He recognised the song immediately—the old classic, 'Can't Take My Eyes Off Of You'.

'I love this. It always makes me think of that movie with Heath Ledger.'

'Me, too. I loved that film,' she said, looking slightly wistful, and started the routine.

Baloo circled round her, circled the other way, then sat in front of her with her head to one side, looking adoringly at her. Luke appreciated the way Jess had matched the lyrics to the dog's actions, particularly when the dog rolled over as if her knees had gone weak, then put her paws on her nose as if shushing her words.

As the chorus began, Jess knelt in front of the dog, who sat up and then played pat-a-cake with her paws against Jess's palms, in a perfect rhythm to the song.

At the end, Baloo put her paws on Jess's shoulders and licked her nose. Jess hugged the dog. 'Good girl. You were brilliant.' She fed the dog a treat, and Baloo wagged her tail happily.

Then she shifted round so she was facing Luke. 'Did you enjoy it?'

He blew out a breath. 'More than enjoyed it. That was stunning. I can't believe you've taught her that in only a couple of days.'

'It's still a bit rough round the edges.'

'Even so, that's an amazing achievement in such a teensy amount of time.' He shook his head, impressed. 'You're an incredible trainer.'

'Baloo's an incredible dog,' Jess corrected. 'She picks things up quickly—when Monica gets her a family, it needs to be one who'll take her to something like agility classes or do this kind of training with her. I guarantee she won't chew, because she won't be lonely or bored if you keep her active like this.'

'She's really blossomed.' He drummed his fingers thoughtfully on the arm of the sofa. 'You ought to show this to my director.'

'Maybe.' But Jess looked pleased and her cheeks went very slightly pink.

'Would she do this with me?' he asked.

'Probably. I'll need to show you the commands. When you want her to circle, you do this.' She showed him the gesture and made him repeat it half a dozen times before she was satisfied. 'Good. She'll sit when you tell her. Then you need to get her to put her head on one side—she'll watch you and mirror you.' She talked him through the rest of the routine, then put the song on again and sat on the sofa, legs curled up, watching them as they went through the routine.

Luke knew his performance wasn't anywhere near as polished as Jess's had been, but even so he was blown away by the way the dog responded. He'd worked with animals before in his career, but it had never been like this. He'd never felt a real connection with the animals before. Not like it was with Baloo.

'You are just brilliant, Baloo.' He made a fuss of the dog and looked up at Jess. 'Can I steal some of your treats for her?'

'Sure.' She fished the bag from her pocket and handed it to him, and Luke took great pleasure in feeding the dog some treats.

'Monica's going to be blown away by this, girl,' he said. He looked up at Jess. 'And it's all thanks to you.'

'Baloo's the one who did all the work,' she said.

'Coffee?' he asked. 'And we can watch the skyline light up.'

She nodded. 'I'd like that. That view's amazing.'

'Yeah.' Oddly, it pleased him that her thoughts were so in tune with his own.

They sat on the balcony with a mug of coffee until it was just too chilly to stay out, then came in to sit on the sofa. Baloo climbed up between them, settling herself with her nose on Jess's knee.

Jess went quiet on him again, but this time it was a different sort of quiet. The sort that made Luke think that she was silently gulping back the tears.

'Are you OK?' he asked.

She swallowed hard. 'Sure.'

But her tone was a little too bright. This was something to do with her ex and their dog, he was sure—

the ones she didn't speak about. 'This is bringing back memories for you?' he guessed.

She nodded.

'Sorry.'

She took a deep breath and looked at him. 'Set rules?'

'Of course. Whatever you tell me stays with me.'

'Thank you.'

He frowned. 'What is it, Jess?'

She looked away. 'You know I was a trainer—well, it was with the police.'

'You were a policewoman?' Luke looked surprised. 'But I thought you said you did a degree in animal behaviour.'

'I did. But you have to do a couple of years on the beat before you can apply to train as a police dog handler,' she explained. 'When I joined the dog handling section, I stayed in touch with my old team. Being in the police—it's kind of like being in a family. You go through a lot together, so you're there for each other, even if you don't see each other every day.'

'A bit like working on a film set—you bond with the crew. Even the difficult ones.'

'I guess.'

'So you worked with sniffer dogs and that sort of thing?' he asked.

'Finding drugs? Yes, but that isn't the only work that the dogs do—they look for missing people, they work in search and rescue, and they track suspects.' Her throat closed when she thought about tracking suspects. That last job…

He waited in silence, and she knew he wasn't going to let her off the hook.

'I trained as a police dog handler. I did a few courses, and I was always involved when we did a display for the public at a show—the sort where you have a cops and robbers chase, and the dog takes the baddie down. Obviously the robber is one of the team and we use a protective sleeve so nobody gets hurt. I used to enjoy choreographing that.

'But it was only part of my job. I was shadowed by a trainee handler, and did some mentoring. That's when I found out how much I liked teaching. My boss asked me to consider training the handlers. I did some instructors' courses, and I loved it.' She shrugged. 'Obviously, if there was a big op, I could still help out as a handler. Most of the dogs are training to work with just their handler, but we also had dogs that were trained to work with several handlers.'

'I know I asked you before, and you said you didn't want to talk about it—but I really don't get why you gave up a job you loved to be a temp,' he said.

'Because…' She closed her eyes. The only way that she could get through telling him was if she could block everything else out. 'My husband was a handler, too. Your police dog lives with you until retirement, then generally becomes your pet. Comet was his. Mine, too, I guess, but Comet really adored Matt. He was a liver and white Springer Spaniel. We'd known him since the day he was born.' She blew out a breath. 'And it was Comet's last year in service. He was eight.'

Only eight. He'd still had years of life in him. His retirement years, when he could've been a much-loved family pet, happy to pad about the house or find himself a sunny spot in the garden where he could drowse the day away. And he hadn't had the chance.

'Matt was called out to a job. He'd had a tip from an informant about a drugs deal—he'd been trying to catch those particular dealers in the act for a while.'

She dragged in a breath. 'But it was a set-up. They were lying in wait for him. They knew Matt would have a dog with him—the informant had fed back just as much information to the dealers as he'd given to the police, if not more.' And, because of that decision, her life had imploded.

'They targeted Comet first, put him out of action, then started beating Matt. Even though they broke his ribs and one of his legs, Comet still came after them and tried to protect Matt.' She swallowed hard. 'They shot him. They shot Matt, too. Then they left them both to die.' The words were getting harder and harder to say. She forced the tears back. 'They smashed Matt's phone so he couldn't call for help. He dragged himself into the street. God only knows how—he must have been in so much pain. But he wanted to try to save Comet. Someone found him and called an ambulance, and he told them as much as he could while they waited for the ambulance and the police to arrive—but he didn't make it to hospital. He died from massive blood loss on the way there.' Her throat felt raw with the effort of holding the tears back. 'Comet didn't make it, either.'

'God, Jess. I don't know what to say. But I'm so sorry you had to go through that.'

'I didn't even get the chance to say goodbye,' she whispered. 'I didn't get to say "I love you" one last time.'

'They knew,' he said fiercely. 'I'm sure they knew how much you loved them.'

Maybe. Except her last words to Matt had been… She squeezed her eyes even more tightly shut to block it out.

'When did it happen?' he asked softly.

'A year ago.' She'd gone completely to pieces afterwards. Especially after she lost the baby. Though she couldn't tell Luke about that.

Even so, to her surprise, words continued to pour out of her mouth, words that just refused to be held back now she'd started telling him about it.

'It's taken me a while to get my life back together. I managed to find a job with a temp agency. Doing pretty much anything and everything. I know it isn't what I was trained for, and I felt so guilty that I was wasting all that time and money and effort—but I needed to do a safe job. Something where nobody ever had a chance of getting hurt.'

'But you miss it, now?'

'I miss working with dogs, yes,' she admitted. 'I haven't been able to admit that there was this huge hole in my life, even to myself. My sister and my best friend have both nagged me about it.'

'Maybe you just needed time to work it out for yourself,' he said softly. 'I'm sorry. Looking after Baloo was the worst thing I could've asked you to do.'

'And the best.' She took a deep breath. 'Looking after her, training her—it's made me think, maybe I *can* go back. Not to the police. I can't handle the idea of training someone who's going to go out and get hurt, maybe killed. I just can't do it. But I could work with people like you. People who've just got their first dogs. Or maybe working with animals on film sets—all the risk assessments will be done to minimise the risk of an accident, and nobody's going to come in and hurt someone deliberately.' Her voice dropped to a raspy whisper. 'Nobody's going to *die*.'

Not only that, every job would have a different crew, Luke thought. Every job would have different animals.

If she set up training classes for new owners, every course would have a different set of people. Which meant she wouldn't get involved, the way you would with a permanent set of colleagues. At heart, she was just like him, scared to get involved again.

Though she had much more reason to be scared. She'd lost everything through circumstances out of her control. He'd lost everything because he hadn't tried hard enough.

'I'm sorry you had to go through that,' he said again. 'And I get that I'm maybe asking you too much. If you know someone else who can help me…?'

'You don't want me to do it?'

'Not if it's going to be too hard for you. If it's going to rip everything open.'

'I'm always going to miss Matt and Comet. That'll never change. But they say that time heals. Every day it gets that tiny bit easier to handle.' She stroked Baloo's head. 'And Baloo here—I never expected that, but she's helped so much.'

'I'm glad,' he said softly, and reached over to squeeze her hand. And funny how it made his skin tingle all over. The lightest, gentlest contact. Crazy. It was almost like being a teenager again—that sense of expectation, of possibilities blooming, of everything being one step further into the exciting unknown.

Was it like this for her, too?

Not that he dared ask. Especially given what she'd just told him. And now he understood what she was struggling to get over: the death of the love of her life. His murder.

Maybe she wasn't ready for another relationship right now. Or maybe she felt the same pull that he did—

despite not wanting to get involved, he found he couldn't help it.

Slowly. They needed to take this slowly. Not push too fast outside their comfort zones. And, right then, he just wanted to savour the moment and enjoy the kind of feeling he hadn't had for a very, very long time.

At the end of the evening, Luke insisted on driving Jess home, with Baloo in her crate in the back, and walked her to her front door. 'Goodnight, Jess,' he said. 'Have a good weekend.'

'You, too. Thank you for tonight.'

Her eyes were huge in the light from the street lamp, and he couldn't resist dipping his head to kiss her goodnight. He brushed his lips against hers. But once wasn't enough, and all his good intentions of taking it slowly just vanished as if they'd never been. He kissed her again. And again, until she kissed him back.

When he finally broke the kiss, they were both shaking.

'I'd better go. Baloo,' he said, gesturing to his car.

'Yeah.' Her voice sounded slightly rusty. Sexy as hell.

It almost made him yank her back into his arms. But his common sense prevailed.

Just.

'See you later,' he said, and fled back to the car, waiting until she'd closed the door behind her before driving away.

CHAPTER SIX

Is Luke lacking?

Luke caught his breath as he saw the headline on Saturday morning.

No. Surely not. Fleur wouldn't have told the press about *that*…would she?

Feeling sick, he read on.

Bad enough. The article was asking if he was lacking confidence, given that his last film was the first one for nearly ten years where he hadn't been nominated for a single award—would the new one be more of the same? The sly insinuation was that he'd passed his peak, this film was his last chance, and he was about to blow it.

He rolled his eyes. That was utterly ridiculous. Every actor or director made at least one film that didn't touch a chord with the audience as much as the others. You couldn't be at the top of the tree for your entire career. Life didn't work that way.

Was this story the handiwork of Fleur's cronies? Or maybe, he thought, Mimi's, given that he hadn't taken her up on her offers of being available. It could be her way of getting back at him, by hitting out at him professionally.

But he was just grateful that it wasn't the article he'd been dreading. The topic that Fleur had promised not to air—though that had been before the guilt kicked in and she'd started vilifying him to make herself feel better about the fact she'd cheated on him.

Is Luke lacking?

Yes.

Because he hadn't been able to give his wife the baby she wanted.

Some people coped with infertility. They had counselling, they tried IVF, they thought about different routes to having a family.

But Fleur hadn't wanted any of that. She'd just wanted a baby of her own, without having to go through invasive therapy or an emotional wringer. So she'd found herself someone who could provide what her husband couldn't.

Baloo wriggled her way onto his lap and licked his face.

He stroked her head. 'Are you trying to cheer me up?'

She wagged her tail hard.

'You're right. I should just stop the pity party and do something useful. Like take you for a walk.'

What had Jess said to him before?

A good run with a dog at your side will definitely put the world to rights. Even if you do have to go out in public wearing dark glasses and a silly hat.

'Do I need dark glasses and a silly hat?' he asked the dog.

Baloo just gave him that dopey doggy grin.

'Wearing dark glasses makes it look as if I've got something to hide.'

Well, he had. His infertility.

'Or as if I'm letting that article get to me—meaning there's some truth in it.'

Which there wasn't. Even though it had got to him, just a bit.

'Right, then. No hat,' he said. 'No glasses. We're going for a run, just as we are.'

He was surprised to discover that Jess was right. Going for a run with the dog by his side made him feel so much better and blew away some of the misery of that article. He had an endorphin rush from the run and he had the companionship of the dog. And other dog owners were smiling at him—not because he was Luke McKenzie, but because he had a dog with him and it was a shared fellowship.

When they got back to his house, Luke was feeling so much better. On impulse, he pulled out his mobile phone and typed a text to Jess. *You were right about taking the dog for a run.*

Then he paused. There was no point in sending this. She'd already said she was busy this weekend, and it wasn't fair to burden her with the way he felt. And sending that text would be pathetic and needy.

He could deal with this himself. Just like he had with every other emotional issue since his marriage imploded.

Grimacing, he pressed a button to delete the text.

You were right about taking the dog for a run.

Jess read the text and frowned.

Why would Luke send her such a cryptic message? And what had she said to him about a run?

She racked her brain, then remembered. It was the evening when she'd teased him about his awful beanie hat. She'd told him that when you'd had a bad day, the best thing you could do was to go for a run with a dog at your side.

Which meant that Luke was having a really bad day—particularly as he'd admitted that she was right.

They weren't shooting at the weekend, as far as she knew, so it couldn't be work. So was it his aunt? Had she taken a turn for the worse?

She called him. 'Hey, it's Jess,' she said when he answered.

'Jess?' He sounded shocked to hear from her.

'You just texted me,' she pointed out.

'No, I didn't.'

'So you haven't just taken Baloo for a run?'

'Ah. *That* text.' He sighed. 'I meant to delete that, not send it. My apologies.'

'Is everything OK?' she asked.

'Sure.'

'So your aunt's all right?' Jess persisted, convinced that something was wrong and he was bluffing. But he'd let her dump a load of stuff on him, last night. The least she could do would be to return the favour.

'Monica's a bit stir-crazy and dying to come home, but they're keeping an eye on her for a while longer yet.'

'That's good. I was worried that something might be wrong.'

'Why?'

She coughed. 'Let's try that again. If I'm right about taking the dog for a run, it means you're having a bad day. So if it's not your aunt…'

He sighed. 'Ignore me. I just let a stupid article get to me, that's all.'

She knew she was probably speaking out of turn, but she couldn't help herself. 'It sounds as if you could do with tea and cake.'

'Tea and cake?' he asked.

'My sister's remedy for absolutely everything.'

'Does it work?'

And that sounded as if the words had come out before he could stop them. 'Usually.' She paused. 'If you have tea, I could bring some cake over.'

'I thought you were busy?'

Most of that had been an excuse so she didn't seem needy. Or like a stalker. 'I can always make time for cake.'

'Then thank you. Cake,' he said, 'sounds perfect.'

'See you in a bit.'

Jess went to the bakery round the corner from her flat to buy a selection of cakes, picked up some dog treats from the pet shop further down the parade of shops, and took the Tube to Luke's place. Remembering that kiss from last night made her feel slightly nervous about it. Was she doing the right thing? Was he going to think that her offer of comforting him with cake was going to be followed up by comforting him with kisses? And did she actually want to kiss him again?

The heat that flooded her skin told her that yes, she did.

Luke was the first man she'd been attracted to since Matt was killed. Part of Jess felt guilty about it—how could she want someone else, when it was only a year since she'd been widowed? And yet she knew that, had it been the other way round, she wouldn't have wanted Matt to spend the rest of his life pining for her.

And then again, how did Luke feel?

Not wanting to think too closely about that, she checked her phone to see if she could find the article that had thrown him off balance. She winced as she read it. How horrible to have people speculating about you in that way, and knocking your confidence. She was glad that she'd never had to deal with anything like that.

When she rang the doorbell, he opened the front door a few seconds later and the Labrador pushed her way in front of him, wriggling and wagging her tail wildly.

She grinned. 'Nice welcome, Baloo. And, yes, I brought something for you.' She smiled at Luke. 'And for you.' She handed him the box.

He glanced inside when he'd ushered her indoors. 'These look wonderful—I don't believe this. Cupcakes with top hats on.'

'Well, with you being such a hat fiend…' she deadpanned.

He grinned. 'Yeah. Thank you. What tea would you like? Earl Grey? Rooibos and vanilla? Chai?'

Clearly he was a man after her own heart; she had a variety of teas in her own cupboard. 'Chai, please.'

'Chai it is.'

Luke had one of those posh glass teapots where you put loose-leaf tea in a basket in the centre that could be taken out when the tea was at the desired strength. And Jess noticed that he was careful not to put the tea into the water until they were both sitting on his balcony with a loaded tea tray in front of them. 'Tea, meet water. Water, meet tea,' he said, and pulled the centre out so he could pour her tea. 'This is basically stinky milk, you know,' he teased. 'All you're getting are the spices.'

'Just how I like it,' she said, and fed Baloo a dog treat while she waited for the tea to brew a bit more for him.

Sitting in the sunshine, overlooking the river, drinking tea and eating cupcakes: it was a perfect English summer afternoon. Apart from the fact that she wouldn't be here if Luke was happy. 'I read that article, by the way,' she said. 'I thought it was mean and underhand.'

He shrugged. 'I just have to let it roll.'

'Why can't you complain to the editor and make them apologise?'

'You know the saying, "Methinks the lady doth protest too much"?' he quoted. 'If I say something about it, then either I'm being stuck-up, or I'm trying to cover up the story. So it's better just to say nothing and not give it any more air.'

'It doesn't seem fair that people can say anything they like about you, and you have to shut up and take it.'

'Part and parcel of my job. Though it's not my favourite bit,' he admitted.

'I don't think any of your fans will agree with that article. They'll all say it's a load of tosh and your next film will be wonderful.'

'Strictly speaking,' he said, 'the last one *wasn't* my best film.'

He'd made it when he was in the middle of splitting up from Fleur, she guessed. So it was totally understandable. 'You can't be perfect all the time, and anyway your fans will forgive you a lot because of—well, what was happening in your life when you made it.'

'I try not to let my personal life get in the way of work,' he said, sounding slightly annoyed.

'I wasn't judging, Luke. Just saying that you're human.'

'Of course. Sorry.' He grimaced. 'I'm being over-sensitive.'

'I guess it must knock your confidence when people give you a harsh review or come out with stuff like this.'

'That depends on how they do it. If they say what doesn't work for them and they're honest, then I can learn from it and make the next film better. I have no problem with that.'

'That's constructive criticism. Whereas this article…'

She grimaced. 'It sounded to me more as if they had an axe to grind.'

'Maybe.' He looked uncomfortable, and she had the distinct impression that she was treading on a sore spot.

'So taking Baloo for a run helped?' she asked.

'Yes, it did,' he said. 'More than I expected.'

'Told you so. Strike two for Baloo,' she said.

'Jess,' he warned softly, 'I can't be her forever owner.'

'Methinks,' she said, throwing his words back at him, 'the lady—well, you're *not a lady, but you know what I mean*—doth protest too much. And I bet your aunt would say the same.'

'I'm just very glad you're not in the same room together,' he said wryly. 'You'd be a force to be reckoned with.'

'Now there's an idea,' she said lightly.

She finished her tea. 'I'd better be going—I'm expected at my sister's, and our parents are going to be there.' For a mad moment, she almost invited him to go with her; she knew Carly wouldn't mind Baloo turning up. But then why would an A-list actor want to hang out with a very ordinary family? 'I guess you'll be busy polishing your lines,' she said.

He gestured to the dog. 'And I have an audience to impress.'

'You'll impress your human audience, too,' she said softly. 'Don't let that article mess with your head. Go for another run with Baloo if you need to.' She paused. 'I'm probably speaking out of turn, here, but someone I know well had a really bad confidence wobble, a couple of years back. She went through a tough time at work. What got her through it was going to the gym and learning to lift weights.'

He raised an eyebrow. 'You're suggesting that's what I need to do? Go to a gym and lift weights?'

'For my friend, it was doing something totally different, something out of her comfort zone. The discipline of training helped her focus and it helped her to get her confidence back.' She looked at him. 'You've hit a tough patch. The discipline of training Baloo might do the same thing for you that the gym did for her—it's out of your comfort zone, but seeing the dog's progress and knowing that you're the one responsible for it...' She wrinkled her nose and shook her head. 'Oh, I'll shut up. I've already said too much.'

'You were right about the running. Maybe you're right about this.' He paused. 'Jess, thanks. I really appreciate you being there for me.'

'Hey. That's what friends are for.' She shrugged off his praise, but secretly it warmed her. 'Thanks for the tea. See you Monday.'

'Thanks for the cake. See you Monday.'

And, when Luke ushered her downstairs, it felt only natural for Jess to pause by the front door. To look at him. He was looking right back at her, his pupils wide and his eyes an incredible silver-grey. Almost in slow motion, his hand came up to cup her face. He rubbed his thumb gently along her lower lip. 'Jess,' he said softly, and she knew he was going to kiss her again. She couldn't help tipping her head back slightly in offering. Softly, gently, he brushed his lips against hers, and that breezy goodbye on his balcony was completely undermined. She opened her mouth, letting him deepen the kiss, and somehow his arms were wrapped tightly round her and her hands were tangled in his hair.

When he broke the kiss, they were both shaking. His gaze held hers and for a moment she thought he was going to ask her to stay. But then he stroked her face again. 'Sorry. I seem to be making a habit of this.'

Jess wasn't sorry in the slightest. 'So you do.' She reached up to touch her mouth to his. 'See you Monday,' she whispered.

He stole another kiss. 'Monday.'

And Jess had the distinct feeling that next Monday wouldn't come fast enough for either of them.

On Sunday, Luke divided his time between training Baloo with the exercises Jess had already taught him, and working on polishing his lines.

But, despite what he'd told Jess the previous day about never letting his personal life distract him, he found himself getting very distracted indeed. Especially when he thought about how Jess had kissed him back yesterday.

This was insane. They both had baggage, valid reasons for not getting involved with someone else. And yet she was so unlike the showbiz women he was used to mixing with; she was utterly straightforward. And she made him laugh. She could tease him out of a dark mood—and comfort him with kisses.

But what could he offer her, beyond a lifestyle? He had no idea whether she wanted children—they were nowhere near the stage of their relationship where they could discuss that—but his infertility could turn out to be a deal-breaker, just like it had with Fleur. Did he really want to let himself fall all the way in love with her, only to have to let her walk away?

As if sensing his mood, Baloo put her paws on his knees and licked his nose.

'You, too,' he said. 'I can't offer you a proper future. And it's mean to let you bond with me. And stupid of me to get used to having you around.' Though one thing had become very clear over the last week—having the dog around had really made his house feel like home, instead of just a place to live.

Maybe there was some way he could find a compromise.

Maybe.

When Luke walked on to the set on Monday, he quickly discovered that everyone was pussyfooting round him; he sighed inwardly, knowing they'd read the article. How many of them agreed with it? he wondered.

The only one who didn't handle him with kid gloves was Jess. She tapped her watch and rolled her eyes, really hamming it up. 'What time do you call this? Talk about messing with a poor, hard done by Labrador's routine. Off to work with you, McKenzie. Baloo here needs a nap.'

He could've hugged her for that. Because the teasing, and the way Jess didn't look at him as if he was so fragile that one word out of place would make him shatter, made all the tension flood out of his muscles. She believed in him.

'My apologies, O Great Animal Expert.' He made a fuss of Baloo. 'See you after shooting. Don't steal or chew anything except a dog toy, OK?'

'As if she would,' Jess teased. 'Break a leg.'

'Thanks.' He blew a kiss at Ayesha. 'See you guys later.'

During filming, he found the rest of the crew were still treating him with kid gloves. When they took a break at the end of the first scene, he said, 'Can I have a quick cast conference, here?'

George, the director, looked surprised. 'What's up?'

'Very, *very* quick cast conference,' Luke said.

George called everyone to gather round.

'I'm guessing you all saw that article at the weekend,' Luke said. 'Guys, you don't have to treat me like a special snowflake. OK, so I didn't get nominated for an award for my last film. So what? It's just one film, and it's not the same as this one. Just so you all know, whatever that article said, this is going to be a great movie. The script is great, we're all doing our jobs to the best of our ability, and our audiences are going to laugh and cry in all the places we want them to. We're a team. And I'm not intending to let any of you down, OK?'

'OK. That's good enough for me.' George clapped his shoulder. 'And I'll talk to the publicity team and see if they can fix up some interviews to show that you're doing just fine.'

The rest of the cast from the scene followed suit, shaking his hand and agreeing with him. Except, he noticed, Mimi. So maybe she'd been the one feeding the information to the journalist. Revenge for turning her down? Or maybe it was because she'd been friendly with Fleur at some point. He didn't know and he didn't care. But he wasn't going to give her any chance to try that kind of stunt again.

CHAPTER SEVEN

ON FRIDAY JESS was taking Baloo for a walk in the park when she felt a tug on her shoulder; acting purely on instinct, she grabbed the top of her bag and looked round. A young lad in a hoodie was tugging on the strap of her bag.

He honestly thought she was just going to let him mug her, in broad daylight, in the middle of the park? 'Get off!' she yelled, expecting him to drop the strap of her bag and run off.

To her shock, he produced a knife. 'Give me your bag,' he demanded.

Her stomach turned to water. So he wasn't just an opportunist thief who could be scared off by attention being drawn to him, then. And, from the slurred sound of his voice, he was taking some kind of drug that clearly made him feel invincible. He'd have no hesitation in sticking that knife straight into her.

Give him the bag.

That would be the sensible thing to do.

But the bag had her phone in it. With photos of Matt and Comet. Texts from Matt that she hadn't been able to bear to delete.

She couldn't lose them. *Especially not today.*

'I said, give me the bag,' he snarled again.

Baloo barked, then growled at him; he turned on the dog and kicked her hard in the ribs. Baloo yelped and hit the ground.

And then Jess's police training kicked in. Everything went into slow motion, as if she were wading through treacle. The next thing she knew, the mugger was on the floor with his arm twisted between his shoulder blades, the knife was safely out of his reach, and her knee was pressed into the small of his back.

'You'd better hope my dog's all right,' she snarled. 'If you've hurt her…'

It would be oh, so easy to pull his arm that little bit tighter and snap the bone. To hurt him as he'd hurt her dog. To grab his hair and keep smacking his head into the ground. To hurt him in revenge for all the thugs like him who hurt people—thugs like the ones who'd beaten Comet and left Matt to bleed to death.

So, so easy.

And so, so wrong.

'Someone call the police,' she yelled. She glanced over at Baloo, who was sitting beside her, shaking.

'It's all right, sweetheart,' she soothed. Please let Baloo be all right. Please don't let the thug have broken her ribs or caused internal bleeding.

Again, she had to resist the urge to grind the mugger's face into the dirt and snap a bone or two.

People crowded round her. She was aware of people offering to help, to take over from her, but she wasn't letting the mugger go or risk the chance of him escaping. She wanted him cuffed and charged. And she wanted him stopped in this way of life, before he really hurt someone.

'Is this his?' one of the bystanders asked, bending towards the knife.

'Yes. Don't touch it,' Jess warned. 'It's evidence and we don't want his fingerprints compromised.'

'What, you're a pig?' the mugger asked with a last bit of drug-induced bravado, using the derogatory nickname for the police.

Not any more, she wasn't, but he didn't need to know that. But she had no intention of engaging in conversation with him. Not until his rights had been read to him, and she couldn't do that herself any more.

At last, she heard the familiar wail of a police siren.

Two police officers came rushing over. 'What's going on here? Oh, Jess!' one of them said in surprise.

She recognised the two officers as colleagues from her old station.

'Mikey, Ray,' she acknowledged them both. 'This guy tried to mug me and grab my bag. He pulled a knife on me—' she nodded to indicate the weapon that he'd dropped earlier '—and he kicked my dog. I'm happy to testify in court, and I want you to make sure animal cruelty is added to the rap sheet.'

'You hurt my arm,' the mugger whined. 'And your dog tried to bite me.'

Jess raised her eyebrows. 'I think you'll find that I've used appropriate force, and no more. And my dog didn't try to bite you. You were threatening me with a knife and she growled at you. You *kicked* her, you bastard.' She felt her muscles go tight. Right at that moment, she wanted to kick the mugger. Where it hurt. Really, really hard.

'OK. We'll take it from here. And we need to take a proper statement from you, Jess,' Mikey said.

She relinquished her hold on the thug. While the officers read the mugger his rights and cuffed him, she checked Baloo, gently feeling the area where the dog had been kicked.

Baloo whined, but Jess hoped that it was because the dog was scared and sore, rather than because she had broken ribs. She couldn't feel anything like a break. But the bastard had kicked her hard. Jess thought again about what had happened to Comet; she only just managed to hold it together, aware that she was shaking now as much as the dog was.

'Are you OK to give a statement here, Jess? Do you need someone to get you a mug of hot sweet tea or something?' Ray asked.

'I'm fine,' Jess said, as if saying it would make it true, and sat on the floor so Baloo could creep onto her lap. So what if a Labrador was way too big to be a lapdog? Right now the dog needed comfort—and so did Jess.

She gave a clear description of exactly what had happened, all the while soothing the dog and holding her close.

'And you'll testify in court, if we need you to?' Ray checked.

'Absolutely.'

'Great. Well, we'll be in touch and let you know what happens.'

She got to her feet again to sign the statement, and he hugged her. 'It's good to see you again. We've all missed you, you know.'

'I missed you all, too. But, after what happened…'

'Yeah, we know. It's…' Ray blew out a breath. 'It's hard.'

He could actually have a lunch break today? Delighted with the news, Luke rang Jess to see if she was free for lunch. No answer. Well, she was probably busy at the production office. He called in to see her, only to discover from Ayesha that Jess had already taken Baloo to the park. Well, OK—it wasn't that huge a park. He'd probably be able to spot them within a couple of minutes.

He signed out of the set and crossed over to the park. He could see a police car parked across the road with blue lights flashing, and there appeared to be a crowd of people in the park. He glanced over briefly, and then stood absolutely still with shock.

Jess was right in the middle of that crowd. With Baloo. And the police were talking to her.

What the…?

Forcing himself to stay calm, he walked over to join her. 'Hey, Jess. Is everything OK?' Stupid question. Of course it wasn't.

'It's fine now,' she said. 'Nothing to worry about.'

But her voice was slightly brittle, and he knew she was keeping something back. Something important.

'You take care, Jessie. And call us. We'd all like to see you,' one of the policemen said, hugging her.

'I will, Mikey.'

'Promise?'

She smiled and patted his shoulder. 'Promise.'

What was going on?

He guessed that maybe Jess had worked with the policemen or their partners in the past, but something was very clearly wrong.

'Are you all right?' he asked again.

'I'm fine.'

He didn't think she was. There was no colour whatsoever in her face and her eyes were huge. 'What's happened, Jess?'

She took a deep breath. 'We were mugged. A guy tried to grab my bag. He had a knife.'

Luke went cold. This could've been much, much worse. Jess could've been seriously hurt. 'Oh, my God.'

She flapped a dismissive hand. 'I disarmed him and it's OK now. He's in custody.'

'You need some hot sweet tea,' he said. 'And some space.' People were crowding round, still. And he didn't think it was just the mugging that had attracted them; people were beginning to nudge each other and point at him, too. 'Let's go back to the set. Find somewhere quiet so you can sit down and catch your breath.' He shepherded her and Baloo out of the park. He'd also noticed that the dog hadn't leapt all over him, the way she usually did; instead, Baloo was subdued and clinging to Jess's side. Clearly the mugging had frightened the dog badly.

He got them both signed back into the set, then bought them both a drink and a sandwich at the catering tent before taking her back to his trailer.

'Thank you,' she said softly, clearly on the edge of tears. He was shocked by how protective it made him feel. He wanted to wrap her up and keep her safe. And he wanted to pin that mugger against the wall and put the fear of God into him so the kid never, ever tried to hurt someone again.

He blew out a breath and unclenched his fists.

'It's hot and sweet. I thought it might help,' he said, pushing the paper cup of tea towards her. 'And, if you want to talk, I'm here.'

Oh, God. He was being so nice, Jess thought. And she was just a mess.

He'd meant well, she knew. Hot sweet tea was supposed to be good for shock. But even the scent of it made her gag, bringing back memories of the last time someone had made her hot sweet tea. Gallons of the stuff, while the bad news unfolded and unfolded and unfolded until it swamped her.

She swallowed hard. 'I'm sorry. I can't drink it.'

He rummaged in the fridge. 'I have sparkling water or milk, or I can make you some instant coffee.'

She shook her head. 'Thanks, but I don't want anything.' Her throat felt swollen from holding back the tears. Right at that moment, she didn't think she could swallow food or drink.

Luke gave her space while she toyed with the sandwich he'd bought her and fed all the chicken to Baloo.

'I have cyber cake,' he said, taking his phone out of his pocket and finding a picture of cake on the internet. 'Not *quite* as good as your sister's remedy, but it'll have to do at short notice.'

She gave him a watery smile. 'Thanks for trying.'

'Talk to me, Jess,' he said softly. 'Better out than in. And it's set rules. It won't go further than me.'

She dragged in a breath. 'I guess today brought a lot of things back to me.' Her voice was shaky. 'The mugger kicked Baloo. I wanted to break his arm and get revenge for Matt and Comet. I really wanted to hurt him, Luke. That's exactly why I can't be a police dog trainer any more. I can't send handlers and dogs into difficult situations where some bastard could put a bullet through them and leave them to die, the way it happened to Matt and Comet. And I can't trust myself to be a good cop and act according to the law.'

'But you didn't hurt the guy,' he reminded her. 'You disarmed him and you got someone to call the police.'

'But I *wanted* to hurt him, and that's the point—what if I'd lost control?'

'I don't think you would,' he said.

'I can't take that risk. It wouldn't be fair on anyone. I'd be a liability to work with.' She shook her head. 'That's why I resigned. I can't go back to the force. Ever.' And for all this to be brought back to her today, of all days...

She was crying silently, tears sliding down her face. The dog was anxious, nudging Jess with her nose and whining.

Luke put his arms round both of them, holding them close. 'Jess. You don't have to go back. You don't have to do anything you don't want to.' He kissed the top of her head. 'It's OK. I'm here. So's Baloo.'

And that made her feel even more guilty. This attraction she felt towards Luke—how much of it was for his sake, and how much was her trying to replace Matt and Comet?

'I'm sorry.' Jess scrubbed at her eyes with the back of her hand. 'I was being wet.'

'Don't be so hard on yourself,' Luke said softly, knowing he was being a hypocrite because he'd done exactly the same thing when his marriage broke up.

She ignored his comment. 'I need to get Baloo to the vet's. I checked her over myself and I'm pretty sure she's just bruised and frightened and shocked, but I want to be double sure that she doesn't have any broken bones.'

Or internal bleeding, he thought—this had clearly brought back everything that had happened to Comet. Hadn't she said that the thugs had broken the dog's ribs and a leg?

'I'll come with you.'

She shook her head. 'You can't. You're expected back on set.' She bit her lip. 'And I've probably already ruined the continuity and what have you—I've made wet patches on your shirt.'

'Wardrobe can sort that out later. This is a question of priorities.'

'Luke, people are depending on you. Baloo will be safe with me.' She gave a mirthless laugh. 'Well, she should have been safe with me in the park, but she wasn't, was she?'

'It isn't your fault.'

'Yes, it is. If the mugger hadn't targeted me she'd be fine.'

'Does it not occur to you,' he pointed out gently, 'that it's actually the mugger's fault? He was the one who chose to try and steal your bag. He could see that you had a dog with you and everyone knows how loyal dogs are. He must've known that the dog would bark or growl at him.'

She dragged in a breath. 'Even so. Look, I'll text you from the vet's. Keep your phone on silent.'

Luke realised that this was her way of saying she wanted some space. Right now she probably wanted to get her equilibrium back. Half of it was the shock of being mugged and half of it was from the memories it had brought back.

So he needed to back off. Now. 'OK. I'll wait to hear from you.'

'And this time,' she said, 'I promise I'll keep your dog safe.'

He didn't have the heart to remind her that Baloo was only his dog temporarily. 'I know. I trust you.'

But the look on her face said it all. She didn't trust herself.

Yeah. He knew what that felt like, too.

Jess texted Luke from the vet's. *All fine. Just bruising. No scary stuff.*

She was surprised to get a text back immediately. *Good. Stop worrying. See you both later.*

Maybe he was on a break between scenes. He wouldn't have ruined a scene just for her, would he?

'Well, *we* are going back to the park on the way to the set,' she told Baloo. 'We're going to face it now, so it doesn't get a chance to scare us and get blown out of proportion.'

The dog just looked trustingly at her.

It was enough to break her heart all over again. Remembering how Comet had looked trustingly at her and Matt. They hadn't been able to keep Comet safe. Matt hadn't been able to keep himself safe, either.

She dragged in a breath. 'Is it ever going to stop hurting, Baloo? Am I ever going to be able to move on?'

The dog licked her.

'I want to, I really do. And I think I want to move on with Luke.' She enjoyed his company. He made her world feel brighter. 'But what if that goes wrong? What if someone hurts him? There are some seriously crazy people out there, people who'll try to hurt others to get their two minutes or whatever of fame.' She sighed. 'I'm a mess. I'm not ready for this. Maybe I need to start backing off.'

Baloo whined.

'Come on. Time for the park. No stupid muggers are going to scare us off,' she said, straightening her shoulders, and set off with the dog.

* * *

Luke walked into the production office as usual after shooting had finished for the day.

'Come and have dinner with us?' he asked.

She wanted to say yes, she really did. But the look of sympathy on his face made the tears prick at the back of her eyelids again. Supposing they went out and she ended up sobbing all over him again? She couldn't face it. It had been bad enough having a meltdown in his trailer. 'Please don't think I'm being rude,' she said carefully, 'and it's really nice of you to ask, but I don't think I can face going out tonight.'

He shrugged. 'OK. We'll go back to mine and I'll cook for you.'

She shook her head. 'That's really kind of you, but no.'

'You've had a horrible day,' he said softly. 'It's brought back a lot of bad memories for you and, although you might think you want to be alone, I think you really need some company.'

Why did he have to be so nice? So understanding? Why couldn't he be the archetypal arrogant millionaire type, the sort who never gave a second thought to anyone else and their needs—the sort she'd want to push into a puddle? Someone as inconsiderate and mean as Luke's leading lady in the film? Someone she could despise instead of want to be with?

She didn't trust herself to answer and just stared mutely at him.

'If you don't want to go to my place, we'll go to yours—and I'll cook.'

Help. The idea of Luke McKenzie in her tiny galley kitchen, working with her in such intimate surroundings… 'You don't have to cook for me. Besides,

I haven't been shopping this week and my fridge is pretty empty.' Way to go, Jess. Couldn't you have come up with a more feeble excuse? she berated herself.

'Then we'll get a pizza delivered,' he said.

She panicked. 'I'm not supposed to have dogs.'

'If your landlord complains, I'll explain that it's my fault and charm him out of giving you any hassle.' He smiled at her. 'Being charming is part of my job description, remember.'

She knew he was right. Although part of her wanted to be alone, left to her own devices she would just curl into a ball and sob herself to sleep. She probably did need company.

'OK,' she said, knowing she was beaten. 'Thank you.' And she followed him and Baloo to his car.

CHAPTER EIGHT

WHEN LUKE PARKED in the street outside Jess's house, she climbed out of the car. 'Bring Baloo in and I'll get you a parking permit.'

She unlocked the front door, very aware of how dark and cramped her flat would seem to him after his light, spacious townhouse, and walked through to the kitchen. She grabbed the parking permit pad from the drawer and swiftly scribbled out the details.

Luke and Baloo came into the kitchen just as she'd finished.

'You just need to add your car registration number,' she said, handing Luke the permit and a pen.

He filled in the last bit, and Baloo whined and barked as he left to put the permit in his car.

Jess dropped to her knees and put her arms round the dog's neck. 'Shh, sweetheart. If next door hears you, then we'll be toast. He'll tell the landlord.'

Baloo whined and licked her cheek.

She made a fuss of the dog and then put the kettle on.

When Luke came back into the kitchen, she didn't look round. 'Sorry, I don't have a posh coffee-making machine like yours, but I do have decent coffee.' She took the jar of ground coffee from the fridge and shook some into a cafetière.

* * *

Jess was really nervous, Luke thought, but he had absolutely no idea why. Did she think he'd look down on her because she didn't have a posh flat with a river view?

'So can you recommend a pizza delivery place?' he asked.

'I guess.' She rummaged in a drawer and took out a flyer. 'I normally get a thin crust.'

'Fine by me. Margherita?'

'Whatever.'

She sounded so tired, so hurt. He wanted to hold her close and tell her that he'd never let anything bad happen to her again. But it was a promise he couldn't keep. Life had a nasty habit of throwing curveballs. Besides, he didn't want to spook her. There was a fine line between being supportive and smothering her.

He called the pizza place to order dinner.

'Would you like some wine?' she asked when he put the phone down again.

'I'm driving, so better stick to something soft—but don't let that stop you.'

She shook her head. 'I'm fine. I'm not going to bother.'

Luke noticed how plain everything was. How bare the kitchen surfaces were. Given how close she'd seemed to her sister and best friend, he'd expected to see photographs of them all together, held to the fridge with magnets—but there was nothing. This didn't feel like a home, and it certainly didn't feel as if it belonged to the Jess he'd come to know. The flat felt as anonymous as a hotel suite, just a place to live.

She ushered him through to the living room; he sat on the small sofa, and Baloo settled herself on the floor by his feet. There was a small bistro table like the one on his balcony, with two chairs. There were a couple of prints on the walls that Luke guessed had come with the furnished flat, because they were as bland and anonymous as the decor. There were no photographs or any kind of ornament on the fireplace—no pictures of her husband or her family or the dog.

It was as if Jess had just shut everything away.

The pizza, when it finally arrived, was really indifferent. Not that Luke cared. He was more worried about Jess. She'd closed off on him.

'Shall I make us some more coffee?' he asked.

She shrugged, as if it was too much effort to disagree.

He couldn't leave her like this. He walked over to her, scooped her out of her chair, and sat down in her place, settling her onto his lap and holding her close. 'Jess, talk to me.'

She just looked at him, her green eyes huge and her face chalk-white again.

'It's better out than in,' he said, knowing himself to be a total hypocrite because he never talked about the real reason he and Fleur had broken up. How often those same words had been said to him, too. *Better out than in.* He wouldn't know.

A tear slid slowly down her cheek. 'It's an anniversary.'

Anniversary? he thought. It couldn't be the murder. She'd said it was over a year ago since she'd lost Matt and Comet.

'I was pregnant when Matt died.'

Luke went cold. The one topic that he never wanted to talk about. Pregnancy.

But if he stopped her talking now, he'd have to explain. He didn't want to do that. He didn't want Jess to know how much of a failure he was.

She dragged in a breath. 'I had a fight with Matt, the morning of the day he was killed. I can't even remember what it was about. Something trivial. I felt sick all morning, and then it hit me that my period was late. I bought a test. It was positive. So I thought maybe that's why I'd been so touchy and we'd had that fight—it was all just stupid hormones. I should've called him and told him right there and then, but I wanted to wait until he got home. I wanted to tell him face to face, and say sorry.'

Except she hadn't had the chance, Luke thought, so Matt had never known that he was going to be a father.

Luke knew he ought to say something but he didn't know what to say. He didn't know how to comfort her. Just as he'd failed to comfort his wife and failed to give her the baby she'd wanted so much.

Not wanting Jess to see his face and guess that something was wrong, he enfolded her in another hug. 'The anniversary?' he prompted.

'I lost the baby.' She dragged in a breath. 'I know miscarriages are really common in early pregnancy, but even so it was the last straw for me. I wanted that baby so much.'

Just like Fleur. Jess had wanted a baby with Matt. If Luke let her get any closer to him, maybe she'd start wanting a baby with him, too. The one thing he couldn't give her.

'I thought I still had something left of him. When I lost the baby, I lost the last link to him. And I felt so guilty.'

'Oh, honey. I don't know what to say.'

And he didn't know how to stop her hurting. How

to stop himself hurting. Though wild horses wouldn't drag that information from him.

How different his life might have been if he hadn't had mumps when he was ten. He could've had a son. A daughter. Maybe one of each.

Then again, he wouldn't have met Jess. He wouldn't have been here with her right now, holding her. So maybe things happened for a reason.

'It wasn't your fault.' He kissed her gently. 'Jess. Is that why you don't have any photos up?'

'Because I feel guilty and I can't face it?' She rested her forehead against his. 'Yes.'

'Do you still have photos?'

'They're packed away.'

'You need to look at them, Jess, not shut them out of your life. They're part of who you are.'

She looked at him, her face full of misery.

'Show me,' he said softly.

He thought she was going to refuse. Then she nodded, slid off his lap and left the room. She was gone for so long that he was at the point of going to look for her; but then she walked in with a large box.

There were framed pictures on the top. She handed him the first one in silence.

Clearly she'd married Matt when they were both in their very early twenties; they both looked young and fresh-faced. Matt looked like a decent guy; and in the photograph his face was full of love.

'You were a beautiful bride,' Luke said softly. 'You look so happy together. Anyone can see how you really loved each other.' He stroked her hair back from her face. 'Hold on to that, Jess. There was always the love there.'

Though in a way he knew he was a hypocrite. He

couldn't stand to look at his own wedding photographs, because he was scared he'd see traces of Fleur's faithlessness in them even then.

More framed photographs: her graduation, and Matt's. A picture of a woman in a wedding dress and Jess in what was clearly a bridesmaid's dress; they resembled each other enough for him to guess that the bride was Jess's sister Carly. A second wedding picture, again with Jess in what looked like a bridesmaid's dress, smiling broadly with a bride. 'Is that Shannon?' he asked.

She nodded. 'My best friend.'

Group pictures—Jess and what he assumed were her family in a garden, with a dog smack in the middle of the group that just had to be Comet. Jess cuddling babies; those pictures made his stomach knot, but he wasn't going to let her know how much it affected him. This was about her, not the mess of his life. It was about her taking control and taking her life back. And he wanted to help her do that. Lend her some of his strength.

After the framed pictures, there were albums. Jess's wedding. An album of family pictures—weddings, christenings, candid shots at Christmas and on summer afternoons. Pictures of a tiny spaniel puppy with a snub nose and floppy ears; more pictures of the dog as he grew up and filled out, his ears and nose growing longer, feathery hair appearing on his legs. Pictures of Matt in uniform with the dog. Another picture that looked as if it commemorated some kind of bravery award.

'Comet,' she whispered.

As if hearing the distress in Jess's voice, Baloo came over to put her chin on Jess's knee.

The tiny gesture was the one to make Jess crack again, and she cried all over Luke and Baloo.

He held her until her sobs died down, and Baloo licked Jess's face anxiously.

'I'm sorry,' she whispered eventually.

'Don't apologise. It's fine.'

'I've given you such a rubbish evening.'

'Actually, you haven't. You've given me trust, and you've told me things you haven't told anyone else. That's worth a lot.' He paused. 'Jess. Do you want me to stay?'

'You can't. Baloo,' she said.

'Then come and stay at mine. You can't be alone tonight.'

She shook her head. 'Right now, I think I need some space. But I appreciate the offer.' She stroked his face. 'Thank you. You've been utterly brilliant.'

'I'm just glad I could be there for you,' Luke said, and was shocked to realise how much he meant that. It wasn't just a kind platitude—he really was glad that he'd made Jess talk to him and open her heart.

Just as long as she didn't expect him to do the same. Because he just couldn't admit to how much of a failure he really was.

'Do you want me to call anyone for you? Carly? Shannon?'

She shook her head. 'I'll be OK. Really. I think I just need a bath and an early night. But thank you for being here.' She hugged him. 'I'll call you tomorrow.'

'OK. If you change your mind, just call me. I'll come and get you.'

'Thank you.'

Maybe he was pushing her now, but he didn't want her to go back into her shell, the way he suspected she'd done after Matt and Comet were killed and she'd lost the baby. 'Are we still on for tomorrow?' he asked.

'Tomorrow?' She looked dazed. 'What about tomorrow?'

'Last weekend, you said you'd cook for me and we'd take Baloo out on the Thames Path.'

For a moment, he thought she was going to back out, but then she gave him a weary smile. 'I swear you're channelling my sister.'

'I am. Nagging's good. And I'll buy cake.'

'You'll leave Baloo on her own in your house, for long enough to go to the shop and buy cake?' she asked.

'Well, someone gave me some very good advice about a toy stuffed with treats. Which will distract her for long enough for me to buy not just cake, but *awesome* cake.' He kissed her very lightly. 'Say yes.'

She dragged in a breath. 'Yes. And I promise not to cry all over you tomorrow.'

'Deal,' he said. What he really wanted to do was to carry her to his car, take her back to his place and just hold her until she slept, but he knew she needed some space. 'Mañana,' he said, kissing her one last time.

When he'd gone, Jess headed to the bathroom, leaving the box of photographs where it was. She couldn't face putting them all away again. Not right now.

The bath didn't help much. She cleaned the kitchen, then dragged herself to bed, and finally fell asleep with tears seeping down her cheeks again.

CHAPTER NINE

JESS WOKE EARLY on Saturday morning with a thumping headache from all the crying the night before. She splashed her face with water and took some paracetamol, then looked at the photographs she'd left in the living room. Did she really want to box her past up like that and shut it away? She remembered what Luke had said. *They're part of who you are.* She knew he was right. Slowly, she picked up the photo frames and put them on the mantelpiece one by one. Comet. Matt. Their wedding day. Graduation. Her sister's wedding. Shannon's wedding.

So much love.

She wouldn't shut it out any more.

After a shower and washing her hair, she went out to buy flowers, then headed for the cemetery where Matt and Comet were buried. The last of the early summer bulbs had finished flowering, and she made a mental note to bring secateurs next time to tidy up the plot.

She put the flowers in the vase in front of the headstone. 'Hey, Matt. I've put the photos back up.' It still hurt to look at the pictures, a reminder of what she'd lost, but she was trying to see it the other way. That they were part of who she was.

'I'm not putting you out of my heart, but I've spent

the last year living in the shadows with everything on hold. And maybe, just maybe, it's time to take my life back.' She swallowed hard. 'I always thought we'd grow old together and raise children. You would've made such a great dad.' Tears threatened to break up her words again. 'And I'm so sorry I couldn't carry our baby to term. So sorry that I couldn't give your parents another generation to love.' She paused. 'If I'd been the one who was killed, then I would've wanted you to meet someone else.' Though she still felt guilty that she was the one left behind. The one who'd met someone else.

She sighed. 'I've kind of met someone else. Though he's way out of my league. As if an international film star's really going to be interested in an ordinary woman like me. But he's had a hard time, too. He's lost someone he loved. So maybe this is a fling, the thing that gets his life and my life back on track. Something to make us both live again.' She rearranged the flowers. 'I'll always love you, Matt. You'll always be part of me, you and Comet. I just—I just wish it hadn't been this way. And I hope you understand.'

There was a soft hiss of wind through the branches of the trees, almost as if someone was whispering the word 'yes'.

Or maybe she was just being way too fanciful.

All the same, Jess went home feeling better. As if someone had taken down a blackout blind from a window and the sun was shining into the room.

Maybe today was the day her life started over.

She'd promised Luke dinner. It didn't take long to get the ingredients at the supermarket. And she found herself humming along to the radio as she cooked. How long had it been since her heart had felt this light?

And she was pretty sure that it was all down to Luke and Baloo.

She put the finished dish in an airtight container so it wouldn't leak in her bag on the way to Luke's, put the rest of the ingredients and a bottle of wine in another bag, and took the Jubilee Line out to Bermondsey.

It was a ten-minute walk from the Tube station to Luke's house. With every step she took, Jess was more and more aware of the adrenaline racing through her bloodstream. By the time she reached his front door and rang the bell, her heart felt as if it were drumming so loudly the whole world must be able to hear it.

Luke opened the door, wearing faded jeans and a white shirt, looking utterly gorgeous. Jess was sure that her face had gone hot and red, betraying her feelings. Please don't let him have any idea about how star-struck she'd become, she begged silently.

Baloo was pattering round his feet and wagged her tail madly; Jess was glad of the excuse to bend down and make a fuss of her.

'Hello, there.' Luke smiled at her.

What she was going to say went straight out of her head. In the end, she gabbled, 'One green Thai chicken curry—I made it this morning so it'll have time for the flavours to mature in the fridge while we're out.' She handed him the bag with the tub of curry. 'I'll make the rice and steamed veg when we get back.' She handed him another bag.

'What's this?' he asked.

'Jasmine rice, coriander, cashews, a lime and some tenderstem broccoli—oh, and a bottle of wine.' Oh, for pity's sake, Jess—how to sound like a gibbering idiot. Stop *talking*, she commanded herself.

He peered into the bag. 'Chablis. How fabulous.'

'It's nice and crisp, so it will go well with a curry.' Matt had always been the wine buff; Jess had just picked up the knowledge from him over the years.

'Thank you. Come up for a minute while I put this in the fridge and sort out Baloo's stuff.'

She followed Luke into the kitchen and waited while he put everything away. Then he took Baloo's leash from a drawer and clipped it onto her collar. 'I've got her bowl, a bottle of water and a supply of plastic bags,' he said, taking a bag from the worktop, 'so I think we're ready. I'm looking forward to playing tour guide.' He smiled at her. 'We've got a nice day for it. I thought we could stop off somewhere and have an ice cream overlooking the river.'

'That sounds lovely.' And please, please, please let her common sense kick in soon. Please let her stop wanting him to hold her hand and kiss her. Please.

'No dark glasses or silly hats?' she asked.

He grinned and produced a fez. 'I was thinking of wearing this one.' His grin broadened. 'Especially for you.'

She couldn't help laughing, every bit of nervousness dispelled. 'No chance. Glasses I'll allow, as it's sunny. But no hat.'

'Spoilsport,' he grumbled, but his eyes were sparkling with amusement.

'Ready to go walkies?' he asked the dog, who woofed and wagged her tail.

When he'd locked the front door, they headed for the riverside path. They stopped by a low tumbledown brick wall at the edge of an uneven green space. 'This was the manor house of Edward III. Most of the ruins are buried under the green behind that wall,' Luke said.

'Just over there's the park named after the stairs that used to lead to the manor—the mudlarks used it, too.'

'Mudlarks?' Jess asked.

'Children who used to scavenge in the river mud for treasures,' he explained. 'This used to be quite a poor area.'

They followed the path along the riverbank. Jess noticed a couple of women nudging each other and looking at Luke. Then one of them came over. 'Excuse me—Mr McKenzie?' she asked.

He smiled at her. 'Luke.'

She went pink. 'Would you, um, mind having a picture taken with me, please?'

'Sure,' he said easily. 'What's your name?'

'Diana,' she said.

'It's lovely to meet you, Diana.'

She went even pinker. 'I loved you in *A Forever Kind of Love.*'

'Thank you,' he said. 'That's really kind of you.'

'Could, um, my friend be in the photo, too, please?' she asked.

He looked at Jess, who nodded and smiled. 'If you can show me how your camera works, I'll take the picture for you.'

When she'd taken the photo and Luke had signed autographs for both women and chatted to them for a little longer, he kissed Diana and her friend on the cheek. 'I think the dog's getting fidgety, if you'll excuse us,' he said with a smile. 'Enjoy the sunshine,' he said, and took Baloo's lead back from Jess.

'Does that happen a lot?' she asked, when the women were out of earshot. 'People coming up and asking for autographs and photos?'

'A bit. But it's fine.' Luke smiled. 'Without people

going to see my films, I wouldn't have a job. The least I can do is spend a bit of time with them in return.'

Jess liked the fact that he was modest and appreciated the support of his fans. 'What about the paparazzi?'

'Most of the time, no. Only if there's some kind of story about me. They tend to follow the people in the news. And I'm very, very boring.'

Jess laughed. 'Is that my cue to tell you that you're terribly interesting and I'm dying to hear more about the history of London?'

He lifted his dark glasses for a second and gave her a speaking look. 'I'm wounded. *Wounded*, I tell you,' he said, clutching one hand theatrically to his chest.

She smiled, knowing that he was teasing. 'Actually, it *is* interesting, walking round with someone who can tell you what you're looking at.'

'Seriously, Jess, if I'm being boring, tell me to shut up. My ego can stand it.'

'I will. For now, you may go back to playing tour guide, Mr McKenzie,' she said with a smile.

'Just remember that you asked for that,' he said, laughing. 'OK. This is the Angel pub—there's been a pub on that spot for more than five hundred years. It's said that the captain of the *Mayflower* hired his crew there, and Captain Cook planned his voyage to Australia there.'

A few minutes later, they came to the Mayflower pub. 'It's named after the ship, I imagine?' she asked.

'Yes. The pilgrims boarded it from the steps nearby—and it's the only place in England that's licensed to sell American postage stamps.'

'Seriously?'

He spread his hands. 'Seriously.'

'How do you know all this stuff?' she asked

He wrinkled his nose. 'Do you want the truth?'

She nodded.

'I've been on a few guided walks over the years. I've got quite a retentive memory, so I've mentally filed away all those little facts.'

'Of course—you're used to remembering things from learning lines.'

'I guess it's the same sort of thing. Learning a spiel, whether it's fact or fiction.'

Jess enjoyed strolling along the river as Luke pointed out various locations to her and told her the stories behind the sculptures.

'Joking apart, if you ever get bored with acting,' she said, 'I think you'd make quite a good tour guide. You really know your stuff.'

'Thank you.' He smiled. 'I'll bear that in mind.'

As they walked, her hand brushed against his a couple of times. It was totally accidental, but Jess felt as if little flames were licking underneath her skin every time they touched.

And then he twined his fingers through hers. For the life of her, she couldn't pull away.

Neither of them said a word, but Jess was intensely aware that she was strolling along the southern bank of the Thames in the brilliant sunshine, holding hands with someone who'd been voted the most beautiful man in the world. It just didn't seem possible; yet, at the same time, it felt incredibly real.

Luke only dropped her hand when they stopped at a park to give Baloo a drink. She took the opportunity to buy them both an ice cream, and they sat on the grass in the sunshine.

'It doesn't get any better than this. Early summer in

England, with flowers out everywhere and bees buzzing lazily,' he said.

Was that a quote? Jess wondered. Not wanting to seem gauche, she didn't ask.

When they'd finished their ice cream, Luke stretched. 'Time to go back, I think.'

This time, when he held her hand, it was very deliberate.

Oh, help.

This felt a lot like old-fashioned courting.

How on earth was she going to explain it to her sister and her best friend—that she was sort of courting the actor they'd both had a huge crush on for years? How, for that matter, was she going to explain it to herself?

This couldn't have a future. Their lives were too different.

But maybe, she thought, maybe this was right for *just now*. No expectations, no promises—just enjoying the kind of closeness that both of them had missed.

They strolled back to his flat and sat on the balcony with a cold drink, enjoying the sunshine.

'I really enjoyed that walk,' she said. 'Thank you.'

'My pleasure.' His smile made her toes curl. He really was one of the most beautiful men she'd ever met; and yet he didn't behave as if he knew it. He was genuinely nice.

Why on earth had Fleur dumped him for someone else?

Not that she was going to ask. It wouldn't be tactful and she didn't want to hurt him by dragging up bad memories.

Eventually, she said, 'I guess I really ought to finish preparing dinner.'

There was a soft woof of agreement from beside them.

Jess laughed, and made a fuss of the Labrador. 'Sorry, curry isn't for dogs—but I did bring you something nice.' She fished in her pocket for a dog biscuit.

Luke smiled. 'I guess you have the tools of your trade on you all the time.'

She shrugged. 'Mine just happen to be visible. I bet you have large tracts of Shakespeare in your head.'

He spread his hands. 'I've spent half my life acting so, yes, I probably do.'

'What's your favourite Shakespeare?' she asked.

'Obviously I've got a soft spot for *Much Ado*, because it got me my big break. But my absolute favourite is probably *Macbeth*. I loved playing Macbeth. The "tomorrow and tomorrow and tomorrow" speech—it's so desolate. It squeezes my heart every time. How much he lost.' He smiled at her. 'What about you? What's your favourite?'

'I like *Much Ado*,' she said. 'Though I think probably everyone does because it's got a happy ending. My sister's an English teacher—she always makes me go to see *Twelfth Night* with her if it's on around Christmas. I always think the other characters are a bit too mean to Malvolio.' She flapped a dismissive hand. 'But I love the start of the play. "If music be the food of love…"'

'"Play on,"' Luke continued. '"Give me excess of it, that surfeiting, The appetite may sicken and so die. That strain again, it had a dying fall; O it came o'er my ear like the sweet sound That breathes upon a bank of violets, Stealing and giving odour. Enough; no more."'

Jess had closed her eyes so she could concentrate on the speech, enjoying the way he quoted. When he stopped, she opened her eyes again and looked at him. 'That was beautiful. Your voice is amazing.'

'Thank you.'

'Did you ever play Orsino?'

'Once. Though—' He wrinkled his nose. 'Well, it's the way he's in love with being in love. I don't have a lot of patience for him. I would much rather have played Feste, the jester. He's the most interesting clown in Shakespeare.'

There was something surreal about this conversation, Jess thought. 'I can't believe I'm talking Shakespeare with a world-famous actor,' she said. 'Especially as I don't really know what I'm talking about, and you do.'

'Actually, your views are just as valid as mine. Shakespeare wrote for his audience,' Luke said.

'But you've studied the plays. The characters. You know what they're all about.' And she'd bet her sister would love discussing Shakespeare with Luke. He'd probably enjoy talking about Shakespeare with Carly, too. They could argue about characters.

'It's my job,' he said. 'I wouldn't have a clue where to start with yours. I wouldn't even have been able to get Baloo to sit still, let alone dance.'

'You danced with her the other night,' she reminded him. 'Anyway. Dinner?'

'Let's go and sort it out. I'll be your sous chef.'

Again, Jess thought how surreal this was. How down-to-earth Luke was. He'd won several Oscars over the years and been nominated for still more—and yet here he was, offering to help her finish making the curry she'd cooked earlier.

He chopped the coriander and the cashews for her while she started preparing the rice and the broccoli. It was strange to work with someone in a kitchen again. It made her think of Matt, and all the times they'd cooked dinner together.

Luke said softly, 'Is this bringing back memories for you?'

'Yes,' she admitted. 'I'd forgotten how much I liked cooking with someone else.' She paused. 'And you?'

He shook his head. 'Fleur wasn't one for the kitchen. She'd rather eat out or get me to cook for us.' He smiled at her. 'And I can cook more than just stir fries. *Really* I can.'

'Yeah, yeah,' she teased back, glad that he'd lightened the atmosphere.

Once she'd finished serving up, he poured them both a glass of wine and ushered her up to the balcony.

'So what's in this?' he asked.

'You're a foodie, right?' she asked. At his nod, she said, 'You tell me.'

He tasted it. 'OK. Obviously coconut milk, green chillies, garlic, lime leaves, lime juice and coriander.' He thought about it a bit more. 'Fish sauce.'

'And?'

He shook his head. 'No. You've beaten me.'

'Lemongrass and galangal.'

He raised his eyebrows. 'This is where you tell me that you cheated and you used a paste from a jar.'

She laughed. 'No. I like cooking from scratch. I like the scent of fresh herbs and spices.'

'I should've taken you the other way on the river path, where all the spice warehouses were,' he said. 'They've all been made into luxury flats and swish eateries now, but the buildings still have the lovely old brickwork and the signs saying what each block was used for. So the story goes, when the buildings were first turned into flats, the first residents could still smell the spices that had been stored there over the past century.'

'That's a nice story, though I guess you'd have to like the scent of the particular spice from your building,' she said with a smile.

When they'd finished the meal and she'd oohed and aahed over the fabulous pavlova Luke had bought, Luke allowed her to help him take the crockery and cutlery downstairs, but flatly refused to let her wash up.

He made them both a mug of strong Italian roast coffee, and they drank it on the balcony, watching the boats go past on the river and seeing the lights go on in the buildings. At one point she stood up to lean on the balcony and get a better view of Tower Bridge; he joined her, his hand resting lightly on her shoulder. She wasn't sure which of them moved first, but then he was kissing her again, just as he'd kissed her last night.

This was when she should be sensible and stop this, she knew. When she should tell him they needed to go back to being just friends and colleagues. But the way he made her feel...

She'd forgotten just how much she liked kissing. Those little tiny nibbling kisses that sent flickers of desire up her spine. Teasing, promising, enticing. How could she resist?

She opened her mouth and let him deepen the kiss, and the flickers turned into flames.

When he broke the kiss, his pupils were huge, his mouth was slightly swollen and reddened, and there was a slash of colour across his cheekbones. She'd guess she was in the same state.

'Well,' he said softly. 'That wasn't supposed to happen.'

'We should be sensible,' she said.

He cupped her cheek, his fingers warm and gentle

against her skin. 'Something about you makes me forget to be sensible, Jess.'

'Me, too,' she whispered, and leaned forward to kiss him.

This time, when she broke the kiss, he asked softly, 'Stay with me tonight?'

Stay with him.

She knew what he meant.

Spend the night with him. Make love. Share a part of herself that had been closed off for so long.

It was tempting. So very tempting.

But this was all happening so fast. They barely knew each other. They came from different worlds. He wasn't just a normal person she'd met at work—he was a film star. Talented, gorgeous, and seriously famous.

'I...'

He brushed his mouth against hers in the sweetest, gentlest kiss. 'I know. Too fast, too soon. And anyway...' His voice tailed off.

'What?' She hadn't seen him look nervous before.

He bit his lip. 'Jess, I like you, and I think you like me.'

She nodded, not quite trusting herself to speak. The 'but' was coming, she was sure of it.

'We haven't known each other that long.'

True.

'And it's way too early for us to have this conversation.'

'What conversation?' she asked carefully.

He sighed. 'It wouldn't be fair of me to let this thing between us carry on without you knowing all the facts. You need to go into this with your eyes wide open.' He paused. 'Set rules?' His expression was intense.

'Set rules,' she confirmed.

* * *

Saying it out loud felt like stepping off a ledge and not knowing how far he was going to fall. But Luke knew he owed it to Jess to be honest about this. 'I don't even know where to start,' he said. 'Whether to ask you or to tell you.'

She looked puzzled. 'Ask me or tell me what?'

'It's not tactful.' Especially after what she'd told him yesterday. 'But I owe you the truth.'

She reached over and took his hand. 'Telling someone something you've kept inside for a long time—it's hard. Like me telling you about…' Her voice wobbled slightly. 'About the baby. But, like you said to me, it's better out than in.'

He wasn't so sure. This could blow everything apart.

She said nothing more, just squeezed his hand and waited.

He dragged in a breath. 'I'm going to tell you something now that nobody else knows, not even Monica. Well, one other person knows, but…' Fleur didn't count, not any more. 'I can't have children.'

'And?'

He couldn't tell a thing from her expression. Whether it was a deal-breaker or not. But he'd started so he might as well finish. 'That's why Fleur and I broke up. I had mumps when I was a kid. It affected my fertility. So I couldn't give her a baby—at least, not without dragging her through IVF, and she was the one who'd have the burden of it, the one who'd have all the invasive medical stuff and have to take the drugs and what have you. And there are no guarantees it would work.' He swallowed hard. 'She wanted a baby, and that's why she went elsewhere. She had an affair with someone who could give her a child. She got pregnant, and that's when I found out about the affair, because the baby obviously wasn't mine. I could've forgiven her, raised the child as mine—but then she told me that she'd only been with me in the first place because she thought it would further her career. She'd never really loved me.'

Jess moved closer. Giving him strength, the way he'd done for her. 'I don't know your ex,' she said, 'but I can't believe anyone could be so selfish and cruel. What she did was—well, words fail me. That's so horrible.' She looked angry, Luke thought—just like she had when she'd taken him to task over the dog, the day he'd first met her. 'Right now I want to shake the woman until her teeth rattle. It's not your fault that you had mumps as a child. How could she hurt you like that?'

'She wanted a baby. Desperately,' he said. 'And I couldn't do that for her.'

'IVF isn't the only way to have a child. There's adoption, fostering. She didn't give you a chance, Luke. And to have an affair, to cheat on you and only think about what she wanted...' She shook her head. 'I don't get it. If you love someone, you make the effort and you talk to each other and you work out a compromise.'

That was what he'd thought, too. 'It's not tactful of me to ask this. Not when yesterday...' He bit his lip. 'Jess, I'd like to get to know you better. A lot better. But I know you were planning to have children. You need to know that I can't do that for you, if we're going to be together. It was a deal-breaker for Fleur.'

'I'm not Fleur,' she pointed out.

He didn't quite dare hope. Because there was another barrier, too. 'And I'm not sure I can live up to Matt. He sounds like an incredible guy.'

'He was, but that isn't quite the way things work,' Jess said. 'You're different people. You have different qualities. It's not fair to compare you and I'm not going to do that.'

'So where,' Luke asked, 'does this leave us?'

'I don't know. I'm just an ordinary woman,' she said.

There was nothing ordinary about Jess Greenacre, Luke thought.

'And you're a film star. People come up to you in the street and ask you for autographs.'

'Is that a problem?'

'Of course not.' She shook her head. 'It's part of your job—part of who you are. But I'm not Hollywood material. I'm not sure I'd fit in to that world.'

'Everyone likes you on set, so that's a pretty good indicator,' he pointed out.

'Mimi doesn't like me.'

He smiled, then. 'That's because you're female. Don't take it personally. She's definitely not the litmus test.' He took her hand. 'I like you. I think you like me. I'd like to see where this goes. So if you can handle the fact that my life can be a bit chaotic, the press can be intrusive, and I can't give you a child—well, not without a lot of medical intervention, and there aren't any guarantees it would happen for us anyway—then maybe we can make this work.'

'There are no guarantees about anything,' Jess said. 'I've learned that over the last year or so.' She took a deep breath. 'So. Me, you and Baloo.'

The dog wagged her tail hopefully.

'Me, you—and Baloo,' Luke echoed. 'Don't decide now. Think about it. I'll take you home, and we'll talk about it again tomorrow.'

'OK. We'll talk tomorrow,' Jess said.

Luke drove her home and was utterly restrained, merely kissing her goodbye on the cheek and waiting in the car until she was safely indoors. She needed to make this decision with a clear head, not when he'd swept her off her feet. He wanted her to make the right choice for *her*.

He just hoped she'd make the same decision he wanted, too.

CHAPTER TEN

JESS THOUGHT ABOUT it. And thought about it some more.

Luke had been honest with her. Totally open.

If she chose to see where this took them, her whole life would change. She'd be dating someone in the public eye. Everything they did would be reported. Sometimes it would be twisted, simply to sell a news story, totally disregarding their feelings. Luke had admitted that sometimes he just had to suck it up and ignore it.

Having a child together could involve yet more intrusiveness, either through medical procedures or through being vetted by an adoption agency: things that would put a strain on any relationship.

And Jess had to be honest: she did want a family, at some point in the future.

But then there was Luke himself. Luke, who'd made her smile again. Luke, who'd given her strength. Luke, who'd listened and who was taking her feelings into account, not expecting her just to drop everything to suit him. Luke, who made her heart beat faster every time she saw him, and not just because he was a handsome movie star with the charm and charisma that went with the job description. It was the man, not the image, that drew her.

Should she say yes? Take the risk?

Or should she play it super-safe and say no?

In the end, she slept on it.

And she woke smiling, thinking of Luke.

That decided her. She grabbed her mobile phone and texted him. *Made my decision.*

Five minutes later, her phone rang.

'Hi,' Luke said. 'I got your text. How did you sleep?'

'Surprisingly well,' she said. 'You?'

'Not answering that one,' he said. 'So you've thought about it?'

'Yes.'

'And?'

'Are you still sure you want to do this?' She needed to know it was still the same for him.

'I'm sure. And you?'

'There are no guarantees. But I do know that I don't want to be sitting here in thirty years' time, wondering what might have been if I'd been brave enough to say yes.'

'Is that an incredibly roundabout way of saying yes, Ms Greenacre?' Luke asked.

'Let me see. That would be…' She paused just long enough to hear him groan. 'Yes.'

'Can Baloo and I come and see you?'

'Yes.'

'Good. Get ready. We'll go out somewhere for lunch.'

On a proper date.

Their first real date as a couple.

'See you soon,' she said.

Showering and washing her hair didn't take long. Deciding what to wear took a lot longer. And then she shook herself. Luke wasn't dating her because of her dress sense. He could've dated a dozen A-list actresses with much better wardrobes than hers. He was dating her because he liked her for herself.

She opted for smart trousers and a pretty summery top. And she was just about ready when the doorbell rang.

Luke stood on her doorstep with an armful of flowers—beautiful summer flowers, bright pink germini, violet-coloured agapanthus, white roses and tiny chrysanthemums.

She looked at them and smiled. 'They're beautiful. Thank you. I'll put them in water.'

He smiled back. 'I thought the chrysanthemums might be appropriate from me. They're called charms.'

'Charming flowers from a charming man.' She liked the wordplay. 'That's great. Can I get you some coffee?'

'No. I thought we could go out for a walk. It's your turn to play tour guide.'

'Bad luck. I don't know this part of London that well,' she said.

He took his phone out of his pocket. 'All righty. We do it the cheat's way. Internet.'

'You really do have an answer for everything, don't you?' she asked.

He spread his hands. 'I try.'

Thanks to the Internet, they found directions to a nearby park, and Jess thoroughly enjoyed sitting in the sun, making a fuss of Baloo. And they managed to find a pub with a dog-friendly garden, so they could eat lunch with the dog sitting patiently under the table.

But when they returned to her flat, Jess hadn't even opened the door when someone walked up the path behind them and coughed. 'Mrs Greenacre. May I remind you that your lease doesn't allow for dogs?'

Oh, no. So her neighbour had talked to their landlord. 'I'm sorry, Mr Bright,' she said.

'Actually, it's my fault,' Luke said. 'I'm looking after Baloo and I can't leave her on her own. I do hope it's not a problem that she's here temporarily.'

Jess's landlord frowned. 'Don't I know you from somewhere?'

'Luke, this is Mr Bright, my landlord. Mr Bright, this is my friend Luke McKenzie,' Jess introduced them dutifully.

'I *knew* I knew you from somewhere! You're my wife's favourite actor. She loves your films. Could I have your autograph for her?'

'With pleasure,' Luke said. 'I can send a signed photo via Jess tomorrow, if you like.'

'That'd really make her day.'

The landlord had moved from slightly aggressive to cheerfully pally, Jess thought with relief. Being a movie star definitely had its plus points.

'What's her name?' Luke asked.

'Mary.'

'Spelled the usual way?' Luke checked. At the landlord's nod, he smiled and made a note in his phone. 'I'll send the photo through Jess.'

'Thank you. Mrs Greenacre, if you could kindly remember the rule, no permanent dogs. But I suppose this one can visit, as long as it's only for a little while,' Mr Bright said. 'No chewing or messing, mind you.'

'I guarantee it,' Luke said.

'That's all right, then. Good day to you.'

Inside Jess's flat, they looked at each other and then burst out laughing.

'I'm sorry,' she said. 'That has to be…'

He flapped a dismissive hand. 'It's fine. I'm the one breaching the rules of your lease.'

'Ah, but we have a temporary permit for Baloo.' Jess made a fuss of the dog. 'So we're fine. Let's get you a drink, girl, and I'll put the kettle on. Go and make yourself at home, Luke.'

He noticed that she'd put the photograph frames up on the mantelpiece. So she'd listened to what he'd said. And when she came in bearing two mugs of coffee, the dog trotting at her heels, he didn't say a word. He just hugged her. Just because.

Over the next week, Jess's world got better and better. She enjoyed her job, even though she was rushed off her feet; she loved having the dog with her all day; and she spent most of her evenings with Luke. Apart from Thursday, when Luke's aunt was finally due home from America and he wanted to meet her from the airport, so Jess arranged to meet her best friend for a drink after work.

Shannon walked into the bar where they'd agreed to meet, did a double take and then said, 'You're glowing. Have you met someone?'

Hmm. How could she tell her best friend that she was seeing Luke McKenzie? 'Sort of.'

'Good.' Shannon smiled. 'It'll do you good, and I knew Matt well so I can say with perfect honesty that he wouldn't have wanted you to shut yourself up in a mausoleum after he died. He would've wanted you to find someone who loves you as much as he did and really live your life to the full.'

'Uh-huh.'

'What's his name? Where did you meet him? When do I get to meet him?'

'That's a lot of questions,' Jess said.

'Which you're obviously not going to answer.' Shannon rolled her eyes. 'I should've trained as a dentist instead of becoming a teacher.'

'Why?'

'Because getting information out of you is like pulling teeth.'

Jess laughed. 'It's not that bad. Look, Shan, it's early days. I don't want to jinx things or rush things.'

'OK. I won't push you any more. But, just so you know, everyone will be pleased for you and nobody's going to say it's too soon or anything stupid like that.' Shannon hugged her. 'We all worry about you being alone.'

Jess raised an eyebrow. 'There's nothing wrong with being single.'

'I know that, honey. That's not what I meant—I don't think you have to be part of a couple to be a valid person. I just worry that you've shut yourself off from life since Matt and Comet were killed. It's good that you've met someone who makes you smile again.'

'Yes, he does.'

'So when do we get to meet him?'

Oh, boy. That would be a meeting and a half. 'Soon,' Jess prevaricated. 'As I said, it's very early days.'

'OK. I won't nag. Even though I'm completely eaten up with curiosity and I have a million and one questions I'm dying to ask. You look happy, and that's enough for me.'

Jess just hugged her. 'Thank you.'

On Friday morning, Luke said, 'So how was last night?'

'Good,' she said. 'How was your aunt?'

'Settling in again.' He smiled. 'Have dinner with me tonight?'

She nodded. 'Thanks. I'd like that.'

'Except,' he said, 'it's a takeaway, and it's not at mine—it's at Monica's.'

He was taking her to meet his aunt? The one he was close to—the one who'd rescued Baloo. Panic flooded through her. OK, so they were officially an item now; but they were keeping it low-profile and they were careful to be professional whenever they met on set.

Meeting the family was tantamount to a declaration of intent.

As if Luke guessed the direction of her thoughts, he said, 'Relax. She just wants to meet you because you've been looking after Baloo. She wants to say thank you herself. It isn't a big deal.'

Jess wasn't so sure. She bought a bouquet of cheerful sunflowers, then had second thoughts when Luke came into the production office at the end of filming. 'Luke, is it OK to take flowers to your aunt?'

'Yes.' He looked at them and smiled. 'She'll love them.'

This time, rather than driving them towards the Thames, he drove them to Notting Hill. Another wealthy part of London, Jess thought. Again she was aware that Luke wasn't just wealthy in his own right, he came from quite a privileged background—one so different from her own, vastly normal background.

The first thing that struck Jess when Luke let them into the house and introduced her to Monica was how like Luke she looked. 'I, um—it's very nice to meet you,' she said, feeling ridiculously shy, and cross with herself for feeling that way.

'And you. Thank you for the flowers. They're beautiful. Luke, can you put them in water for me?' Monica asked.

'And arrange the takeaway. Sure. Chinese OK with you, Jess?' he asked.

'It'll be lovely, thanks.'

She made polite small talk with Monica while Luke was in the kitchen. When he came back, he said, 'Jess, are you going to show Mon what you've taught Baloo?'

'I—well, if you think I should.'

'Definitely.'

Feeling even more nervous, Jess switched on the music and took Baloo through their routine.

'That's incredible,' Monica said, making a fuss of the dog. 'So clever.'

'I can't take all the credit,' Jess said. 'It was a little girl in the park who gave me the idea. I was giving Baloo some basic training, and the little girl said she'd seen a dancing dog on the television and asked me if I was going to teach Baloo to dance. I gave it a go and it turns out she's a natural.'

'She's a very clever girl indeed.' Monica gave Luke a speaking look. 'She'd fit well into a showbiz life.'

'We've had this conversation,' Luke reminded her. 'And don't you gang up with her, Jess.'

'As if I would,' Jess said, and gave him a wicked grin.

The ice was thoroughly broken, and Jess told Monica about some of the training work and exhibitions she'd done.

'I wanted to say thank you,' Monica said, when Luke took Baloo out into the garden. 'For making Luke smile again.'

'Me? I haven't done anything,' Jess said.

'Hmm.' Monica looked unconvinced. 'OK, so you're keeping it between yourselves for now. Fair enough.'

Jess felt the colour flood into her face. Oh, help.

Monica patted her hand. 'I won't tell him I know. Even though he must know I would've guessed.'

'I know you're close to him,' Jess said. 'He talks about you a lot.' And he said hardly anything about his parents.

'He's the best nephew I could've had,' Monica said.

'The only nephew, according to him.'

'He's the nearest I have to a child of my own, and I love him dearly.' Monica sighed. 'Much as I love my sister Erica, she wouldn't win any prizes for maternal feeling.'

Jess, knowing that this was immensely private, said softly, 'Set rules.'

'Set rules? Oh—what you hear and what you see stays with you.' Monica nodded. 'Thank you. Let's just say that Luke grew up in a house with white carpets.'

'High maintenance,' Jess said, wondering how his mother would have reacted to the inevitable spills.

'You can say that again. He grew up disappointing her. And his father.' Monica rolled her eyes. 'Even now they'd like him to give up his acting and go back to being a lawyer, so he'd fit in to their expectations of him.'

'He would've made a good barrister. He's meticulous and he's got stage presence,' Jess pointed out.

'True,' Monica said.

'But you're right—it wouldn't have made him happy.' Jess sighed. 'I come from a materially much poorer background, but I think I was the lucky one. My parents said that as long as my sister and I were happy in what we did, then they were happy—that was all they wanted.'

'Very sensible,' Monica said. 'I agree with them.' She

grimaced. 'I wasn't able to have children myself, so I was always happy to borrow Luke and do messy stuff with him at my place—painting, glitter and glue, play dough and making cupcakes with icing and sprinkles.'

'And I bet you supported him when he said he wanted to act,' Jess said.

'It was the first time I'd seen him really come alive,' Monica said. 'Of course I was going to support him. He'd found the thing of his heart. So I ran interference with his parents as much as I could.' She smiled. 'I still do. His mother's always giving dinner parties where he can meet someone suitable.'

Luke's parents are definitely *not* going to approve of me, Jess thought.

Either she'd said it aloud or Luke's aunt was immensely perceptive, because Monica said softly, 'It doesn't matter what they think about you, it matters what Luke thinks about you—and right now he's happier than I've seen him in a very, very long time.'

It was the same for Jess. But right now she didn't want to talk about that. 'I was going to ask you about Baloo. Were all the kennels really full?'

'No,' Monica admitted, 'and I was taking a huge risk.'

'Giving a rescue dog with special needs to a total novice—that could really have blown up in your face, Monica. Big time.'

Monica laughed. 'I like you, Jess. You tell it like it is and yes, you're right. It could have blown up in my face. Especially as I wasn't here to rescue them if it went wrong.' She glanced ruefully at her cast. 'And especially as this happened. I hate being stuck in a cast and having to rely on other people to do even basic stuff for me.'

'That's what Luke said—he'd give you a day of being in hospital before you were climbing the walls.'

'He got that right,' Monica said wryly.

'Got what right?' Luke asked, coming in to hear the tail end of the conversation.

'Being stuck in hospital drove me crazy. At least I can do things, now I'm home.'

'Just promise me you'll be sensible and ask me for help when you need it,' Luke said. 'And I mean that, Mon.'

She rolled her eyes. 'Don't fuss. I'm fine.'

'I mean it,' Luke said. 'Otherwise I'll let my dog loose on your shoe cupboard.'

Monica exchanged a glance with Jess and smiled. And Jess knew exactly why the older woman was smiling: Luke was definitely near to accepting Baloo as his permanent dog.

Jess felt as if their relationship had turned a corner; over the next week, she and Luke grew closer, and she was really starting to think that, despite the huge differences between their lives, this might just work for both of them.

On Saturday night, she was sitting on the balcony with him, wrapped in his arms, when he nuzzled her ear. 'Stay with me tonight, Jess.'

Stay with him.

Her pulse skipped a beat, and then another.

Stay with him. Fall asleep in his arms, and wake up with him.

Part of her wanted to. Yet part of her was scared. It had been a long time. Supposing she disappointed him? 'I—I don't have anything with me,' she prevaricated.

He shrugged. 'Well, I have a spare toothbrush and a

washing machine. And, although I probably can't produce anything like moisturiser, you're very welcome to use whatever you need in the bathroom.'

'You make it sound so easy,' she whispered.

'It *is* easy.' He kissed her. 'Stay, Jess. No pressure. We don't have to do anything you don't want to do. You can use the spare room if you'd rather.'

Time to meet him halfway, Jess thought. 'I want to stay.'

'But?'

'It's been a while,' she said. 'What if I disappoint you?'

'You won't disappoint me. Ever,' he said.

And it really was that easy.

Baloo, for once, stayed on her own bed when she was told, and didn't do her usual trick of opening the door and escaping upstairs.

And Jess discovered that Luke's bedroom had the best view in the house. When she told him, he laughed and pulled the blind. 'I have a better one right now.'

He undressed her slowly, gently, stroking every inch of skin as he uncovered it. Jess in turn enjoyed taking his clothes off, discovering how soft his skin was, finding out where he liked being touched and how she could make him gasp with pleasure.

'Just so you know, I wasn't taking this for granted,' Luke said as he removed a condom from his wallet. 'And the Press seriously over-report how many women I sleep with.'

She liked the fact that he'd guessed at some of her reservations—and he'd guessed correctly. But she also wanted to keep this light. So neither of them would feel pressured. 'Are you trying to tell me you have a stunt double for Most Beautiful Man in the World, Mr Mc-Kenzie?' she teased.

He groaned. 'That accolade's very flattering, but I'm not sure I live up to their expectations. They haven't seen me first thing in the morning, with bed hair and stubble and being grumpy before my first cup of coffee.' He stole a kiss. 'You've been warned, by the way.'

'Noted,' she said, and let him carry her to his bed.

The next morning, Jess woke feeling sated and happier than she'd felt in a long, long time.

'Morning.' Luke drew her closer and kissed her. 'OK?'

'Very OK.' She snuggled against him. 'I thought you said you looked a mess and were grumpy, first thing?'

'Bed hair, stubble, shadows under my eyes because I didn't get a lot of sleep last night…'

She laughed. 'You know, if the award-givers could see you right now…' She stole a kiss. 'They'd cancel all future awards on the grounds that nobody could look as good as this ever again.'

'I wasn't fishing.'

'And I wasn't flattering,' she said softly. 'You're beautiful, Luke.'

'And so,' he said, 'are you.'

She scoffed. 'Come off it. I'm ordinary. You work with some of the most gorgeous women in the world.'

'Most of which is achieved with make-up and good lighting. It isn't real. You are. And it's not just about looks. It's about how you make me feel.' He kissed her. 'Waking up with you, I don't feel grumpy and in need of coffee. I'm with you, so I know it's going to be a glorious day.'

It was one of the nicest compliments Jess had ever been paid, and she felt her face go pink with pleasure. 'Thank you.' And it was the same for her. Being with him had taught her how to be happy again.

He kissed her again. 'Much as I want to do all sorts of wicked things with you right now, I have a dog who needs to go out and who's probably trashed my kitchen cupboards because I turned the door handle upside down so she had to stay put last night.' He rolled his eyes. 'Stay there. I'll make us a coffee while I clear up.'

'Are you sure you don't want a hand?'

'I'm sure.'

Jess lay back against the deep pillows and drowned until Luke appeared in the doorway with two mugs of coffee. A second later there was a flying leap and a thud as Baloo landed on the bed.

'So how was your kitchen?' she asked Luke as she made a fuss of the dog.

'Perfect,' he said. 'I was expecting rice and pasta everywhere. She hadn't opened a single door or chewed a single packet.'

Because, Jess thought, the dog was finally feeling secure. She knew she was *home*.

'Good girl,' Jess said, and made a fuss of the dog.

'You don't mind?' Luke asked, gesturing to Baloo.

She smiled. 'This was how Sunday mornings were at home if we weren't on duty. Coffee, the papers, and lazing the morning away in bed with Comet snoring his head off at the bottom of the bed.'

His eyes widened for a moment. 'I didn't think. Sorry. I'll—'

'No, it's fine,' Jess said. 'They're happy memories. Like you said, it's part of who I am.' She kissed him lightly. 'And, like you said, it's going to be a glorious day.'

* * *

Over the next couple of weeks, Jess ended up staying most of the time at Luke's house, only dropping back to hers occasionally to pick up fresh clothes. The one day she did stay at home was when she'd been in court to testify at the hearing of the man who'd mugged her, and Luke had planned to pick up Baloo from Monica before meeting Jess at her flat.

When the doorbell went, Jess rushed to answer it—and was surprised to see her sister standing there. 'Oh—Carly!'

'Is now not a good time?' Carly asked.

'No, it's fine. I just wasn't expecting you, that's all.'

Carly raised her eyebrows. 'Well, you've been so unavailable lately, I just wanted to call round and check you were actually OK.'

'I'm fine.' Jess hugged her sister. 'Come in. I'll put the kettle on.'

Hopefully Luke would end up chatting to Monica and running late, and Carly would be gone by the time he arrived. Much as Jess loved her sister, she wasn't quite ready to admit that she was seeing Luke. This was all still too new.

But Carly was in the mood to talk, and when the doorbell went again Jess knew that it was Luke.

'It's probably a neighbour with a parcel delivery or something,' she fibbed, and went to answer the door.

'My sister's here,' she told Luke.

He raised an eyebrow. 'Is that a problem? Will she think it's too soon for you to be seeing someone?'

'I—um...'

'Jessie, is everything all right?' Carly came out into the hallway and gasped as she saw who was standing at the front door. 'Oh, my God! Luke McKenzie.'

'You must be Carly. Lovely to meet you.' He held out his hand to shake hers.

'I—you—oh, my God,' Carly said again.

'I should be recording this,' Jess said. 'The first time our Carly's ever been lost for words.'

Carly cuffed her. 'Luke McKenzie,' she said again.

'And Baloo.' He introduced the dog to her. 'Though I imagine you know all about her, as Jess has been looking after her for me.'

'She has?' Carly stared at the dog and then at Jess, who was making a fuss of the dog. 'You said you were working on a film set.'

'I am. I'm in the production team,' Jess said. 'One of my duties is looking after the leading actor's dog and stopping her munching on expensive designer shoes. Luke, come in. I'll get you a coffee.'

'Thank you,' He kissed her lingeringly.

Jess felt her face flame. If Carly had been under any illusions that her relationship with Luke was strictly professional, they were well and truly blown, now. Because that most definitely hadn't been a business kiss or an actor's air kiss.

Carly appeared to have recovered herself. 'Come and sit down, Luke. As Jess said, she'll make coffee.'

'Carly,' Jess began, but her sister shooed her away, clearly in bossy teacher mode.

'Sorry,' she mouthed at Luke, and went to make coffee at double speed.

'So you're seeing my little sister,' Carly said.

'Yes. Is that a problem?' Luke asked.

'I hope not.' Carly folded her arms. 'I don't mean to be rude, but I'm her big sister and it's my job to look out for her.'

As an only child, Luke didn't have a clue about sibling relationships. But he liked the fact that Carly obviously loved her sister very much and worried about her.

'Has she told you about last year?' Carly asked.

Straight to the point. Luke liked that, too. 'About Matt and Comet?' He nodded. 'She trusted me with that much. And...' He gestured to the mantelpiece.

'She's finally put the photos back.' Carly's eyes filmed with tears. 'Was that anything to do with you?'

Jess clearly hadn't mentioned the mugging or the trial today, and it wasn't his place to tell Carly about it. 'A bit,' he said. 'And I want you to know that I have no intention of hurting your sister.'

'Good. Jess has been in a bad place and I don't want her going back there. Ever again.'

'She won't be there on my account,' he assured her.

'Thank you—and she seems to be bonding with your dog.'

'Temporary dog,' he corrected. 'Once my aunt's back on her feet, she's going to find Baloo a proper home.'

Carly looked at him. 'Hmm. I know a good home— and I also know that Jess's lease is up in a couple of months. There's no reason why she can't find another place that *will* allow her to have a dog.'

He smiled. 'She said you'd nagged her about her job.'

'She hated it, Luke—she was so miserable, and even now she refuses to go to our parents' house because she can't face seeing the dog. She makes them come here or sees them at mine. Maybe now that will change.' She bit her lip. 'I know Mum and Dad understand—we've all been worried about her. We all think this new job has been good for her, but she kept it quiet that she was looking after your dog.'

'Maybe she needs time to work things out for herself,' Luke suggested. 'And you do know she'd be cross with both of us for talking about her.'

'Yes, I am,' Jess said, walking into the room in time to overhear the last bit. 'Don't talk about me. I'm a grown-up and I can make my own decisions.'

Carly spread her hands, 'Jessie, I love you, and you know we've all worried ourselves sick about you since Matt died.'

'I'm fine,' Jess said. 'Really.'

'I think,' Carly said, 'I believe you. For the first time in months.'

'Good. Shut up and drink your coffee.' She scowled at Carly. 'You were supposed to be so dazzled at meeting your idol that you'd stay lost for words.'

Luke laughed. 'No way is your sister ever going to be lost for words, Jess.'

'Charming.' Carly rolled her eyes, but she was laughing. 'I still can't quite take in that my sister's dating a movie star—oh, and thank you for the signed photos, Luke. Shannon and I both appreciated it.'

'My pleasure.' He smiled at her. 'I know you're an English teacher. Jess tells me you take her to see *Twelfth Night* every year.'

Carly nodded. 'I can imagine you as Orsino.'

He smiled. 'Yes, I've done that. But I want to play Feste.'

'Can you sing?'

He launched into Feste's song from the end of the play.

'That,' Carly said when he'd finished, 'was lovely. Did you ever think about auditioning for *Les Mis*?'

'My singing voice isn't good enough, not for a full-blown musical,' Luke said. 'Though I have to admit I'd love to do *The Sound of Music*.'

'Captain von Trapp.' Carly grinned. 'Yes. I can see that. You've got that lovely rich voice, like Christopher Plummer. You know, you might be the only person who could do a better Captain von Trapp than him.'

Jess groaned. 'Luke, just make her the head of your fan club now, will you?'

He laughed. 'I don't have a fan club. But thank you both for the compliment.'

The conversation turned to favourite films and plays. Carly and Luke were both animated, and Jess thought how well Luke fitted in to this side of her life. Maybe, just maybe, this was going to work out.

'I ought to go,' Carly said finally. 'Jessie, see me out?'

Jess knew what her sister meant. Time to be grilled.

She went to the front door with Carly.

'Shannon said you were seeing someone, but she didn't push you for details because she didn't want you to go back into your shell. I can't believe it's Luke McKenzie.' Carly smiled. 'You're right—he lives up to all my expectations and Shannon's. He's fabulous.'

'Are you going to tell her?'

'That's your place, love, not mine.'

Luke walked into the hallway and overheard the last bit. 'Let's make it easier. Why don't both of you come for dinner at my place on Saturday? Bring your husband—and Shannon can bring hers, too.'

'Oh, my God. Luke, I'm so sorry. I wasn't angling for an invite,' Carly said, looking aghast.

'I know, but Jess is close to you, and of course you want to know more about the person she's seeing.' Luke looked at her. 'Invite your parents, too, Jess. We'll eat in the garden if it's good weather.'

This was it: they'd be outing their relationship as a real one. It was a huge step. For both of them.

'Are you sure about this?' she asked.

'I'm sure.' He paused. 'Are you?'

She nodded. 'I think so.'

When Carly had gone, Jess said again, 'Are you really sure about this?'

'Yes.'

'You've invited my parents—what about yours?'

He shook his head. 'I'm not ready for you to meet them—and that's not because I'm ashamed of you or anything remotely like it, but because my parents are a bit difficult and I think we need some time to get used to this thing between us before you meet them.'

She thought about what Monica said about his mother always being disappointed in him and it didn't matter what his parents thought about her, it mattered what Luke thought. Not that she was going to tell him, because she didn't want him to feel she'd been gossiping about him. Even though he'd been gossiping about her with her sister.

'But I will invite Monica,' Luke said. 'The bathroom and garden are both on the ground floor, so she won't have to negotiate stairs.'

'What if it rains?' Jess asked.

He smiled. 'We'll all just have to pile into my office. Or I can really annoy Mon by playing the superhero and carrying her upstairs.'

Everyone was free on Saturday. And Luke made everyone feel totally at home rather than that they were trespassing in a movie star's pad.

He talked Jess into doing the performance she'd choreographed with Baloo, and everyone sang along with the song—and then made a huge fuss of the dog, who was in a state of utter bliss from all the attention.

Monica and Jess exchanged a glance. They both knew that Baloo had definitely found her permanent home. Luke just needed to realise that, too.

At the end of the evening, Jess's parents dropped her home. 'He's lovely,' Jess's mother said.

'And he's good for you, which is the most important thing for us. We like him,' Jess's father added.

'Yes. Luke's special,' Jess said, smiling.

They'd cleared the first hurdle with ease.

So maybe, just maybe, this was going to work out just fine.

'She's lovely,' Monica said to Luke when everyone had gone. 'And she's good for you. She loves dogs. She's perfect.'

He grimaced. 'Mon, it's still early days.'

'I know, love,' she reassured him. 'The fact you've introduced her to me, and you asked me here when you met her family and best friend, tells me a lot. I like her.' She gave him a hug. 'I think she makes you happy, and you make her happy. And that's all that matters.'

CHAPTER ELEVEN

THE DOORBELL RANG insistently.

Luke, presuming that it was a delivery of some sort, opened the front door. To his shock, flashlights started going off in his face and microphones were shoved at him. There were people six deep on the doorstep, all talking at once, and the noise was incredible.

'So is it true?' one of them called.

Uh-oh. If he was being papped, that could only mean one thing. Another story. A juicy one, this time. Had Fleur found out somehow that he was seeing someone, and implied to her tame journo that it was a relationship that predated the end of their marriage, to let her off the hook of her own perfidy? Oh, hell. If that was the case, he'd need to handle this quickly and carefully to make sure that Jess didn't get hurt.

'No comment,' he said, and closed the door.

The doorbell rang again, but this time he ignored it. Instead, he grabbed his phone and flicked into the Internet to look at the news gossip pages and find out exactly what was going on before he called the publicity team at the film company and asked them to start damage limitation.

The headline leapt out at him: *Luke McManly?*

Oh, God, no.

The story wasn't about Jess, but that was small comfort. Because now the one thing Luke had spent the last year worrying about had actually happened.

Someone had broken the story about his infertility. And now the press was saying he was less of a man because he couldn't father a child.

He scrolled through the story, his temper simmering more and more as he read. He wasn't sure what made him angriest—the invasion of his privacy, or the way the gossip rag implied that the reason he'd not done as well in his last film was because he'd played a father and, not being able to become a father himself, hadn't been able to get into the role properly. His personal life had got in the way of his job.

What made it worse was his inner fear that there was some truth in it. That maybe he hadn't done as well in the role because he couldn't identify with what it was like to be a father. That he'd done his research and knew what it would be like intellectually, but he hadn't managed to transfer it emotionally. He hadn't been able to feel it—or make his audience feel it.

Life on set was going to be unbearable. People would be whispering in corners and then going silent as soon as they saw him. Pitying him. And they'd make the connection with Fleur and pity him even more.

Luke *hated* this.

And right now there was a pack of journalists and photographers waiting outside his front door. No doubt there would be a gaggle of them at the entrance to the set, too. This was a nightmare. Just like it had been when he'd split up with Fleur; he'd been shadowed every minute of the day and everyone had wanted to dig, dig, dig into his private life and his feelings.

As if Baloo could sense his mood, she whined and lay on her back at his feet.

'It's not you, girl,' he said.

He couldn't take the dog out through the back gate; it would mean having to take her on public transport during the rush hour. So they were going to have to drive out of the garage at the front of the house, as they normally did, and he'd have to hope that the paparazzi were sensible enough to get out of his way.

Thank God he always reversed into his garage rather than driving straight in.

He put the dog in her crate in the back of the car, put a pair of dark glasses on as he got behind the wheel of the car, then opened the garage door with the remote control.

The photographers crowded round him as the door opened, bulbs flashing everywhere. He opened his side window just enough to tell them to get out of his way or he'd call the police and have them removed from the street for causing a public obstruction.

One of them made a snippy comment and his temper snapped. 'Or maybe it'd be quicker to just drive over the lot of you,' he snarled.

By the time he got to the set the pictures were on the Internet from this morning—describing him as 'mean and moody'. And there was a headline to go with it: *Un-Daddy Un-Cool*.

The scumbags, he thought, gritting his teeth. They were so busy thinking of snarky words and poking fun at people, congratulating themselves on their cleverness, that they ignored the fact there was actually a person behind the story. Someone who could get hurt.

Sticks and stones may break my bones…The old rhyme ran through his head. And how wrong it was.

Because names could hurt. Words could cut deeper than anything else, seeping into your head and freezing you.

This was a total nightmare. Luke was used to press conferences and interviews and photographs, but he hated this side of the business—the muck-raking and the way the press acted as if the public owned you and you had to live every last little detail of your life under the glare of a photographer's flashlight.

As he walked onto the set, Luke could tell that everyone had seen the article. The way they stopped talking as soon as they saw him, the pitying glances. He did his best to ignore it and walked into the production office—but even Jess was looking anxious when she saw him, treating him with kid gloves.

He couldn't handle this. Jess was the one person he'd told about this, the one person he'd expected to understand—and yet she was behaving like all the rest of them, pitying him.

'Are you OK?' she asked.

His temper finally snapped. 'Of course I'm not OK! My private life's being dragged through the gutter yet again. How the hell do you think I feel?'

Her face went white. And then she lifted her chin. 'Does it not occur to you that maybe I'm concerned about you?'

Luke knew that he was completely in the wrong, but he couldn't stop himself. His mouth was on a roll. All the pent-up anger and bitterness of the last year poured out of him. 'Maybe I don't need your concern. Maybe I don't *want* your concern.' And then the words he knew he shouldn't say came out anyway. 'Maybe I'm better off on my own. Without you.'

She flinched as if he'd struck her physically. 'If that's the way you feel,' she said quietly, 'then you probably are.' She looked over at Ayesha, the production manager. 'I'm sorry to let you down, but I'm afraid I can't work today.'

And then she simply picked up her things and walked out.

Baloo whined and tugged at her lead, desperate to be with Jess, but Luke didn't move a muscle to stop Jess leaving. Even though he knew he was in the wrong and should apologise, he was too angry to focus on anything else but how he felt right at that moment. He glared at the dog. 'You'll have to be on set with me today, and if you so much as look at a single shoe, let alone steal one and chew it, you're going back to the dogs' home as fast as I can drive you there.'

'Mr McKenzie,' Ayesha said, 'just leave the dog with me for now.'

The cool, clipped tone of her voice registered, and he looked at the production manager.

'Baloo's used to me,' Ayesha said. 'She'll be fine.'

Luke was about to thank her when she cut in. 'It's none of my business,' she said, 'but I think you've just made the biggest mistake of your life.'

'No, I don't think so,' he said coldly. Because maybe he *was* better off on his own. And, from this evening, his aunt would just have to pay someone to look after Baloo until she could find the dog a new home. He didn't need anything or anyone in his life. Not now, not ever.

Anger kept Jess going until she was inside her flat. Sure, she could understand that Luke was angry and hurt by the story—but that didn't give him the right to take it out on her. Would this be what their life would've been like had they stayed together, Luke going off at the deep end whenever something upset him in the press? She didn't want to have to spend the rest of her life treading on eggshells. She wanted an equal partnership, like the one she'd had with Matt. Of course she wasn't looking for someone to be a carbon copy of her late husband— that wouldn't be healthy or reasonable to expect. But she didn't want a tempestuous relationship either; an on-again, off-again showbiz drama really wasn't her idea of a happy life.

Right now, it hurt that Luke could turn on her like that and dump her just because he was in a bad mood. But it would've been far, far worse if she'd actually married Luke and maybe adopted a child with him before something like this happened.

'I'm better off without him,' she told herself briskly.

And if she kept telling herself that, eventually she'd believe it.

'Right. Cut.' George, the director, rolled his eyes. 'Go home, Luke. We're not going to get anything filmed today. You've messed up every single take so far.'

Luke could taste the bitterness in his mouth. His whole life was on the brink of collapse. He couldn't even do his job any more. And how long would it be before the media picked up on that? How long would it be before directors decided that Luke McKenzie had passed his sell-by date—that Luke McKenzie was no longer a virile male lead but an infertile man, an object of pity?

'Go and get your head sorted out. Talk to your girl,' George advised.

'My girl?' Luke prevaricated. They'd been careful to keep their relationship quiet, on set.

'Everyone knows you're seeing Jess.' George rolled his eyes. 'Just let her talk some sense into you.'

Except Jess wasn't his girl any more, was she? Luke had blown it. Pushed her away. Lashed out at her.

He'd lashed out at Baloo, too. Threatened to send her back to Death Row. And he'd called the press scumbags when his own behaviour had been far, far worse. Shame flooded through him. How could he have been so selfish? How could he have hurt the woman he loved like that?

'Luke?' George asked.

Luke rubbed a hand over his eyes. 'Sorry. I've screwed a lot of things up today, and not just these takes.'

'Yeah, I heard you'd had a fight with Jess and she'd walked out of the office,' George said.

'I'm an idiot,' Luke told him. 'And I'm not sure she's going to give me the chance to explain myself.'

George looked sympathetic. 'I reckon you're going to need something a hell of a lot better than flowers or chocolates to fix this one.'

'You're telling me,' Luke said wryly. 'I'll see you tomorrow. And I'm sorry, George. I won't screw up tomorrow.'

'Glad to hear it,' George said. 'It would've been helpful if you'd given us some kind of warning about the situation, so the press office could've had contingency plans in place. But the damage is out there, so you might as well go and sort things out with your girl first.'

But before that Luke needed to pick up his dog and apologise to the production manager.

Baloo whined when she saw him, but she stayed by Ayesha's feet, almost cowed.

He sighed. 'I'm sorry, girl. And I apologise for the way I behaved to you, Ayesha.'

'Water off a duck's back. I'm used to stroppy thesps

throwing a hissy fit,' Ayesha said. 'But I think there's someone else who deserves a hell of a lot more of an apology.'

'There is,' Luke said. 'And I'm going to be eating humble pie, believe me.'

'If she'll let you.'

'If.' Luke sighed. That was the crunch question. 'Thank you for looking after my dog. And, again, I'm sorry, Ayesha.' He stooped down to make a fuss of Baloo. 'Let's go, sweetie. I'm going to fix this.' Even if he had to sit on Jess's doorstep all day and all night, he'd get her to talk to him. He'd apologise. And hopefully she'd let them start again.

He tried calling her from the car park. There was no answer from her landline or her mobile. Well, that wasn't so surprising. In her shoes, he wouldn't want to talk to him, either. Leaving a message felt too impersonal, so he just put Baloo into her cage so she was safely secured in the back of his car.

What was it Jess had once told him?

When you've had a day of dealing with people you have to be civil to, but really you want to shake them until their teeth rattle and tell them to grow up... That's when a good run with a dog at your side will definitely put the world to rights.

Maybe it would clear his head, too. And he could work out the right words to convince Jess to give him a second chance.

He managed to evade the paparazzi by using one of the back entrances to the set, and found a park a few miles away where nobody would bother him. Not if he had his beanie hat and glasses on. It would give him just a little while of anonymity. Space to work things out.

He texted Jess before he let Baloo out of the car. *Sorry, I was wrong, please can we talk?*

There was no answer by the time he and Baloo had finished their run. The endorphins had made him feel better, but the guilt was like a heavy sack on his back, weighing him down.

'What am I going to do, Baloo?' he asked.

The dog whined, sat up and put both paws up. Just like in the routine to the song she'd done with Jess.

I love you.

Three simple little words.

OK, Jess was angry with him—and rightfully so— but maybe she'd listen to the dog.

He frowned. It was a long shot. Totally crazy. But if there was the tiniest, tiniest chance, he'd take it.

He downloaded the song he needed and looked at the dog.

'I,' he said, 'am going to teach you something. Something that you've taught me, Baloo, and I'm sorry it took me so long to work it out.'

The dog looked quizzically at him, her head on one side.

'We're going to dance,' he said.

Not at his place—the paparazzi would have it staked out and he wanted a bit of privacy for this, not someone snooping into his house with a telescopic lens—but he could work with Baloo at Monica's. He called his aunt. 'I need help,' he said. 'I've been an idiot. And I'm being papped so my house is a no-go area right now. Please can I borrow your living room—and maybe ask for a bit of advice?'

To his relief, it turned out that the one other person in his life who meant something to him was still talking to him. Though Monica, too, wasn't impressed with him when he explained what he'd done.

'I know they say you always lash out at the person closest to you—but, Lukey, that was insane.'

'You're telling me,' he said wryly. 'And this is how I'm going to fix it.' He explained his plan to her.

'It's a long shot,' Monica said. 'But I think it's about your only chance, now.'

It took the rest of the afternoon, and it wasn't his best performance ever, but he didn't have time to polish it—and, besides, polish wasn't what Jess needed now. She needed unvarnished honesty.

He drove Baloo over to her flat and rang her doorbell.

No answer.

OK. If she was out, then he'd wait for her. He sat on her front doorstep with Baloo by his side.

Her nosey neighbour came out. 'You do realise dogs aren't allowed?'

'Actually,' Luke said, 'Mr Bright happens to have given this particular dog special dispensation.'

The neighbour stared at him in obvious disbelief.

'What have you got against dogs, anyway?' Luke asked.

'They bite.'

'When they're hurt and scared, maybe,' Luke said. And he was guiltily aware that was what he'd done. He'd bitten Jess metaphorically, like a dog who was scared of being hurt again.

'They're savage beasts,' the neighbour said.

'Most of them aren't, just those who haven't been treated properly or trained. That's what Jess does, trains them.'

'I had to have years of skin grafts,' the neighbour said.

'I'm sorry,' Luke said softly, 'that you had such a bad

experience, but not all dogs are bad. Come and meet Baloo. You can't be scared of a dog called Baloo. It's a ridiculous name and she's a ridiculously sweet dog, I promise.'

The neighbour flinched. 'They bite.'

'This one doesn't.' He lifted her up and she licked his face. 'See?'

The neighbour still looked wary.

'Here.' Luke took a dog biscuit from his pocket. 'Put this on your hand and she'll take it from you.'

The neighbour flinched. 'She'll bite me.'

'She won't. I'll stake a thousand pounds on that. A million. Watch.' He put the biscuit in his flattened palm and Baloo took it gently from his hand. 'She won't hurt you,' he reassured the neighbour. Clearly the man had been badly hurt as a child, and nobody had tried to help him overcome his fear of dogs by introducing him to a gentle, kind, ordinary dog.

Maybe Baloo could help him overcome his fear of being hurt again.

The same fear that Luke had to face—except it was emotional rather than physical hurt. And, yes, the dog might just help him, too.

His dog.

'Try it,' Luke said. 'Can we come into your garden?'

'I...' The man shrugged helplessly.

'Thank you,' Luke said, and took Baloo into the garden. 'Sorry, I should've introduced us properly. I'm Luke and this is Baloo.'

'I'm Paul.'

'Nice to meet you, Paul.' Luke shook his hand. 'Baloo, sit and shake hands with Paul.'

The dog dutifully sat and put one paw up.

Paul looked amazed.

'Shake hands,' Luke said softly.

Paul did so—and looked shocked and pleased and amazed, all at the same time.

'Do you want to give her a biscuit to say "well done"?' he asked.

Paul nodded. Luke took another biscuit from his pocket and handed it to Paul.

His hand shaking, Paul gave the dog the biscuit on the flat of his palm.

Baloo was duly gentle and polite as she took it.

'It's OK to stroke her,' Luke said. 'She won't hurt you.'

Paul's hand was unsteady, but he stroked the dog—then flinched as the dog turned her head and licked him. He stared at the dog, and then at Luke. 'She licked me.'

'She's a good dog,' Luke said. 'My dog.'

Jess walked into her garden and frowned. What was her neighbour doing, out in the front garden? And why was he talking to Luke? What was Luke doing here?

'What's going on?' she asked.

'I'm introducing my dog to Paul,' Luke said.

His dog? He was calling Baloo *his* dog?

And…since when had Luke been on first-name terms with her difficult neighbour?

'While we were waiting for you. Baloo and I have things to say to you.'

'She's a nice dog,' Paul said, shocking her further. 'Listen to what they have to say. And I'm not going to call the landlord.'

'What?' This was totally surreal.

'Will you, Jess? Listen to us?' Luke asked.

'Like you listened to me this morning, you mean?' She couldn't stop the caustic comment bursting out.

He grimaced. 'I'm an idiot. I got things very, very wrong. I'm sorry I hurt you, and—' He broke off and looked at Paul. 'Sorry, do you mind if this is a private conversation?'

'You're in his garden,' Jess said. 'You can't order the poor man to go indoors.'

'I'm not ordering anyone.' He sighed. 'Jess, please, I need to talk to you—just give me five minutes.'

'Five minutes,' Paul echoed. 'Or I *will* call the land-lord—and I'll tell him you have cats as well and they're using the sofa as a scratching post.'

She stared at him. 'You've fallen for the movie star charm as well, have you?'

'Movie star? Who's a movie star? *Him*?' Paul asked, pointing with his thumb at Luke and scoffing. 'He's just a man with a dog.'

'He's right,' Luke agreed. 'I'm just an ordinary man with a dog.'

There was nothing ordinary about Luke, and she was damn sure he knew it. But the Luke McKenzie she'd fallen in love with was nothing like the cold, hard man who'd pushed her away this morning. Which was the real Luke? Could she trust that the Luke she'd fallen for was the real Luke?

'And a gerbil,' Paul added. 'Which has eaten through some of the wiring.'

She put her hands up in the age-old sign of surrender. 'OK. I give in. Five minutes.'

'Shake hands, Baloo,' Paul said, and shook hands with first Baloo and then with Luke. 'Listen to him, Jess.'

'That was surreal—what did you do to him?' she asked Luke when they were inside her flat.

'You were right about him being lonely—and he was

savaged by a dog when he was little. Skin grafts,' Luke said economically.

'Poor man. If I'd realised…'

'Sometimes,' he said, 'we keep our hurt inside and we don't let it out when we should.' He sighed. 'I'm sorry, I've been horrendously unfair to you and I know I don't deserve your time, but please hear us out.'

He fiddled with his phone and then put it on the table. Jess recognised the song from *The Jungle Book* as soon as it started playing, because she'd loved it as a child—'Bare Necessities'. How appropriate for a dog named Baloo.

Baloo was on her hind legs, following Luke, almost like Jess remembered the bear doing in the animated film.

Then she sat down, doing something like the pat-a-cake routine Jess had taught Baloo, for the chorus of the song.

Was this Luke's way of telling her that he loved her?

Could she believe him?

'You're our bare necessity,' he said. 'You're all we want. All we need. And we both love you and want you in our lives.'

'I…I don't know what to say,' she said.

'Baloo's taught me that everyone deserves a second chance. She's my dog, most definitely. I'm giving her that second chance.' He dragged in a breath. 'Will you give me a second chance, Jess?'

'What—so, next time there's a story in the press that upsets you, you can dump me all over again?' she asked.

'No. I was wrong. I guess I've been really angry, this past year. I've damped it all down and told myself that I was over it all—and then today the story was everywhere, and all that anger stopped being buried. It forced its way out, and I took it out on the wrong person. I lashed out at you because…' He wrinkled his nose. 'Well, I guess because I feel close to you.'

She folded her arms and looked at him. No way was she letting him get away with trying to look cute. It wasn't enough.

He grimaced. 'I know just how lame that sounds. I haven't got a script, or flowery words, or anything except what's in my heart, right now, and I hope that's going to be enough.' He blew out a breath. 'I love you, Jess. You make my world a better place. And I'm so sorry I overreacted this morning and took it out on you.'

'Why did you do it?' she asked.

'Honest truth? Because I'm terrified that they might be right. That I'm not enough of a man.'

She frowned. 'Just because you can't father children, it doesn't mean you're not a man. Fleur was totally wrong about that. Or are you still in love with her?'

'I'm not talking about Fleur. And I'm not in love with her. No way. I love *you*,' he said. 'I'm talking about how Hollywood sees things. What about all the actors and actresses fifty-odd years ago who had to pretend they were straight? If the truth had come out, they would never have worked again. And acting… that's not just what I do, it's who I am. If they don't think I'm enough of a man, then that's the end of me playing the romantic male lead with the slightly posh accent and floppy hair.'

'You honestly think the directors would do that?'

'It's not necessarily the directors. It's the marketing

people. The people with the money.' He shrugged. 'I don't have any control over that.'

'Your fans would be pretty upset if you didn't work again,' she said. 'And does it have to be Hollywood? Why can't you make your own low-budget film here in England? Direct it yourself?'

'That,' he said, 'never occurred to me.' He looked thoughtful. 'An indie film. If the script was right. Direct. Yes, I could.'

'So the worst doesn't *have* to be the worst.'

'No,' he admitted.

'You've built up this huge fear of losing your career—like my neighbour being scared of dogs. You just need someone to show you that things aren't as bad as you think they are,' she said.

'Maybe not in career terms, but the rest of my life's pretty much a train wreck at the moment. I finally find someone I can be myself with—someone who makes me smile for all the right reasons, someone who makes me want to be a better man. And then I'm stupid enough to let her go. Can you forgive me, Jess? Can we wipe the slate clean and start again?'

'You really want to be with me?'

'I really want to be with you,' he said. 'But sometimes I can be a real idiot. I can't necessarily offer you an easy time. I can't give you children. I have to go where my work is, and the location isn't always in England. And, any time we have a fight, there's a good chance it'll be splashed right across the press, because that's the kind of garbage they thrive on.'

She looked thoughtful. 'OK. Those are the cons. And the pros?'

He frowned. 'Pros?'

'If you're doing a risk assessment, there are always good points as well as bad,' she said.

She was going to listen to him. Maybe give him that second chance, if he was honest with her and kept nothing else back.

Luke's heart felt as if it had swollen to twice its normal size. He knew it was anatomically impossible, but he could still feel the hope blooming out, filling him.

'Good points. OK. I've got a nice view from my living room and great walks on my doorstep. I live with the best dog in the world—a dog who can dance with you if you're feeling down, and who seems to be developing a bit of a bossy streak and tells you what to do.' He smiled at her. 'And I love you. I hope that counts for something.'

'It counts,' she said. 'OK. The pros all work for me. Back to the cons.'

Where it could all go wrong. But he knew that they needed to sort this out.

'You're an idiot—agreed, and we can work on that. Life isn't easy—well, that's true whether you're a movie star or not. Children...' She spread her hands. 'Yes. I do want children. But this is the twenty-first century. We have options. We can foster, we can adopt, we can try IVF—if it's what we both want, we'll find a way to make it work.' She frowned. 'You don't work all the time in England. OK. Sometimes I can be with you on location, sometimes I'll be here with Baloo, and there's always the phone and Skype when we're apart. The world's a much smaller place now, so you working away isn't that big a deal. And the press...' She sighed. 'I guess we'll just have to put up with that. As long as we know the truth and the people who matter to us know the truth, and we talk about things instead of jumping to conclusions or going off in a strop, that's enough.'

Thank God.

She was going to let him be enough for her.

He dropped to one knee. 'Jess Greenacre, despite the fact that I'm an idiot, I'm prepared to work on it. I love you. Will you marry me and spend your life with me—me and you and a dog named Baloo?' He smacked a palm to his forehead. 'I'm supposed to have a ring when I do this. I told you I was an idiot.'

'Not an idiot. Maybe just a little under-rehearsed.' But she was laughing as she dropped to her knees to meet him. 'Luke McKenzie—I love you, too, and yes, I'll marry you.'

And Baloo put her paws up as if to echo both of them.

I love you.

* * * * *